Outlaws

Kevin Sampson lives and works on Merseyside. His chequered career has embraced the production line at Cadbury's, film production at Channel Four, and the music business front-line of Produce Records, as manager of Liverpool band The Farm. His first novel, *Awaydays*, is being adapted for the screen. He is the author of two other novels, *Powder* and *Leisure*.

Kevin Sampson

OUTLAWS

V

VINTAGE

Published by Vintage 2002

2 4 6 8 10 9 7 5 3 1

First published in Great Britain by
Jonathan Cape 2001

Vintage
Random House, 20 Vauxhall Bridge Road,
London SW1V 2SA

Random House Australia (Pty) Limited
20 Alfred Street, Milsons Point, Sydney
New South Wales 2061, Australia

Random House New Zealand Limited
18 Poland Road, Glenfield,
Auckland 10, New Zealand

Random House (Pty) Limited
Endulini, 5A Jubilee Road, Parktown 2193,
South Africa

The Random House Group Limited Reg. No. 954009
www.randomhouse.co.uk

A CIP catalogue record for this book
is available from the British Library

ISBN 0 09 942223 9

Papers used by Random House are natural, recyclable
products made from wood grown in sustainable forests.
The manufacturing processes conform to the environ-
mental regulations of the country of origin

Printed and bound in Great Britain by
Bookmarque Ltd, Croydon, Surrey

THIS ONE'S FOR MY DREAM TEAM – DF AND CD

Sunday

Fat Francis

Standing here now, I can see it all over again. It's like a real-time flashback it's so clear and true. I remember it like it was yesterday. It was Ged that kicked the whole thing off. It was all him, he was the one that realised how far we could go, what we could all pull off just by virtue of who we were. Or *what* we were. It was completely Ged's thing. He was the Kiddie. I owe him big time. I owe him everything. Or I did. Maybe I don't owe him no more.

It's a funny one, standing here now. I've done what I've done, it's over, problem solved and I now find myself tackling a new problem: whether to go join them all in there. I don't feel nostalgic, not remotely – but I do feel a strong sense that I'm apart from them, now. I can hear Moby's big laugh from here and it gives me no end of glad feelings – but it's things from the past. It feels right that I just carry on walking.

But I stop and lean back against the wall and light up a ciggy. I find myself looking at my bushes again and out over the Garden Festival site. It seems mad me standing here now, like this. I can see the first proper robbery Ged done. All him, it was. That was the one, by the way. I doubt that anyone else has ever given it a minute's thought, but it was purely Ged that started all this. The others shit themselves. They probably didn't even know I was there in the bushes, watching, seeing

I

everything. But I was always there. I saw it all. He was unbeatable, Ged was. He was an untouchable.

After, when it was all over, we said that from that point on, this'd be our place. All our meetings would take place here. And that's how it happened, more or less. Not just business meetings and planning meetings and that – as we grew up, all of our big days happened here. Wedding receptions, christenings, birthday parties, everything – it all happened at the Britannia. Funerals and all too, every now and then. We always said that the day one of us didn't show up for one of these, for something big – that'd be the day it was all over. I think I understood that more instinctively than any of the others, if you know where I'm going. I was the outsider at that time, and I just knew in some way that there was nothing the lads couldn't do together. I just never thought I'd be the one to break the whole thing up.

Monday

Ged

I fucking hate driving, I do. I'm not cut out for it. That is a fact, by the way. Just not cut out to drive a car, myself. I'm a hothead. I get wound up too easy as it is, to be fair, but one thing guaranteed to pure do my head in is selfish driving. Little pricks in souped-up E-Reg Polos and that, divvy hatchbacks and that, thinking they're fucking somebodies, driving like cunts and expecting decent people to move aside so's they can steam past like you're not even *on* the fucking road. I fucking *hate* them cunts, by the way. I hate the way they drive with just one hand on the fucking wheel and the other one dangling out the window, with their head cocked to one side trying to look dead fucking bored with all the other poor cunts on the road holding them up. I hate their fucking baseball caps. Everything about them makes myself want to kill them with my fists every time I set out in this fucking car. You can guarantee there'll be one of them gobshites at least, any fucking time you go out. Look at this twat. Look at him! He's coming right up behind myself now, almost touching my fucking bumper trying to get us to move out the way. If I weren't so late for the lads I fucking *would* pull over and I'd pull that little shit-car cunt over for a little word and all, too. Does he want to get to know myself? Is that it? Does he want to drive right through my backside and that, come and have a proper look? 'What you got on the CD, Gerrard? Jamarakie? He's sound him, isn't he, Ged?' Is that why he's right up my arse? Wants to see what I'm playing and that? Twat! Come 'ead – look at us then, you gobshite! Here in the wing mirror! Here I am, you! D'you want to say something to myself? D'you want bollocks? Little cunt!

I shouldn't drive.

Moby

One day I'll have to be late myself, mind you. It's not supposed to be coolio to be early all the time, but it does always seem to work out that I'm the first one there. I don't mind so much today. Considering that it's nearly Christmas and that, it's a boss fucking day. You could almost get a bronzie off've that sun. That's the God's honest truth. Not quite, mind you, but walking down here just now it was good to feel the sun on the back

3

of my bonce again. I would not mind if it was a longer trot on days like this, and I mean that.

I love these meetings. I don't mind admitting it. We only come here when there's something happening, know where I'm going. To be fair, we do have all the kids' birthdays and christenings and communion parties and that down here, that's just part and parcel. But for Ged to call us out and that – well, it can only be good news, in fairness. He'll never tell you nothing over the phone, mind you. Tells you fuck all, our Gerrard, by the way. Para to fuck he is. But suffice it to say, we half get the picture by now, know where I'm going. A call out to the Britannia can mean just the one thing for us boys. It means there's a blag on the horizon. Not before time in fairness, know where I'm going. Can't wait, lar. I mean it. I can not fucking wait. Could use the tank and all too just now, to be fair.

We've half grown up with that Britannia. I remember it getting built at the same time as the Garden Festival site and that. It was the making of us, that Garden Festival.

Ratter

I can see the big dope now. Sat outside holding his dick, first there as usual. I don't know what he's good for, the soft cunt. I'd have well fucked him off by now. He can have a fight and that, but the world's changing. It's not about who can have a fight no more. It's about the bigger picture. It's about ambition. I think our Ged's gone soft and all, too. I don't think he's got no ambition these days. Not since he moved over there. He's more arsed about fucking Fun Runs and that, playing golf with his *Brookie* B-list cronies, doing his bit for charidee and that. Makes you fucking sick sometimes he does, Gerrard. What a

4

fucking phoney, by the way. He's made widows of three sub-post-office mistresses by my reckoning, and there he is hassling us all to do his half-marathon for that thing, Riverside Single Parent Families' holiday fund or something. Thinks he's fucking Robin Hood, he does. His ideas are about as modern as Robin Hood, to be fair. He's a fucking dinosaur.

'Ratts!'

Look how pleased he is to see YT, the big galloot. Fucking Lurch, he is. I sling him a big mad wave back. Made his day, the soft cunt. He's come ambling towards us now to give us the big bear hug and that. Trademark Moby greeting, that is. Should've stopped all that about ten years ago, to be fair. That's them for you though, the lot of them. Living in the past they are.

I speed up my stride in case he sees the Shogun parked behind us. That's another thing about fucking Gerrard. Will he fuck let you enjoy your ill-gotten gains. If he knew old JPB had that Shogun he'd run us over with it, no word of a lie. He was bad enough when I had the Prelude, but a four-be-four – he'd fucking keel over. I've had to park it round the corner by the Dome, out of sight of Big Brother. He'd pure have a fit. He would. He'd be frothing at the mouth like a mad person. Ostentatious symbols of prosperity, he'd say.

State of him, by the way. *Hates* the idea of anything that might bring us a second glance. *Pa*ranoid, he is. Like, it's his big thing that we should all have some visible means of income, something that, at face value at least, seems to justify our lifestyle. So I have the great presence of mind to go into property in a small way. Gets myself a few grants and that, gets my photo in the *Echo* every now and then for bringing some fucked old warehouse back into community usage and that. Is he made up? Is Big Brother in some small way pleased for the runt of the litter? Is he fuck. Just says how fucking glad he is we've got different surnames. I'll fucking love the day the cunt finds out what I really do to keep the wolves from the door. I'll love it. He's not even my brother, by the way. Don't know why I call him Our Ged. Well, I do. Force of habit and that, isn't it – half taking the piss out of the cunt. Our Ged and that.

Fuck the twat, anyway. This is my last one of these. Can't be doing with it. It was good cover at one time. Perfecto, it were. Placed YT with the right people and that, and as for image – Alistair fucking Campbell couldn't've give us a better profile. But it's not for John-Paul Brennan no more, this. Our Gerrard and that – he's a dinosaur. Over and out.

Ged

Sight of that Britannia always, *always* gives myself half a glad-on. It's like all these things rushing you, all at once. The river right down behind it, so close it looks like the pub's sailing on it. I've always loved that river – even when it was brown, by the way. Always loved it. Something in the way it moves and that. It's a magical river, to be fair. Mystical and that. Can't explain it. There's just something about it. There's fucking dolphins in the Mersey now, by the way. Flipper and that coming up to have a mosey at the pondlife in the Britannia. Is right. Am I ever more glad to see any gaff anywhere, though? Don't think so, matey. The way that pub just seems to loom round the corner, like it's moving on casters. One minute you're on the Riverside Drive, car salesrooms, warehouse apartments, software development companies, casinos, all of that, then – just the slightest little incline to the left and the faintest pull away up the hill and there it is. The Britannia. The Garden Festival. Where It All Started.

So maybe I'm one of these twats that's just given to nostalgia. Maybe I am, but I swear the sight of that pub will always give myself a jump. I can see us, little rats, scallying around that Garden Festival. Pure fucking manna, it were. Dips, snatches, cameras, purses, the odd Barbour jacket – the Garden Festival sent these hordes of tourists and trippers right into our own backyard, from all over the world, expressly to be had off. By us. Japs, Yanks, Krauts, Aussies – you name it, we robbed them.

I know I'm not meant to say Krauts and that. One thing I myself am not is a racialist. But, in all fairness, I've grown up with the lot of them. Turks, Pakis, Filipinos, fucking Somalis, everything. Round by ours we had a Akinbyi, we had Ahmeds, Alis, Ades, Adus, Albertinas, Ancianos, Appels, Allens, Agars, Arrecifes, Ananas, Amins, Assifs, Aziz – and that was just the As by the way. United nations it were round the Southern Neighbourhoods. Pitt Street and that for a e.g. – mainly Filipino families when we was growing up. Sometimes they'd get called dagos and that. Nothing was meant by it.

It was a Jock that was the making of us.

Ratter'd been on this one's case all afternoon. He looked like one of them stereotype American tourists – big mad camera and that, all sorts of fuck-off lenses and fucking secret tricky bits built in – and he was *dead* loud. He had two old girls with him and he was shouting his head off, very keen to impress these two auld 'uns with

7

his knowledge of hibiscus and hardy perennials and that. He was starting to make Ratter extremely cross, by the way. He'd had enough, to be fair. Wanted to just do him in, with or without goodies. You couldn't talk to Ratter when he got like that, not in them days. He'd only ever listen to myself, and even then it was a hard rap. But I won him over that day. I told him. Told him it'd be sound – it was a case of waiting. I think that murderous hot sunshine helped, to be fair. I made him just sit and watch and wait it out. Wait for the moment. He weren't happy. He was a horrible kid, Ratter. Fucking wretch he were, in all fairness.

The last hour was always good for muggings. We weren't really like that, ourselves. We would never've done that round by ours. But this was just easy pickings. It weren't real muggings to be fair – you didn't have to hurt them or nothing – just scream at them, shake them up a bit. Anything, really, but you had to sound like as though you meant it. Sometimes we just pure caved in with the giggles, specially the glueheads in the company, but more often than not we could pull it off, in fairness. What you'd do is you'd just grab what you was after and scream: 'Give us your fucking bag, you bitch!'

And it was yours. Pronto, by the way. They was nice people and that. They didn't want to get hurt. And they'd never come across nothing like that before – they was there to look at plants. The more we done it, the more I realised what we was on to. I used to watch for different people's reactions and that, but to be fair, there weren't that much of a variation. They'd go white. They'd hand over their goodies. End of.

Except for the Jock. He was a fucking hero, that Jock was. He was fucking Braveheart. He'd read about

8

vermin like us, preying on decent people and lowering their standards of living and there was no way he was bowing down to lowlifes like us. Not in front of his two elderly babes at least, anyway.

We got them right down by the Japanese Garden, away from most of the crowds. It was still hot enough and there was still plenty of people around, but we had this arrangement with Go-Inhead that we'd meet him in the Britannia at half seven every night to divvy up whatever he'd managed to get for the swag. Never would've entered your head that Go-In'd skim you. Just would not have happened, by the way. Happy just to be involved, Go-Inhead was. Made up to be one of the lads. Weird thinking of him how he was back then, just driving down here, now.

So every hour on the hour we'd go over to the delivery gate by the Dome and lob whatever we'd got to Go-Inhead. He'd whack it all in a extra big Head bag and cart it up through Priory Wood to Freddie Woan's in Dingle Vale. Freddie was just a minty cunt. He did like to think of himself as a fence and that, but he always used to pay way over the odds for gear in all fairness. I think he just wanted to be thought of as a face and that, someone you'd half let on to in the street and that. He's still a fucking mingo, by the way, Freddie, but he has got better at the game as time's gone by, in fairness to the cunt.

Soon as the Jock strayed away from the main gardens, that was it. Three of us was around him like jackals pillaging the cunt, hands in his pockets, no fucking about, wrenching that fucking camera off his neck — but this hero was not going to take it. He wasn't having none of it. He starts throwing big mad fucking haymakers and kicking out and shouting and that, screaming blue murder. The two old dears starts screaming and all, too. People are looking over, having a little look-see what's going on and that. Know what – not one of the cunts made a move to help the poor cunt. Not one of them. They was rooted to the spot. Horrified, they was. Terrorised. Pure could not, would not go to his help. That's when I knew.

But Moby and Ratter had half started backing off by then, by the way.

'Come 'ead! Basta! Let's do one!'

That's all I can remember anyone saying, apart from the big fat Jock. *Basta.* We got that one off've Joey Anciano from by ours. He was always coming out with things like that, basta and what have you. Pronto.

Can still see the Jock now, by the way. Could never hardly forget the cunt, to be fair. He looked like that Boss Hogg off've *The Dukes of Hazzard.* Cunt was going to take some convincing and in that half-second, with all these people stood there staring and knowing that Old Bill'd be along any second, I makes a big decision. And for us boys, this is what turns out to be the moment.

I still do not know how – it was just a instinctive thing – but I knew big and loud in my own head that this was a tussle I fucking had to win. Had to do it, there and then. So I slashed him. I hadn't used a Stanley for years. I thought they was for kids by that time but I still had it on myself and that, just as a prop and that – and I was glad of it, by the way. I never even thought it through. I knew I had to make my point and make it quick and my point was this:

I've just cut your face.

You don't know what you're fucking with here.

This is not like any single thing you've ever known in your life so far.

You can not win.

You'd better do as I say.

And he did, to be fair. He put his hand to his face and he seen the blood, seen it was steady and he just went down on his knees and started crying and handed over every last fucking thing that belonged to him. Good as gold he were, at the end of the day – just give his swag over nice and easy. Still no cunt moved to help him, by the way. All them onlookers, all them ghouls stood around at a safe distance, not one of them lifted a limb. They was frozen to the spot. They shit themselves. It was unbelievable – but it was fucking fantastic and all, too. That was the moment. I knew from then on that, if we weren't soft about it and that, if we got our heads together and done this proper, we could get away with whatever the fuck we wanted. We was a law unto ourselves.

A lot of the time since then I have felt chocker about some of the jobs we've pulled, to be fair. I try to make it all as painless as possible now, for everyone. In general I *am* full of remorse, full of regrets. I don't like what I've done and I try, I really do try to use my knowledge and that to help the good, decent people have a better life, these days. But somehow I can never feel too bad about that Jock. He was asking for it. Cunt had it coming to him.

I pulls up outside the Britannia. Ratter's trying to look as though he's got better things to do, as per fucking usual. Kite on the twat, by the way. Big long moody gob on him. But Moby – Big Moby's buzzing his nuts off. He knows there's something cooking.

And there is. There is. I sticks my head out the window.

'Now then!'

That's more *like* it. Smiles all round. Grins for Uncle Ged. Half happy faces. I locks up and strolls over towards the pub, giving the boys a nice big beamer back to let them know we're rocking again – more for Moby, to be fair. Funny thing with nicknames, by the way. People think they've got them for different reasons. Ratter thinks his is because he used to go out by the canal bank digging for rats and that, or it's because he's a bit of a cad with the Judies, bit of a rake and that. But that's not it. It's purely and only because of his teeth. Our Ratter's nickname is down to his fangs. They slope back slightly and the thingy, his dracs and that, are pointed as fuck. They are. And they always do tend to look that bit on the wet side, to be fair, Ratter's gnashers. He's got very wet teeth.

And poor old Moby has forgotten just how long he's had that name. He thinks it's because he's always on his fucking mobile. Not quite, by the way. My cousin Anthony (that's An-thonn-knee, God willing) is called Moby because of his dick. When we was growing up and that, his dick was half deformed. That is the truth. Moby Dick. Kids are fucking savages, by the way. Won't let nothing go. I'm his fucking cousin and his best mate and I was at it myself. Maybe deformed is a bit harsh. It was hairy from age nine, Moby's dick. Not just his towns and that, by the way. The whole package. The shaft and that, right up to his bell. Hairy as fuck. Not the actual bell-end itself, to be fair, but the rest of it – yeti's knob is right, no back answers. Fact. Lad had a big mad hairy dobber on him.

Weird how he's bald as Gary Mac now. Coolio bald, though. He's *knowingly* bald, Moby. There's only myself and Go-Inhead don't have a nickname no more. Go-Inhead filled out and his head don't go in any more. Only a bit. And they did start trying to call myself Ravanelli a few years back but it never really did catch on. In all fairness no one can really expect to give the heavy hitters nicknames unless they confer it on themselves, know what I mean.

But they are looking well, the lads. Moby, six-four, dressed in his usual doorman-style clobber. Head completely shaven shiny bald, with that little Chicano beard of his neatly styled and spruced. Ratter, slick and sly as ever. Nice suit, if you will. Prada, in all probability. It's Prada everything for Ratter. He's even got Prada trainies, the beaut. Now to me, trainies equals adidas. I don't even like Nikes, by the way. Not a Liverpool shoe. Half for basketball players, the Nike is. But Ratter don't give a fuck. He'll wear any fucking thing if it's got a label. If it's got that little red Prada flash, he's made up. Give us three, love – and don't bother wrapping them up. He wears these white Prada foot glove efforts – them or his Patrick Cox loafers and always a smart whistle. He spends a fucking fortune on them suits of his. I can get Jimmy the Stitch to whip us up a Paul Smith copy or a Nicole Farhi or whatever for a fraction of the cost and no one's any the wiser. Anyone'd take it for the real thing except for one little slight drawback. I look shite in that kind of clobber. Strictly for weddings and funerals, whistles. Other than that I'm happy in a old Lacoste and a decent pair of trainies.

He does always looks sound though, Ratter, to be fair – always did. Proper Guido, he is. Whatever we made, even if it was coppers, you knew that his'd be gone by teatime, spent on clobber. He looks a tiny little bit like Frankie Dettori, the jockey lad, Ratter does. Just a passing resemblance. Ratter's bigger and that.

'Now then, boys!'

I gets right up to them and go half posh on them. Dickie Attenborough is what I'm thinking.

'My boys! My dear, dear boys! I've missed you!'

That always gets Ratter twitching, that sort of thing. Don't know why I do it to the lad, to be fair. I just like winding the cunt up. He thinks I don't give a toss no more since I've been living over there. I know he thinks that. I always know what he's thinking. You have to. An arm around each of them, I steers them into the pub. It feels great to be back. I can't feel sorry for that plucky Scotsman. All I feel is glad that we met him.

Moby

Ged goes over the blag. Well, he doesn't, to be fair. He just tells us that there's something coming up. He never really tells us nothing, by the way. Not until nearer the time, and even then he tells us fuck all. Just what kind of blag, who's going to do what and that.

There's only really two kinds that we do, nowadays. Most of them are inside jobs from the top down. By that I mean that maybe, say, if it's a haulage firm or a delivery blag or something then the dispatch manager will be in, the driver is always in and sometimes, I think, there's a copper or two getting paid off for info or looking the other way or something, know where I'm going. I don't know how it all adds up. Don't want to know neither, mind you. Ged takes care of that side. Ged has always took care of the organisational end of things. The only thing that's changed is the type of blags.

In the old days we was like fucking Jesse James, out in the back of beyond holding up sleepy little post offices and that. For a while we was on easy street with all the tom in Manchester. Fuck knows why the Manc boys never got on it theirselves and that – fucking easy-peasy, it were. All the wholesalers used to be in Strangeways and that, right by Victoria. Tell you though, lar, them boys was the slackest cunts you ever saw. It was half as though they wanted to be robbed, know where I'm going. They probably did if our Gerrard was anything to do with it. Great big fuck-off trays of tom, briefcases full of watches and bracelets and raw stones. You'd tail one, run the cunt off've the road and have him off. Simple as that, no back answers. One of the beauts left his briefcase on the back seat of his jalopy this one time while he popped into Burtonwood for a fucking cuppa. Fucking easy street, it were. Didn't last all that long, though. Got a bit wise to the caper after they'd lost about a million pound to us boys.

Did we care? Did we fuck. We just moved on. Started doing the payrolls and that until they fucked it all up with CCTV and that, red dye and fucking dummy runs and all their other little tricks. You wouldn't think it was worth their while, but they used to send out vans with fuck all in them. We'd cut them off – there was more of us in the crew back then – and jemmy the back doors open and, well I never, by the way. Empty. In fact this one time, right, we pulls a Transit over and before we could even get to the doors they bursts open and out jumps this little firm, hired in and that, tool-handed, proper mob they were. We was so mad about these cunts wasting our time that we probably filled them in worse than what they really deserved. We give it to them, good style – I don't mind admitting it. Ratter wanted to cut the driver's ear off and send it back to his boss, but that sort of behaviour, well – it's for savages, that. That was the day Drought got his voice, that job.

Our most famous blag was the transporter with all the Mercs on, just off've the Humber Bridge that time. That was us. Eli the Mensch had got shot of all fourteen cars – over a million's worth of Mercs – within two hours of the blag. He's a fucking legend, old Eli is. He can shift any fucking thing you care to throw at the cunt.

I miss all of that. Ged's blags for the last few years have been just like in the pictures. It's all planning and timing and stopwatches. There's hardly any knuckle at all. I don't even know when the last time was that I put a gun in someone's mouth. I love that. Their eyes go dead mad and white – you can see they've shit themselves. Smell it too half the time, to be fair. You don't *have* to stick it in their mouth in fairness, but I always do. It does help you get to where you want to be. The only good bit now is when we have to give the lad a few digs to make it look thingy, just mark him up a bit and that, know where I'm going. But it's all about mobility now. That's Ged's big thing. Mobility.

Ratter

Just listen to him. Monsieur Mob. Signor Blag. The fucking Man. Half a fucking mill he's talking about here. Half a mill. I've fucking lost half a mill in the time I've spent down here, nodding my stupid head and trying to look like I give a fuck. In the time I've been down here I could've bought a couple of warehouses, sewn up a development grant and had a nice massage down the Crowne Plaza. I could've taken Councillor Benefit out on the sloop – I need to arrange something for the good councillor soon, by the way. There's all kinds sniffing round him now. No bother, like – no one can entertain quite like YT, and I do know exactly how the Bennett likes to be looked after. I should get on to him.

But I'm here, aren't I? I'm sitting here, listening intently, thinking – I'm going to go down for this. Why in fuck's name am I even pretending to have this shite? And from him and all, too! It's a blinding realisation. The truth is, I don't know why. It's not even habit. It's nonsense. *Mobility*, for fuck's sake! It's been worth my while coming down here after all. Today has been The Day for JPB. It's been in the back of my mind since Gerrard give us the call, but the penny has finally now at long last dropped. Today is when the Ratter finally came to his senses.

Ged

'The beauty of this one, boys, is the volume. Or lack of. We're so agile with this blag that you could put the whole fucking job in your coat pocket!'

Ratter looks at the floor. Moby looks out the window, staring at a slovenly oil tanker for inspiration. Always had a liking for that word, slovenly. Teacher at Martin's was always using it about myself, always calling myself slovenly. That was before Moby got into trouble and we both got moved on to Shorefields. I can see I'm losing their attention. Don't know why I even bother bringing them in on the planning. Well, I do. I want them to be a part of it. They're my brothers. They *are* a part of it. I want them to enjoy this as much as what I do myself.

'This one is beautiful, lar! See them knobs hauling beak round the city? You'd need to be Geoff Capes to make a living on that weight! What'd you get for a key of gack, eh? What's that go for? Sixty grand? Maybe walk away with a half of that in readies?'

They're all eyes and ears now. Even Ratter's woke up now.

Ratter

He's not wrong about the weight. Cocaine can be a hefty lug, to be fair. Profits though – cunt's way out. Out of whack, out of time. He's from the Dark Ages, he is. I seen this holiday programme about the Hebrides a couple of weeks ago and, out there on the Isle of Harris, there's this one funny auld fella that still makes tweed on a pedal loom. That's our Gerrard to a tee. A dying breed.

Ged

'With all the gimmes and dropsies and once we've factored in Eli's take we'll be left with a good half million. Easy. And the beauty of it is, we're nimble. No lifting. No trucks. No storage. We're in there, we do it, we're out, we're rich. Happy Christmas, one and all! Agility. Mobility. Perfecto.'

Ratter

I hate the way he uses big words when he thinks we're getting close to him. Like, I could give a cultured guess what this heist is going to be. It's probably tom. If it's that light and that easy for that kind of tank, it's got to be diamonds. Tom of one sort or another at least, anyway. Any cunt could work it out. So he comes back with 'nimble' and 'agility' and that. 'Factored in.' Any twat can use them words. Mobility! Cunt's losing it. I know he is. The Year of the Ratt is nigh.

Moby

We're close, the three of us. We've been a team since forever. Even before we was a firm, we was a tidy little crew. Round the Holylands, in school, at the match – everyone knew who we was. But for all of that, Ged will only tell us so much. This job and that, it's a bit like one of them. Bit of a downer. You're mad keen and you want something, just something to chew on and that but he won't give you nothing. Just that it's soon. He won't tell us who he's paying off, whether there's law on board, nothing. We've just got to roll with him. It's always worked before. I'm all right with that, mind you. I'd do anything for our Gerrard.

But one thing that does do my head in is when he gets all para. Like, we all know what's coming next. He's going to dish out new mobies, isn't he? Just as you've started to get used to your last number he's giving you another new one – and only he's got all the numbers, know where I'm going. So by the time, say, my good self, Ratter, Drought, Spit if he's involved – by the time we've started into these new numbers he'll go and change them over again. New phones all round. And it's all pay-as-you-go gear, mind you. No billing addresses, nothing. He must spend a fortune on fucking mobiles. He gives us new phones about every two or three weeks – even when there's fuck all going on. How's your kids going to get hold of you when they need you if your phone number's getting changed every two or three weeks? That's the one thing that does my head in about Ged. Always making plans, he is. Always looking for the catch.

Ratter

I'm starting to feel quite chipper. The meet's nearly done and, knowing that I don't have to listen to his I-am-a-big-mad-mobster spiel for much longer, I don't feel so bad no more. But the worst bit's still to come. The Lecture.

Ged

'Right, boys, youse've got your handsets. Use them only when you need to, will you? Only for business, this time. Yeah? I don't want to find them phones clogged up with personal calls when I need you. I have to be sure of that, boys. All right? I need to know I can get at you straight away, as soon as I need you. This is coming off in a week or so, God willing. Stay in. Keep a low profile. I know that's not easy – especially not this time of year, by the way, I know all that. I know the invites are going to be pouring in and I know youse're both popular fellas and it's hard to keep out of town and that. But just think of the job and that, if you will. It still might be short notice, this one, so just be ready and that, yeah? Just keep your noses wiped and stay out of trouble. All right?'

I'm looking at Moby, but it applies even more to Ratter, in a way. Compared to how he used to be, he's hardly even one of the crew no more. He don't bother going training, doesn't go to none of the fights, didn't even come to Vegas last year. Cunt was apologetic enough and that, but he never come. Let me down there.

I weren't supposed to know too much about the trip anyway, but Ratter should've been there in fairness. He should've well been there. And he's only half going the match and that nowadays, goes in the exec boxes, doesn't he, knocks around with corporate hospitality cunts and all of that. It happens though, doesn't it? In all walks of life, people drift apart. So long as he can do a job for us, that's all that matters. So long as he still wants to. I'm looking at our Anthony, but I mean this for John-Paul.

Ratter
Here it comes . . .

Ged
'Everyone loves us in this city, don't they? People still want to shake your hand, don't they, Mobe?'

He grins.

'Even the new faces and that, the young bucks and that, all the lads on the door, all of them boys want to walk us right into their gaff and buy us champagne, don't they? Every musher in town wants to know the Brennan boys. Why d'youse think that is, well?'

Ratter
Me, sir! Me, sir! Because we're not a threat, sir! Knobhead . . .

Ged
'Because we're not taking nothing away from them, are we? We don't ask for nothing from them and we don't take nothing. We're not queering no one's pitch. Plus they like to think of us boys as half thingy. They think

we're the wild bunch and that. They want to be able to let on to lads like us, introduce us to their cronies, buy us all a drink and that, don't they?'

I looks at the pair of them. Right into their faces.

'So we'll keep it that way. Keep every cunt madly in love with us, God willing. Ay?'

I start laughing. Moby grins and nods. Ratter gets up and shakes hands – or, rather, he places both of his hands over my right one and clasps us, warmly and that – like he loves myself. Like I'm his brother.

Moby

Ratter seems all right today. He's a hard one to make out, our Ratts is. After all our Gerrard's done for him and that he should be laying down his life for him in all fairness – well, for me Auntie Eileen and all too, to be fair. I hear all sorts about him when I'm out, mind you. Oh aye. It's one of them – 'Moby this, Moby that, you wanna have a little look at your Ratts and that, not saying nothing and that' – all of that carry-on, know where I'm going. Little bits and pieces of hints and that. No one'll come out and say nothing, just little bits of hints and rumours. But to be fair you hear rumours about every cunt in this city. There isn't no one you don't get told about. You'd half be worried if you wasn't hearing tales about lads like Ratter. He's always half been one for putting himself about a bit. I think maybe he's just that bit in awe of Ged. Always has been, by the way. If I thought there was something serious with him then I'd do something. But there's fuck all going down with him, I'm fucking certain about that. He couldn't work a thing like that. Hasn't got it in him. He's nothing, Ratter. Bullshitter, if anything. Billy Bluff merchant. No way is he a Name.

Maybe I should just give him a smack for old times' sake anyway, just to remind him what that's like. Fucking remind the lad who he is and all too, mind you. Who he works for. He used to bring in all sorts of leads, Ratter – freelance jobs and that. Not any more, he doesn't.

That's the other sort of job we do – the occasional freelance. Those are the fun ones. They're risky, but we've never had one blow up on us yet, touch wood. These ones, Ged just has to judge on their merits. Someone might come to him with a schedule and a proposal and that. Ged'll look at it and maybe ask around a bit about the fella and what have you, although I can only ever remember two times when he's taken on a lead from someone that he didn't half know a little bit, know where I'm going. And they both come with references, them two, by the way. They were sound. Good heists and all, too. One was representing a lad from the postie that reckoned he knew when a new batch of Visas was coming in. Pure kite it were – clean as a whistle, not signed or nothing yet, obviously. Beautiful gear that was, just waiting to be knocked off. He wanted us to knock him over for ten grand. It was good business. Ged sold the kite on for ten times that.

The other lad was from one of the parcel services, UVF or UDA or one of them. He'd been making routine drops at some of the big jewellers in town, Boodles and all of that. He said he could tip us off when he was doing something chunky – Rolexes or something, gear we could shift like that. You don't even need Eli when it's Rolexes, but Ged still brings him in. He knows what he's doing, Ged. This lad from the courier firm, he wanted ten grand and all. That must be what they talk about, these lads, when they're getting a bit greedy. Get knocked over, get paid. Ten grand. But this lad didn't want us to mark him up too bad. Big crazy wool from Warrington, he were. Or maybe Widnes. Out that way, whatever. I can still see the cunt now. Mad red Brillo-pad head, half a Afro it were, big sticky-out wire-wool head, big ears and this big mad woolly accent.

'Mek it lewk good,' he said. 'But not *tew* good!'

We did and all, too. We kicked fuck out of the cunt. Freelances. Fucking laugh they are. Ratter used to bring loads of them in. Doesn't seem to give much of a fuck now. Seemed all right this morning, though. Almost jolly, by his own standards.

Ged

Moby asks us for a lift back to theirs, says come on in and have a cuppa with him and their Marie (that's 'Marry', by the way). We haven't seen you round ours for a while lad, he's going. You haven't seen the new taps and that, have you? Their Marie's put these new gold-leaf taps in, upstairs and down, with swans' heads where the water comes out. To be fair, Marie's always doing something new to their ken. They've still got the same little gaff in Beaufort Street that they've had since they was married. It's theirs now and that – oh aye. Bought it a while back, they did. All that's changed is they've had a extension built on the back. More for the hounds, to be fair. It's only little, their place, for a couple of dogs that size. Bigger than dingos, them dogs of theirs are. Proper hounds, by the way – can see the muscle packed into the bastards. Beautiful, they are, classy – but savage. Proper Dingle hounds.

People in the North End try to say the Dingle lads

have our own way of talking, but that's shite, really. We do have sayings and that, to be fair – the lads at the match used to slaughter us for the way we'd say 'a accident' or 'a escort' and that. What we'd do to properly wind them up is we'd drop a aitch and all, too. A amburger and that. A atchet. But we don't talk no different to any other cunt, in fairness. That's the Tocky lads. It's the Granby firm's got the patter, all the black boys and that, all the lads with race, if you will. Now them lads have got their own thing going on. The black lads that we grew up with round the South End, once they got to a certain age they did all start talking that bit more Yardie, to be fair. They'd be saying 'I axed him' and that instead of 'I asked him'. Perfectly A-OK saying 'I asked him' the year before, but once they started getting older it was all the other thing. 'Ah axthed 'im for thum thkunk.' Putting on a lisp, by the way. Oh yis. *Pretending* to have a speech defect. That was just a handful of them, to be fair – Granby Street and round there. Lisps and Jamaican accents. We haven't really got a accent. We use a bit of backslang, to be fair, now and then and that, but we don't really talk no different to the Scotty Road crew. 'Stotty Road', that's what they used to say up there. And 'the Stratford End'. Them North End beauts, always going on about taking the Stratford End, they were. You'd give up telling the cunts it weren't called that.

The Holylands was considered posh compared to the other side of Harlow Street, where Marie was from. And as for Debbi, by the way – she was fucking *common*. She'd crucify me if I told any of her posh friends from that school, but Debbi's from Tocky. Windsor Street. Tocky proper. The Holylands was sweet suburbia compared with that barrio. It's only a few auld streets, the Holylands

– ours was Moses Street – but clean, always just so. Spick and span. It's where *Bread* was filmed. *Bread*'d have you believe that the Holylands was this tight-knit neighbourhood full of lovable rascals and that, all keeping the wolves from the door by any means necessary. And they was all dead principled, by the way – they'd only rip off the 'haves' and they'd always hand it all over to Mam. They had Mancs, homs and Billy Idol lookalikes all living under one roof, all up to this and that and getting away with it, Mancs and tits getting respect on the street. We used to love it though, especially when our Billy used to punch his fist into his palm to show that he was about to get tough. He was a better ted, our Billy. Fucking whopper and then some.

One thing that *was* true about *Bread*, though – it was houseproud round there. Still is. Them streets are immaculate. Moby lived in Jacob Street and we was in Moses and there weren't a minty family between us. All of them houses was well looked after. Still are, by the way – you can see that just by looking. Even though people do move away and that, not everyone does. And nice people tend to move in, anyway – people are always wanting to move in around there. Some people only move a couple of streets away, just for a change – or to try a new house and that, with all the mod cons.

Moby and Marie, right, they've had this little gaff, from new, to be fair, little grass lawn in the back, little pond and that, but you'd think it was Buckingham Palace. The money she's spent doing that place up, mind you – she must've put more money into that place than what they spent buying it off've the council. Well more. They've got these sort of Grecian pillars outside the front door, a little sort of ornate porch, and no end of brass handles and lion's-head brass knockers and brass buzzer bells. Door furniture is what Marie calls it. She's always got her head in some brochure or other, paint charts and wallpaper samples and all of that. Good gear too, by the way. I told her I can get all that swag for her, but she likes going down to Robinson and Neal and that, spending the day in there collecting brochures and samples and what have you. She says fuck all to you, Marie, unless you ask her if she wants a ciggy or you ask her the difference between magnolia and off-white. They're always half having a barney about the amount she's spending on the house and that, her and Moby, but he does dote on her, in all fairness. She on him and all, too. They're potty about each other, them two. That much is fact.

But I'm not wild about the notion of running into their Marie at the minute, to be fair. She's properly flapping about their Liam's first communion and I doubt very much that sight of myself is going to suddenly soothe matters. Nice lad our Liam is and all, too. They haven't let him get too wild, Liam. I still can't bring myself to call the boy Fitzy – only to our Anthony, well. I know Marie's driving him daft over the arrangements. You'd think it was a royal wedding the way she's going on about it. I'll be surprised if David Dimbleby doesn't turn up with a flower in the appropriate lapel and ask her for a few words for the nation. Fitzwilliam, for the love of God! What a name to saddle a young lad with. I'd hate to think that was Moby's idea. I know he weren't that crazy about Billy-Chantal and Kerry-Louise for the girls, but he went with it in the end. Anything for a bit of P&Q. Fitzwilliam, though – know what I mean?

We turns into Beaufort Street and he sees McKenna,

his next-door neighbour on this side lugging in a big mad set of Chrimbo lights. Not just any old lights these, by the way. This is a full-size fuck-off Santa Claus and you can be sure that by six bells tonight he's going to be sat up there on McKenna's roof, all lit up and shouting 'ho-ho-ho' at weary passers-by. Moby goes white and slumps back in his seat.

'Tell you what though, lad – drop us off in town, will you?'

I can't help laughing at him.

'Scared that little cunt's going to have you up his ladders tying Santa to the chimney?'

'What? Fuck off, will you! It's not that. It's just . . . *her*. She'll want me to go straight out and buy one for ours. Bigger.'

'One that sings carols and that?'

'If you could get one that took confession and that, she'd have it, lad, I tell you! She'd well have it!'

He slides down low as we pass by. I turn right, back up towards Park Road. He's still a bit quiet, to be fair. Bit pale by his own standards.

'You all right there, lad?'

'I'm sound.'

'OK.'

He does a big mad sigh. Sighs out loud, he does.

'Just – she's doing me head in a bit. Over the communion. Wants it to be just so. You know what she's like, man.'

Don't I though.

'That's only normal, though, eh?'

'Nothing's fucking normal with her. She doesn't want normal, lad.'

'She's just excited, isn't she? Doesn't want to let no one down and that.'

28

'Oh, don't you worry about that, lar. No one's going to get let down. I don't want her making a cunt out of us, though.'

'How d'you mean?'

'If I don't watch her and that. If I give her a free hand she'll turn it into fucking Beckham's wedding. She will, though. She'll spunk thirty grand on this do. Easy. She'll go well over the top, know where I'm going. You want to see the dresses that she's having made for the girls. And your Cheyenne and all, too. Wants them all to have the same and that. Then it's flowers, photos, cars, carriages, and the *do* . . . just don't even take us there, lad!'

I don't want to insult the lad, but with his betting and that, with all his knocking about town and all of that carry-on, you never can tell. And I'm his brother at the end of the day. In a way, I am his brother.

'Have you got money?'

I can see four things in his reaction, if you will. He's pretending to be insulted. He's not at all insulted. He's not OK for money. He's not that bothered, neither. Can see all of that by the way, just in the way he goes, 'Fuck off, will you, Gerrard,' as though I've took terrible liberties with him.

But he'll live. He's sound. I still can't help myself having a smile at him. It's half amusing to see the big lad in a flap over the nice things in life. It's not him, all this. It's just not Moby.

'We'd better make extra sure the lads are coming down, ay? Make sure Didi and Sander and Tinhead are deffo coming and get *Hello!* round to take the sting out of the bottom line for you.'

He tries to make himself laugh, but the lad is worried

in fairness. She can't seriously spend that much money on one day, can she? On a communion? We cross Parly, past the cathedral and I puts him out at the top of Bold Street. I buzz the window down.

'Stay out of that Buro!'

I'm laughing. He winks.

'I'll tell them I don't see you no more. Tell them you're devoting all your spare time to charidee . . . you and Vince Earl and Tarbie!'

Now it's my own turn to laugh like I mean it.

Ratter

I can not get hold of the excellent Councillor Bennett. That's not unusual. The guy's been a breath of fresh air for Liverpool since the Lib-Dems got in, and this man has helped green-light some of the most imaginative and progressive regeneration schemes in town. JPB is honoured to have worked with him on a variety of them projects. I do mean that, by the way. Each one has surpassed the previous job in terms of scale and ambition. We're working on a joint venture now that will see forty acres of supposedly derelict industrial wasteland brought back into public usage. South Village (working title), just up from the Cain's brewery site, will be a cosmopolitan melange of vibrant student life at its best alongside up-and-coming new media start-ups. It's going to transform that part of the city, which has lay dying on its arse for decades.

The northern side of the village, running up towards Jamaica Street, will comprise high-spec student accommodation on secured-rent terms. It'll half be too good for students – elegant and adaptable inner-city accommodation at highly affordable prices. In the core central area we're opening up a warren of little side streets, streets that've been blocked off or bricked up for years. We're going to let them breathe again. They'll be alive with bars and cafés, a small live venue for bands maybe, live comedy and that, acoustic sets – that sort of thing. Little specialist shops selling nothing but tea or malt whisky and that. Nice. What living cities should be all about.

And then the south side, running down towards the Queen's Dock, is going to be creative commercial space. We're just about finished on this phase. It makes me unbelievably proud to stand and look at that thing and know it was all my own idea. Only a fool would've took it on, to be fair. It was this *yowge* storage block, immense it were, one unspeakable vast tram shed full of rusted railway sleepers and dead pigeons. A million pigeon carcasses in there, there was. The soft cunts manage to get in, but they can't get out. To say we've transformed that shithole is not even a understatement. It doesn't get you near to the truth of the way we've redesigned this place. In my own opinion, we've added to the architectural stock of the city, the way our designers have used glass and light and the river view. Stunning work, I think. Brilliant. After the work we've done on designing and remodelling and reinventing that space, it seems a shame to call the units offices. They're not even units. We've been working alongside a handful of very exciting young software and new media entrepreneurs to help provide them with exactly the sort of working spaces they need, from basic shell spaces to fully geared cyberrooms. YT was among the first to get on the Scallicon Valley trail. Oh yes. Pure visionary, I am. First thing I done was to cable the whole gaff. Fully ISDN'd up, the whole fucking site. So we'll be looking towards the e-commerce kids mainly, but we expect the fashion and television and film production sectors to take up space, too. Will not be a problem. They'll be biting our hands off to be part of the Village, knowmean. In ten years' time it'll be getting referred to as one of the main attractions of tourist-friendly media-city Liverpool. South Village. *The Village.* Created from a vision by John-Paul Brennan. Something like this would never enter Ged's empty head.

Councillor Benefit has aided this venture with several millions of EEC and local government funds, allowing the developers (see Brennan, John-Paul, aka 'Ratter', and Lascelles, Margueritte, currently trading as Byzantium Holdings) to keep rents viable for the community South Village has targeted. Bennett is a very forward-thinking councillor. It's not surprising his mobile's turned off. Someone or other will be lunching him at 60 Hope Street or his other favourite, Bijou – but that's only fair. The competition should be allowed to have a crack at him, too.

That said, I'm now at a loose end, in all fairness. I was half counting on catching up with the councillor – there's something I need to berate him about and something I need his blessing for also – but that's life. He ain't picking up just now. And with no other plans and no real desire to head back to the office and run the gauntlet of Margueritte being 'focused' or 'driven', whichever she is today, I get this sudden impulse to head out to the country. I'll call up Terry to get the dogs ready and we'll have a afternoon out among the wildlife. Rabbits, voles, maybe badgers once it gets dark – no creature can rest easy when me and Terry go wild.

It's what I always used to do, when I first got took in by Mrs Brennan. Never could call her mam, to be fair.

She never pushed that side of it, neither. She's a good auld girl. Great what she done for us and that. But the truth is that I don't feel nothing for her. I don't. I can't say that I do feel something – or if I do, it's something not good. It's the way I feel with Ged and all, too. All they ever done was take us in and look after us. And all's I feel back is that I despise them for it. Can't do nothing about that. It's just the way I feel inside about what's happened. That's all. Haven't given it hardly no thought for years. Been a busy lad, JPB has.

That's the one good thing to come of all this, by the way, getting taken in and that. That surname, Brennan. Done us no harm, in fairness. Carries a bit of weight, it does, which is no disadvantage in business. And it's better than Buggabi, which I've been told is what my ma was called. My mother disappeared. That's all I know and all that matters. Don't know if she's alive or what. Really do not give a fuck, in all fairness. If she walked in through that door right now and said, all right, son, sorry about that, lost it a bit – I don't know what I'd do. Knock her out. Take her on a world cruise. Come what may I can never love Ged Brennan and his ma will never be my ma. Fucking doolally she is now, anyway.

In them days though, in some barrios – most parts of town in fairness – they had kids that was 'taken'. I was a taken kid. The authorities weren't that organised back then and, so long as a kid turned up for school and didn't have nits and seemed to be well fed and that, there was nothing to get that worked up about. So Mrs Brennan just took us in and, abracadabra! I was Ged's little brother. A brand new little brother to make up for the other little brother, the one that got run over, the apple of their eye. Nobody wasted a moment in telling us what a little cracker he'd been, how Mrs B and Ged and the girls was all made up with that little lad. And here was me brought in to try and lighten the load for them. That's the way I seen it, anyway. I'm not that arsed, by the way. That's not the thing that I hold against them. I don't know what I hold against them, in all fairness. I never hardly give it no thought nowadays, knowmean. All's I know is that all of sudden Ged was my brother and Moby was my cousin, just like that. I should've been made up to get dropped right into a set-up like that, knowmean, two of the hardest lads in the South End there to look after little John-Paul. But I couldn't take to it. Not at first. They was scary, knowmean. I'd shy away from them. I thought they was all too thingy and that. I kept bunking off school, bunking the train out to Aughton and Ormy and I'd spend all day setting traps and catching birds and mice and rats.

I got to know all the lads that went out there, hunting. Lads from Kirkby and Crocky and Skem, all on the dole, all dressed in Barbours and Harris tweeds and that, all out in the countryside with mad, vicious dogs. They was working dogs by the way – Kerries and lurchers and Lakeland terriers. Forget beagles and Dobermanns and Staffs. Them dogs are fuck all, man. The hardest dog in the world is a Kerry blue – no back answers. This one time myself and Terry and Ned was walking back to Town Green station. We'd been digging at the canal bank out by Downholland Cross, digging for rats mainly, but sometimes you'd come across a stoat and that was one fuck of a brawl. A stoat can have a proper fucking go, but Ned and Terry's dogs knew how to work them.

We'd cut back across all sorts of fields to get back to the station and, because the dogs had done well that day, instead of kicking them and hitting them with sticks, Terry and Ned let them run ahead through the fields. We was all talking and that, so we didn't see what was coming. Over this stile and suddenly you're in this very quiet suburban area on the outskirts. We hears this yapping. Up ahead a little peke has come out to warn the dogs off, let them know this is his patch. This peke is the cock of Town Green and he doesn't care who knows it. I'm first over the stile and I sees the little Pekinese showing his teeth, eyeballs all pulled back and wild like he really wants to have the Kerries off. I probably could've stopped it, but I wanted to see what'd happen, in all fairness. I was glad I stood off. Hilarious, it were. One second the peke's there, yapping at the two Kerries, and his mummy comes out to see what the matter is. Next thing there's a mad squeal from the peke and suddenly it's all just fur and blood. There's just this little mess of guts and fur and blood and there's one mad stary peke eye in the middle and all, too. The dogs have pure torn it apart – literally torn its head away from its shoulders and tossed it from side to side like a beanbag. We couldn't stop laughing. All the way back, every time one of us went to say something it was more fits of giggles. What it was, was – the nice lady whose peke it was had to sort of retrieve the mess that was left of it. She was in bits about her darling little pooch, trembling and half about to cave in and that. We weren't hanging around, by the way, and we managed to shuffle past, all dead serious and that, stony-faced so's we wouldn't laugh in her face. But then, just as we're about at the end of her road, she shouts after us, in this dead high-pitched sort of schoolteacher's voice: 'Excuse me!'

Trembling still. Could hear that bit of tremble in

her voice, like she was half crying but trying to stay on top of it.

'Do those dogs belong to you?'

That done it. We just legged it. We was in bulk, though. Fucking killing ourselves, we was. Never stopped running or laughing until we got to the station. Every few minutes on the train Terry'd go: 'Ex-cuse me! Do them dogs belong to you!'

One of my own little luxuries today is that I've set Terry up in a kennels out near Billinge. It's a totally legit KC-registered operation and turns over a nice little profit while we're at it – but obviously he keeps our own dogs, too. Every so often he'll organise a Badger Night or something, or if I'm in the mood I'll just call him up and we'll take the dogs out for a lurch and that. It's one brilliant fucking way to unwind. Can't be beat, in all fairness.

Moby

If I have got a fault it's that I'm too sociable. I'm a amiable guy and lots of people want to buy my good self a drink. That's the problem. For a big fella, I don't half take the knock easy when it comes to the demon drink. And once I'm half-canned, I don't mind admitting it – I'm punyani crazy. I have got to have a lady, lar. It's not that I don't love Marie an that, it's just thingy. We've been together since dinosaurs ruled the earth is right. I see it as myself doing her a service. If I can get my end away while I'm out, I'm not going to be bothering her in that department when I come in, am I?

The thing is, because I'm half a musher and that, bit of a face out and about, I can have my pick of what clubs I want to go into. And when the girls see the doormen making a fuss of you and the manager of the club sends

36

you a bottle of champagne or whatever, comes over and gives you the big howdy-doody, they know straight off that you're a Somebody. I don't mind saying so – I love it. I do not half mind being a Somebody in Liverpool, to be fair. You can see all these little honeys lined up trying to work out where they know you from. Is he the new fella off've *Hollyoaks*? Is he Everton's new goalie? And the truth is, they don't care. They do not give a fuck whether they can put a name to your kite. So long as the management is sending you a bottle of champagne, they want to suck you off. They want to put your dick in their mouth and suck it. That's how it is, by the way. That is a fact.

But I'm mad, I must be, I swear to God I am. I've got all of that or I can have it like that whenever the fuck the desire so takes my dozy self – and I don't want fucking none of it! Straight up. Since the lap-dance bars opened up in town, that's all's I'm interested in. Poledance punyani. I fucking *love* them girls. That's true – I am in love with them. I love everything about them. I love their made-up names like Danielle and Sapphire and fucking Lycra. Are they names or what? Fucking Dara! I love the smell of their talcum powder and that thick, cheap perfume that they spray all over themselves to keep the old bodily odours at bay. What a fucking mix that is! That slick, glistening skin sweat just starting to come through under the eau de bargain. Fucking love it! If places like Nirvana brought out their own perfume – the stuff the girls use in there – and sold it over the bar I swear to God there'd be no end of randy fellas taking a bottle home for their ladies. I don't mind it when one of the girls has a bit of stale breath and all, too. That's what I like, by the way. Heavenly creatures with down-to-earth vices. BO. Bad breath. Brutal sex drives. Love it.

Best of all, though, I love the way the girls in Nirvana do their borders. It's like they're having a little contest to see who can shave their minge in the most eye-catching way. I've got so many little favourites in there, I love them all, but there used to be this girl Laetitia that had hers done in a Nike swoosh and that. Straight up. And there was Niagara, little Latino-looking girl who trimmed her beaver down to one little strip, a tiny oblong, just like Huey's beard out of the Fun Loving Criminals. It says Touch And Go all over the place in there, but it was an act of penance to keep my thumb out of her cunt, in all fairness. It's just *there*, right in front of you, and you can't help but feel that these girls want it and all. I know they dream about getting rammed by big, hard lads like me. I know they do. They like bad lads, hard lads, lads with big knobs and lads who've got a few bob. And they like a lad in a nice whistle. That's about it. Anyone else can join the waiting list.

I did ask Purple Fonzie this one time if there was anyone in there that's mentioned my good self in conversation. He's all right, Alphonse. Bit of a musher in his day. Can have a fight if he feels like. Been doing the door for Mikey Green for years. I'm not one of these guys that's got any beef with Mikey Green. People say he brings smack into the city but it's never been proved to be fair and, in saying that, plenty enough white lads are bringing gear in, too. Lads I grew up with are meant to be heavily into that caper, by the way. I wouldn't go as far as to say good luck to them and that, but it's life, isn't it? There'll always be some cunt bringing junk into the city so why not let your own thrive if anyone's got to.

I've always got on with Mikey more or less. We all went through a bit of a spell when we first left

Shorefields and there was a whole summer of big black v white tear-ups going on. Shorefields was about the most mixed school in the Barrio and we all grew up all right with each other. It was just when we got to about fourteen, fifteen, we all started kicking off on each other – girls, music, all the usual things. Mikey Green could always have a fight and that but so could I. Last day of school we had a big one-on-one right outside the gates. The traffic woman was in bits, screaming at us to stop it. I had him off quite easy, really, and we was at it all summer. There was this one *yowge* tear-up outside the sports centre. They come down and that, looking for us. I think they thought we was going to run when we seen how many there was, but that just made us into loonies. Mad persons, we were. Fucking psychopaths. We went through them like marge. It was only the riots brought everyone back on line. Mikey took off after that. He was away for a year or two, no end of stories about him going to New York and Jamaica and then he come back rich. Nice fucking car. Opened some clubs up. Good luck to the cunt, by the way.

Alphonse isn't from the South End, I think he's off've the boat. So black he's almost blue he is. Purple Fonzie. He don't say much, tries to look hard and that – not difficult with them mad Charles Bronson eyes – but he's all right. I've never had a peep out of him. He's one fella whose hands are almost as big as mine, Fonzie. I noticed that the first time I shook hands with him. We was both trying to get our hands round each other's and I only just stole it on him. Could I fuck squeeze his knuckles though, by the way. Tried and that, to be fair. Had a grip on the cunt. Could not make any impression on him. I sometimes get the impression he's frowning at us, but in fairness it's probably just his eyes. He's fine with my good self, Fonzie is.

That time I asked him if any of the girls had made mention of old Moby he half admitted it. He said a few of the girls had started giggling when I went out and they was saying things and that. Like getting blood out of a stone, by the way. When I asked him who in particular he pointed up a girl from Leeds, Nadia (like fuck!), and she was all for it, to be fair. The other girls cleared out of the changies – just about big enough to roast a girl it were, never mind two dozen of them all getting changed and shaved and that – and I give it to her standing up in there. She stood with her back to us and put one foot up on the little table and bent forward a bit to help us in and that, and pulled her lips right open with one hand like she was putting on my own little peep show. I don't mind admitting it – I'm not at all that patient when it comes to Judies. I'm very easily aroused and I just don't have the discipline to take my time and enjoy it. I mean, I fucking *enjoy* it is right – I fucking love it. I just think I'd enjoy it more if I weren't so fucking excited the whole time, know where I'm going. No complaints from little Nadia, though. She was squealing and screaming at us to really give it to her. I never seen her in there after that.

I think that was down to Derek. Now Dajun Derek's a sly one. See, Fonzie knows the score. He knows who to oblige and that. Derek, though – Derek thinks he's a Player. Derek thinks he's a big hitter because he works directly for Mikey Green. He's like a sort of under-manager, a group manager that looks after part of the operation. He's hardly ever in Nirvana, but you can see the girls' attitude change whenever he walks in.

Suddenly, they're not chatting to the punters no more, they're all work, work, work, money, money, money. They won't even look you in the eye when Derek's in there. Not that they do with most punters. Angelina, one of my own little favourites, told us that the best way they can keep their pride and dignity in there is just to look past the fella's shoulder and think of him as just a piece of meat and that. Reverse psychology, she said. She was at the Liverpool Uni, that Angelina. Smart girl. Derek was in there when I come out, the day I walloped Nadia. He must've heard us. You couldn't *not* hear us, in fairness. Nice kid, that Nadia. Nice, tight, gushy fanny.

In spite of our Ged I do have a couple of drinks in the Buro after all. It's not that unusual to see a few of the players in there after training on a Monday – if they've had Monday training, that is. More often than not these days they'll have had a Sunday game or they're preparing for a Monday-night match or a trip to Europe – the Liverpool lads, that is. They don't come out and socialise so much since Houllier's been in charge. Fair play to the lad, though. Just look at the results. He's stopped the Chrimbo party and all, too – thinks he has by the way, anyway. Ho ho ho! The lads still know where Santa's hanging, though. I was at the one the other year, fucking cracker it were, the one at the Pen & Wig where everything got a bit thingy and the press was on top. Gentlemen's Evening? Don't think so, lar. Lads have been a bit quiet since that one in fairness.

You still see the Everton boys round and about, though. One of them's in a bit of lumber right now. He half took liberties with a young girl and that girl happened to be still going with one of the lads. Girl only finished with the kid a week and a half ago. Still half going with him as far as he's concerned and next thing she's in Baby Blue with this Everton cunt, tongue halfway down her throat and that, making a proper cunt out of the kid. So what's happening is, one of the lads went along to Bellfield to catch him after training and he goes to him, basically, this city can still be a good experience for you and that but you're going to have to behave yourself. And you're going to have to put £50,000 in the kitty. That's the sticking point. He only wants to give twenty. Cheek of the cunt, by the way. The money them twats are on.

Anyway, no players in there this afternoon but I do have a good old chinwag with the Count, who asks to be remembered to our Gerrard and before I know it it's after four and I'm randy as hell. Always cracks me up, that one does. Randy as hell! Always stuck with us. Some lad from over the water that used to go the aways with us was always coming out with stuff like that. Had his own rhyming slang and that, Wirral Rhyming Slang. Guinea Gap was crap. Raby Mere – queer. Made us lot laugh, he did. What was his name? Funny cunt. *Milo!* Milo, that was him. He'd look at you and go: 'Gentlemen, I have an uncommon thirst!'

Our Gerrard used to love all that. I know he did. Rubbed off on him a lot, all of that. He still comes out with 'if you will' and 'gentlemen' and shite like that. They was all Milo's. Randy as hell. Cracks me up, that.

Nirvana opens at four of a weekday, and early doors is a good time to go down there. There's only a few suits and pervs in there at that time, so you can have a good natter with the girls, get a dance then take one of them back to the changies. Dajun Derek hardly ever goes down there early doors. It's as good a time as any to get one of them backstage.

This puts me in mind of Ged. Our Gerrard reads a lot, by the way. He's a bit deep sometimes, young Ged is. But something he said this one time done my head in good style. It was when I first told him I was half getting sweet on little Angelina. He said that throughout history, know where I'm going, throughout the history of wise guys and goodfellas and that, there's always been lads knocking on the dressing-room door after the show. Pure done my head in, it did, thinking I was just doing what some handy lad from Brooklyn might've been up to a half a century ago. It's like thinking about the edges of the universe and how it never ends ever and that. You shouldn't let yourself think about that shite. And it's not as though I'm bringing flowers, by the way.

Nirvana's pretty busy already, to be fair. All sorts of bevvied-up beauts in cheap work suits, out on the Christmas piss-up. Fonzie's not exactly knocked out to see my own cheery grid knocking at the door but he's polite, and that's all you can ask for. I half think that I sees him raise a eyebrow at one of the girls, but that would involve his face moving and is therefore not on. It's not the greatest ever time I've had in there. Too many piss artists. I select Palmeira who says she's from Madrid and get it over with. I tries to slip Fonzie a dropsy on the way out but he shakes his head and won't look us in the eye. Funny cunt, he is. Proud, I suppose. Is right and all too, to be fair.

Tuesday

Ged

I do like to keep fit, but one thing I can't stand is gymnasiums. The old sort are all right, places like Vic's and the old Powerhouse by the Bully. Places with benches and free weights and that, sweatboxes if you will. But these new gaffs that're springing up in every disused council building and church and picture house, Bodyfirst and Slenderline and that, tarts' places with all the aerobic cardiac machinery, they're just shite. They do all the work for you. That's not keeping fit. That's half a hour on the treadmill at four mile an hour then straight on to the sunbed. Or the beautician's. Or into the bar to talk about the gym instructor's steel-hard arse. Shite.

Margueritte

This site is perfect. Ideally I'd have preferred it a little closer to either the Strand or Castle Street and we're stuck in between, but with Beetham's Plaza and the new Grosvenor Estates development we're lucky to get anything in this area at all. This one will certainly be our flagship Uptone. I've been trying to catch John-Paul's eye and get him to piss off, but he's too busy staring out at the river. That vista alone will add another £50 to the membership fee. It really is a spectacular view to work out to. I have no doubt; this site can be terrific for us – if John-Paul doesn't blow the whole thing with his damn slobbering. I used to love that unadulterated desire in him but now he's just fucking embarrassing. Success has not improved him. He's still raw goods. Guys like this young real-estate agent can see right through him. He's always wanted things too badly,

John-Paul has. It'll be his undoing if he doesn't watch himself.

Ratter

What I've always loved about Margueritte is that she wants it as bad as what I do. Even at Shorefields she was aloof. She was the best-looking black girl in our year and did she know it, by the way. Would she fuck show out to any of the mushers or the knuckle-draggers. She hated all them roid-heads and plazzy gangsters as much as she hated druggies. Which makes it poetic that we should be putting so much investment into sunbed salons and gymnasiums at the moment. She used to despise them places! Club 18 to 70, she used to call them. Now we call them Uptone and toast them with Cristal.

I used to walk her home most nights after school. Follow her home, in fairness, the speed she used to walk. She's slowed down a bit now, but her legs are still fantastic. Long and smooth and tapered they are, just perfect. I love her legs. Her mam used to say she walked so fast 'cos she was trying to leave one life behind and get to the next one as soon as possible. I'd have to say here and now that I used to whack off over her mam all the time. Thinking about it, she must only've been about thirty-five when I started calling round there, if that. She was good enough to be a model – better-looking than Naomi Campbell's ma, and she's better-looking than Naomi in my own book.

Margueritte Lascelles. I used to write her name over and over on my school books, then rub it out in case anyone seen it. The chances of someone like myself going with her was so laughable that you would've got slaughtered if anyone'd seen her name wrote there.

45

There was only three Haitian families round by ours and every one of the girls was knockout gorgeous, by the way, but Margueritte – she was something else. She was cut out to live the high life and everyone seemed to know she'd do it. No one and nothing was going to stop her. Pure class, she were. The hard girls never even picked on her. She was treated like a sort of special case, to be fair. Like one of our own was going to break out and do something boss with their life. No one ever called her Margi, neither. It was always Margueritte.

I thought I'd lost her when she passed her A levels and I never. She was off to Manchester Uni to study law. I thought that was that. But then I seen her in the *Echo* about eight years ago, little piece about her practice in Lodge Lane, how she was specialising in women's cases – battered wives, maintenance, immigration, all of that. She's still a ardent feminist to this day, just a slightly more materialistic one.

But that was it. It was a second chance I never thought I'd get. I called right round to her office to see her and, to be fair, she was pretty glad to see us and all, too. Over the years I've levelled with her where the venture capital comes from. She's OK with it. She knew, I think, anyway. She's a realist. We've got the place she always wanted in Cressington Park and all the neighbours just think she's this classy, high-powered lawyer and I'm her fella that works away a lot. Which I do, by the way. I've got my place in the Dock and I don't even have to square it with her when I stay there. To be fair, I think she's sometimes glad of it when I don't come home. We understand each other. It's a solid bond that we've got. We're much more of a partnership, a real close equal partnership, than loads of the orthodox married couples you see queuing up at Costco at the weekend. I do half regret that I haven't give her a baby, though. I know that is the one thing what she wants more than any of this. But I just don't. I don't like kids. I don't want a kid. Not even for her. I can feel her eyes in my back now, giving me the nod to fuck off while she talks about the lease with the agent.

Ged

Now this is exercise, lar – this is a proper fucking go-around, by the way. I'm keeping up with them three twats, but only just. Moby and Drought are miles behind. What we're doing just now, couple of times a week at the moment, is we're going out with Robbie Loughlan doing roadwork. Robbie's got a big fight coming up at York Hall a week on Saturday. All hands are going down for it. Liverpool are away at West Ham and all too, so it's going to be a bit of a do. He's only on the undercard, Robbie, but he's a good little lad. He might do it.

Today we're doing the Holylands circuit. Fucking grueller it is – no two ways about it. Sorts the men from the boys, this fucking circuit does. There's myself and Robbie, his regular spar Carl Igo and their trainer Willie McDermott, plus our Moby and Drought. Drought just comes so's he can sit in the Nutty and tell all hands he's been out training with Robbie Laughlan. My own name'll figure and all, too. Likes to let everyone know he keeps company, Drought does. But he's welcome. He's a good lad, mind you. He got slashed right across the windpipe on a job of ours that went wrong, this one time. This delivery firm sent a van out with some boys riding shotgun for them. It weren't even shotgun – there was fuck all in the van when we got it open, only the heavy mob waiting on. Of course, we proper took it out on them, but Drought got hurt in the tear-up. That's how come he's called Drought and that, now. He half sounds thirsty all the time. Croaky.

So what we're doing with this circuit today is we start on the corner by the sports centre, jog down Harlow Street, left into Mill Street, left into Welly Road and sprint back up on to Park Road. Then it's right into Beresford and a jog down on to Mill Street then hard sprint up Moses right across Grace Street up to Park Road and down again into Isaac, jogging this time, letting the heart catch up again. By the time we're at the top of Jacob Street and turning back for David Street, Moby and Drought are right at the bottom of the hill. He could've been a fighter, Moby. He used to box. He had a terrific dig on him – he broke this lad's thigh once, pure snapped it in two with one dig – but he weren't dedicated. Girls was his undoing – girls and the ale. Once he started going out that was it for Moby and boxing. Boxing never got a second look-in.

I could have a fight myself but I weren't no boxer. I had no skill. I could never keep a reign on my temper. I was all out attack from the first bell and any cunt that had the suss to play us out a bit, that was it. I was gone. My worst moment was getting put on my arse by this little lad from Salford. It was in front of the lads and all too, over at Everton Park. He was a clever cunt, this Manc, sucked us in good style, got myself going, wore myself down, knocked us out. I still love all the roadwork, to be fair. It's real exercise. It's you that's doing all the work.

Moby

I'm fucked, by the way. I'm looking forward to a nice drink. I don't mind saying so.

Ratter

I had to leave anyway. I'm more than happy to let Margueritte take care of the legalities, but I had to get off. I'm picking Paul the Hom up at twelve bells and we're off on a drop to Kirkby.

A couple of my regulars have asked why I take the risk, making the drops myself. I just tells them I like taking risks, but that's not it at all. It's the pure fucking opposite of that. The truth is I don't like leaving nothing to chance. Nothing. I've got this thing that, if I take my eye off the ball then it's liable to disappear. I've worked fucking hard to build up this line of revenue and I don't intend to spunk it through being careless. I've seen it happen that many times. Lads get past a point where the money doesn't mean a fucking thing to them. They drink or they fuck around or whatever, they don't pay attention to what they're doing and that, don't have their eye on the ball. And then it's gone. They're gone with it and all, by the way.

I'm not coy. What we're talking is drugs. Class-A drugs. It's me that brings them in and it's me that drops them off. The only time I can't see the fucking gear is when it's all dressed up in the boot of my vehicle. I've done it up as all sorts. I've taken fucking massive packages of caper round in the boot, done up like a kid's birthday present. This one time I was delivering to Telford and I gets stopped on the M54. I was properly khaziing it, I don't mind saying so. I didn't know if I'd been stitched up or what. Plod asks where I'm going and

49

that, what I'm doing and all of that. I tells 'em it's my godson's birthday and keep on smiling like a gobshite. Not good enough for one of the fucking goons, mind you. Nowhere near good enough for Telford muzzie man. Asks if he can have a shuftie in the boot. Sees the prezzie. Asks what it is, who it's for and that. I'm just going 'act normal, act normal' and I tells him it's a Winnie-the-Pooh wheelbarrow and garden set and tries to get a laugh out of the twat. Even though my accent isn't as strong as, say, Moby's or something and I'm trying to disguise it even more it's obvious he's twigged I'm a Scouser and, what with the Shogun and that, it's a nap that I'm going to get his undivided attention now.

'Mind if I take a look?' he goes.

My heart is pure bursting through my ribcage now but I'm just trying to think – what would you be like if you *was* off to a kid's party? So I just goes: 'By all means. But if you *could* just be that bit careful with the wrapping. You know what children are like about presents.'

This seemed to do it. He still ripped a tiny bit of the wrapping paper off, just to show that he was thingio, the kiddie and that, but it was YT he was looking at, searching for my reaction instead of looking at the package. Not even apologetic or nothing, by the way, he just goes, OK. Off you go. I couldn't even flop out and relax even then, mind you. Cunt followed us all the way at sixty-nine-mile a hour. Twat.

So I always *always* ship it out myself. If I sit on top of the gear myself then I've got no one to blame if it all goes wrong, have I? And who else could've come up with the godson's birthday rap, by the way? No one is who. It's terrible that I won't trust no cunt, but there you go. I'm not a trusting sort of a guy. I don't even trust Paul the Hom and he's the most loyal cunt you could wish to have by your side. Pretty fucking thick, to be fair – and cake and properly a sex case – but loyal as fuck and coming with good repute, and all.

He just loves being a gangster, Paul does. That's what's in it for him. He doesn't drive a big car, hasn't left the barrio or nothing. He does like his labels in fairness but, apart from that, he seems happy enough with his lot. He's being a legitimate gangster. He's the real thing. He's not a hired hand or a door fella or whatever. Paul the Hom, by gift of JPB, is involved in the day-to-day supply of class-A narcotics on a moderate to large scale.

He's the perfect Batman, Paul, because you don't have to pay him a fortune and he doesn't ask for nothing and people think he's hard. He's not, strictly speaking. He's not a Hard Man, to be fair – not one on one. But he's mad. He's done loads of mad things over the years, run into mobs on his own and bitten police horses' arses and capers like that, so people are half afraid of him. That does no harm in our business. And he's not like a typical homosexual, Paul, neither. He's not camp. You wouldn't know he was queer if it weren't for the name, and that stuck with him from when he was in Preston. All the subbies from Burnley and Blackpool and that thought it was hilarious. *Pour l'homme*. Paul the Hom. Funny. But it stuck.

I always treat him well, Paul. I'll throw him a couple of puck of black every now and then, and a few tablets so he can be seen to be a dealer around Walton where he's from, and he's happy as fuck. Fucking delirious he is. He'd do anything for YT. But I don't need him to.

All I need is for him to ride shotgun with us once or twice a month and keep his mouth shut.

That's where I think my own operation is a step ahead. I'm not a drug dealer as such. What I'm offering is in the grand tradition of Liverpool brokers. I'm really just a frontiersman, setting a tariff, bringing goods in through the port and effecting a distribution network. My role is simple. I'm a consolidator, that's all – a consolidator. I'm at the high-risk, high-profit, zero-labour end of the market. I bring the shite in. Almost immediately, I move it on to the boys that make the real money. But I'm happy with the ratio of risk-to-gain that I deal with. I'm somewhere near the high-to-middle end of this particular chain. I deal via Bernie and mainly through Ireland. Almost all of my trade comes via the Bhoys, the Dubliners, the Irish connection. Now, these lads are fucking tasty, they are. If it weren't for the nod from Bernie I'd half have the horrors having to deal with the cunts. Nobody's ever come out and said it's the Provos or whatever, and I'm certainly not asking no questions but let me just say they're not like most of the lads you deal with. Don't dress up. Don't make a fuss of you. Only have a laugh and joke over something horrible, and even then they only have a laugh with one another. You never really feel like you're their mate – which you're not in fairness, even though you do get them no end of tickets for the match. That's their one indulgence, the Bhoys – they love the match.

I've always left the Bhoys and Bernie to make the actual deal, the big one, the import from source. They sort it out with Turkey or Amsterdam or Colombia, depending on what the crop is, then I'll make my deal with them. And once I've dealt, I move it and fast.

Mainly to firms in Kirkby, Skem or Crocky – lads I've known for years, in fairness. But I'll also supply reliable outfits from as far away as Middlesbrough and Norwich and Southampton. I'm a broker and I'll go wherever there's a sustainable and relatively docile market. One thing I'm not crazy about is stirring up the competition, by the way. Even with Bernie's say-so, I'd rather go where there's no feathers to ruffle. A guardian angel can't protect you all of the time.

But I do always clear everything with Bernie. Bernie's one of our own, a very heavy hitter in London nowadays and everything I've ever done has been with his blessing. Right from the off. I as good as asked his permission when I moved in on them little places at the start. I targeted these little sleepy places where there was a population centre and that, but no cunt seemed to be taking care of business. Just because it's only Nantwich or whatever, doesn't mean the kids don't want droogs. In actual fact, it means they *double* want droogs. I put that to Bernie. I said to him, if I'm standing on anybody's toes it's only going to be some wool dealing a little bit of weed and that. I won't even zap 'em. I'll gently move them over, knowmean. That's what I put to Bernie that first time. He knew Ged'd be against it, but he stood back and took a view. He was cool-headed, not rash and emotional like our Gerrard. Bernie told us to stay well away from Windsford but he okayed Whitchurch and Northwich and a bit of Telford for YT, cleared it with the Wolverhampton mob and that's how I got started. Not kicking off. Not trying to take over. But supplementing. Having the arse to come in when others are hesitant. Securitising.

He's in business, Bernie, and that is his only criterion

for decision-making. He told us that at the start, when we was talking about Cheshire and that. Does it make sense? is all he asks himself. Is it business? Not like one of them played out Mafia things where they go on about it being, like, business and not personal and all of that baloney. The fact is that drugs IS business. Big fucking potatoes. And what I put to Bernie a couple of years ago – weird calling him Bernie after all that time, but, that's what they call him down there, that's what he likes to be called by the trade – is that there was a gap in the market. There was a demand for a sort of service industry – a well-capitalised mini wholesaler who would supply the suppliers. Bit like selling on a debt, if we're being crude about it. It'd be a specialised field but a pretty fucking handy one. I'd have to state here and now that I did devise that whole concept, by the way, but there's a few fellas specialising in this area now. Truth is I don't mind a few people getting on the scheme, in fact it's been more help than hindrance. There's been times, quite a few of them, when Ireland has wanted me to take more than I strictly want to bring in, knowmean. But I'm adamant about the right way of bringing it into this city and the right amount to ship. One thing I do know is how the Port of Liverpool works. But there's been times when I've sensed that the Bhoys are getting a bit frustrated with old JPB, little bit impatient with my safety-first tactics, and at that point it's easy enough to bring in the fella in Ayr whose money's burning a fucking hole in his pocket. Or there's the young lad in Southampton and one or two others who're playing this particular market now. Lay some or all of the risk off against them boys. And then there's always the Boro Brothers. They don't even recognise the word risk, by the way. To them lads, it's all a case of jam today. I love them boys to death. I really do personally enjoy being around them. Their attitude to life is the same as their attitude to business. Go for it, lar. Is right. Go for it big. And while I tend to get a bit thingy about huge quantities and the possible repercussions of my name being stamped on a deal like that, the Brothers will dive all over it. As they often do, by the way.

But that's all it is that we do. It's Futures. It's just another way of playing the money markets is the way I look at it, and just look at the money market. Completely deregulated now, it is. Retired fellas playing it from their bedrooms on little PCs. People like me are, in practice, nothing more than a second wave of suppliers who serve to supplement the main guys, and only then when the need arises. It's a risk-free proposition. I don't undermine no one, I don't take from them – I fucking *pay* to *help* them. Get that. And it adds up. I've taken every word of Ged's teachings and turned it into big business. *Big* fucking business, by the way. None of his scatty-arsed heavy-duty blags for no money. I'm into big dough with all of this – and I know how it works at the other end and all too, by the way. I've got half an eye on the sell-by date. The smartest deal a real wiseguy will ever do is to get out. Not that I madly want to get out, by the way, but it's just the law of averages. You do – you have to quit before you get quitted. Couple more jobs like this one today and I can maybe begin to think that way.

So I'm outside Paul the Hom's gaff and here he comes. I don't mind Paul's company. He's quite a good laugh, Paul is. Queggs always seem to have a good sense of humour. And it is no bad thing to have someone sat next to you on days like these. Years and years of carrying large amounts of cash or drugs or both in the car does get to you. It does make you very wary. I'm forever looking in the mirror, for instance, on the case for any cunt trying to tail me. You can never be too sure. But that's one area where I'm a Luddite. I have to, have to, *have* to handle all cargo myself. I wouldn't ever trust no other cunt to make a delivery on my behalf. Never.

Paul jumps in. Just the one drop today, but it's a biggie. Enough smack to keep fucking Kirkby pinned right into the New Year. I should wear a bushy white beard and shout ho-ho-ho as I come down Valley Road. I hate smack. I fucking hate fucking bagheads even worse, but what are you going to do? I don't like to have to do this for a living but some cunt's got to do the scummy jobs. Paul gives us his lairy grin.

'D'you know the gag about Tony Blair and William Hague in the brewery? Hague goes to Blair, I can drink fifteen fucking pints . . .'

'Heard it.'

I haven't, like, but droll as he is at times, I'm no longer in the mood for Paul the Hom's quips. The thought of all those lowlifes cutting each other's throats for smack has started to fill me with despair. It's true. I hate the cunts. I try to think of the money instead. After we've dropped off in Kirkby we're driving straight up to Edinburgh to bank. I deposit funds with one of the oldest and most august financial institutions in Scotland. They ask zero questions. They never have done. Eli put their name forward, among others, and he knows all about clearing banks. Byzantium Holdings. That's us. I always wanted to be a Holdings, right from way back. Jonesy from by ours whose dad had a roofing business once paid for his summer football school by cheque. It was only three fifty. *Nobody* had bank accounts in them days. I always remember the wording. It was Williams & Glynn Bank – Jones Bros. Holdings. It made its mark. The bank up in Edinburgh are quite happy that we're Byzantium Holdings and quite happy to accept large deposits in cash. They may be a august establishment, but they don't give a fuck.

If there's time, we might even drop in on the Boro Brothers on the way back. If anyone can put a smile back on my face, it's them boys.

Ged

I love the bones of my Deborah but she does make us cringe at times, to be fair. One such time is every fucking time I get our answerphone. State of her voice on that message, by the way. Thank fuck the lads haven't got our private number. If they heard that, they'd slaughter myself. You'd think she was brought up in Windsor Castle, not Windsor Street. She sounds like she's got a broom pole up her arse.

'Helleow – regrettably neither Mrs Deborah nor Mr Gerrard Brennan is able to accept your call. Leave a message please or try again later.'

'Regrettably', for fuck's sake! '*Accept*' your call! I've argued it through with her but she's adamant. She thinks the people who've got that number – the other mothers from that fucking school, basically – are going to be impressed by the message. She reckons it's a honest message. It doesn't say, like, we're not in. It says we're not talking to you just now.

When I get mad with her she just gets nasty and says how I don't like it because it sounds like courtroom lingo. Well, it does. Half sounds like a magistrate giving you a KB – I said that when I first fucking heard it. I nearly went white. I *would've* gone white if I weren't already white.

'Regrettably, Mr Brennan, this court does not accept your plea . . .'

That's what it sounds like. She won't have it. She says it's my criminal mentality getting things all bent out of shape. Criminal mentality, if you will! How many times do I have to tell her? We are not criminals. *I'm* not, anyway. I just operate outside of the accepted sense of what the law is. I *interpret* the law different, is all. If the law weren't bent against barrio kiddies like ourselves in the first place then we wouldn't have to do nothing about it.

I told her last night, anyway. If she doesn't change that fucking message I'm going to change it for her – and she wouldn't like that. My message'd go:

'Phone us later. All right?'

That's all's I'd say.

I switch off the mobile and manage to get back through the tunnel without encountering any more maniac drivers. The M53 is fine. Everyone's keeping a sensible braking distance, no one tailgating or overtaking on the inside lane. Nice and civilised, just how it should be. It's a nice car for cruising on the motorway, this. It's a classy car, the Saab. It hardly attracts no attention at all, except from odd people here and there with a bit of taste. It's elegant without being flash, the 9–5, and safe as houses. Anyone passing by would just take myself for another moderately successful businessman. Which I am, God willing. I decide to put my good mood to good use. It's not arranged, but I fancy I might just surprise Coley. Can pop in on the girls to kill a hour, then it's a nap that Coley will be sat in the snug. And what *is* the point of being a respectable businessman, by the way, if you don't feel you can pop in for a drink every now and then with the likes of Ray Cole, CID. I sail past the Heswall turn-off and head straight on for Bromborough.

Ratter

I'm on him straight away. One of the drawbacks of driving a purple SLK is that you're never inconspicuous and I catch a flash of him over on the left, hardly moving at all. I clock the rear-view mirror. I'm not imagining this one – it's definitely him. It's Stanton, and he's got back-up. Three lads in a Discovery right behind him. What the fuck is occurring here? I rack my brains. Only Paul and me know about this drop. Paul wouldn't tell a soul. Would not say a fucking dicky bird to no cunt. So can it be just a bad coincidence that we're now being tailed through Kirkby by Alan fucking Stanton? Al Stanton is not a drug dealer – not last time I looked. To the best of my knowledge he's still into loan-sharking. There's no sense to this at all. Al Stanton on my case? Can not be. I drive on, slowly.

I glance at Paul. He's oblivious. He's fuck all to do with this. Thank fuck for small mercies, by the way. If you can't rely on the likes of your Pauls then you're fucked. That's all. I check the wing mirror so as not to make it obvious. Fuck coincidence. He's tailing us. No doubt about it. This cunt behind, one of the most ruthless cut-throats in north Liverpool, is going to try and have our gear off. For what? Or for who, more likely. Think, think, think. What's in this for Stanton? To stop his clients spending the money they owe him on drugs? Just because he can? Whatever, he's taking a crazy fucking pop with this one. Any and every cunt knows I'm green-lighted by Bernie.

I sly another look at Stanton's Merc. Twat of a colour that, by the way. Big mad purple I Am. Sums the cunt up. Can I fuck get my head around his game, though. Cunt knows I'm elect. So what's his thingy here? Can only be a gypsy heist. He's going to pure rough-house it, that's all's it can be – take the fucking gear off've us and see what happens next. He'd do that, Stanton, by the way. Fucking wretch, he is. Wrong 'un through and through. Fucking bully, he is. And not that clever, neither. Cunt's stupid enough to start a war with this. If there's one no-mark bully in town that'll cut your throat and have your gear off and to fuck with the ever-after, it's Alan Stanton. Who is on my case, by the way.

And then, suddenly, a opportunity up ahead. I sees it in a flash. We're approaching Brubakers. Outside Brubakers it's like a doormen's convention. There's loads of them, about eighty lads waiting outside, hands in pockets, shuffling about laughing. I suss it straight off. They're way too relaxed for this to be a call-out. They're waiting for their lift. They're going into town for their big Christmas hoolie and they're waiting for the fleet of look-at-me's to turn up. They're on Paul's side. I buzz his window down.

'Let on!' I hiss at Paul. He jerks out of his stupor. He weren't on to the Stanton thing at all. He looks out of the window, frantic.

'Who to?'

'Just give it the big one! Really fucking let on!'

'I don't know none of them!'

'Fuck off! Have you ever known a firm of doormen not to let on to a Shogun? They'll be falling all over themselves to make out like they know you! By the time we've driven past we'll be Robbie Fowler, fucking Carra's auld fella, fucking . . . Shea Neary's trainer's mate – just make it fucking, loud, all right!'

And he doesn't let us down, in fairness. He looks the part anyway in his fucking doorman swag. Probably all they see is a black glove waving out the window and a fella in a Kevlar hat shouting, 'Macca! Go easy on them Judies, lar!' in this big, mad accent. Loads of lads turn round and let on. You can see them all going 'fuck's that?' and that, but a good few of them starts to wave back. I slows down. Stanton's slowed up, too, but he's still behind. A couple of the door lads start walking over to us. Is all fucking Stanton needs, by the way. Him and his back-up fuck off down the next side street pronto and that's them, gone. The two lads from Brubakers are up to the window now. Too late for YT to scat in fairness, but no worries. Paul pulls out a wad and peels off five twenties. He hangs his arm out the window, doesn't look them the eye, doesn't act like he's their mate. He's good.

'Pass that to Macca for us, will you? Tell him I'll win it back off him tonight.'

They're immediately on their guard. They don't want to touch the money. But Paul's played it spot-on – they don't want to risk fronting him neither, just in case, even though there's loads of them. The first doorman points back to the big congregation outside the club.

'He's only there, lad.'

The lad puts two fingers in his mouth and gives the familiar whistle. Two blasts, one high, one low, like a duck-call. No response. He whistles again, then shouts

61

for this Macca one. Whoever he is, cunt's mutton. The young lad looks mortified. He half apologises to Paul.

'Here y'are, lad, I'll just get him for you.'

The doorman turns to jog back. Paul grips him by the arm and pulls him back. Only now does he look at him. He does look hard, Paul. You can see this lad's not sure about him. I've been ready to put my foot down and get out of there since Stanton done his offski, but Paul's into his role, now. He's De Niro. He's fucking Method Man. He presses the money back into the lad's hand, all smiles.

'Ah, tell you what though, lad – he'll be chocker if I pay him off in front of the lads and that. Know where I'm going? You know what he's like, lad. He'll feel a cunt. He won't take it off've us. Just pass it on, will you?'

The lad looks at the money in his hand. Sold.

'Good one, man. Say it's from Sammy, will you? Good one. All the best lads. You take it easy now.'

The two young lads seem happy enough. The window goes up and I start to drive. In the mirror I can see the doormen going into a huddle. A bit of an auld coach arrives. No stretches for this crew. Whoever they work for, he's a cheapskate.

'Who's fucking Macca then?'

'Eh?'

'Who's Macca?'

He shrugs and grins at me.

'Fuck knows. There's got to be one Macca in a platoon of fucking Kirkby mushers, hasn't there?'

I crack up laughing. I've got to take my hat off to him and that – he is fucking good, Paul is. I should let him do more. But that encounter with Stanton has only served to steady my feeling that there ain't going to *be* much more. That was too close for comfort, that were, however you want look at it. Something's happened, and it's happened over the last few days. Think. Can't. Doesn't make no sense at all. Either my Kirkby end has ratted me out to Stanton – which, by the way, would be suicide. Fucking death warrant, that'd be – or he's after pure moving in regardless, anyway. That'll be curtains if someone like Alan Stanton moves in on the drug trade. You can not do business with a animal like that. Or with Kirkby from now on, sad as it is. Just procedure, by the way. Just common sense, eliminate risk and that. Whatever, this little ep has served as one almighty wakey-wakey for JPB. Time to get my arse in gear. I'll have to have a ponder about Byzantium and Margueritte and that. But from this moment right now one thing is fucking Waterford. I, Ratticus, need to get my personal account back into the healthy eights then I'm out.

Ged

Setting up on this leisure park was one of the best moves I ever made. No doubt about it. Like all good business ideas, it sprang from personal experience. Me and Debbi had been the Odeon to see that *Usual Suspects*, then we went for a blackened chicken in that Louisiana, next door. It weren't even a mad time of year, by the way, but could we fuck get a taxi home! The nearest firm was in Eastham, the next nearest was in fucking Bebington! There we was, stood there like two soft cunts outside one of the biggest leisure complexes in the Wirral – cinema, Yatesies, skittles, two nightclubs, video-game arcade and three restaurants – and that's just the night-time, mind you. During the day there's all kinds of offices and factory units and all, too. There's Boots, Dixons, Comet, Homebase, McDonald's, Halfords and all of that, and of course there's the Asda. All the mams and pensioners that haven't got cars, struggling to get their shopping back from the big Asda. I could not believe that there weren't one fucking taxi firm on site. We'd only just started moving the money into taxis, but I knew for certain where our next office was going to be. Here.

The rents are a bit stiff, to be fair – you pay premium going rate for a site like that, but, as these things go, you can pass that on in your tariff. Punters know we're not the cheapest firm around. That's not the thing with A-Line. In fact, our regular Billies know full well that we are nothing other than the *dearest* firm around. A-Line cars are a pricey ride, is right, but folk round here are so fucking ecstatic at being able to just get a cab, immediately, just like that, at long last, that they don't mind paying four pound or so for a three-fifty ride.

Obviously I do have to charge my drivers a slightly higher settle than they'd give in, say, New Brighton, to be fair. But they do know that the work is guaranteed. It's fucking non-stop here, nearly twenty-four seven. And the Billies are mainly regs and all, too. Even if it's just a auld dear that wants taking home from the Asda twice a week, she ain't going to be doing no runners and them little home runs soon add up. My lads are very happy here at A-Line, to be fair to us, and I've got drivers banging on my door every day of the week. I've got thirty-two lads now and I could easy take on another twenty tomorrow. But my lot'd just kick off, wouldn't they, and, in fairness, they'd be right. I don't really need no more lads. Couple of girl drivers I could find a case for but other than that it'd just be greed on my part.

It's going fine how it is. Thirty-two drivers giving us a £70-a-week settle. Take away Trudi and Mandi's wages, my operators, take away the office overhead and that still leaves myself pounds in. It answers all the questions that have to be answered. It tells the world how I can afford the house, the school fees, the holidays and all the trimmings – and it gives complete control to my good self. It's perfect. Nobody knows a fucking thing. Nobody *needs* to know nothing. And the bottom line is that I know what's coming in, each and every week. No cunt can shortchange us or rip us off, know what I mean. The only thing that runs it close for peace of mind is the tanning studios, but that's asking for it nowadays. You open a tanning studio and you may as well have Money Washed Here on the sign outside. Don't want none of that, to be fair. Don't want no funny fellas with briefcases knocking on your door.

And I know plenty enough lads that's ploughed their money into bars, restaurants, clubs and all of that carry-on. Whenever you're out with them, their face and body might be there with you but they're miles away themselves. They're wondering what capers the staff are up to this time. They're trying to work out how that lad behind the bar is skimming two ton off've the take. It's not that they're going to *miss* the two ton, by the way, but the principle of some little cunt thinking he can walk in and have them off is quite preoccupying. It drives them potty, to be fair. They don't want to think that some lad with spots can stand there under their own roof and take off've them. But that's what's happening. That's what they've got to deal with day in, day out. That's the hassle that I've managed to bypass.

Same goes for the job in general, by the way. We

could've easy run the doors, me and Moby. We could get a crew of lads together like that. Proper firm and all, too. But then you're into staff, you're into wages and all of that, and the more people you've got under you the higher the likelihood is that one of the cunts is plotting your downfall.

That is a fact, by the way. You give a lad of eighteen a job and what he's thinking is not, how do I repay this man? How do I show him my gratitude for giving myself this half a chance? No no no, lar. He's not sat thinking that. He's thinking – how can I fuck his wife? What about the daughter? When do I take over? How soon can I be *him*? That's all's the young lads are thinking. That's the God's honest truth, by the way. Or they're looking to skim off 've you, at the very least. And, even if your own boys aren't looking to fuck you, there's always the other side. With nightclubs and the doors and that, there's no status quo to be fair. There's always going to be competition. There's always going to be grief, whether it's just pissheads kicking off or it's a younger firm looking to take your door off 've you. And that day will come. That day will come. You'll be stood outside of your door one night having a smoke and a laugh with the lads, clocking the gear on the little honeys in the queue and a younger lad will walk up to you and just pure have you off. That's how it'll go, by the way. Pop you. Zap you in the leg. Knock you out if you're lucky. Might take a year, might take ten but it will happen. It *will* happen.

That's the way it is with the tartan and all, too. I could've got rich through tartan, easy. Sometimes, when I look at the no-marks calling themselves gangsters in this fucking city, I think I should've gone after it – run the whole thing, like. Run it proper. But that's only odd days. Same thing applies. Staff. Enemies. Restless nights. Don't get none of that in this game. There's always talk about Taxi Wars and all of that, all the stunts that rival firms will pull on each other to get the upper hand. They might make loads of bogus calls and that, order cabs from non-existent customers. They might come in with hammers and smash up the switchboard. Whatever, none of that shite has ever happened with myself. I asked Dools to make sure that every cunt over here knew who I was – just so's they didn't end up embarrassing themselves, mind you – and, to be fair, the lad done a good job. I sleep easy.

And I do live a easy life. Every Wednesday I take two thousand, two hundred and forty pounds from my drivers. That is a fact. There is no variable. They give us seventy nicker a car, midweek every week, if they want to keep on being a A-Line driver. It's up to them how much they make after that. But for myself it's two-two-four-oh, each week, every Wednesday, on the nail. I declares about a half of that. Bit less – that's what I'll put in the bank. That's my regular income as far as the regular world is bothered. Any accountant looking at myself, my lifestyle, my business would have to shrug his shoulders and go: 'Yes. That's a fifty-grand-a-year man, that is.' That's the way I want to be seen by the world. Just another hard-working lad that's done all right for himself.

And this week I have double reasons to be cheerful. This Wednesday is Week One of that most excellent Yule tradition, the Double Settle. On account of the extra income them thieving bastards will be raking in, on account of their invented double-clocks after midnight and clock-and-a-halfs and ten-pound-minimum fares and all of that caper, as well as the obscene number and amount of tips they will make, none of which is ever channelled back to myself, by the way – because of all this we, the misunderstood guardians of the taxi industry, gets it all out of our systems by imposing a double settle on the twats for the three weeks starting 12 December. This, in fairness, gives myself something of a spring in my step as I enter the office.

Ratter

Ritchie was so fucking weird when I made that drop that I started to feel a bit thingy. Just thought okey-dokey, here we go. Backs to the wall time. They want my swag they're going have to fucking take it off've us. I cancelled Edinburgh straight off. That's a long, lonely drive if there's fellas on your case. Many a spot to pick you off with Brewster's in the boo. Ritchie paid up and that, to be fair. There weren't no nonsense. But I just felt like he was surprised to see YT. Nothing you could put your finger on, just a half beat and that. He weren't normal with us. Whatever was going on with Al Stanton, Ritchie was in on it. And it's not like he had a choice about paying, by the way. There are higher beings than JPB pulling the strings in all of this and if I've learnt one thing it's that they just want things to go to plan. They want people who'll do what they say they're going to do. It can be very simple and very rewarding. Fucking Ritchie's no mug. He should know all of this by now.

So I takes the money across to the kennels instead. It's the only safe place now, and we're right by Billinge anyway. Even if Ritchie Mahon and co *are* half thinking they wouldn't mind a instant return on their lolly, hijack opportunities are limited. We can be there at the kennels in twelve minutes flat. Terry wouldn't even dream of asking what goes in and out of that little strongroom, by the way. He's another good one, Terry. You need them around you. You've got to have lads like that.

I pays Paul off and drop him back at his mam's, but as soon as he's gone I start thinking I'm being followed again. I'm hardly watching the road ahead I'm that busy with what's behind and what's behind that and all, too. This black BM has been right on my tail all the way down County Road. It's not like he hasn't had chances to get past, neither. I've just been cruising and that, give him all the time in the world to fuck off past into town to be a gangster, but he's tucked in good and happy to sit. With no indication to the cunt I does a sudden big mad youie by the Clock and screeches off down Bradewell, across Westminster Road and on to Orwell then back to the dock that way. And once I'm inside the apartment and I've locked all the doors I find that this has all got to me, bad style. From as soon as I dropped Paul off I've felt the lowie coming on and now it's pure crashing down on us, a fucking murderous black downer. I can't stop fucking pondering on it, over and over and over. Who's behind this? Which cunt is backing this cowboy up?

And it's not just that, by the way. It's not just that some cunt is trying to have JPB off and I've got a fucking shrewd idea who, by the way – it's bagheads. It's the life I lead and the world I fucking live it in. It's a downer and it does get to us on and off, depression and that. I'd never, ever go and see the quack about it. No way. It's too easy to cop out and take Prozac and that, jellies or whatever. I don't need no doctor to tell us the score. It's just a occupational hazard. I've worked out the mood pattern and that. I do tend to get depressed when I've had dealings with bagheads. Anything to do with the cunts, it pure brings us down, it truly does. I fucking hate them. They fill my soul with despair. I hate their pallid white skin and their oversized heads and their sunken, saucer eyes and their wide fucking mouths. And the lies they tell. The lies they tell themselves and every other poor cunt that comes into range with the low-life raggedy-arsed bastards. I hate them. There's only one way I can deal with this. It's time for another cull.

Ged

Ray's there in the Thatch, usual spec. He's half startled to see us by the way, but I have good reason to conflab with him. Ray Cole, Detective Inspector Cole, by the way, is a very valued member of the Allied Charities Commission, of which I am President this year and fully fucking expect to be voted in unopposed for the coming year and all too, God willing. We've almost doubled our income and distributions since I've been on board. That's no fluke. Some of the older puritans don't like my style and that, to be fair, but I am a doer. No cunt can argue with that. I get results. I haven't hardly started yet, neither. I've got big ideas of where we can go and what we can do with this charity. I know that some of the fucking posh cunts don't want the likes of myself showing them how it's done, but deep down they can't help but be impressed. They'll come around to me in their own good time. I've got no doubts about that, by the way. I half wants it that way. I wouldn't go jumping all over some new lad that I didn't hardly know, to be fair, so why should they? I am the new lad. That is a fact. If I want in to the golf club and that, secret handshakes and all of that, then I know I've got to prove myself. I've got to show that I am worthy. And in the meantime them cunts can call myself what the fuck they want behind my back. It means fuck all compared to the work we do for them poor children. When you see them little kiddies faces light up it's all worth it, school tie or not.

In fairness, Ray Cole is with me one hundred per cent on all of this. That is one guy who *does* like my style, by the way. He's not just a good colleague, he's become a friend and all too, Ray has. I have never and I would never compromise that friendship with the Ray Coles of this world by leaning on them or asking for no favours. With myself and Ray it's always strictly off duty. We just seem to happen to enjoy one another's company, in fairness. That's allowed and that. Is right. A copper and a blagger − so what? Life is what it is. My only rule *is* that there is no rules. And in any fucking walk of life you has to have some R&R, some little thing that's your own, something away from the grit and toil of your day-to-day scenario and that. That's how it is with myself and Coley. To be fair, the work that I do with Ray and that is the best bit about my life just now, own kids excepted. It's a buzz for a lad like myself that I am putting something back. I am making a difference and that.

'D'you hear back from Robbie?'

I shakes my head, half thingy, bit embarrassed, to be fair. Ray wobbles his empty glass around as though it might magically refill itself. One of the reasons we get on so well is that we have a shared ideology about charity. Bottom line − it's all about raising money, charity. Forget worthy causes. It means fuck all if you can't bankroll it. Kidney machine for Alder Hey? Give us a hundred grand. Where's it coming from? Show us the money. It's just another business, charity is – there is no point in avoiding or denying that fact. It's a business. It's all about your product. You do have to give people something they want, whether it's for a good cause or not. People don't want to just hand you their lolly for fuck all. They want something for their fucking money and right and all, too. We understand that, myself and Raymondo. Most of the committee do not.

There's a prevailing wisdom in charity circles that if you pack a event with half a dozen has-beens, a few never-did-quite-make-its and get the weather reporter off've the local hospital radio to compere the event, then punters are going to turn out in their droves, fivers in hand. Not quite. Punters are very picky. Teenage girls, say, will come out in their droves if Adam *Ricke*tts is going to show up. Now you're talking. But even then, they still want something to do besides just standing in line waiting for a photo. They want to see Adam make a cunt of himself, get custard pies or wet cloths thrown at him and all of that carry-on. One of my own big initiatives is the Allied Charities Festival every Whit bank holiday. I gets the big bands down to play, a few of the footballers'll come down for Penalty Prize and that and we'll have six-a-side matches between, like, *Hollyoaks* and Five or something like that, with the players going in goal or taking turns to referee. And that works, by the way. It works a fucking treat. It's a fucking nice family day out, to be fair. I half know a lot of the lads socially and that, half let on in the Baby Blue or the Mello or whatever. Moby knows them all better than myself, in fairness. He's always knocking about town, our Anthony, bit of a face, if you will. I don't like asking Robbie, to be fair. I do know the lad. He's from the barrio and that. Moby knows him good. But I half gets a feeling he's thingy about our Ratter. I just get the notion that Ratter's queered his pitch, somewhere along the line. He's never said nothing in fairness, but he is distinctly cooler with myself than maybe he is with some of the other lads. It'll be nothing, in the long run. He's from the barrio, Robbie. He's one of our own. It's good to see the lad doing so well for himself. Ray's made up that I know him. I've told Coley that Robbie'll deffo put in a appearance at the kids' panto, commitments allowing. He's made up with myself, to be fair, but that's never stopped the lad from asking for more.

'How am I fixed for Boro?'

Fortunately, Mr Brennan delivers again.

'Sorted. You're in Mick Malloy's box.'

'Malloy? Remind me which one he is again . . .'

'Scrap metal.'

'Nothing dodgy?'

Dodgy, by the way. Who the fuck says dodgy these days?

'Mickey's sound. He'll make a great big fuss of you, brush the crumbs off've your jacket and he'll have you picked up and sent home in a car of your choice. So long as it's a limo!'

'Smashing.'

We both has a little chuckle at this. Ray Cole half puts his arm around us. It's like he's going to half tell us something for a second, but then he doesn't. It's just a bit of a hug. Just a nice, warm gesture and that. More than words and that, to be fair. I think twice about it and then I think what the fuck, we're getting along sound, he's my mate, he's not going to fucking mind. I don't want to do nothing to rock the apple cart, but I do just think fuck it in the end.

'Did you, erm. Did my application come up for consideration and that, at all?'

He doesn't even pause, by the way. Doesn't fanny us for a second, to be fair to the lad.

'Not yet, Ged. It will do, though.'

Ged, by the way. Not Gerrard and that. Not Mr Brennan. I'm his mate. He thinks something of us. I'm in good here. I really fucking would like to fuck off a lot of the scummy stuff that I have to do and just spend more time with the likes of Ray Cole, to be fair. I wouldn't say I'm desperado and that, but I wouldn't mind joining that Royal Liverpool. I half go for it, in fairness. We play quite a bit of golf together during the summer as it is, Ray and me, but never there. I tell my Barbara that I play at Hoylake with him and she's made up and tells her mates and that, but the truth is we play at the Hoylake Muni. Nice course and that, by the way. Would not knock it for one second. End of the day though it ain't the Royal and that is where I want to hang my hat. Membership's rock though, Ray says. They're strict as fuck who they'll let in. Doesn't matter who the fuck you are, by the way. Helps if you went to public school and that, Merchant Taylor's or Birkenhead or one of them. Our Stephen'll be all right on that score. He'll waltz in. He's had the best of everything, Stephen. They both have. We was right not to send him the Annie's. He'll get into the Royal Liverpool, our Stephen. I won't. Women can't get in neither, by the way, so you couldn't say they're making it up as they go along. Not as full members with voting rights and all of that, they can't. Last bastion it is, the Royal. Wouldn't mind getting in there, to be fair. Debbi'd be pure fucking made up. Made. Up, she'd be.

'Time for one more?'

'Thought you'd never ask.'

He's a fucking good lad, Coley. I shuffles up to the bar, trying not to knock into no one, not wanting to disturb the auld regulars and that. One auld fella half lets on to us, just a little half-nod of the head and that, all right and that. Nice crowd in the Thatch. Very nice people in here. I'm wishing I'd thought to say 'one for the road' instead of 'time for one more'. One for the road would've sounded well fucking better. I'm a bit gutted about that, in fairness.

Dajun Derek

'Don't want you letting the man in no more, Fonzie. Seen?'

'Im nod but don't look me in the eye. He just don't like to be told off, this bwoy. 'Im bad awight. I like 'im.

'Or if 'im come then 'im pay like normal punter, yah? 'Im not a special case, yah? 'Im NOT a special case.'

Fonzie nod again.

Ratter

You only need a car-full for a cull. The bagheads don't fight back. Don't get a chance to, in fairness – cunts don't know what's hit them. You don't even need the best lads for a do like this. Just need one or two boys that don't like bagheads or just pure like hurting people. They've got to want to hurt the bagheads bad, smash their hands and that, shatter their knuckles or something.

Cunts are fucking useless anyway but you have to leave them even more fucking useless. I've never had to pay for a cull. Never.

So I gets on to Paul and he's made up, as per usual. Fucking head case, Paul is. Loves anything like this. He gets a little crew together and we're off. There's a shooting gallery up by the Brow. Shaw Street, just off 've. It's a risky do taking direct action in that particular barrio, by the way. It's a strong Lodge area and they do like to police it themselves, knowmean. But it's not like we're going to sending a advance posse, in all fairness. We're not firing no warning shots. And it isn't as though the smackheads are going to go crying to the UDA, is it?

'Some mad fellas come round and mashed us without green-lighting it with yourself, Johnny.'

Not going to happen, by the way.

I've got bats in the car. Not basies. Basies are a bit unwieldly. I like to use these customised little half-bats. Like a kiddie's basie, but with a bit of weight in it. It's shaped like a basie and that, but flexible as fuck with it. What I do is, I bore out a hole at the thick end and pour in a few spoonfuls of molten lead – lead melts dead easy, to be fair, you can do it on the stove with a old pan. The effect though, lar – fucking stunning, by the way. You can knock a lad clean out without hardly no backlift – break his jaw and that, smash his teeth with just one or two smacks. One of the lads has got like a cattle prod and all, too – not a prod and that, to be fair, more like a stun gun. One of them things where you ram it into a horse's mouth or something, calm the monster down, knock him out and that. One of them.

We parks up by the Red Triangle and mooch up over to the estate, what there is of it. The notions them councillors used to come up with, by the way – this place was meant to be themed on a Cornish Fishing Village when it was first built. Fucking state of the place now. Purely a disaster, it's nothing but. Old Tommy White Gardens up the road had its problems, but the flats was all right. They was decent. They pull down places like Tommy White and do what? Fishing villages. Blowing it out of their arses, they are.

If bagheads are good for one thing, it's strong doors. They don't want Old Bill giving them a unexpected knock and they double don't want no other heads coming in and zapping their gear. It's easier getting into the Cream. But I do have a advantage. I do happen to know the name of their main fella and that. Their Bag Man. So I just sticks my mouth to the letterbox and go: 'It's Phillo.'

Abracadabra! The door's open. We're in. And it fucking mings. The stench inside that gaff is knockout, proper bad, bad stink and that's no word of a lie. Fucking murderous, it is. It's like a blowback when you walk through that door, all the stink of all them miserable, unwashed, unproud bodies cabbaging on smack for day after day after day. They're not just smackheads nowadays, by the way, neither. They like the brown and the white, these cunts. They're just pure monged day and night, on their way up or on their way down. Bit of crack to make them high, bit of bag to lull the comedown. Out of it, they are. They're not of this world and that's the God's honest truth. You can believe the bit in that *Trainspotting* film. You can believe that a little baby would be allowed to corpse in a place like this. No cunt'd give a fuck. They wouldn't even fucking notice, by the way.

We don't fuck about in there. No one wants to stay any longer than we had to. Straight away we're booting and smashing all these yellow, wretched, yellow-toothed creatures all around the gaff. Even the tarts – they get it, too. This skinny one is half game and half out of it and she stands back against the wall sucking her finger. Asking for it, by the way, the baghead slag. Was probably good-looking a year ago. You'd still let her suck you off if you found her over the bridge and that. Her eyes are doing something. They're half going 'come 'ead'. Asking for it, she is. Paul gets her before I can. She makes a horrible fucking moan when she goes down. He proper fucking twats her with his bat and from the way she goes down it looks like he's done her skull. Her eyes roll right into the back of her head. This cunt on the deck tries to grab my shin and pull himself up. Fucking horrible he is, big fucking Belsen head looking up at us, half pleading and that. I takes a step back and ram the toe of my PCs into the cunt's mouth and think thank fuck it weren't the white Pradas and that. He's down and whimpering like a shot dog. Probably all kinds of snot and fucking smackhead slobber on my snakies. We're out of there. Six or seven of the sick fucks are left doubled up on the floor, whining and spluttering and crying. Probably only what they're like when they can't score, knowmean. We was in there less than five minutes and the results are devastating. I'm a awful lot happier when I get back to the dock. I gets my clothes off and set myself up on the sling and call up one of the chat lines.

Ged

I don't know who's worse getting ready for bed, her or me. I'll admit it, I do like to have a shave before I go to bed, half to scrape off all the day's shite and that. I do feel that bit better for it, in fairness. And I will slap on a bit of a moisturiser afterwards and all, too. Just whatever she's bought us for my birthday or back from the duty-free or whatever, but the whole shebang only takes myself a minute. But her? She takes hours. Exfoliators and tonics and balancers and re-fruition creams. I've usually read three chapters by the time she's ready. I always has a book by the bedside. I like history books and that, biographies, military histories and that, but I do read novels, too. I read that Ian Rankin's books, they're sound, and I like that Kathy Reichs. Patricia Cornwell. Detective thrillers and that, mainly. I'm reading about Bismarck at the minute and all, too. AJP Taylor. He was a Scouser, AJP was. He fucking done it, didn't he? Did go to Merchant Taylor's though, to be fair. He would've got in at the golf club if he'd wanted, AJP would've.

'Are you going to be reading long?'

'Doubt it. Can't hardly keep me eyes open.'

'*Can* hardly.'

If she could only see myself grinning from ear to ear. *So* fucking hard to wind up, Debbi is.

'What d'you want for Chrimbo?'

Big, huffy sigh. I fucking love this one. I got lucky the day I seen this girl.

'D'you have to cheapen everything, Gerrard? Does everything have to be dummered down?'

One of the big things that I love about her is that she is deluded to fuck. Does my head in at times, to be fair, but I've got to hand it to her. This girl does not know her place. Is right and all, too. We're fuck all without our dreams and that, are we? I'm with her all the fucking way, God willing. If that's her thing then I am fucking well behind her one hundred per cent and I don't give a fuck what any other snide cunt says.

'I'm trying to be nice,' I go.

She gives us a lovely little twitchy smile and goes: 'I know you are.'

She snuggles up into my back. Fuck. She's in the mood. I weren't counting on that. Haven't got a shag in me, to be fair. Not sure I can pull it off – not even if I think of Nina Perkins-West. Best get myself snoring, pronto. Debbi whispers in my ear. 'Just get us something classy.'

I start the heavy-breathing routine and she leaves us alone.

Wednesday

Moby

We always have bacon and eggs. Always. I know we get told it's bad for us and the cholesterol and all of that. Even the lads down the gym are all clued up about CPRs and cholesterol and the balance of your diet. The way I see it is, if you have your bacon and eggs first thing in the morning then you've got all day to work it off. Is right, isn't it?

And look at my good self, by the way. Six-four and a half, sixteen stone dead, know where I'm going. There's hardly a pick on us. I'm a lean, mean fighting machine. Shagging machine, by the way, these days. And to be that, you need feeding up. It's the one meal we're sure to have sitting down together. The taxi comes for the kids – school's only about a five-minute walk but you can't be too careful these days with all the psychos and pervs and that running round town. Our Billy-Chantal's old enough to get them all into class, now, and I just give the lad his dropsie at the end of the week. Marie picks them up in the afternoon, in fairness. It's just the mornings she doesn't fancy. And I think it does next door's head in by the way, our three going to school in a taxi. I'm waiting for Marie to finish off her brekkie and fuck off out so's I can watch that *Aerobics Oz Style* in peace and that. I'm not saying that I *always* have a morning tug to get the day started, but it'd be a unusual day if I didn't wake up with punyani on the mind, know where I'm going. I like that *Aerobics Oz Style*. Their thighs are a bit on the hefty side, to be fair, but I'm all in favour of a joust with a athletic Judy and that.

'Did you see their lights?'

Fuckinell – she speaks! She's stuck into the *Mirror* and dunking her toast into a fresh mug of rosie, but she did definitely make a noise in my direction.

'Next door's?'

A grunt from Marie. She bursts through her egg with a wedge of toast and carries on munching. She makes another sound. I think it was: 'Well?'

'Well what?'

Now she looks up.

'Fuck off! When are we getting ours?'

I'm not in the mood for a barney. I just want her out the house and that.

'We want something boss, don't we?'

She shrugs. I've got her.

'So? I'm waiting on this set that's coming in . . .'

'Who off?'

'Never you mind who off. If they're anything like the lad says they are, then we're the San Siro, they're fucking Prenton Park!'

I haven't even given lights a second thought, to be fair, other than when it's rubbed in my face. This should buy us another couple of days though. She's half on my side now.

'Well? When are they coming in?'

'That's what you can never tell with quality stuff like this. But I'm first on the list. No messing.'

She looks us in the eye. No, I'm not certain she does, but she's well on the way to lukewarm. I'd swear she's having a laugh and joke with us.

'It *will* be before Chrimbo, like?'

I gets up from the table and gives her a peck on the head.

'I'll give the lad another couple of days. Say, what – fifteenth? That's well long enough. If he hasn't come through with them by then I'll go to Freddie.'

'Freddie Woan? I'm not having no fucking swag from fucking Freddie Woan! What's that auld-arse going to have that's so special?'

'Ay – don't knock Freddie, by the way. He's got all kinds.'

'All kinds of fucking diseases . . .'

I know her well enough. I'm off the hook. For a few days at least, anyway. But I'd better get the feelers out for some lights, and yesterday and all, too. It's sly on the kids anyway, isn't it? They want lights and that, kids do. I'll have to proper start putting some lines down. Drought's usually good for any jarg gear like that that's knocking around. It's going to have to be good gear, to be fair, though. I don't mind admitting it – better than that little knobhead next door's, at the end of the day. Maybe try Chinatown. They go in for all of that, don't they? Lights and that.

'Are we inviting next door?'

She's fucking paranormal, Marie is. I swear she is.

'To the communion?'

'Unless you're throwing any other fucking parties that you haven't told us about . . .'

I don't know why she's like this. Always has been, in fairness. Half a nark she is, to be fair. Everything has to be turned into a fight. Good girl, though. She used to bring the dosh in for us when I was in Walton. She don't need to work now, wouldn't want any cunt to think she had to neither but when times was hard she was a boss bringer-backer, Marie was. She was the best. Every cunt knew her grid, Markies, Next, George Henrys, the lot of them – but nothing ever phazed her. She could front the lot of them and every single time they'd have to give her the money back. Hard-faced and that, but you have to be. She can have a fight and all, too, by the way. She'll have a little go around with any cunt, Marie will.

'We should invite them. They'll be chocker.'

I gives it a second.

'Not chocker that we didn't invite them, by the way. Chocker that we did.'

That half gets a grin from her. More of a leer it is, in fairness.

'Wait till they see the carriage. They'll fucking khazi it!'

Get this, by the way. We've ordered a horse-drawn carriage, all decked out in white orchids and lilies and that to take me, her, our Fitz and the girls down to

83

the church. Costing us Brewster's, by the way. It's going to look sound. Our Ged and Frank are going to be sponsors and that, but I did want to ask the Count and Robbie, in fairness. Now that *would* have done next door's heads in, that would. They'd've been denouncing all worldly goods and running up the white flag if I'd've gone ahead with that, Robbie as sponsor and that. I think he would've said yes if I'd've gone ahead, to be fair. Still, says he's coming to the do and that if he can make it. Good enough for YT. And Sander's coming along, I think, and Didi and Christian, God willing. Jamie and Louise are going to be down south, which is fair enough what with his knee and that. That's where their mams and dads are at the end of the day, isn't it? Michael don't drink, neither does Nicky. Don't know them boys so well, to be fair. Don't knock about that much. Nicky wouldn't, would he, to be fair, not with all the shite with the Shite. Macca says he'll come if he's back in town by then. He fucking should be. That's why we stuck out for the Christmas Eve, so's as many of the lads could make it as possible. Father Lacey was a bit thingy about it at first what with it coming into the advent and all of that, but he weren't going to make a issue of it. He could see the reasoning of it. Christmas Eve on a fucking Sunday is one day every cunt should be able to make. Macca's got no excuses, lar. Falls on the Sunday wherever the fuck you are, Christmas Eve does this year. That's the God's honest truth.

'Invite them.'

That must be the right answer, because her head goes down to the *Mirror* again and that's that. Don't look like I'm going to be seeing my little chunky-thigh Aussie babes today, well. I picks up my bag and head out to the gym.

Ged

I've just started having a nice wet shave when the front doorbell goes. I've just got a good auld lather up, proper soapy Joe jobbie with the auld shaving brush and that. They can fuck off, whoever the fuck it is. I'm not going down like this. Bell goes again. No let-up, this time. Whoever it is does not realise that they are now exactly fifteen seconds from a slap. Bastard! I was fucking starting to enjoy that and all, too. It's not often that you get the time to give your grid a proper fucking scrape. I manage to slosh most of the soap off and I'm downstairs and at the door in four big bounds.

It's our Stephen. He looks like he's been crying. He's fourteen, our Stephen, but he is a bit soft. Half a tart he is, at times. He cries if we won't let him stay up and that. Cried when I thrown out that *Marshall Mathers* one. Don't want him listening to shite like that in this house. Fucking lingo on the cunt, by the way. Kill your ma and that. Carve your bird up. He is easily upset, our Stephen is.

'What's to do, lad?'

He steps inside, snuffling. The situation is that Stephen's at Birkenhead. I'd gladly run him down there and that, but he likes to get the bus with his mates, now. It works out fine, God willing. Little Cheyenne's still at Heswall Prep for another year, so Debbi can drop Stephen at the bus stop on the way. I'll pick him up if he's staying late for chess or drama, but other than that he doesn't ask for lifts. Not from myself, though. He's a good lad. I'm proud of him. I wish could've had a half of what he's had. I'd be fucking prime minister by now, in all fairness.

'Come 'ead, lad – what's happened? Has some lad picked on you?'

He shakes his head. Fucking – relief. Very big let-off, by the way. I can not abide the thought of any cunt laying a finger on the lad. He tries to force a little smile for us. Smashing little lad, he is.

'I'm sorry, Dad. I'm going to need to blag a ride to school or I'll be late. I'll tell you all about it in the car . . .'

Wish he wouldn't use that word in this house. He's got half a trace of a accent, Stephen has. I know he only talks like that to try and please myself. He should know I'm not arsed. I'm fucking proud of the posh little cunt. He doesn't have to talk down for the auld fella.

I gets my trackies on and we get mobile, pronto. What he tells myself is that he tried to pay his bus fare in coppers. The driver made out he was 2p short and threw him off the bus. There was fuck all he could do about it. Just pure threw the lad off, no back answers. Obviously the driver was saying to him: 'Think you can take the piss? Think you can get me to count out your slummy? Let's see who's smirking now then . . .'

Obviously I don't tell our Stephen what I'm going to do. He'd only make us promise not to. He'd say I was making it worse. But the truth is that, much as I don't want to make a show of our Stephen, it's quite clear that this driver needs to be reprimanded.

Ratter

My life has just changed. Truly, this has been a life-changing moment. I was planning to have cross words with the good councillor over the Williamson Tunnels, but that phone call has jingled us up so much, I can hardly concentrate on lunch.

If I do have a fault, then it's caution. I am a bold lad to be fair, but I will not take foolish risks. Risk is not a idea that interests YT. I can live with that – it's a bind and that, I've had to pass some nice ones on, but it's better than having a fatal flaw, knowmean. I am cagey, I don't mind admitting it – and my deals to date have tended half to reflect that. People I deal with know my limits – or they appreciate my field of expertise is how I see it. I'm known for shifting a bit here, a bit there. I'm reliable. I do what it says on the label. I'm *very* fucking reliable, by the way. But if there's one thing I agreed with fucking Gerrard over, it was never to stick your neck out. Don't be a name. No need. Let everyone else kill each other and, so long as you're not treading on their grass, you can carry on until your luck runs out.

That was until yesterday. The first thing I done, first thing even before calling out the cull, was to let it be known that the Ratter might not be averse to upping the ante. For his own good reasons, J-P Brennan might be looking to improve his own cash-flow situation, knowmean. And twelve million is a amount of money such as will free me up big time. For ever would be more like it. I'm not without my reservations about this, by the way. For a long time I've had a system and a formula that works just fine for us. Good as gold, my little set-up indeed. But I have put out for a do like this and, even if it has come back a little bit faster than what I was expecting I am one hundred per cent having it. This is it. This is the moment. This fast-tracks me to the very point where I need to be. This deal frees me.

Ged

It doesn't take hardly any snooping at all to find out who the driver was. I'm down there straight from dropping our Stephen off. I just pops my head round the door at Woodside and ask did anyone by chance find a schoolbag on the back seat of the Birkenhead school bus this morning? The Heswall bus. They obligingly point us to Tommy. So this is him. This is the cunt who thinks he's going to do something to my lad. He's not even fit to *say* something to my lad. It's wrote all over this one's face, he's a wretch this fella, pure wrong 'un. But I goes on over and asks him about the bag, anyway, just to get one good look at him. He shrugs his shoulders, says it's not his job to check the bus over once he's light and goes back to the *Daily Sport*. If I was in any doubt about how to deal with this Tommy one, he seals his own fate with that one. Fella's properly a shithouse. He's just a horrible fucking horrible wretch and he's about to have a day he will never, ever forget.

Ratter

Twelve million, at a quick guesstimate, is what I'm going to clear on this. I'm not arsed about the whys and wherefores. The Bhoys mentioned a bit about excess quantities coming in to take account of Christmas and that, more than they was expecting and all of that – but I don't give a fuck. I don't need to know. What I need to know is this: can I raise the ante? Yes I can. Can I get shut easy enough? Oh yes.

They want eights for it, which is toppy in today's market, but with a bit of cutting and what have you I can get rid for twenty, no fucking worries. Off the top of my head I can think of four guys who'll be only too happy to take a bag like that at this time of year. I haven't decided yet which way to go with it – four lots of five maybe, or just a straight twenty. I know enough ambitious young lads out there that'll take it off my hands without a second thought. Plenty of them, by the way. But it's a case of finding the right firm. Twelve million pounds is not nothing, and a story like that is going to go round in no time if I don't play it right. My mind is going faster than I can make thoughts. I'm racing ahead, computing one thing into another, looking for the cause and effect and the possible repercussions. The whole picture is falling into place, and one thing above all is fucking Waterford – it's all just a matter of timing. It's a big fucking deal by the way, but it's nothing and all, too. Planning and timing, that's all it is. It's no fucking different to none of the other dos I've had through this port. That's the only way to think about it. If you think about it any other way, you'd go potty. Because this is, at the end of the day, the full whack. It's half the fucking Christmas gear for the whole of the mainland north of Birmingham. Every little dealer from Inverary to Darlington is going to have a piece of this – and I, for one, am fucking right off once I've hauled it in. That'll do me. Twelve million Not Out will do the Ratter very nicely indeed. All in the timing, it is.

But I'm putting all that to the back of my mind, for now. As luck would have it, we're having a sandwich down at the Harbour Club of all places, so I can start to put the wheels in motion with Arthur post-haste, just as soon as I've waved off Señor Benefit. And to think I was going to tick him off. All's it was was, I did hear that the Williamson Tunnels project is deffo going ahead. One hundred per cent green-light jobbie. This is a network of tunnels, by the way, commissioned by one of our enlightened forefathers, Joseph Williamson, after the Napoleonic Wars. There is, literally, dozens of them, all leading from the site of his old town house in Edge Hill down to various points on the riverfront. Some of them start from his stables and all, too. At the time, Williamson claimed he only built the tunnels to give work to decommissioned soldiers arriving back in Liverpool and that. But the thing was that he was obsessed with Napoleon escaping and invading Liverpool. But he weren't getting the better of old Willo, la. The lad constructed a whole sort of underworld village – there was even supposed to be a pub down there. A inn, at least, anyway.

We used to play down there. Didn't go down too far, in fairness. Most of it was blocked off and that. The bits that you could wriggle into was dead spooky. Your eyes wouldn't get used to the dark, even after about a quarter of a hour. I shut Go-Inhead in there, this one time. It was bad enough trying to get the fat cunt through the hole into the tunnel, never mind get him out again. I just blocked the hole up with these big planks of wood. I only meant to leave him a hour. Weird to be thinking on that, today of all days.

I mentioned to Bennett a few years ago that there was a potential tourist attraction in them tunnels. He'd only just really got his feet under the table and I'd met him a couple of times at Ramblers' functions and that and I don't think – well, I *didn't* think – he took us that serious. At the end of the day he fobbed us off with some stuffed shirt in Leisure & Tourism and it was never going nowhere from that point on, to be fair. Imagine my surprise, as they say, when the tunnels become the subject of a major initiative – EEC money, heritage grants, the works. I just like the idea of a attraction called the Liverpool Underworld, knowmean. To be fair, he did tell myself way back then that some old-timer had made the tunnels his lifetime's mission – been at it since the eighties or something. So hats off to the auld cunt if it's him. I can afford to feel generous. I have twelve million reasons.

Ged

Fucking weird it is sitting it out, waiting for that maggot to clock off. Haven't done this in a long while, to be fair, staking some cunt out like this. Twat's out there, driving his bus, making people's lives harder than what they need be and he has not got a inkling of what's about to happen to him. I think that's what that *Magnolia*'s all about. It's about the moment before it happens. Whatever's going to happen *will* happen, that is a fact and *Magnolia*'s about the moment before it does happen. Here he comes now, the gobshite. He's zapped his bus door shut, he's walking away and he's half thinking about having a bet or a bevvy or going home to give his missus stick. What he isn't thinking is that he's about to be thrown in the dock.

It's not plain sailing at first. Far from, to be fair. He comes walking right past the car. I leans over and shout to him. He recognises us. He's not quite so thingy now he's off the patch, but he starts up making his excuses about the bag again and how it's not his problem and all of that. I open the door and ask him to get in.

He completely fucking khazis it. Straight up, pure shits himself and starts trying to walk off, walks dead fast without actually running. Didn't count on that, to be fair, but I'm out and after him and I've caught him before he's five yards away from the car. I'm looking around me all the time. There's a bizzy station just up from here and, while the bus terminus isn't that busy no more since they opened up Conway Street, I'm still a bit thingy about eye witnesses.

But I've done this before. I've done it lots of times. I know what the fuck I'm doing and I know how to get the best result in the quickest fucking time with the least fuss. I just give him one hard fucking backhander to the grid. Lip bursts. Half think I can hear the little snap as it goes. Blood all over his chin. Cunt starts snivelling.

'You've got the wrong fella. I don't know what you think . . .'

'It's you, you fucking shithouse! Listen to this. It. Is. You. You're the fella I'm after. Shut your fucking mouth and get in!'

He starts acting like a baby, making his legs go dead so's I half have to drag him into the car. I'll admit, I give him another crack, harder than what I should've in fairness. I should've built it up more and that. If I'd've just pure told him then and there why he was getting hauled in he probably would've let our Stephen on free for the rest of his life. But I want to show him. I want him to learn something.

We drives in silence for a minute down Canning Street, past Tower Quays and over the Four Bridges on to the dock road. It's only now I speak to him again.

'No idea what this is all about?'

But the fella is a proper worm. He doesn't see this

as a step towards his own rehabilitation and that. He just sees it as a chink of light, a possible get-out for his runny arse.

Times like this – and there's been a few, to be fair, good few and all, too – I always find myself thinking about that one time in the park when we was just kiddies. Terrifying, it were. It was nothing else. Fucking horrific. It was a nightmare mainly because the lads was so calm, so certain about what they was going to do to us – but they never told us. They hinted that it was going to be fucking monstrous and that, but would they fuck tell us what they was going to do with us. And that made it horrible, know what I mean. I've never forgot that.

'Can not for the life of you think why I'm driving you off some place?'

'No. No idea. None at all.'

Cunt's a bit cheeky still, to be fair, little bit insolent. Pure does not want to learn a lesson here. I decide not to go easy on him.

'No idea, well?'

I shake my head and say it again.

'No idea.'

He starts to whimper.

'Look . . .'

I cut him dead.

'You haven't done nothing today that you think was, maybe, now you think about it, a little bit out of order?'

He shakes his head. He's grovelling.

'No! *Nothing* . . .'

Wretch has done it so many times it don't stand out in his mind as something bad. Won't help himself, this one. Will not make it easy on himself.

'OK.'

We drive on in silence for a bit longer. We're approaching the Duke Street bridge. It's quiet down here, this time down of day. As we turn left towards the bridge I ask him.

'Can you swim?'

Now he is fucking terrified.

'No!'

He makes the word last ten seconds, he's crying that much. I stroke his head with my free hand, try to soothe him a little bit.

'It's all right, Tommy, lad. I'm not going to drown you.'

This seems to cheer him up a bit.

'You might drown yourself and that – if you really can't swim.'

That does him. That's when he finally twigs that this is something bad. He's not talking his way out of this and he now knows that. Cunt starts wailing like a baby. I slap his head, hard.

'Shut the fuck up, you!'

I pull up in the little car park right opposite the old café. I stare straight ahead. I don't want to look at him. I speak to the windscreen.

'So. Nothing you regret, well?'

He shakes his head and dabs at his lip. Bleeding free again from that last crack I give him. Cunt's world has gone topsy-turvy. He can not get a grip on what's happening here. He won't try neither, though – he won't even try to understand. I feel nothing.

'What have I done? Please – just tell me what I've done and I'll make it up to you . . .'

Fear of the unknown. Terror. Proper nightmare. I

tell him nothing. Just stand there and look at him, like a headmaster.

'Please! I'll do anything . . .'

I can't stand much more of this.

'You can't think of no little incident or nothing like that? Nothing that maybe happened in the heat of the moment?'

He shakes his head again and shudders. There is no helping this lad. He's just a eel. He's a out-and-out shitbag that preys on old ladies and defenceless school-boys. He does it for all the usual reasons – because he's shite and his life is shite and all he knows is shite. Time to enlighten the cunt.

'OK. Here's the thing. Someone that I know or someone that I work for has put in a complaint about you, Tom. They say you threw a lad off the bus this morning because he was tuppence short on his bus fare. That right?'

Don't mind admitting it. The moment of realisation is always a sight to behold. Tommy doesn't let us down, to be fair. The horror is dawning on him. He did do something. He does deserve this. He's got sneaky, piggy eyes and they're now darting around his head like pinball bollies, still looking for the way out.

'I, well . . . he . . . he was . . .'

'What?'

He just slumps and gives this horrible, craven look out the window, pleading for someone to come to his rescue.

'What was he, Tommy?'

I grab his foxy face in one hand and make him look at myself. I feel like biting through him, just pure chew his horrible face off.

'Listen, you fucking bully. I'm going to do something to you now.'

His face was white enough anyway, sickly cunt, but now the blood has drained. For the first time in his life, this cunt thinks he's going to die. He might and all, too. It's up to himself, to be fair. He starts crying again, really sobbing now, begging me to let him go. I try to soothe him again.

'I'm going to hurt you a little bit now. OK?'

His shoulders are in convulsions. I never expected nothing like this, to be fair. He is fucking his chewing his fist off. Terrified isn't in it. Cunt's fucking delirious. I stroke his head and try to talk calm to him.

'That's only right though, isn't it, Tommy? You deserve to be punished. Because otherwise there'd be no stopping you, would there?'

He half nods his head. He's more quiet now. He's starting to accept it.

'Come 'ead. Let's get this done. This might make you think again next time you drive past some old girl laden down with shopping who didn't put her hand out quick enough. That's you, isn't it, Tom? You hate your passengers and you take it out on them, don't you, lad?'

He doesn't deny it. He's in bits, sobbing and snivelling quietly, snot and snivel all over his nasty face. I'm still stroking his head and that, trying to shush the wretch.

'Don't get yourself upset, lad. This is for your own good. You'll be a better man once it's done.'

He looks up. He's not sure if there's still half a chance. I give him a little squeeze and try to look into his eyes.

'Let's go and do something to you. Yeah?'

He breaks down.

'WHAT! Wha-ha-ha-hot! What are you going to do to me!'

'Shhhhhh! Come 'ead now. There, there. Let's get it all over and done with, shall we? You know you had this coming to you, lad. It'll all be over soon.'

All's I can see are his red ears. He's buried his head under his arms and all's you can see of him is these two mad red ears. In a sly sort of a way it's half touching, just that little sight of Tommy's ears, pulsing a bit with his sobbing. I pulls his head up and make him look at myself again, make the miserable cunt take a long look at the fella that's going to hurt him.

'But listen. I know you now. I'm a very bad man. I'm a very bad man indeed and you do not even want to *think* about trying to do anything about this. You know what I mean, don't you?'

He tries to nod and then I pull the swaddling out. I bind his hands tight behind his back. He's quite cooperative, now. I gives him a little punch and open the car door.

'Come 'ead. Let's go and sort you out.'

Now the cunt really does start off again, wailing like fuck he is and I have to give him a proper dig to wind him and shut the crying bastard up. I help him out of the car and, arm around him like he's my mate, I walk him over to the bridge. It's a lovely old bridge. It still goes up and divides in the middle when a ship needs to pass. They can hold the traffic up for about a half a hour, but it never bothers me. I'm happy to sit and wait and that. I love seeing the ships come in and out.

Now I put his blindfold on. I give him a leg up and make him stand on the ledge of the bridge. Below him on one side is the deep, slick dock. It's deadly still. Deep dock still. From when I was very little I've always had a thingy about docks. They hypnotise me, they do. I always half want to jump in and that – they're so flat and deep and still. Tommy, blindfold, is stood on a foot-thick bridge girder only a few foot above that dock. On his other side is the cargo road. It's not a busy road, these days. He'd be unlucky to be run over if he fell that way.

'OK now, Tommy, lad. You're on the bridge. You're tied up. If you fall in the water, you're dead. So my advice to you is that you stay still and don't make no fuss and wait for someone to come and get you down again. Someone's bound to pass by, sooner or later. While you're waiting, just try and think about what you've done today. And all them other days. Remember what I said. Don't try to do *nothing* about this. God bless.'

I strolls back to the car and do a slow three-point turn. I have one last look at the trembling figure of Tommy the bus driver, then I'm off. Our Stephen'd be proud of what I done for him today.

Ratter

I meet Benefit at the club, but the weather's that good. I put it to the councillor that we repair to the sloop. He's double up for that, to be fair – and we do have a nice afternoon of it up on the deck with a bottle of bubbly and some crab butties brought over from the bar. The sun's still mellow and we just chill out there and have a nice general natter about the state of play with the village and that. There's one or two other opportunities about to open up that he thinks I might like. He can think what he wants, by the way. Obviously I make out like I'm into it and that, play it like I want to know more, but I've half got my mind on Arthur and winter tides and that, to be fair.

I manage to keep it quite tight, though. My main thing from now on in is to just act normal and that. More than likely nothing'd come of it, by the way, but why take a risk? Why would I just suddenly change routine and that, cancel meetings I've been grafting for? So, much as I dearly wish to be fucking elsewhere and getting on with my new life and that, auld Bennett gets the same attentive, charming JPB he's become accustomed to. If the councillor wants to just sit and bullshit and drop a hint that he wants this or that, hasn't been the new casino in a while or whatever, then I'm the fella who's just pure going to sit here and have it from the cunt until he gets bored. And in the meantime it's a lovely day to be out on the sloop. Life is good.

Two things you know for sure about the sloop: you're not going to get seen, and you will never be overheard. It's pukka out here. I bought her for other uses this is true, but I've done more dinners than drugs on her of late, to be fair. Mr Bennett does love to get out the office for a nice, long meeting *al fresco*. He mentions again that he hasn't had a decent night out in ages and this time I puts the auld crook out of his misery. I ask whether he'd care to join me at the casino Friday night. I can't think of better cover for a fella who's going to land a big 'un next week than to act like he's still grafting for Objective One money off've the council. I'll come over polite and nervy and right up the cunt's arse, I will. He'll shake us down for five large before the night's out, but really – the pleasure will be all mine. So Friday night it is, well. I know a few girls down there, as luck would have it, as Councillor Bennett is a very partial man. Punyani daft he is once he's had a glass of champagne, the good councillor.

The second I've waved him off I shuts up the hatch and hotfoots it down the King's Parade to find Arthur. This is now crucial, by the way. There's a lot of trivia I've got to straighten out with him on the landing front and that. Tide charts and that, does the extra weight have any effect, will the sloop be up to the job and that, do we need a deeper dock? I don't know, do I? That's what I pays Arturo for. We're not exactly strapped for time, not yet, but the sooner we gets plotting the smoother the plot, knowmean.

And that's just exactly what I do. I gets right to work. Arthur's straight as a stiff, no problem, no questions. Twenty grand in cash, no matter that the haul is going to be that much bigger than usual. He will not hear of taking more, by the way. He's half superstitious, half religious, Arthur is. All seamen are to be fair. I've always told him it's Tom we're bringing in, always blagged it that it's only a little VAT sting and that but he must know in his heart of hearts that that's bullshit. He must know. Maybe he's not that religious at all, in fairness.

The weather's that good that I gets a mad rush of a idea just to walk it back through the barrio to ours. Just for old times' sake. Margueritte won't be back until well gone six and I'm half thinking I'll surprise her with one of my Thai curries. I can cook up a scran and all too, by the way. And that's it – once the idea's been thought then it's a fact. It's happening. I'm not a lad that goes in for mad surges of happiness and that, but I do feel all right, the day's gone that well. So by three o'clock I'm strolling down Caryl Street, up on to Grafton and before you know it I'm back on Harlow Street, scene of one of my worst atrocities. Brings a smile to my face just standing here, it does.

It's almost as hot as that day and all, too. Debbi'd just that minute got back from Corfu – think it was Corfu, in fairness. Close my eyes and I can smell the fucking coconut lotion on her now. Her skin was fucking slick with it. Fucking *shining* as she got out of that cab, she were. She had good skin anyway and that, to be fair, Debbi did, and she was in good nick. Her skin always seemed stretched tight, she was so toned up. We should thank her, Margueritte and me, by the way. She was one of the first ones into all of that, Debbi was – real obsessive fucking body vanity and that. She was a fucking pioneer, Debbi. The likes of her, they started this whole fitness caper off. Not just the gym but toning tables, that was the fashion back then and she used to fucking live on the sunbeds and all, Debbi, and she used to wax herself to fuck. There was not a trace of a hair on that girl. She used to pure fucking glisten. Shining she were, when she got back from Corfu that day. The heat and the coconut lotion and her good skin – she looked fantastic.

I seen her getting out of the taxi and that. The driver was half trying it on with her and she obviously said something saucy back because he was laughing and that, slapping his own wrists. He tried to help her carry her case inside, but she wasn't having none of it. Debbi'd just moved in with Marie. Exciting times, it were. I used to always be on the lookout for the pair of them. I'd be there at the window whenever they'd come down the street, in fairness, just to get a blimp of the two of them. Two really boss-looking, shiny brown blondes walking round in ra-ra skirts and that. I used to wank myself daft over them. Debbi more than Marie, to be fair.

I watched her go inside. I was locked out and bored as a cunt and just milling about the barrio. I was half on heat as it were, by the way. I must've been fifteen. I was still at school – or I was meant to be, but it was the start of summer and they was long schooldays, them hot, fuck-all sort of days. Sometimes I'd just bunk off and walk the length of Mill Street and up to round by the Proddie cathedral just to look at the brasses. They looked well better in the summer with their vest tops and that, little minis. Even the old grannies was in minis.

Our Ged had just starting seeing Debbi round about that time. He didn't want her to go to Corfu, to be fair, but she'd already booked and paid. She was even more strong-willed back then and all too, by the way. I think she thought of YT as being the cute, shy little brother, so she had no qualms about inviting us in. Her mistake was she tried to tease me. She thought she was going to have a bit of fun with little JPB. She'd brought back this fucking huge bottle of ouzo and she was giving us the tales of what she'd got up to over there and that. There was some quite horny stuff she was saying by the way, then she'd just flick her hair and look directly right at us and go: 'But you wouldn't understand that, would you, John-Paul?'

She kept telling me it was our little secret and she did keep on pouring that ouzo, in fairness. Thing is, I didn't like the stuff. Proper didn't like it one bit, so as she's getting more bevvied, I'm tipping mine in the plant pot. And she's getting more relaxed and more flirty, I'm getting a hard-on. And I know where I'm going with this hard-on.

It's not a bad thing for me to be properly fucking Waterford about this. There's nothing in it for me to kid myself on it, knowmean. What happened next was, I asked her if she had a all-over tan. She didn't take much persuading. She was wearing a orange vest and her arms looked beautiful against it. Dead slim brown arms she had, just a little bump of muscle and that and just a strip of flat brown tummy and all, too. I'm churning up inside, by the way. I'm breathing dead fucking hard and my knob is pulsing like fuck and all, too. I want to jump on her so bad it feels like torture, it's a ordeal to just sit there and try and act calm with her so close and so fucking sexual.

'Go 'ead, Debs. I'm just a little lad, aren't I? I've never seen anyone as beautiful as you in my life.'

She half tries to look bored and that, but she goes ahead with it. Just a quick flash, to be fair. She just pulls her top up and holds it up for a second and shows me her brown tits. This is important. Looking back on it now and that – because obviously what happened did affect the way me and her was together after that – she did only give us a little look. She didn't take her vest off, to be fair, she weren't saying come 'ead or nothing. So looking it at from a distance now, the truth is probably that she was proud of her lovely tits and she did want to show us them and her tan and that and she half wanted to tease YT a bit, show us what a woman is and what I couldn't have and that.

But I was on fire. I come across the room to her and I asked her if I could just feel them and she took that bit too long to say no. That's the God's honest truth. I really thought that she half wanted us to push it a bit, just start feeling them and maybe she could blame the drink and that. Her brown tits are right in front of us, perfect and shining with coconut oil, and she's looking at us and I don't know what she's thinking. I've got the whole thing stored in my mind, frame by frame. I still think about it now when I'm wanking or if there's no fireworks with the girl I'm with. It's still my favourite spark scene, me and their Debbi that time. What happened was, I ducked my head down to start sucking her tits. She put her forearm between herself and my head, trying to force us back. I'm out of fucking control by now, I'm fifteen and I am just dying to fuck her. I can't stop. No way can I stop myself now. I've got to fuck this coconut-oil girl here in front of me now. And I've still half got the notion that she's into it, by the way – she just don't want to make it too easy and that. I got her down on the floor easy enough. I was stone in love with her. She was just perfect in every way. I was so in love with her, so madly into her that I come almost as soon as I got inside of her. She was all right about it. Just dead quiet and that, to be fair. Dignified as you can be with cum drooling down your inner thigh which, against her copper skin, looked amazing. Could not take my eyes off've it until it trickled away. She was defiant, by the way, Debbi. Never done none of that thing off've the movies, shaking and covering up her flesh and that. Sat there proud, she did. Still sticking them tits out, by the way. Then she just gets her stuff together and goes: 'Get out. You've had what you wanted.'

I walked around for hours after that, all sorts going through my head. I *was* in love with Debbi. That's a fact. I would've done anything for her. But I was shitting it that she'd tell Ged. I had a weird thing with Gerrard Brennan by then. I was in awe of him, what with his reputation and all of that, course I was. And I was grateful for all the kudos he give us and the times when

he directly bailed us out when I was half being a brat
and things was getting thingy on us. I should have no
gripes in fairness – he was fucking great with us. He let
us knock around with his crew and go the match with
them and, when they copped for a bundle they always
boxed JPB off, too. Well, our Gerrard boxed us off. I
distinctly remember fucking mad dick having something
to say about that, by the way.

But I hated him. Every living moment I hated Ged.
The closest I ever get to making sense of that is the film,
the one that's always on this time of year, thingio – the
Dickens one. The little matchstick lad is pressing his nose
up against the window, looking in. That's how I felt, to
be fair. All the fucking time, by the way. Nothing was
mine. It had all been give to us by Ged or his ma. For
all that they pure went out of their way for us, done
everything to make us one of their own – I weren't.
That was all his, in there. It was his. Is that fucking crazy
or what? I just used to spend my waking hours fantasising
about the day when *I* could bail *him* out. I wanted him
to need something, anything that only I myself could
give. But he never needed nothing. He never needed
help from no one. He had it all, didn't he?

That day with Debbi I ended up in tears, wandered
all the way up Lodge Lane, not arsed about where I was,
just fucked up by the whole thing, Ged, Debbi, all of it.
Didn't care where the fuck I was or who jumped us. But
by the time I eventually got back to Moses Street that
night, there'd been a change in us. I was clear-sighted.
I had a understanding that there was nothing a man can
not justify. I still refer to the Debbi thing as a atrocity
because that was what I was thinking about coming back
down Lodge Lane that night. If four black lads knocked

fuck out of us, there and then, they'd think that was all right. They'd all be thinking the same thing at the same time, knowmean, so it'd half make sense and that. Just – do it. Who the fuck cares? Maybe one of them'd think it was tight and that, but they'd basically all throw the boot in and have us off. Because they was all thinking the same, then it'd seem like a OK thing to do. Take it further. Soldier raping a mother in front of her kids. He knows it's not *right*. Of course he does. But he does have a sense of why he's doing it and all, too. It's thingy – have *that*, you bastards. This is what I think of you and your fucking code, la. He can justify it. A man can justify any fucking thing he wants to. I come to understand that by the time I got back to the Holylands that night. So it was a important day for JPB, that were. And not just for the wanking fodder.

I'm bored of walking. My feet are getting sore. These shoes weren't designed to do anything other than get looked at in restaurants and nightclubs, by the way. And my body – well, my body needs more proper exercise, end of. I cuts along Dingle Vale to St Michael's station and I'm back at ours, feet soaking in a steaming bowl of salt water a quarter of a hour later.

Ged

So I'm sat in the Saab outside Heswall Prep. Our Cheyenne's got her dress rehearsal and that, so hence she's not out until six bells. No probs, I've told her. I love picking little Cheyenne up. It never does anything but amaze me that this little princess is mine. And she *is* a princess, by the way. She's pure quality, our Cheyenne.

We still argue over that name, me and Debbi. I chose it a full five years before she was born, making that fifteen-odd years ago. Debs was all for it back then.

Now she says she always wanted to call the girl Clarissa. We always knew we'd have a girl and a lad and leave it at that. We had a good ding-dong over the names. Stephen weren't my idea. But she was right. We was still living in the barrio when he was born. He would've had a hard time with Napoleon.

A little group of mums and dads has started to cluster outside the school. I've never been in any hurry to get to know that school crowd. I'm polite enough and that, but they're not really my sort of people. I fucking hate some of them dads. Fellas with names like Steve Lancaster and Warwick Burne, four-wheel-drive types who tell you to open greeting card shops because it's a guaranteed three hundred per cent vig on greeting cards. Tits, the pair of them, them two. Always let you know they've got a few bob. Fucking personalised plates and highlights and that, respectable golf handicaps, know what I mean. One of their crew, this Mal Randall beaut, bad-tinted swede, bad tan, bad white kecks – this cunt's got a plate that says Raz 1. *Raz* for fuck's sake, by the way! You can see the better-looking Heswall Prep mams falling over theirselves to talk to that Steve Lancaster when the cunt finally flips that fucking mobile off and lowers himself out of that beautmobile and ambles fucking over. And he *does* fucking amble, by the way – walks like he's got a cock-and-a-half. He's one of these fellas that's half a fucking celebrity round here. They fucking love the cunt! It's fucking 'Hi, Steve, hi, Steve, how was Puerto Banus, Steve?' All of that. Right up the cunt, they are. Everybody's heard of him, everybody knows one crucial fact about Stevie Lancaster and that is that he's *rrrrrrich*. That's all they care about round here, by the way. I've got my doubts about whether he IS all that well off, but I've got to hand it to the twat, he does do a decent impression, in fairness. He's the one lad I know that can look all right in a pair of tight, salmon-pink slacks.

He makes out he's fucking loaded and that, but nobody knows a fucking thing about him. He does fuck all for charity – not a fucking thing that I know of. It's a good name for a rich fella with a decent golf handicap though, Steve Lancaster. Gerrard Brennan doesn't have quite the same stud-u-like ring to it, to be fair.

I'm watching them all wishing each other a happy Christmas and that, shrinking their shoulders against the cold and what have you, grabbing sly looks at each other and just being *nice*. I can not fathom it why I can't just go out there and be nice and all, too. It's not that hard. They're all being nice to each other and even if it *is* as phoney as fuck they don't seem to know it. They seem to all like each other. They seem to think they've got a part to play.

I'm watching them, trying to work out the real difference between them and me. I can't see too much that sets us apart. Except one thing, maybe. For as long as I can remember, I've woke up every day not having to do nothing that I don't want to do. That might sound like fuck all. It sounds like a white-tooth announcement in a Warwick Burne Financial Services pamphlet. But that's straight up. It's the real thing and it's what sets me apart. I don't *ever* do nothing I don't want to do. If I wanted to, I could play golf with fucking Ray Cole every day of my life. If I fucking wanted to, by the way. Take that Tommy though, the bus driver lad. He'll do. That cunt has to drive a bus every morning, whether he likes it or not, and the routine of it, his lack of any fucking choice in the matter has turned the lad into a gobshite. That is a fact, by the way. Whether the cunt feels like it or not, he has got to drive a bus. Got to do it. Maybe on his first day and that, first week or two he's made up, to be fair, got a job, got no worries and that. But then it *becomes* a job, know what I mean. Most of these here are the same – however they want to put it to you they've all got *jobs*. They'd try to say that they can have a round of golf and that whenever they feel like it. They can take off on a holiday, whatever. In one way that might be true, though in reality they always, always has to pay themselves back. Stole a hour here? Give it back. Nipped off for a week, did you? Stay in the office 'til nine every night then, you cunt – and work weekends and all, too. Me though, I can fuck about every day of my life if I want, even if I live to be eighty. I can't make a song and dance about the loot I've got but, to be fair, I have got some fucking potatoes. I don't really need no more. The lads need it, to be fair. But it's me decides when we go out and take some more. No one else. I decide. That's the main difference between me and Stevie Stud and Warwick the Secret Fag. That and the fact that I terrorise people for a living.

I sit and wait and start to get a bit restless with all the sitting and waiting and watching these phoneys hugging each other and that, doing that kiss-on-both-cheeks routine and wishing each other all the best. They all seem so at ease with the phonus balonus. I'm just starting to think that maybe I'll donate the school about ten fucking PCs, just to fuck Steve Lancaster off – even if I have to buy them, in fairness – when suddenly it's all worth it. It's worth being sat here watching Raz and Lancaster and fucking Warwick Sad-Shoes in action, worth being here for the moment when she gets out of her car. What a lady. I was half hoping I'd see her.

We're talking class now, by the way. We're talking about Nina Perkins-West, fittest ma at this school by a long way, and I ain't the only that thinks so judging by Raz Randall's sudden twitchy smile. Nina blanks him – fucking class. Now that is a lady. Blanking the likes of fucking Randall is nothing bar quality. She is, though – she's fucking quality. Nina Perkins-West, to me, is a walking embodiment of what a class lady is all about. She always wears boots, by the way, always looks horny as fuck but somehow she never looks tarty. I hate to say it, but for me Debbi can look half-brash at times, in fairness. I'm not sure about all that having a tan in fucking December and that, to be fair. But for all that Nina's quite upfront – silver-grey fur coat, miniskirt, leggings, boots, expensively shaggy hair – she's . . . *classy*. That's the only word for it. She looks like a high-class Goldie Hawn.

But her *fella*, la! For fuck's sake. That old cunt is Geriatrix, I swear he is. No way is he putting the plank to the lovely Nina. No way in the world. If Nina Perkins-West is getting sorted then it's not her fella that's doing the honours. That old lad takes a half a hour to walk their Oliver up the school path. He looks like Michael fucking Foot, dithering with his car keys and that, trembling all the way to the gate. Nice enough fella, I'm sure, but he has got a Douglas Hurd ice-cream swede and a fucking MCC tie, in all fairness. Has it on every time you see him, soft cunt. I'm quite fucking keen on the Reds, aren't I, but I don't wear a scarf to pick the kids up. Ah fuck it, though – I feel sly. He's probably a real gent. Maybe he teaches her loads, and that – maybe she's into him for his brain or his wallet. But no way in the world is he sorting Nina. Someone must be. You couldn't see a dame like her going without. Someone must be putting it to her. Out of my league, though. I could live for ever and never get close to a lady like that, in fairness. Class is what she is, plain and simple. Quality.

Cheyenne gets in and gives us a little peck. She fucking idolises me, our Cheyenne.

'Did you see that old tart?'

Her accent cracks me up. Posher than Princess Eugenie she is, and I'm not fucking messing. I try to sound cross.

'What sort of language is that?'

She takes no notice. She's the only person I know who isn't even a little bit scared of me.

'Didn't you see her? She was wearing *mink*, Daddy! I've got a good mind to spit in her raddled old face next time I see her, the tart. I've *told* Oliver, but he's so ineffectual!'

Ineffectual, if you will. That's my little girl saying that and I don't mind saying it, it gives myself a proper glad-on. But one thing the fragrant Nina isn't is auld. Probably my side of forty, to be fair, but does she look fucking good on it. Cheyenne puts down the window and screws up her pretty little nose as Nina herds their deathly white Oliver into her Land Cruiser. Oliver, by the way. Cheyenne makes a purring noise as Nina passes by and I half feel a bit thingy with her now. Taking it too far, she is. She's all sorts of green, Cheyenne is. Veggie, Friends of the Earth, Greenpeace and that. Got to take your titfer off to the girl. Cracks me up, she does. Ten going on twenty-ten. But there's no need for her to make a holy show of us in front of Nina Perkins-West.

Moby

I have an uncommon horn. That was one of Milo's, the mad Wirral cunt. But it's true. I have. I'm randy as hell. I do not know what the fuck is up with me, and that's the God's honest truth. It's not like it's fucking spring or something. It's fucking Christmas, by the way. Everywhere you look there's little posses of hooched-up schoolies and shop girls and what have you, all having it, all showing their tummies and their arses and their legs and their tits – but it's like that in town all the time. There's just more of them at Chrimbo, and they're out on the ale earlier.

This one here in the Retro is giving my good self the eye big time. Little doll she is, quite tall, good figure on her, fucking honey, by the way, and it's times like this I wish I was into the tartan. It's wrote all over her. She's properly a tartan fiend, this one. That's your password with a Judy like this – cocaine. There is a sort of doll that's into big, hard-looking fellas with shiny bald domes like my own, to be fair, but this girl ain't one of them. She's a beak-baby, plain and simple. She thinks I've got loads and in fairness to her, I probably do look like the sort of fella that would have.

I don't know whether it's the Christmas spirit or what, but I pass her on to Alvin. Alvin's about the only doorman round here that's got any hair at all. He's a fucking psychopath, I swear to God he is. He has his swede half in a rockabilly quiff and he always wears black gloves. He does a few tablets and that, small amounts of whizz and beak. I tells him about the girl giving us these coke-crazy smiles and he's right on it. Takes the girl downstairs and doesn't come back. He owes us one, Alvin Stardust does. This crew in the corner starts singing along to the Slade one, 'Here It Is Merry Christmas' and that does it for me. I'm out of there.

I wasn't going to come back to Nirvana until after New Year's. Too many beauts in town at this time of year, office divvies full of Dutch courage and that, start thinking they're hard after a few slurps. They think they're walking on the wildside by going up to Nirvana and all, too – make loads of fucking noise about it, they do. I hate teds like that but, to be fair, Fonzie and Derek have got a job to do. Christmas pissheads will spend money in the gaff and they have got to make up their subs to Mikey. Same time, they don't need some cunt like me hitting their margins. I could pay and that, to be fair, but that'd half be a insult to Derek, know where I'm going. But, like I say, I've got a lob-on like the mole in *Thunderbirds*, drilling away at my kecks, demanding answers of my good self.

'Where's da grumble, Daddy?' it's going. 'Show us da punyani!'

So there isn't really no choice in the matter, is there? Nirvana it is.

And the place is hopping. Fonzie's busy trying to quieten down some rowdies when I come up the stairs. The young lad, Willie, lets us straight in. I asks him if he thinks Fonzie needs a hand with the kick-offs but Willie says no, they've just got a bit touchy-feely with the girls and that, Purple's just marking their card for them. I goes over and stands with him anyway, just to let them know. Fonzie looks shocked-as to see my big bald head. Someone as black as fucking he is can't exactly go white, but it's like I'm dead for a second there. It's like he's seen a ghost.

'Fuckinell, Fonzie, lad! Don't stop taking them pills . . .'

He looks fucking dumbstruck at the best of times, by the way, Fonzie, but he's just stood there with his gob open. I ask him if he wants a bevvy. He just goes no and fucks off up the back stairs somewhere.

Purple Fonzie

''Im here. Narr, 'im here right now. Sem ting, yah narr? 'Im tek bockle of beer an' 'im stan' right up close to girl. Narr. Narr shampenn. Yah. Was going to but jus' checkin' yah–narr. Yah-yah. Will do. Narr, got dat. Narr call out. Narr call out.'

Ged

I'm not talking to none of them. There's times, to be fair, when I think that the whole three of them is embarrassed by myself. They clan up and try to freeze us out. All's I said was I was going to video the school play and Debbi and Cheyenne goes ballistic on us. Cheek of fucking Debbi, by the way! Common! Her brought up in fucking Windsor Street gobbling every black cock in Granby turns round and says *I'm* fucking common. State of her! One thing I am *not* is common, by the way.

I think about it some more. I'm still livid. That little bitch and all, too, with her blocked-up-fucking-nose voice.

'Daddy, that's just, like, *so* gross! Like do not even contemplate bringing a handicam anywhere *near* that production, yeah?'

Fucking lingo on her. Pro*duction*, by the way! It's a

fucking school *play*! I stomps off upstairs loud as I can to make them all feel guilty.

Moby

Hallelujah! Little Angelina's in! Don't know whether she's back for good or she's been off studying or what, but today? Today's she's here, and that's all's I could ever have asked for. We had a good little routine going there, me and Ange did. Like I said, she's a psychology student, something to do with your innermost thoughts and that. Whatever it is she studies, she knows what makes your mind tick. She told us that what she likes about being with a big strong lad like Mr Moby is the feeling that there's fuck all she can do about it. It's pure submission and that. She's said she doesn't mind admitting it, just the thought of being overpowered makes her wet.

That's exactly the way it goes and all too, by the way. I has a little word with her and first she's going, like, they're dead busy and that, Derek's been in and all of that, Fonzie's on her case to get the punters drinking more. I tell her Fonzie's gone on a errand and she looks around and checks and sees I'm right. Then she gives us this little look that tells us she's half up for it herself as it goes, and that's it – I'm on. She said this one time that I should try and think about who really ends up dominating who, but in fairness I couldn't be arsed. I'm just after ramming her, myself. That's part of the thing that we've got going, by the way. I've got to be that bit greedy and forceful and that for it to work for her. So I'll shut the door behind us and she'll back herself right up against the far wall trying to look dead scared and that and she'll go: 'What are you going to do?'

And I go: 'I'm going to ram you.'

And she swoons. She does, by the way – pure swoons. It's a old-fashioned word and that but it's exactly how she goes, in all fairness. She just – she half turns into another Judy. She's so fucking bang up for it that she looks like she'll pass out with wanting us to give it to her – and that's what happens now. She's breathing heavy and her chest is heaving, too. Her tits, small as they are, are jammed together in this red bra, firm as fuck, just slightly flushed from the dancing and that. She backs into the wall and waits for us. She's said she loves the way I walks over to her – dead calm, but threatening, she says. I'm hard inside my kecks. Fucking stiff hard I am, and ready for a go-around with her. I've got a nice pair of black Armani jeans on. I unbuttons them, pulls my dick out, sees her look at it and walks towards to her. Her face is flushed, but what I like best is the way her eyes keep darting down and back, and the way her little bosom is heaving.

'I am. I'm going to ram you hard.'

Little gasp from her. Slides her arse up against the wall. I pull her towards myself and slams her back on to the wall and, quite rough to be fair, I just puts my hand there between her legs. Soaking. Fucking soaking she is, already. She clamps her legs together hard on my hand.

'Not yet!' she goes. She tries to kiss us but I keeps on ducking my head this way and that, like a boxer. She's curling her lip at us. She's got a lovely curved top lip. Bit of a snarl to it, but it fits in with our thing. The snarly top lip seems to be saying: 'Bastard! Go 'ead! Fucking take what you want . . .'

She's got beautiful tiny tits, Angelina. The left one has a mini, mini birthmark just on the lip of the bra-cup.

She's driving us wild just standing here. I pure have to make a restraining order not to drag up that bra and proper eat her tits, bite fuck out them, mark them up bad. She'd fucking love that and all, too. I do though, I have to have a word with myself, she drives us that mad.

Angelina just stood there in this red fucking get-up is more than I can cope with today. I put my hands on her a bit rough and pull the whole bra up and take one tit then another right inside in my mouth and I suck them dead hard, harder than I should. She punches us in the side of the head but I can't stop sucking and then I feels her shudder and give in and start to go with it. I put my hand in between her legs again and the heat and the stink is powerful. She wants it bad as what I do. I sit on the table and let her get on top of us and then, when she's into her rhythm and we're sliding into each other nice and smooth, I walks us over to the far wall, rest her back against it and start to pummel her. I don't mind saying so – I can go fucking hard and fast and for a long fucking time. My thighs are taking a lot of stick, here, but I'm all right. I just keep going – bang, bang, bang, bang, bang, and the noises and the tearing and the clawing out of her are properly vicious. She's going mental. Some of the things she's saying are mad.

'Go on! Murder me! Fucking murder me you big, big fucking stupid fucking bastard!'

I say fuck all myself.

I'm not proud of it afterwards, but it comes into my head that I want to spray her. All over her and that, good style. Make her go back in there and perform with Moby on her, even once she's washed it off. And that's what I do. I pulls out and stands back. Two strong jets of cum, one after another, right into her face. She's well into it and all, too. She's looking up at us with them eyes again and she is *well* pleased by the whole caper. She lets it run down her face on to her shoulders. She looks right into my face and she massages it all into her little tits, looking right at us the whole time, never taking her eyes off've Mr Anthony Brennan. And then she seems depressed. She just slumps down in the plazzy chair and hangs her head. I half want to ask her what's up and that, but I don't bother at the end of the day. She's not soft. She'll tell us what she wants, when she wants. I starts doing my kecks up.

'That's me fucked then,' she goes. 'I may as well get me things.'

'How d'you mean, well?'

She looks up at us.

'Ah, nothing. Fucking dive anyway.'

She stands up.

'Come on. I'll buy you a drink.'

I shrug. She's doing all the talking, to be fair, and I'm just thinking on how I can shake her off. I'm not being funny and that but I don't like this idea of us having a noggin together. That'd be a bit like having a tart know where I'm going.

'Meet us in The Revolution then. Ten minutes.'

She's cool. She's all right. I shrug again. Yeah. Sound and that. She's a nice-looking girl, to be fair. *Extremely* tidy, by the way – would not be ashamed to be seen out with her. But it's not really me, all of that – mistresses and bits of strange and what have you. I'm not someone the lads'd expect to see on the arm in town – not unless I was out with her, in fairness. Marie. I take the stairs four or five at a time, still half not sure about a drink with her.

It might just be me, in fairness, but there's a feeling I gets just that split, split second before I bumps into something. It might be the hairs on my nose or thingio, a mad feeling right on the surface of my skin, sort of a tingling that tells us there's something there. That's what I felt just before I got zapped in Temple Street. It was dark, but not *dark* dark. Not black. Some drunks had passed us going the other way and then, I just become aware of something coming up behind and that. I went to turn but that was it. This hand just come crashing down on us. I come round not in the hozzy but in the back of a cab, a few streets away from ours. The lad, the cab driver and that, told us I'd flagged him down on Victoria Street. Give him the name of the road and that and then sparked out. I paid him off and told him keep the change. Made up, he was. He'd've just thought I was pallatic blacking out in his cab like that, giving him two and a half pound out of a flim.

In fairness, it didn't feel like I'd been too badly done in. I could immediately remember two things, by the way. One was that there was a good few of them. I don't know for sure how many, but a good few. The other thing that I do know for sure is that the hand that zapped my good self was Fonzie's.

Thursday

Moby

I don't mind admitting it, I'm chocker. Chocker at myself sitting here all marked up in front of her and the kids. Just the way she's looking at us is making us feel last. She doesn't say nothing though. She wouldn't. And she's not one for the silent treatment neither, by the way. Let's you know all about it, Marie does. She's just chocker herself. That's all there is to it. She wishes her fella weren't someone that comes in at all hours smelling of ale, with cuts and bruises all over his kite. She asks us for the taxi money and half shuffles Billy-Chantal and Kerry-Louise out the house. I'm not even in the mood for the Aussie girls.

Ged

This call-out is all's I fucking need. I don't believe him. I swear, I don't know what gets into our Anthony and that's the God's honest truth. It was Drought told us what happened. Moby'd never even mention something like that. Even if it's getting whacked from behind by a few handy lads, his pride is too much to ask for back-up. He'd go after them himself. Drought found out about it from some of the lads in Vic's, if you will. Everyone knew about it before I did. Little things like that do tend to start making myself feel that maybe the day has come, at long last. It's not that long ago I would've known about it before Moby fucking come round. But I never heard nothing – and now we're sat here in Dooley's deciding what to do about it.

It's not straightforward, by the way. For a start Fonzie is one of Mikey's men and Mikey is a very big hitter these days. And for another thing, it's a black-on-white scenario. The city's only just simmering down from the last spate of black-on-white kerfuffles. I know full well it's going to be hard as fuck to get anything sanctioned. We've got no dice. He's a fucking prick, our Anthony. Moby by fucking name, fucking dickhead by fucking nature.

'What was you thinking of, Mobe?'

He stirs his tea. He's already put four sugars in a small cup. Dool brings the sarnies over and more milk and sugar, keeping a eye on the door. He was going to give us a lock-in but I said no, thanks – but not required. No need for the lad to lose custom at the end of the day. Moby peels the bread back off've his butty and smothers the bacon in brown sauce. Anything to keep the heat off've him, by the way.

'What did I tell you?'

'Leave it out, kid. It's done. It's not like I done it on purpose, eh? Did I go out with a "Zap Moby" sign on?'

This, in all fairness, does my fucking swede in. I nearly fucking choke.

'I fucking told you not to *go* fucking out! And what d'you do? You go out! You fucking go out!'

I'm fucking cross, by the way. Moby, big fucking musher that he is, just looks down at the table and carries on stirring his tea. It's good that we remind ourselves every now and then just which one of us is the boss, and why it is that he *is* the fucking boss, by the way.

'How many days to the thingy?'

Moby shrugs. Still doesn't look up. I look at the others.

'He fucking goes out!'

I have to pick up one of my butties to keep my hands out of trouble. I takes a deep breath and tries get myself straight. Drought's keeping a diplomatic silence. I take one bite out of my bacon and tom and a bite out of my bacon and egg. Fucking gorgeous. Bacon and egg and tomato can put a lot of the world's fucking evils to bed, I swear it can.

'Where's Ratter?'

Shrugs.

'Couldn't get hold of him.'

I chew and wave the butty.

'Probably just as well. He'd've shot some cunt by now.'

'Probably the wrong man 'n' all, too.'

Drought, trying to draw my anger. They don't get it, these lads. I'm banging my head against a brick wall with the cunts. They pure do not get it. I have one last try.

'We DO this, lads, we CHOOSE this fucking caper so that shite like that DOES NOT happen to US!'

Moby's stifling a grin. I know I've half gone red in the face and that.

'*Club* owners get whacked. *Drug* dealers get whacked. That's the law of averages in their caper. We do not get zapped, gents. It's not a part of our thing.'

Another big sigh from myself. My shoulders slump forward and I start chewing the rest of my sarnie, thinking out the way ahead. Whatever is done, it is imperative that it's done right. I just can't see it, though. Proper can not see a way ahead with this one. I ask the Dool to sit with us. He glances around like the menus are bugged and comes to join us. He knows everyone, the Dool does, knows all the mushers and what have you. Whenever I've asked him before he's always known the right thing to do. I ask him what he'd do and he shrugs, modest.

'Go and see George.'

And he's only fucking right, by the way. I don't know why I didn't fucking think of it myself. I've known Georgie O'Farrell since I could walk. He's been out of the main game for a while now – still has a few good boys on his books, to be fair, does a bit of building-site security, low key sort of stuff. Still lives in Caryl Street, Georgie does. I gives him a tinkle there and then, he's in, he's heard and he says he'll see us in the Nutty. I'm off.

'Purple Fonzie, Mobe,' I say as I get up to go. 'Of all fucking people.'

I shakes my head and I'm out of there.

Ratter

I'm always relieved when it's morning. It makes them horrible illusions from the night before seem purely pathetic. I always see things in the night. Always have done, in fairness. I just don't sleep good. Last night, I lay in bed with Margueritte spark out like a baby next to me, waiting for the windows to go in. My windows have never been put in, by the way, but at least once a week the thought comes to me that it's about to happen, knowmean. I'm listening to the silence before the crash and that. I've been in a pub that was bricked by Arsenal fans before the League Cup semi in 1978. Everyone jumped when they first went in, then we all got together and run out. I remember Drought: 'Get stooled up!' he's going. 'No twat go out without a fucking stool!'

Stooled up, by the way.

But it's so peaceful here in Salisbury Road at night that you're just waiting for that quiet to be shattered. I fully expect it to happen. I do, I think to myself as I'm lying there that, if I'm ready for it, if I can get a sense of the sound the shattering glass will make then I won't jump like I done in the Cock Tavern that time. I'll be ready. I wait and wait for it to come. *Crash!* But it never does. The loudest noise is my heart beating.

Thump-thump-thump! I'm going to make myself ill. These nights are too long. Too long.

Ged

I haven't been in the Nutty in a *long* while. It hasn't changed so much, except I don't think you can cash a giro in here no more.

George is already by the bar, having a half of mild. Honest George is one of the few in his line of business who's survived to relative old age relatively unscathed. He's a legend, Georgie. Neither really white nor black, really. He was one of the first lads from the South End to set up his own firm of doormen. Tell you, man – could write a fucking bestseller about his stories. He looks a bit like that footballer Terry Phelan, used to play for the Shite, but he's got white hair. And he's whiter and all, too. But he does look a bit like that Terry Phelan, in fairness.

He come to be known as Honest George because he is dead straight. Almost religious, he is. I remember him after the riots knocking on our door and telling us that whatever we took, we better take it back. I laughed at him in fairness – I used to think I was a bit of a buck back in them days, I would've rather had a straightener with him than take any swag back. But I was scared of him, deep down, or, if not scared, then I was in awe of him. He struck myself as being invincible, know what I mean. I never took them tellies back, though.

And he always weighed his lads in. That was the news about George – he was never a bully and he always seen the lads right. Even in the seventies he was giving his lads twenties a night. He knows every cunt, George. He's retired, now, good as. Strictly non-frontline stuff, building-site security, odd job here and there. People like the Cream'll have Georgie in to do some of their events, but as much to have him there as a statement, to be fair. Like he's half a attraction in himself the gentleman heavy guy and what have you. Good luck to him. I ask him if he wants a pint. He doesn't, so I gets him another half and we go and sit in the corner.

'I've got to tell you, kid, I hear he was out of order, your Anthony.'

Great fucking Dingle accent the lad's got. When you hear Georgie talk then maybe it's right what they say. Maybe we do talk different. His accent is on the verge of a Terry McDermott. There's no thingy or nothing like that, no impediment and that, but he pushes his words right through the roof of his palate. Like I say, almost a Terry Mac.

'Can you not just let this one go?'

I shakes my head.

'You know I can't, Georgie. Just can't do it.'

He takes a swig of his mild. Now *he* shakes his head.

'He's not like he was when you was growing up, you know.'

He means Mikey.

'I know he's not.'

'Could lead to all sorts.'

'Not if we do it right.'

'How d'you mean, kidder?'

But he knows, all right. He looks right into my eyes, them piercing death-blue lights probing myself. Raking my kite, he is – eyes on the cunt never stay still for a second.

'Straightener?'

I nods and look away from him, using my pint as

a excuse. He thinks about it. When I look back at him he's weighing the whole thing up, half ducking little imaginary punches. He does like a shrug-nod, his bottom lip hanging out while he weighs it all up.

'Could work, I suppose. I don't see Mikey going out on a limb for Fonzie. He won't want to risk things getting out of hand again round here.'

He shrug-nods again. He points at myself.

'You'd have to set it up, like.'

I give him my straightest look.

'Would you not be able to make that call yourself, George?'

My straightest look is not a tenth as straight as his own. He dazzles us with them beams of his.

'No, kidder. That's down to yourself.'

I take another swig and try my own little shrug-nod. Mine's a nod-shrug, and all the while I'm swilling my pint around the glass and looking at it at the same time, trying to look casual.

'Sound. Where will I find him?'

'Today?'

'Say . . .' I look at my watch. 'Nine or ten tonight.'

He gives it due consideration.

'Well, if it's *after* ten he'll be at the Blues.'

'Where, like?'

'Murray Kiwara's tonight.'

'Murray Sad Kecks?'

Murray's basically just a ladies' man. Bad gambler and that too, always owes out all sorts but he's harmless, God willing. George nods.

'Lives in Lime Grove now.'

He scribbles down the address in a auld fella's writing. Good job I know the Lime Grove bit.

'Go on your tod. You'll be sound.'

I drink up and offer him another. He doesn't want one. He's off to feed his mate's pigeons. Fucking Honest George tending to all creatures great and small. He shakes my hand as I gets up to leave.

'Good luck, kidder.'

'Ta. And thanks for this.'

I hold the piece of paper out then pocket it.

'No sweat. Let us know how you get on.'

We shake again then I'm gone.

Ratter

I'm late paying in this dropsy. We've had a sudden cold snap and the gritting lorries are out and I've had to take a back way into town, up Parly and through into Rodney Street. It's never like it's en route at the best of times, by the way, but this time I've come close to just fucking him off. But more than ever before, things have to be just so, just how they always are. This is going to be hard enough to pull off without me blowing the whistle on the whole caper by bringing extra glare on myself. One thing missing a instalment will most certainly do is bring the glare in on JPB. But he's a fucking pest, that Bennett is. I could well fucking do without this detour, to be fair.

In all truth I don't know what the councillor'd do if I turned Turk on him. It's not like he can go running to plod. It's not that I don't want to pay the greedy cunt, by the way. It's just a fucking nuisance the *way* he wants paying. I don't even pretend to understand the trail of bank accounts he's got going and I don't want to know, neither. All's I know is that I have to pay in on the 10th of every month at the Leece Street Post Office and it's never anything bar a hassle to make it over there. I've got a lot to do today and all, too. But if I plays all this like a dream between now and Chrimbo, there'll be no more of this. JPB will be out of here. *That's* why I'm making the effort. No more Leece Street, no Councillor Benefit, no Gerrard Brennan, none of it. Outski. I find myself smiling as I half sort of skid-walk on the melting ice down the hill towards Pilgrim Street, digging my soles in hard to stop myself from slipping. The younger brasses are starting to take up their specs. They must be frozen. I hardly even look over, by the way. Too much to do. I needs to start planning the rest of my life.

Ged

In spite of them, I've got the camcorder hidden between my legs, trained on our Cheyenne. I can see her perfect through the periscope. I just have to glance down and, whenever she moves, I just gives it a little tilt and I'm on her again. No cunt's going to take that away from myself. What have you got if you haven't got no memories? Is right. And she's a star, by the way, our Cheyenne. She is proper fucking stealing this production. She must be able to see myself sat here, made up with her. She can hardly fucking miss us. I'm right in the front row next to the headmaster who's been very nice, in fairness, and has been calling myself 'Mr Brennan' and that, shaking my hand and saying have a good Christmas and all of that. I'm going to give him them PCs, by the way. He's a nice fella. It's a lovely little school they've got going here, lovely the way they put so much into the kiddies' well-being. Does cost a few bob, in fairness.

I'm just starting to fill up at the bit where our Shy gives her big speech to fucking thingio, Death Head,

Nina's little puff. *Oliver!* Suddenly I gets this shove in the back. Hard, by the way. Proper dig. Not even that polite, to be fair. I half jerk around in my seat to see who's trying to aquaint themselves, but I half can't swivel with the camcorder and that. He probably doesn't mean it as rough as it comes, to be fair, but you don't have time to consider when you get a jab like that. I places the camcorder flat on the floor then turns round nice and slow to have a little word. I don't want to embarrass no one – specially not in front of the head, so I'm just going to tell him I'll see him outside if he wants to prod myself some more. Talk about taking the wind out of your sails. It's only fucking Nina herself sitting there – looking *gorgeous*, by the way. That woman is just the last word in sophisticated. I can feel myself getting a hard-on just being so close her. I can see right inside her blouse. I don't know that she needs to have all those many buttons open and that, but fuck – I'm glad she does. I can smell her and all, too. That beautiful, perfumed, expensive fucking cleavage of hers. Fuck, I would *cane* that woman if I got her in a place somewhere.

I don't know if it's Nina or her near-geriatric fella that's prodding me, but neither of them looks that ecstatic, if you will. To be fair, it is a twat of a spec they've got there, she can't hardly be able see that well at all with all us in front of her. Don't know why they don't space the seats out in staggered rows at things like this. At the end of the day, if you ain't on the front row, you can't fucking see. I think about offering her my seat, but that'd fuck the video up and there's another big speech about to come so I just sort of mugs up to her. The old boy's got a gob on him. I can see his point, I really can. I tries to slide down as much as I can to give them a better view, but I can still see our Cheyenne in the viewfinder.

Moby

The thing is, The Montrose is cracker on a Thursday night, never mind that the Chrimbo lunacy season has kicked off good and proper. The grumble in that place, by the way! Untold, it is – untold. There's all sorts – auld 'uns out with their girls, up for anything they are. I know I'm meant to be lying low and that, but just the thought of the tarts in there, all partied-up, ready for their once-a-year goose on the sly is half starting to get to us, in all fairness. That's for Moby, that is – I don't mind admitting it. I'm the fella that takes giggly women from Old Swan outside the Montrose at Chrimbo. I'm the lad that can get them to perform a sex act in a back jigger, no back answers. I just don't know what to do, in fairness. I should just stay in, do some Christmas things with the kids and that, watch *Jingle all the Way* with them, watch *Harry Potter* or something. Qual is a bit bad, to be fair, but they can make out what's going on and that. I could do that, watch a film with them, get over the Montrose, just get a nosh or something and still be back before midnight. They'll have that, by the way. With a lad like my good self there'll be a little posse of them around us, to be fair. Start off a bit giggly, they will, all kissing me dome and that, taking turns to polish me head and then I'll push it with one of them. Just go, like: 'You know you're the best-looking one of all you lot. I can't stop looking at you and imagining you without no clothes on. I bet you're even more of a doll without your kit on.'

Cheesy as fuck, by the way, and you'll get a big mad

'Oh-my-God' sort of face back from her, hand clamped over her gob and that, 'I feel ashamed' and that. But it's a nap that she'll come outside and put it in her mouth. It's a certain thing. Pound to a penny she'll be on her knees sucking Moby's knob. I won't even have to get a taxi back to hers.

Ged

I've had to leave them in the restaurant. In a way it's a blessing in disguise because I never knew fucking Paleface was coming. How was I to know she was seeing him? Tells us fuck all, by the way. Debbi gives us what's meant to be her withering look and goes: 'A cultured guess might've served you well . . .'

A *what*? A cultured fucking guess! *You?*

So it's all backfiring on myself a little bit, in fairness. I told our Cheyenne when she first got the part that I'd take her to Ego's after her first night, but I think even she would rather I done one. You can just see her looking at myself, mortified, just thinking: 'Shut *up*, Daddy! Don't say another *thing*!'

And now she's invited fucking Olly Death Head. I'm surprised that he even eats. He looks like he fucking lives in bed getting spoonfed and that, the freak. I could well see Nina leaning over him, giving him a good look down that beautiful front, feeding him rusks and milk and that, stroking his sickly head the whole time. Maybe she suckles him and all, too. I sit there, thinking this because not one of them is even looking in my general direction. Me that's paying the fucking bill, by the way. Made up with each other is what they are – made up with their clever talk about this and that, films they've seen that I've never fucking heard of. Do not know what

131

Deborah's so pleased with herself for. Any cunt can see she's winging it. Like fuck has she seen *Three Colours: Red*. She'll be telling them it's about the 1996 Cup Final any minute, the fucking phoney. I'm not sorry I've got to nip off, in fairness. Do not like being blanked by my own kiddies and double do not like seeing my good lady wife grovelling on her back for respect. Fuck that, by the way. I tell them I'll try to get back there for pudding, but no one seems that arsed. Debbi's got cards if I'm unavoidably detained. Pay – that's what I do. Basically, my thing in this family is to pay. End of.

Ratter

Just what the doctor ordered. He does show up at the most opportune times, old Paulie. Hom or no hom, this is a lad that understands. He knows the score, this lad does. Big crazy grin on his grid as he stands there in the doorway with these two waifs he's got. It's a chemical grin if ever there was one. Maybe a crystal meth grin, maybe just the beak but excitable as fuck, whatever.

'Just passing and that, like. I got these two.'

What he's got is two kids, lad and a girl, cute as fuck the pair of them. Can't be more than fourteen if they're that. Paul says he got them by the bridge. Well I fucking never and that. He's said he'll give them a pony each if they'll fuck for him and a mate and then let the pair of us get into them. I takes Paul to one side.

'Do they know the score?'

'Oh aye. They're bang up for it.'

'Does the lad know about you?'

Paul grins. It's more a embarrassed grin than anything sick or malicious.

'If he hasn't took the hint then he'll find out soon enough.'

This cracks him up. Fucking slays him, it does. Laughing like a twat for ages and then, just when you think he's got over it and it might be down to business, cunt starts chuckling again. The kids don't seem that nervous, to be fair, but they're acting that cocky they must have their doubts. I takes them a glass of wine each, nice cold Mâcon-Villages straight out the fridge and we all just sit and chat. The girl drinks her wine down like lemmo so I go get her another. She gives us a lovely little shy smile when I ask her does she want another, but shy she most deffo is not. Little honey, this one, even in a tracky. She's wearing the uniform – white Lacoste tracky, no socks even at this time year, tracky bottoms pulled up over her ankles and a nice pair of Nastase. The lad's dressed almost identical, only he's wearing a Carhartt fleecy sweatshirt and a fleece hat. The girl keeps darting little looks at YT. No way is this one a novice. She's impressed by the apartment, that much is pretty fucking obvious and my guess is that she's already thinking ahead, thinking Sugar Daddy and that. I can't help but clock the figure on her and I'm starting to feel like I want to fuck the Paul thing off, get him and the lad out of here and pure start getting into her, just me and the girl.

We've done this sort of thing before. Paul will knock around with lowlife that he's picked up, bagheads and that, young brasses or just girls and lads in need of a few bob. I'm happy to just sit back and let him MC the whole show.

He says something to the girl and she gives one short nod. Now that it's time for action, she is shaking a bit in fairness. She's more nervous than she's been letting on. Younger than fourteen, too, looking at her now – or maybe it's just her hair making her look young. She's got long, straight brown hair, cut in a high fringe across her forehead. Dead fucking cute, no two ways about it.

The lad starts necking her and feeling her tits. They're necking like proper revolting teens, just gulping each other, no sensitivity or nothing. His hand goes right between her legs ten seconds after they've started kissing and again it's rough stuff to watch. He's just scumffing her with his four fingers, just fucking rubbing her and grabbing her – but she seems to be into it. Every now and then there's a faint little moan out of her and the lad starts necking her faster and harder. He's on one himself now, pulling at the elastic waist on her tracky bottoms trying to get to her flesh. He can't quite get his hand inside, the way she's lying. But saying that, she then just pushes herself up off've the couch a little bit so's he can get into her better.

Paul's up, now. He goes over and stands her up and pulls down her trackies. No please or thank you, he just basically strips her, tugs them right down. I'd have rather he'd just let the two of them get on with it, but it does just move things on, to be fair. The lad takes off his own bottoms. He's standing out like fuck, really fucking erect. He goes to start necking her again. I see Paul's got a hard-on himself. He shouts over.

'Might as well both get the rest of your kit off, ay?'

They just do it, by the way. Do not think twice. Off with their togs, no messing about. She's a tiny bit coy, but only in the way that she knows she's got a beautiful body, she knows my eyes are going to be all over her, she knows she's got some power here but she doesn't quite know how to use it yet, not proper.

The lad starts to straightforward fuck her, him on top planting her dead hard and dead fast – can't half go, this kiddie, to be fair – and the girl is properly starting to lose it. Fucking sounds out of her, by the way! Profane isn't in it. I don't remember girls of fourteen going for it like that when I was their age. She's a pure pro and all too, this one. She's got this one little movement where she takes her weight on the flat of her hands and her heels and sort of lifts herself into him, boning him back with this little flex of her hips. She's got to me, lar, I tell you. I'd have been hypnotised, but Paul, who's just been standing there bollocko, wanking himself off looking at the lad's tough little arse in action, goes and whispers something to him. The lad nods and seems to take a deep breath. He says something to the girl and she gets up and goes on her knees, forearms resting on the couch, head resting on her forearms. The way she just quietly gets on with it, just accepts what's coming to her is one of the best turn-ons I've had in a long time. I'm ready for this now. The lad starts to give her one from behind. I don't think it's in the arse, he's into his rhythm too quick and she's right back into it, too, whimpering and proper starting to fuck him back. But next thing Paul's there, positioning himself behind the lad, coaxing him and stroking his chest from underneath, trying to relax him. You can see the lad wince as Paul's putting it in. He tries to bang the girl harder, but you can see he's screwing his face up to make the pain go away. He doesn't like Paul's knob in him one little bit.

The girl beckons YT over with a flick of her head. It's supposed to be a cool come-on but with her down there on her hands and knees getting rammed by what looks like two lads it doesn't quite come off. I go over. I'm still fully dressed, but she don't hesitate. She feels me through the material, traces the outline of my hard-on with the palms of her hands and gives us a knowing little smile when she feels how stiff I am for her. I don't like that smile, by the way. It makes me feel like she's won us in some way. But she has my cock out and in her mouth pronto, yanking it with her fist and gobbling that bit too fast, slurping and all of that. I wraps some of her hair around my fingers to harness her and slow her down. I pulls her head back nice and slow and let her forward, sucking us, sucking us good and deep and slow. What is getting to us now, getting right to the nerve ends of my knob is the sight of the curve of her back, and the small peach of her bottom moving back and forth to take the sex. The taut skin on her back is starting to glisten. That pure, natural arch of her spine, collecting the sweat as she gets to work on my knob, is mesmerising. I am half in a dreamworld until I become conscious of her brown eyes seeking my approval. I expressly told her not to do that. Told her all of five minutes ago, if that. One thing I can not stand is a girl looking up at us while she's giving us a nosh. I hate that coy little suggestion, knowmean – 'Is this how you like it?' and that. They're not to know unless you tell them, but this one I told. No two ways about it. I expressly tells her not to look up and she fucking looks up – leaving JPB no choice in the matter. I only punch her the once, and I'm careful to hit her on the side of the face so's I don't mark her up too bad but maybe I do hit her that bit too hard. She goes down and she doesn't get up.

Moby

I don't know which one of these two I'll go for. Maybe the both of them. The way they're dancing, they're plenty game. I'm dancing with the both of them, two bubbly tan-queens from Kenny, drunk as fuck and having a whale of a time. They're glittered up to fuck, by the way. They aren't wearing nothing that hasn't got glitter on it somewhere and they haven't stopped dancing since I got here. They must think I'm a lovely, happy-go-lucky sort of a fella, the way I'm dancing and grinning and that. I must look like Soft fucking Joe. The thing is though, we're dancing to that one 'Fresh' by Kool and the Gang and it's just brought it all back to us, when we used to go the Grafton and that when we was kiddies. We used to dance next to the auld 'uns and that, have a laugh and a joke with them, kidding on like we wasn't interested and when 'Fresh' used to come on we'd go: 'She's rrrrruff! (Ruff!) But I'd *shaaag* her!'

That's why I'm grinning like a gobshite.

Ged

To be fair, I'm a little tense now I'm outside Murray's gaff. I could hear the music even before I'd parked up. If I weren't sure where this particular blues was going down, it's not like the Granby heads are keeping it under wraps, by the way. There's old black boys in hats clustered around by Murray's front door trying to look like they can still have a fight, and more again making their way up Lime Grove. It's not that big a place to take a party like this. I recognise Maxwell Laurie coming up the street. I know Laurie from years back. He's all right. He's not that thrilled about seeing myself and having to

137

let on in front of his Yardie hombres, but he says all right anyway. He says it head down and that, says it to the floor but he's got no choice, God willing. Until he's told different, Laurie is not someone that's going to blank a lad such as myself. Oh no he ain't – Maxwell Laurie is going to let on whether he likes that or not. He mumbles his 'a'right' and tries to shuffle past us, half humiliated. It's not like I'm the only white fella around there, by the way, but I'm definitely getting a few looks and that. I pulls Laurie to one side and tell him the score. Obviously I'm on my jack, I'm not here on the bounce. I just need two ticks with Mikey. I tell him to frisk us, but he can see I'm not messing about. Sad case, Max Laurie – sad fucking case. He was with us side by side, helping get all the tellies away on the second night of the riots, Laurie was. Look at the cunt now. Half shady with us, can't wait to get away. Sad, it is. He says he'll see what he can do and that. His mates raise their voices as they all go inside, obviously making remarks about myself in some kind of mad Yardie backslang. I sits on the wall and wait and try to ignore the looks from the old boys on the door. My feet feel like keeping time with the dubby soundtrack that comes oozing out from Murray's, but I don't want to come over like some white groover desperate to get down with the homies. So I sit dead still and wait.

Mikey keeps us as long as he can decently get away with. I'm just getting up to go and thinking that maybe I'll need to call in some favours when there he is out there next to myself. Still a shithouse, by the way. He doesn't bring them right out with him but I can see his back-up just inside of the front door. The same front door that was closed a few minutes ago to all but the chosen few with a flim to hand is now kept ajar so's the back-up can see what's happening with Mikey.

It's kept quite civil, to be fair. He does try for a minute to pretend he didn't know what's happened with our Anthony, then he's shaking his head, all anguished at the stupidity of man. Any trace of his Liverpool accent has well gone. He's Superyardie.

'Ah tell 'im narr Call Out. Ah fucking *tell* 'im dat.'

He's deadly serious with it and all, too, even though he knows I know him. He sounds like fucking Bob Marley, by the way. It's as much as I can do to keep it nailed in but, to be fair, Mikey's not someone you'd laugh at these days. I'm not kissing his ringpiece, mind you, but he is a hard hitter now, Mikey. He's a fucking *big* hitter. That is a fact. Even with that accent, I'm not going to laugh in the cunt's face.

No, if anything I works the play completely opposite to that. To my mind, I play the man and the situation perfect. I don't demean myself or nothing, but it's done as though it's Mikey's idea that Moby and Fonzie have a straightener. He's coming over all Corleone with Honour this and Respect that – and before we know it he's given his permission for a straightener next Monday morning in the Mystery. No seconds. No weapons. They'll just stand up and have a one-on-one.

We shake and he asks us inside for a drink. The back-up starts to melt away. They look chocker. All this time they could've been dancing and drinking and getting jiggy with it and there weren't even a cross word to report between Mikey and myself. His accent's changed again now the naughty stuff's dealt with, by the way. He's half a thrusting young businessman. Blair'd fucking love the cunt. Fucking Eubank, he is. He's saying there's 'bithnith' we can 'deethcuth', but I lays it on thick about Debbi and little Cheyenne. I'm figuring that he must know *Godfather I* and *II* off by heart the way he's been gabbing on, so I goes with more respect, more family and all of that. My feeling is that he won't mind the likes of myself turning down a drink in his yard if it's to go and be with my Family – specially if I tell him about the school play and that. I'm not wrong.

'Where you meet with them, Ged boy?'

Boy, by the way. I tell him Ego's in Heswall. He does this ridiculous fucking nod of approval and goes: 'Exthellent choyth.'

Worse than Eubank. The black lad in *Rising Damp*. He's him. I take his hand and shake and I place my free hand warmly over both our hands.

'Thanks, Mikey la. You're a wise man.'

He accepts the compliment with one nod of the head. I knew he'd like that one, 'wise man' and that. People like Mikey want to be thought of as wise. As I drive away, I start to let myself think that this straightener might turn out to be a pukka smokescreen in the run-up to our little thingy anyway, at the end of the day. Plod'll know all about it by tomorrow dinner time, by the way. They'll leave that well alone, the straightener – Old Bill never goes anywhere near a private affair like that. But it's possible – far from certain, in fairness, but more than fucking possible that they'll start thinking that's it for the winter for Ged Brennan's boys. If one of us is chalked up for a little go-around in the Mystery then we can't have much else on, can we? They'll think we're winding down for the holiday. Turned out nice again then.

Friday

Ged

I'll never tire of that view. You come out of the Scotty tunnel and swing left to go back into town. Even on a shitty day, the first thing you see is the gold dome and then, rising up behind, towering over the whole port and all the financial district is the Liver Building. Majestic, it is. No other word for it, in fairness. Makes you feel small.

I'm just enjoying the sight, still amazed like a kid at the way it changes its look the closer or further away you are. Close up it seems to squat in watch over the city, but from a distance it looks like it's turning its back, looking out for a better offer over the Atlantic. I'm trying to look up at the actual Liver Birds themselves when this black-and-fucking-chrome menace comes right up in my mirror. I look hard at him. It's half a decent fucking car for once, this time. A Audi – nice one and all, too. They're usually kids in souped-up Fiestas and 205s, these pricks. Baseball caps, chewing gum, ciggy and that, skinhead mate looking out the fucking window – all that palaver. This guy just looks – he looks fucking angry, to be fair. He's got his fucking angry head on.

I'm just about to call him over on to the hard shoulder to have a word when he changes down hard and lurches off into the inside lane then he's back in my lane again, right in front of myself. And then, just in case he hadn't already signed his own fucking warrant, by the way, he then goes and slams on. I have to brake hard and it's just a good job there's no one too close behind myself. If they didn't have proper brakes they would've had no chance.

One thing I can not fucking abide is a Sammy Slam-On. Cunts are usually waiting to get out of a side street. There's fuck all behind you, by the way, but they decide to hell with it and fucking pull out right in front of you, screech into third at forty mile an hour then, once they're sure they're in and that, they just pure slam on. Slow you down, by the way. Tick you off and that. Thirty mile an hour round here, sir. Watch your speed, if you will. All's you see for the next ten minutes is their fucking red light as they tells you again and again and again don't get too close, by the way. If the cunts want to go twenty-five why the fuck don't they wait five seconds and tuck in behind us where there's no fucking traffic? Cunts.

And fuck knows what this twat here's braking for, by the way. The lights at Pall Mall and up ahead at Old Hall Street are on green still. I'm half out the car to pull him when he takes off again. I'm after him good style. I'm right up behind the cunt and I can see him now, see him clock myself in his mirror. I can see it all starting to sink in. He knows, now. I flashes him to pull over. Cunt doesn't know it just yet, but he's about to get shot. That's what he's drove me to, by the way – there's no talking to twats like this. I can see it all with him. I know all about him from his car and his hair and his clothes. He thinks he can do what the fuck he wants because he's driving a Audi. He's beyond reason and I'm not the fella that's going to try and talk reason to him. I'm going to walk over to him and put one in his leg. Maybe put it in his thigh, half give him a chance and that. But this cunt is not driving on these roads again. Fucking menace, he is.

I feel for the weapon as I walk over to him. I still

use the same little Browning as what I always have. I like it. I like the look of it and the feel of it. Young lads today trying to make a rep for themselves all seem to go for the name guns – the Uzis and that, Kalashies and all the Eastern Bloc gear. Not for my own good self, though. My little fella's never jammed on me, never let us down in any way – and it's cute enough to stash anywhere, by the way. Proper little Sam Spade piece, it is. I don't know why any cunt even thinks of using anything else.

In the second or two it takes me to walk over to him, checking this way and that, the fella gets himself a second chance. It's just the way he's sat there, shaking, properly shitting himself. He looks like a decent enough fella now I've got a proper look at him. Half looks like a lecturer or something – woolly, wispy hair and that, like a mad professor. Fuck knows why he's driving a car like that – cunt should be in one of them bubble cars, them 2CV lads, not a fuck-off Audi, know what I mean. I decide I'm going to put his fate in his own hands. He can be judge and jury to himself and I'll just act on whatever he says. I'm going to give him the chance to apologise. If he holds his hand up and admits he's been driving like a cunt and if he says he's sorry and that, then, what can you do? To be fair, he's not a young lad, now I'm close up.

I taps on his window. The fella's holding his head in his hands. Tears *streaming* down his face, by the way. Fucking *floods* of tears there is. He takes his gigs off and gives them a wipe, then opens his window.

'I'm so terribly sorry,' he starts.

Dead fucking posh. Poshest cunt I've ever heard, to be fair. Fuck! I can't shoot a fella like that.

'Fucking right you're sorry, you gobshite!'

He starts to shake again and then it all comes out. He's from down south, but his auld fella's come back to town to die. Come back to his Liverpool birthplace to meet his maker, by the way. He's had a call from the hozzy. His da's had a stroke. He's belted up here to be with him, got confused by the ring road, crying his eyes out in frustration and that and he can't even see proper, and then – fuck! Do I feel last! Tell you – I'm in fucking bits, lar. I whistles over a black hack and gives the lad a flim and tell him to show this fella to the Royal. I'm shaking a little bit myself when I get back in the Saab, I don't mind saying so. I can't help thinking about it. I'm on my way to see my own mother myself and what nearly happens? Fella nearly gets himself shot, is what. Fella thats auld fella's come back to the city to die. Makes you think, to be fair.

Moby

Really looking forward to the match and that tomorrow. We haven't had a good London away since the start of the season anyway, but this one's going to be a epic. Love going to West Ham, by the way, always have to be fair, and then Robbie's fighting at the York Hall. Only on the undercard and that, but all hands are going. All the Scottie crew'll be there, Breck Road, big firm from Kirkby going. Going to be fucking proper. The London lads have always been OK with us for years now. The villains, by the way, the *boys*, especially that Marty from Stratford, the mad cunt. Fucking *loves* our Gerrard, he does. Thinks he's the bee's knees. Remembers him from being a bit of a skin at the match, doesn't he – that time the ICF tried to come round the Kop and got legged down Oakfield Road. Good on them and all, by the way. Hadn't had that for years, to be fair, another team's boys coming down to have a little go-around. Ged was in the fucking thick of it as per fucking usual and that Marty'll never let him forget it. Thinks our Gerrard's fucking wonderful, by the way. Bit slow, he is, that Marty. And with Franner Mr Big down there now and all, it's just going to be a party. We'll be well looked after, in fairness. And all eyes'll be on my own good self with the Fonzie thing.

Ged

Fucking depressing me coming here every week. Depressing that no one hardly bothers except for myself and our Patricia and their Lauren. I know that, as the youngest, duties like this do fall on myself but the others could make more of a effort. None of them lives that far away. To be fair, our Ratter gets down here when he can. He's never said nothing, not a word of it, but you do get to know about these things. The rest don't give a fuck, by the way. They're all fucking quick enough with their tales of her legendary generosity and that, her big soft heart and all of that. But will they come here? Will they fuck. Our Anthony greatly disappoints me. It's not his own ma, to be fair, but she may as well have been, the times he stayed over at ours and the fucking scrans he's had out of her. She's young and all, to get like this. She'll be like this for a while yet.

She's young to have what she's got at least anyway, my mother – young for a woman and that. It doesn't usually hit women until a lot later, in fairness. I remember the day I brought her here. It was like a kid's first day at school. Showing her where she was going to sit and that.

All them rows of faces that was going to be her mates from now on. Face after mad, fucking cuckoo fucking face. All of them was looking at myself because I was new and that, looking right *into* myself but through me at the same time, know what I mean. I don't mind saying it – proper freaked me out, it did. Their eyes was the thing, all of them scanning us but with nothing behind the beams, know what I mean. They'd pure lost the plot. Simple as that, by the way. There was this one auld girl – passed away now, God rest her soul. She used to sit there day in, day out just shouting: 'Terry? Terry!'

Just like that. The first 'Terry''d be half angry, half '*there* you are' or 'where've you been' and that. There was a note of hope and that. But the second one, la – fucking hell. Pure emptiness. Never known such despair in one word. It was a wailing, desperate plea for someone, *anyone*, to make some sort of sense of what was going on with her. They was all the same, more or less. They didn't know who they was and there I was signing my mother over to be one of them until the day she died. I caved in, to be fair. I just had to get out of there.

What depresses myself most is the days when she's half normal. She's a hair's breadth away from normality in the way that she looks at you, her patter and that, everything. I go away thinking I was maybe hasty putting her in there. Like, she'll be quite enthusiastic telling a story about when she was a kid and she'll remember *every* detail, street names, who had the sweet shop, all of it. Or she'll suddenly turn to us and go: 'Did I lend you a tenner? Or was it twenty?'

I'll half shrug and humour her, which is deadly, by the way.

She'll go: 'Yes. It was twenty. I'd better have it back, anyway.'

I'd give it her just to keep her happy, but you know she's just going to give it to one of the part-time girls. I seen her this one time, sticking a flim down one of the girls' blouses. Girl was chocker, in fairness, but she had to let her do it, at the end of the day.

I park up, takes a deep breath and stride on in there. It's something that I have to do, and I will myself into a frame of mind where I'm just half cruising it. No matter how much I don't like being here, I know that it's got to be done. I've brought flowers and little Chrimbo presents for the staff, and a big box of Milk Tray for my mam and her posse. I notice a lot of the windows are boarded up on the side that backs on to where I'm parked. The main lady, Mrs Anderson confirms it.

'Same every Thursday. They're supposed be nice children as well, at the Dunstan's. It's not so much them – it's the crowd they get at the discotheque. If you're not standing out here at chucking out time, you've had it. They'll break into your car, dig up the bedding plants, anything.'

'You're saying this is the kids from the youth club? They're the ones put the windows in?'

Mrs A nods. She seems not that bothered. It makes me feel sick. That's the God's honest truth – I'm fucking chocker about this.

'They smash in the windows of a old folks' home?'

'It was pretty bad last night. But it's been worse.'

I'm boiling up. I do a quick scan to try and remember if we ever done anything like that. Not really. We caused murder in Sevvy Park with the Palm House and the parkies and all that. But we was *dead* young, in fairness.

Seven, eight we was. And the parkies had uniforms. But we liked auld fellas and that. Or no, we didn't exactly *like* them, but we'd never prey on them. Never.

'Little bastards.'

She's not thrilled by the language. I apologise.

'Does it affect the patients bad?'

'The residents? Some of them don't seem to notice. Others are scared witless.'

She thanks me for the bouquet and goes about her business. When I go through to see my mother she says yes, she was terrified, thought it was the Jerries again – but she's far more interested in the Milk Tray, to be fair. 'When am I coming home?' she's going. Only says it to do my head in. That's a fact, that is.

Ratter

I swear here and now that the good councillor is the most immoral man I have ever known. One of the teachers at Shorefields used to have a word for behaviour like this. Fuck did he used to call us? *Licentious!* That was it! That's what he used to call us when we was caught sagging off. He used to go into these big mad speeches about Nero and decadence and Adam and Eve and that. There was hardly anyone who *wasn't* fucking licentious by the time he'd finished. I only wish he'd met the good Councillor fucking Bennett. The man is that decadent he's crumbling. Fella is plain mad for punyani. As I look at him now, he has two very palatable blondes and one redhead in his company, each of which is being promised weekends in Capri, pearl necklaces and champagne. He's good for two of them things, at least.

This evening my esteemed benefactor has consumed, almost single-handedly, four bottles of Krug. To be fair, he has had very little to eat, but what he *has* consumed has been either lobster or fucking caviare. Nothing to look at, that caviare, by the way – just these little crackers spread with what looks like mini blackcurrants but is in actual fact fucking fish eggs. A platter of these, with other titbits, weighs in at £75, by the way. And that's before he's ordered up his chips.

So far, and it's not even midnight, he's had three grand's worth courtesy JPB. He'll have that again before he collapses, especially if these pros have him over good style. It's OK. It's what we're here for. Likes of YT, we do know our place, to be fair. We pay. I just have to keep smiling and repeat the words 'twelve' and 'million'.

But I do nearly khazi it when Mikey fucking Green comes over to the table, in fairness. If he says anything about Moby I'm going to lay it straight out in front of him. Nothing to do with YT, lar. Hardly even see the soft cunt these days. Not even related to him, by the way. Not proper.

But he does not so much as mention *none* of that. Not at first. He smiles a lot, offers around mad-coloured cigarettes out of a highly elegant gold-plated case and sort of seduces the councillor's permission to steer YT away. Bennett looks dazed for a second. He's obviously down on his chips and needs more but can't put the bite on us just like that in company. So he just does his usual, half-caned Bill Clinton-style grin, waves us away and returns to his game of roulette.

Mikey's conversation is unsettling, but I think that's the idea. He wants to unsettle us. Fair dinkum, by the way. Reason why I've done fair to middling as a hood is that I do pride myself on knowing what the opposition knows. That is fucking crucial, by the way. That is everything. It's the one thing of value that I've taken from Ged. Know thine enemy and that. And I'm sure as can be that Mikey is a) not my friend and b) knows fuck all – not one thing, by the way – about what's due to pass through this port. Of course people shoot their mouths off, there's knobheads everywhere – but not at this level. If there is anything then people can only be guessing. Shots in the dark is all's it is. Maybe people *have* got a whiff of something. The Kirkby thingio would seem to bear that out. But that's all's it is. People have got wind, they're trying to shake down a bit of info but they're firing blind. I can see from Mikey that he's as good as convinced that I know fuck all. He keeps his arm tight around my shoulder, patronising us, steering us around like I'm his boy. Lots of people see it, but I'm cool with it. I'm relaxed. Again, I'm thinking: 'Not long, now.'

Mikey spies someone he'd rather talk to. He takes his big fucking arm from around my neck and suddenly turns all sincere on us.

'I like you, John-Paul. I do. I always liked you. Just you be careful, yeah?'

'I'm always careful.'

'You surely are. But you're running with a rough crowd. They do you no credit.'

'I keep my distance.'

'Maybe not far enough. You shouldn't play out with such bad boys, period.'

Period, by the way. Cunt's been watching too many films. But I don't mind playing him along. Do not mind that at all, in fairness.

'Our Anthony's a loose cannon, Mikey. He always has been. You know that.'

What he does next, though, properly does fucking

unnerve me, whether it's a act or not. He just looks at us really close and that, looks at us like I'm really fucking stupid, pulls a amused face and starts laughing. *Really* fucking laughing, by the way. Half pissing his self. When he can finally catch his breath I think I hears him say something like: 'He's the least of your problems!' or 'That's the least of your problems!'

But he's already turned away from us to let on to someone else and he says it so quick I can't be certain and the next thing he's steering YT round again and I'm starting to feel a little bit para. So it comes as some relief when he points out this very done-up lady, fortyish, and asks me if I know her. I look her over. Brass, possibly – but tasteful. Expensive, sluttish clothes. Fuck-me shoes. I'm into her. Very much so, by the way – she's fucking horny-looking, this girl. Nice fucking half-smile, knows what she's all about, knowmean. Confident. I tells Mikey I don't believe I've had the pleasure and that's him in his fucking element. He likes it when you get girlie-girlie with him, Mikey. He's another one. *Loves* his women. Proper fucking loves them, by the way, pure fatal flaw jobbie. Always had boss-looking girls, he did, even when he was dead young. He's supposed to have started goosing when he was eight, by the way. He pats me on the arse, which I do not like, and sends us over to her. He gives a little phoney three-fingered wave and goes: '*Very* interesting lady. Go and meet with her.'

Which gives me all of three seconds to compose myself. Less. She's clocked Mikey putting us on to her. So I just looks her straight in the eye. I'm successful with women. Certain types of women at least, anyway – and she is most certainly of that type. She's filth. Rich filth. She doesn't try to hide that, by the way. She's half made up about it, head held high and that, knowmean. I like that. Self-recognition is a fine quality and this one knows exactly who she is. I'm going to do just fine with this lady.

'What are you thinking?' I says to her.

I won't pretend this just jumps up off've my cuff, by the way. It's one I've used before. It gets one of three types of response, all of which mean: 'I want to fuck you.'

That's how it is. That's the reality. Some women might feign a bashful little look away, trying to make out they can't believe what I've just asked them. It's not like I've asked them if they're wearing knickers or something. The second type will try and say something clever back: 'I'm just thinking what a twat you are,' something like that.

Usually they're the pissed ones, but they'll go for it anyway, they'll think they're being risky. The best ones are the women who'll look you right back in the eye and answer the question directly. I can think of three or four times when the answer has been sexually explicit. This woman tonight, Mikey's woman, half falls into that category. She's asking YT to take her back to the apartment, but she's clever with it. She does look us in the eye and she goes: 'I'm thinking: at last. He's plucked up the courage to talk to me.'

And then little smile again. Clever, by the way. The 'plucked up the courage' bit puts her in control. Makes me into a boy. But not for long.

Ged

Our Stephen's telling us this story about the origins of *The Magnificent Seven*. Knows all sorts, by the way, our Stephen. Who directed this, who wrote that, all of that carry-on. Japanese samurai he's saying, but to myself it's just a boss film. Not as good as *Bring Us the Head of that Alfredo Garcia*, but a fucking good film to just sit back and watch with your lad. And I'm glad we've done that. It's been nice, just the two of us. Debs and little Cheyenne have been upstairs trying these face masks and toners and what have you, but I haven't heard nothing for a while. They must've sparked out. Should be getting up there myself too, by the way. We're on the 8.45 tomorrow. I could've done with a early night, but our Stephen wanted us to watch the film with him. And I'm glad I done that.

Ratter

She's deranged. I fucking love her. Had a struggle with myself not to just push her down by the door when she kicked her shoes off and that. I told her the no-shoes rule as we was coming up the steps. Not that I'm a fanatic or something – I just love women's feet. I love to look at them. I love birds' shoes and all, too. They tell you everything. Not that I needed much more info, by the way, but this one – her fucking CV was stamped on the inside her shoes. Manolo's by the way. Slut's shoes, no back answers. No two ways about it. No matter how people think they're the last word in classy and that, sophisticated footwear and all of that, your Manolo is a basic fuck-me shoe. That's all's it is, by the way. And this one is wearing Manolo's. *Was* wearing Manolo's.

And now she's telling YT her favourite scene in a movie is the whole build-up to the Angie Dickinson shagging scene. What a waste of Angie Dickinson, by the way! Never would've thought she'd buy the farm by scene three and that. But this old girl who is fit as

153

fuck for her age, slim as a feather, great perky tits and that, tight silk blouse, beautifully cut arse, she's telling me that the very thought of it, the glove hanging out the limousine window and the way that Michael Caine pure tears into her on the back seat, it can make her wet just thinking about it. The conversation has been nothing but pervitude since we left the casino, by the way. Which was three minutes after we met. Fuck the Bennett – he's done fine and dandy out of YT for one night. Cunt won't even have noticed us go, the state he was in.

She kicks her high-class tart shoes off and I takes her straight over to the bench and I just know it – I know her well enough to tell her what I want. That I want to be thrashed. That I want to be humiliated. I'm not wrong about her, neither. She is totally into it. More than. Asks us if I'll stand there and wet myself for her – proper, by the way. She wants JPB to piss in his shorts so that she can get into the part and punish him. This is not a hard sell as far as YT is concerned. I do it. I'm wet and warm and exposed in front of her, pathetic like a boy. She turns her back on me then whips round again and slaps my face, hard.

'Take them off! I said take them off, you disgusting child!'

Fuck-ing hell! Do I take them off! I'm hard, by the way, so fucking hard it hurts. I throw my wet kecks and undies on the deck.

'You nauseate me, you disgusting fuck!'

Steely-posh, by the way, half Thatcher, but with undertones. There's a accent there, but there's menace and all, too. She walks towards us.

'Kneel down!'

I kneel. I'm so into her, into all of this that I don't feel thingy, half don't mind being knelt there with my red end stood up erect in front of her, P.O.W. stylee. She puts her foot on my shoulder so's I can see right up the length of her legs. She digs her toes in for a second then pushes us over with her foot and follows up with a hard kick up the arse. The kick don't hurt that much – falling right on my knob does. My head is a foot away from the pissed undies and that.

'Smell them! Smell what you've done!'

I'm momentarily confused. Where's she going with this? But she's on us like a flash, kicking my backside and slapping my face and the back of my head. Slapping us hard, to be fair. Sharp, stinging whacks here and there and everywhere, proper laying into us.

'You little fuck!'

She gets hold of my soaked boxies and rubs them in my face.

'Smell it, you little fuck! Smell your piss!'

I rolls over to let her see how hard she's made us. Her eyes are shining mad, she's fucking madly into this whole carry-on and I feel like I'm going to come my load any second. She eyes my cock and brings her head down slowly and, just as I'm starting to relax and expect the warmth of her lips over my bell, her hand flashes past and I experience the sharpest pain I've ever known. Ever, by the way. Agony, but it's gone as quick as it come, and now my knob is warm, warm and tenderised by the slap she's give it. She kneels down. She lets out a groan and starts to run her tongue down the smarting shaft.

'I'm sorry, baby.'

Fuck. She pulls my hand up to feel her. My fingers slip right inside, she's that wet. The desire in my stomach is something ruthless. Again I want to just get up and on top and fuck her hard, but I manages to control myself. She licks and sucks and, as I'm trying to hold on, she gives us this knowing, slut-dirty look. I gets to my feet. She's startled and that – looks up to see what's wrong.

Ged

It's one of them – I'm dog tired, so I can't fucking sleep. Something's bugging myself but I'm fucked if I can get to it. I'm going over and over what it might be. I'm that desperate for sleep that my mind, my fucking brain is pure aching but still I try to trace my thoughts back to when I was last OK. That way, I can go back through all the shite that's cropped up since. Considering how much there is for myself to deal with, now that I lie back and think about it all, it half comes as a surprise when I finally uncover that one little thing that more than any other is niggling away. It's the thought of them little cunts stoning the old folks' home. Throwing stones at my mother, by the way.

Ratter

I lie in the sling. The sponk I rubbed into my belly has gone dry and flaky white, but I'm still half tossing myself off. The gentle sway of the sling is just what I need. Soothing. Her face was more confused than anything. She tried to put her arms around us, tell us it was OK and that. I shrugged her off. She just lowered her head. Sad, like. Dignified. She started trying to ask what had happened but I turned my back and walked away from her. She weren't sure if I'd come and I was chocker about that – but it weren't that. I never, anyway. I didn't come.

I made it plain she had to go. Just wanted her out the place. She scribbled something and left it by the phone. I know she was looking at us the whole time. Could sense it. Wish I never had turned around, by the way. I just caught her eye as she was letting herself out. Still specks of blood on her face. Mainly around her nose still, and her mouth. Her lip was starting to swell up and all, too. It looked bad. She stopped in the doorway and just looked at us, sort of: '*Why?* What the fuck happened! We was having such a great time . . .'

And we was and all, too. The two of us would've rocked if we'd've got going proper. This is a dame that's up for all kinds, by the way. Don't even know why I give her a slap, in fairness. Can't help smiling about it now she's gone.

'Smell them!' by the way. Think we sorted out who the boss was.

Saturday

Ged

What a shower of phoneys! Big massive crew of lads. Some good heads here, by the way, but there's way too many Tommy twice-a-season types, if you will. There's all the usual gang of roidheads and half-mushers in their fantastical selection of puffa jackets and that. It's a width competition with this crew. These boys with their fucking horrible yellow and fucking orange puffa jackets, they look like they're proud of how much fucking *room* they're taking up. It's like that thing in Turkey in the olden days – it was the fat fellas that got respect. There's a couple of hefty lads here in them fucking tragic green, ultra-padded snorkel parkas who just look fucking outrageous. They're *yowge*! Snorkels, by the way. That's what they are, them ultra-puffa jobbies – fucking snorkels is all's they are! Put a bit of a reflector flash on and that, slap a label on and it's three and a half hundred pound. Must be a fucking clever lad that designed that coat. Three and a half hundred pound, by the way. Must be some designer. Tommy Fullfigure, by the looks of them two greedyguts. Labels fucking everywhere. All in favour of taking care and that, I am – but it's got to be done right. A label should serve a apprenticeship, same as anything. They shouldn't be able to just have a shave, leave school and take a pitch at Wade's. They should be time-served. Lacoste. Bass. John Smedley. Classics and that. Time-served. One of the lads at Vic's turned up this one time in a tracky top with YMC in big mad letters. Paul told us it stands for Young Man's Cock. Which is a bit cake, to be fair.

Time was not so long ago that you were lucky to muster up fifty for the last away before Chrimbo, by the way. Even if it was fucking Villa or West Brom – you'd struggle to get a crew together and if it was London, forget it. People was always looking for a excuse not to go to Chelsea or West Ham and Father Christmas was the perfect outro. I said it myself this one year, in fairness. We had Tottenham away, didn't we, just at the time that their fucking donkey-jacket crew had started having a bit of a go-around with all and sundry. They'd just had that famous one in the Shed, only a handful of them and that, but they half had a go at Chelsea. They was game as fuck, what there was of them, and I just didn't fancy it, to be fair. Wasn't scared or nothing, by the way. Just wasn't arsed. Christmas and that.

'I'd well go, like, but I've got a kid to think of, now – prezzies and all that.'

That's the blag I come up with. I did have tank at the end of the day. Fucking Moby sprung for the dough. Had to go, didn't I? We done all right. Got legged a bit on Seven Sisters, but we got together afterwards and ragged them. Only about eighty of us, in fairness, but they was all good lads.

Look at this shower now. There's fifty-odd here and that's just first class. There must be close on two hundred just on this one train. Gang of phoneys. Wouldn't be here if the ICF was still at it. Good crew, though. Man U are at Southampton. Wouldn't be the end of the world if we run into them, to be fair.

Moby

All hands are in first fucking class. You can get a weekend first for a extra tenner each way. That's what we always do. There's no need to be flash, know where I'm going. There's no need to pay £450 for something you can get for thirty–forty pound. Some of these lads here though, they *want* to pay top whack. It's the big I Am and that, isn't it? They're looking to slaughter the ones that's got Virgin Value Firsts off've the Internet, or lads who've just gone for the upgrade. Some of that lot are a fucking nightmare to be around when they've got beak in them and that, but they're good lads, to be fair. Proper Reds, the lot of them. Been going for years, by the way. Go fucking everywhere with Liverpool, they do. There's this little crew from Soho Street who're just pure grafters. They'll come back from London with tank. They make money wherever they go with Liverpool. They made money in fucking Accra. They went to the

Tyson–Julius Francis fight then jumped on a plane to watch Rigobert Song playing for Cameroon in the African Nations. Mad as sand, they are. African Nations, by the way! Come back with all kinds of gold. That's the riff at least, anyway.

There's a few of the lads that come to our Gerrard's fortieth in Vegas last year, Jonah and that from Topsite. Couple of the Burly crew sat with them. Funny as fuck, they are. They're sat there phoning each other up on their mobiles when they're right finninst them and that, only a arm's distance away and that. Mad cunts. They do get you laughing though, them lads. Stories you get out of the cunts, by the way. They went to Glastonbury last year with a, like, sort of printing factory. They got stung, didn't they, the previous year when the pass-out stamps was luminous. That was the one type of ink that they never had – luminous. Every year they've been stamping the Billies' hands with these jarg pass-outs for a twenty spot a pop and it's worth grands to them – then fucking Glastonbury, fucking hippy-dippy heaven come up with this aggressive anti-piracy stance! Luminous ink, by the way! So last year the Burly go down with every shade under the sun covered. Luminous, infra-red, ultra-violet, the works. They've got every fucking ink known to man. But the evil hippies are one step ahead again, aren't they? What do they do this time? They've got holograms! Fucking holograms, by the way! And what they're basically saying to the lads is, don't waste your time, boys. We've got youse covered. Or so they think, know where I'm going. The Burlington posse drives off to the nearest B&Q, don't they, Texas Homecare and that, and buys themselves the strongest bolt cutters you can get. And they cuts a basic door in the perimeter fence

and the game's back on. In you go, sir. That'll be twenty
pounds, please. Thank you very much, sir. Entrance to
the Glastonbury Festival of Contemporary Performing
Arts, madam? That'll be twenty pounds. The Gooch
turned up this one time wearing *Scream* masks and that,
half tried to take the door off've them. Only a couple of
our lads and that but they never stood down – would not
have none of that. Nice mask and that, lad. How's your
ma keeping. Good little crew, they are. They'd have to
cancel the fucking festival to keep them out.

Ratter

Looking around this carriage and there's hardly no one
who's totally legit. There's kites, dippers, dealers, spivs,
all kinds. There's two lads over there that run the Alpha.
Making Brewster's, they are, by the way. Everyone's
got their angle, but all bets are off when it comes to
the match. It's brilliant. There's lads from Scotty and
Burlington Gardens that we used to fight with in Scamps,
all that North End–South End palaver, and we're still a
little bit thingy with each other now. Just half wary and
that, to be fair – but you know that the match is like a
NATO zone. There's nothing comes close to the crack
you have on the train down to a London match. Might
not be so fucking great on the way back, in fairness,
but nine o'clock on match-day morning every cunt's
buzzing. You can feel it.

'Who's got that tartan? Fucking pass it back, you, you
cheeky twat!'

We're not even past Runcorn and the crew at the end
of the carriage are on one. They're very keen to impress,
these boys. They're all around about twenty-five or so,
and they're talking dead loud, letting everyone know

that they think they're players. They're not even going through the motions of sloping off to the WC for their bugle, these lads. It's right there, racked out in fat lines on the table. Does not bother my good self for one minute, by the way. So long it's not smack I don't give a fuck, but I know for a fact that Ged'll be going mad. He hates cunts like that. Young bucks and that – them most of all. I glance up from my *Guardian* to see if he's clocked them, but our Ged's in a world of his own, having a laugh and a joke with Drought and Jimmy Rico.

Now Jimmy Richardson is a class fucking hombre. I love him to bits, I do, he's one of our own – but he's unreliable. He's just that little bit talkative, knowmean. He's not a discreet lad, Jimmy. Bit of a bully too, in fairness – always was. One of them lads that's a loudmouth and a bully, but funny with it. You'd be made up if you was in with Jimmy Rico, but God help you if he had it in for you, knowmean. He'd slaughter you for anything. Lads with gigs, lads with red hair, fat lads, anything – he'd fucking cane them. Go-Inhead used to get it off've him bad style. Used to have him in tears. I've kept a bit of a distance from Rico for a while now, but only because he's in and out of the nick. He's always in the *Echo*, quoted as: 'alleged to be involved in the supply of narcotics'.

Alleged, by the way. Every cunt knows he's bang at it, but he's fucking daft as well. *Far* too open with his play, Jimmy Rico is. Every time we see him he's getting slaughtered, usually along the lines of that 'alleged to be involved in the supply of narcotics' thing. I'd like to be a better friend to him, but you can't have a guy like that too close to you, in fairness. Great laugh, though, Jimmy.

And we have got a great little crew here, by the way. All the lads are on board. Drought's there, Paul the Hom, our Moby, Jonah, Spit and Rico – all reliable boys. All's that's missing is Steady but he'll be out and all soon, too. Look at them faces, though. Those are hard faces. Hard from years of fights and self-defence and looking after number one and scowling and knock-backs and disappointment and smacks and zero expectations from day one. Not one of us here has given in to that. Not one lad in this carriage has let himself get dragged under. I love that. Lads with fuck all down for them sticking together and making a living for themselves. I love the match. It's the one thing about the old days that I'd never give up. I think it keeps us sharp, in a way. I could get very complacent very quickly if it was just deals with the Benefit and dinner with Margueritte.

Spit's arguing with Jonah about the noise it makes when you whack someone with a bat. He's a handy lad, Spit. You wouldn't think it the way every cunt slaughters him, but he won't be took for no mug. He can have a run around with any cunt, Spit can. Knows how to have a fight, he does. He's half had his day in a way – used to be the top jockey around L8 when he was a kiddie. Best in town to be fair. During the riots he was ruthless – James Bond had nothing on him, lar. He was getting down entries, squeezing through roadblocks, loading up with swag and dropping it off at warehouses in Speke ten minutes later. Untold, he were. That time the surveillance copter got rammed? Everyone said that was Spit.

He used to look like Bob Carolgees, years ago, when he had a bad muzzy and a sheepie. Bob Carolgees with a sleepy eye. That's why people think they can get away with all kinds of shite with him – because he's got a sleepy eye and he once went by the name of Spit the Dog. The lads used to shout: 'Shoshijizz!' whenever they seen him. The eye does make him look slow, to be fair. But he's far from it – he seen *Once Upon a Time in America* twenty-four times when it first come out. The full version, by the way. He tried to steer us away from 'Spit' and on to 'Cockeye' instead. Didn't work. Did not work, to be fair. Cunt could've had two gammy eyes for all's we cared. He was staying Spit.

But him and Jonah, the baseball bat noises and that – everyone's crowding round their table, laughing and adding their own impressions. Jonah's a big lad. Blind as fuck and all. The lenses on the cunt's gigs are about a foot thick. None of us has ever seen his eyes, by the way. There's just these two mad wedges of glass staring up at you, and that kite with that fucking barnet. He's got a full fringe like a monk's tonsure, Jonah – like one of them Three Stooges. Mind you, no one's about to call him Bootsy or something at the end of the day, are they? Not him. Fucking head the ball, he is. Totally different animal to Spit. He's a animal, Jonah, full-stop. He always wears a long shirt, Lacoste or Armani, something obvious, always wears it untucked over his gut to try and disguise that mountain of blubber. He's a big fat cunt but has he got a dig on him! Fuck. No backlift or nothing. He's just . . . bang! Can not see the cunt's eyes for the want of looking, though. Two pieces of glass looking at you. He's a pair of glasses, Jonah is. Spit used to be a bit of a slasher. It's to be hoped they can settle their sound-effects dispute amicably. Spit's blowing out and slapping the side of his neck to make a kind of a hollow thud noise with a bit of a echo, but Jonah's having none of that.

'No, you soft cunt, that's not it. Haven't you ever used a basie?'

'Have I? I'll use it on you in a minute you gobshite!'

'What's it go like, then? What's the noise like?'

'I've told you! That's it! That's it, exactly like what I done!'

Everyone's laughing and crowding round.

'Is it fuck! It's this . . .'

Jonah tips his head back, that mad fringe opening up like curtains and he just holds his mouth hard open and hits the side of his neck with three fingers:

'Thwok! Thwok!'

The lads all start clicking their fingers and cracking up.

'That's it! That's fucken it! That's the noise!'

'Is it fuck!'

Jonah indicates his audience with two outstretched arms. He doesn't say nothing else but it's half thingy – two dozen lemmings can't be wrong and that. Spit shuts the fuck up and goes into a big mad sulk, staring out the train window. I love the match. I fucking love it. I'll always go.

Moby

On the way back from the bog I sees these couple of lads from Kirkby that's been going for years. They was in the Monty the other night, trying to pull these two fatties. These are two heavy lads, by the way. Bullies. I'm all right with them and that, but they're the sort of lads who'll let on to you one day and pure fucking blank you another. It depends on who they're with or what they've had up their nose. To be fair, they always do have cracking stories. Always getting off without paying at some brasshouse or getting sisters to go down on each other or something. Never nothing normal, mind you. Never just a nosh or trying to shag some young mother quietly while her kids are asleep. Our Gerrard thinks it's all baloney, but he's not exactly in the marketplace, know where I'm going. He don't mind talking to them, to be fair, but I think they're straight up. They go the fucking Montrose. Say no more.

'How d'you get on with them two?'

They mean these couple of scrots from Kenny.

'I was made a offer I couldn't refuse.'

They half start to have a go at the accent, start that old 'Ah axed a ironmonger for a 'ammer an' a 'atchet', but they're with us. They're laughing. This Christmas must get to every cunt.

The Kirkby growlers are in good spirits. I hovers over their table, palms pressed flat down. Overfamiliar and I know it, but I feel more relaxed for it. I tell them about these two from the other night. One of them fucked off with one of the fellas off've the door. The rip. The other one, though – she looked boss when we was in the club, but once I got back to hers she was *auld*. Know the auld one in that *Something About Mary*? Her. Dead orange and that from the sunbed and the tits was like a bunch of grapes, to be fair. Not nice to look at, but I weren't arsed. The Kirkby lads love this story. One of them's in tears, by the way – he's chortling that much he's half crying. I tells them how I starts giving her one and then she starts talking dirty and asks my good self to put it in her arse. I'm thinking, well, we aim to please and that, and she turns over and that's where it starts to get gruesome. I can't miss it. There's a big chunk of chopped tomato right in the middle of her Gary Glitter. The lads start groaning, making out like they're disgusted and this only brings the lads from the table behind over, wanting the story again. Next thing half the carriage is down by the Kirkby table, throwing their own stories in. These lads Jonah knows from Breck Road have just got back from a fucking swingers club outside of Oldham. It's always fucking places like that, by the way. Ramsbottom and that, Clitheroe – places like that. They reckon it got thingy when one of them starting spanking this fella's wife's arse dead hard. Said she was all for it at first, but then she started crying and that, pleading with him to stop. He didn't want to stop, did he, and they ends up getting chased through the club in their boxies, with half their clobber still in the lockers. Whole fucking carriage is in bulk about this, by the way.

Ged

My heart goes out to these poor people that's paid for first class and finds themselves having to listen to that lot. Poor bastards – you can see them cringing, not wanting to catch no one's eye or cause offence. These are nice people, by the way. Nice auld fella taking his wife Christmas shopping, see the lights and that, Chrimbo treat for the auld girl. Family just behind them off to see a show or something – they don't want their kids hearing things like that, language and all of that carry-on. Poor cunts are half grinning, making out they're not bothered and they've got the spirit of Wacker themselves and that, but you can see they just want to go: 'Shut the fuck up, will youse! There's kiddies and that here!'

They say fuck all, though. They just sit there and take it.

Ratter

I know that a lot of the match-heads have got a bit of a take on me. They'll see my grid in the *Echo* every now and then, me wearing a hard hat, digging a ditch or shaking some councillor's hand and that. The lads here probably think I've got Brewster's (which I have) but they think I've lost touch, too (which I most certainly have not). I can hear all the silly sex talk from a couple of tables away, and decide that my own episode from last night might buy JPB his place at the table, buy us a weekend pass and that. I think I might leave out the bloody grand finale, to be fair. I've been told that these football hooligans have got weak stomachs.

So I ambles over and recount the heavy stereotype of the dirty, older rich bird that wanted it hard and fast. I gives her a few extra lines of dialogue and go in big with the wet-your-kecks element. They love it. I'm putting on my best posh Wirral madam accent, telling how wet she were and how her legs was wide open, begging for it. And then I tell them the new ending. In fairness, I do resist the temptation to half make myself into a stud and that. I inform my tittering gallery that I suddenly despised this woman that lay spreadeagled before us and, instead of giving her one single moment of pleasure, I took care of YT and come all over her instead. It takes a second to sink in and then they're roaring with laughter and shaking my hand. While one of them shouts to be careful not to shake my wanking hand, another voice asks where he can meet this lady. I remember that she scrawled down her number. I fishes it out.

'Nina Perkins-West. Fuckinell – that classy or what, by the way?'

I see Big Brother is suddenly extremely interested.

The fucking goat – never thought he was like that, our Gerrard. Tut-tut, and that. I shout over to him.

'Here y'are, Ged. It's a 342 number. That's by yours, isn't it? You should get round there!'

But he's not playing. Typical of that cunt, by the way – the lights are on and then they're off again, just like that. He's half a fucking control freak, he is. Kite on him now, mind you. You'd think I'd just told a tale about his bird's sister or something. I haven't seen the cunt go so white in a long time. If ever a person could be said to have been in shock, seen a ghost, stunned into silence, whatever, then my dearly despised bro-by-default has just shit his good self.

Ged

That greasy-haired twat! I've never liked that John-Paul. Wrong 'un. Wrong 'un, through and through. What them nice folk on the next table must be thinking of us, I don't know. Bad one, Ratter. Bad one.

Moby

We're past Watford. I've been sitting with the Kirkby boys since Nuneaton and that, but I gets up now to go back to ma homies. They've been all right, these two, by the way. Had a good natter with them about the old days and faces from the match that you don't see no more. We had a laugh trying to think up some of Milo's best ones. 'Randy as hell' is still the one everyone remembers – 'Gentlemen, I am as randy as hell' and that. Then I slaughters them over that 'Kirkby Do All The Rucking At Aways' spray at the side of the Kop. They're all right. Even as I'm getting off one of them goes good luck for Monday and that. Every face on this fucking train knows

169

about me and Fonzie and the thing on Monday. I don't even hate the cunt but I'm going to have to do him in good style now.

Bernie

I'd really been looking forward to this one. I love it when Ged and the boys come down. Gives me a chance to do something for them, if you know where I'm going. Ged really, to be fair. All the stuff he done for me in the old days – none of this could've happened without him. But he's like an Untouchable. He's like De Niro in *A Bronx Tale*, you can't get to him, he won't take nothing from you. You'd think he was a priest or just an ordinary hard-working fella the way he keeps you at arm's length. Can't even get the kids decent presents or nothing. He don't exactly tell you he disapproves, it ain't like that – he's just *Ged*. He's a one-off. So I do love it when they all come down for the match and I can make a proper fuss of them. And I suppose I don't mind them all seeing how far the lad's come – people like Rico and that, lads who give us hell when I was the run-around. I don't mind looking into their eyes nowadays and seeing that thing that isn't respect and isn't envy but is nothing other than stone-cold fear. I don't mind that one little bit, in fairness.

So I was looking forward to this one – Ged, the match, the fight, big crazy banquet, girls, the works – then that sly cunt goes and phones us. Ratter. Wants to see us. Dead important, by the way – can not wait. Taken the shine off things, I don't mind saying. Hope the cunt hasn't rumbled us. No chance – he don't know we're on to him.

Ged

As we're heading up the platform all the lads from the back of the train start running forward, getting a shout going. It still sounds boss, that. They just have to go: 'LI!'

And then every other cunt gives it a big mad: 'VER! POOL!'

The way it echoes round the station sends your everyday Billy Bunters scurrying for the food plaza until we've gone. I don't mind admitting it – it doesn't half give myself a tingle and that, arriving at Euston with the boys. Still gives us one fuck of a charge, it does. The Nina thing's forgotten already. Fucking stupid, anyway – this is what it's all about for lads like me, not pathetic wet dreams about the likes of Nina Perkins-West.

Some kids jog past, eyes darting everywhere, but they've well missed Man U. Missed 'em by a good hour, I'd say. They'll be at Waterloo by now if they want to get to Southampton today. A couple of them recognise myself and Moby and start getting cheeky with us.

'Where's the limo, mate?'

We went to the Cup game at Man U in a limo a few seasons back. The fucking Solskjaer one, it were. Started at my fortieth, to be fair. There's all kinds out in Vegas spending Brewster's and that, and it half become our motto for the weekend – we'd go: 'Terrible poverty in Liverpool, by the way' and crack up laughing. Some of the lads was tipping hundreds and that, lighting ceegars with fifties – all of that. Could not quite bring myself to spunk money like that, to be fair, but some lads are just like that, aren't they? Anyway, our little firm and the touts all decides we've had enough of this 'in your Liverpool slums' rap, so a few of us went in limos and that. We got dropped off at the Quays, in fairness, so's we're visible, so no cunt could say we was door-to-door. We had a drink in that Pier 9. No cunt come near us on the day, but the touts are all fine with the Mancs, anyway. It's spivs of the world unite and split the cake up with them fellas. It is with the Salford lads at least, anyway. They're not so sure where they stand when the Gooch come into the picture. Them boys don't mess around, by the way. They don't abide by no cunt's rules. That is a fact.

'Gizza lift in your limo, mate!'

'No limos today, my friend.'

'Ah, go 'ead, mate. I'll look after you. I'll make sure none of them East End hoodlums worries you.'

'Do one, kidder.'

Just then we spot Franner, looking every inch the East End hoodlum himself in his Crombie and silk scarf. He's even got a Homburg on, the flash cunt. All the lads get on his case straight away, talking in cockney accents and calling him all kinds of slags and nonces.

'Oi, Bernie you kant where we going for a Lilly?'

'A fucking what?'

'A facking Lilly the Pink, you slay-agg!'

Moby whips Franner's hat off and tries to shove it on his own fat bonce. He makes a move on Franner's head.

'Here y'are, get his spot. Get his fucking evil alien spot!'

'Look! It's fucking pulsing! Exterminate! Extermi-nate!'

Fran laughs it all off, but you can see the impatience. He's not that amused, to be fair. He's not used to getting slaughtered so much these days. Howls of laughter as he leads us under Euston to a vast, fuck-off white stretch limo. A chauffeur waits with the door held open. You can just see this little walnut door wide open on a fridge full of miniatures and that. The drinks ledge has been pulled down and there's four or five white lines, ready and waiting. Can see how Franner's got on so well, by the way. Lad's got a bit of class about him, to be fair.

Moby

The hotel's sound. I take it all back. I was all for staying by that Marble Arch, like we always do – loads of brasses, dead handy for everything and that. Our Gerrard was the one that sussed that we wouldn't be going nowhere near the West End. It's West Ham today, Robbie's show's at the York Hall, and Franner's taken over a restaurant in the Docklands for after the fight. If we'd gone for the Metropole we'd've spent the fucking weekend in taxis. Ged tried for that Jury's in Islington so's we'd be in a barrio we half knew and that, but we've landed on our feet with this place. Big glass tower right in the heart of Canary Wharf. No matter how bad we end up tonight, we're only a stagger away. That's why Ged's the boss. He *is* the man with the fucking plan.

Ged

All the talk in the Globe is about how Moby and Jonah and Paul the Hom got hassle off've a load of kids. They're getting torn apart by the lads, they are. Paul the Hom's dead quiet, mind you, he's just taking it, but Jonah's not having none of it. He's saying that six of them run the lot. He's getting very agitated about this. His glass is going to shatter, he's squeezing it that hard. The veins in his neck are standing out the more he tries to get it across that they never ran. It just half got a bit iffy for a minute. Even though we're in company, we're starting get a few looks from across the bar. The Globe's right by Stepney Green station. Not the worst part of town by a long way, not since all the yupsters moved in, but it ain't Sloane Square, neither.

Moby

I don't mind admitting it. My arse went for a second back there. There was just so many of the little cunts. Not just that, by the way – it just doesn't *happen* like that no more. Twenty years ago, fair enough. If we brought a mob to West Ham we'd expect to be on our toes after the match. But this *was* the old days, know where I'm going. It reminded me of us lot, how we used to be and that. One minute we're with all the boys, shuffling out the ground, half not concentrating and that, just made up about the goal. Franner's told us to look out for white Hacks with Dial-a-Cab on the side. He's got a platoon of them standing off just up Green Street. Couldn't see none of that, though, couldn't see the lads, neither. Knew we was all meeting at this Globe and then Paul the Hom – who does know London well, in fairness – says that it's about four or five stops on the Tube. We'll be there before them. So we keeps going up the road to hop on a Tube at that Upton Park. We're all having a laugh and a joke about the game while we're waiting on the platform when this little shower of tykes starts looking over. Then one of them comes over to Jonah and goes: 'Got the time, have you, Scouse?'

Jonah starts laughing and brings us lot in on it. He gives the lad a bit of a lecture on how to be a stand-off. Makes a bit of a cunt out of him, to be fair. He goes:

'No, lad – your job is to suss whether we *are* Scousers, right? You're supposed to be making out like you're a nice geezer, you don't give a fuck where we're from. Hasn't entered your fucking head, yeah? Does not even come into it, Scousers and that. That's your riff, lad. You just need to know the time and that, don't you?'

Fair to say the lad weren't expecting that. Jonah's on one. Doesn't give a fuck, by the way, Jonah. Pure does not give a fuck about nothing.

'So all's you've got do is ask us the time. That's not too hard, is it?'

More and more of them starts to crowd around. Jonah either hasn't noticed or he knows what he's going to do. There's fucking loads of the little cunts now. They can smell it. It's going to go off. Jonah just carries on bullying the lad. He's not arsed that there might be too many of them, by the way. Hasn't given none of that a second thought. That's the beak for you. Any last trace of a sense of danger is blown away. You're not on borrowed time so much – but you're not on *real* time, neither. You're not dealing with reality, to be fair. That's it with Jonah – he can't sense nothing, he doesn't give a fuck.

'So, d'you want to try again, lad? Just walk away, come back and go . . .'

He puts on a big mad Dick Van Dyke accent. It's more like James Coburn in *The Great Escape*.

'Got the time have you, me old mucker.'

I can't help myself, to be fair. I'm in bulk. Pure can not stop myself from laughing – just Jonah's mad voice and that. The lad doesn't know what to do. He's looking into Jonah's treble-thicks, trying to get a clue. A lot of people have made that mistake, and people will carry on doing it. They see Jonah's gigs and they half think he might be easy. The lad gives his mates a little signal. This is it. They all walk over, nice and slow. No noise. They start to spread out a bit as they get near to us. I've seen this happen, by the way. Doesn't matter how handy you are, sometimes – doesn't mean a fucking thing if you get rounded on by a pack of little street rats that know the score. Doesn't matter if you're Charlie and Reggie, they'll get you.

Bolton, that was one. When they was at the other gaff, thingy, Burnden Park. Freezing cold. Match had to be called off because the snow was that bad, but there was a hundred of us already there on the ordinary, fucking frozen in grandad shirts and bib and brace and that, trainies with no socks. February 1979, six inches of snow and we're wearing Nastase with no fucking socks. These ten fellas come walking out the alehouse and they're like the Ready Brek Kids – only fellas. Muzzies. Donkey jackets and that. Big red glow on their kites and steam coming off 've them as they come out, all full of ale. Sees us and they're half up for it. They're not arsed either way. Makes you feel a bit sly, now, what was done to them. Bad, it were – we was only little scallies, like, but we knew what we was doing.

This little West Ham firm are like that. They've done this before. Before anyone has chance to think, Paul the Hom runs in, eyes bulging like a lunatic.

'COME 'EAD THEN!'

He's bouncing around the platform, fronting the biggest of them. They're kids and that, sixteen or seventeen, but some of them look like they can have a go. Some of the young black boys with them, they're as big as we are, to be fair. I'm in there next to Paul and next thing we're all there, only the six of us and that, back to back, waiting for them to make a move. They don't know what to do. It just needs one of the cunts to run in, throw a kick in, anything, and we're fucked. But they don't. They stand off on the balls of their feet.

'WHAT'S UP, BOYS? DON'T YOU FANCY IT NO MORE?'

Then Jonah runs in, and so does Paul. Whop! Wham! Bang! Some haymakers get thrown and one of the kids goes down. They start to back off. I'm looking round for the Number One and that, the daddy. If I can spark him I know full well what'll come next. I run round the side of them and there he is, this big, handy-looking cunt. No doubt about it. That's him. The Kiddie. I chin him, get him good, by the way. He goes woozy, but he stays on his feet. I go to whack him again but he turns and runs and, with that, they all run. We start to go down the platform after them but, to be fair, we weren't expecting a tear-up and we're all a little bit fucked, bit out of breath and that. The train comes anyway. There's no problem finding a seat. As soon as the doors shut they all comes back down the platform again, lobbing anything they can find at our compartment. One window gets a bit of a crackline. That's it. We're in the Globe ten minutes later. Wish to fuck Jonah would've kept it all under his hat. Not exactly the most diplomatic thing to be rubbing in fucking Marty's face. Might have had a little nephew in that pack, Marty. His fucking lad might've been one of them, to be fair.

Ratter

Did I say I love the match and I'll always carry on going, come what may? I'm a liar. I've got nothing in common with these low-life twats. I want nothing to do with them, and fucking soon I won't need to *have* nothing to do with them. I've come on this trip expressly to see Bernie. My own personal fixer. I need to run something by him. Not to put too fine a point on it, I need his support over something. I need his permission. I think he'll see the sense in it all, too. I know he will. He's said he'll see us as soon as he gets everyone sat down with a drink their hand, and the floor show's under way. Suits me, sir. Ooh!

Ged

Good atmosphere. Great day all round. Some of Franner's colleagues are circulating, introducing themselves and that. There's some lovely fucking women in here, by the way. I don't want to insult Fran, but I take it he's brought them in. Class, they are. You can tell by their waistlines. They've got them elegant, supple waists that look like a drawn-out S-shape. It takes work to look like that, and money. Lots of it.

It's a class place and all, this – like one of them Ken Hom places he's took us to before. Always takes us somewhere boss when we're in town by the way, Franner does. Puts on a proper Gentlemen's Evening he does, grub, floor show, the lot. Turned into a very stylish guy, to be fair. When he first started off down here, he used to take us to that Phoenix in Stratford. That's where we first got to know Marty and that crew, all having a laugh and a joke with Frank McAvennie and Charlie Nicholas and that. He loves his Chinese, though, Franner. Always did. Drought's making a cunt of his waiter. Slaughtering the poor cunt, he is.

'This beef is not sizzling! I asked you for *sizzling* beef! It has to sizzle! Zzzzzzzzz! Take it away and bring me *sizzling* beef!'

It's the beak. Every cunt's been hammering it since the train left Lime Street and now they all think they're Tarby. Even Stratford Marty's getting it. They started off just having a go at the Turks, how you can't do business with them and that, and Marty's saying that, to be fair, he's always found them very honourable. He says they was very good to him when he used to smuggle cars. That does it. Spit's on him in a flash.

'Must've had fucking big kecks, Marty!'

'What you on about, you soppy-looking cunt?'

'Your kecks and that. Must've been some Birmos if you was smuggling cars in them!'

Marty shakes his head, smiling and that. He looks a little bit like that Sean Bean, Stratford Marty does. A auld Sean Bean, if you will.

'You know what? I fucking hate you Scouse cunts! Can't you just go back to Liverpool and nick hubcaps instead of coming down here bothering respectable businessmen!' That gets a big raucous laugh and it's champagne all round. The women all smile all the time, smiling, smiling and looking terrified. Before long I know why. A stunning-looking black girl and this presentable blonde starts up a floor show. They're fucking boss movers, mind you, and after a minute or two they starts getting into each other. First it's just necking and that, sucking each other's fingertips and running them around their nipples. I don't mind admitting it, they're horny as fuck, these two, and I has to adjust my sitting position. Then the whole kit comes off and they're stroking each other's bush. That's like a signal. Most of these are no strangers to a Gentlemen's Evening, they know the score and that – but I thought they might've been a bit more restrained on someone else's yard. No such thing, mind you. Jonah's got his lash out then Spit's whipped his out then all kinds are at it, stood up right by the girls giving: 'Go 'ead, love! Get into her! Fucking get right into that juicy quim!'

The two girls gives it the best they can with two dozen fellas wanking themselves soft, to be fair, but you have to feel sorry for the pair of them. They're fucking covered in it. They have to sit there smiling as the lads all finish. Half have to pretend they're into it, they do, when it's going everywhere, in their hair, in their eyes, fucking everywhere. The black girl in particular is covered from head to foot in it. She's done a Janet Jackson, to be fair.

While the evening gentlemen are otherwise engaged, one of Bernie's Boys comes over. We call them Bernie's Boys, these silent, say-fuck-all gophers that work for Franner. Mr Big wants to see myself pronto. He's in the bar.

Moby

There's a big cheer from the boys when Robbie comes in. He done well. It was a tough little lad he was up against and he give him a good go-around, but Robbie done everything right. He comes in now with Willie Mac and Carl Igo, and Stratford Marty makes room at his own table straight away. He signals some of the girls to come over. They sit by Robbie, chatting away and touching his cuts and bruises with their long fingers. Every one of these Judies has got long fingers, by the way.

Ratter

Everything seemed to go all right with Bernie. I always call him that. Bernie. That's his name now. That's what the trade calls him. He seemed to see where I was coming from with my little conundrum, mind you. Seemed more than sympathetic, to be fair. I know I was raving a bit with the beak and that, but I think I put my case over well. I've made a good impression tonight. Job's a good 'un.

Ged

In fairness, he's more like a brother to myself than a mate, Franner is. We just sits in the bar for ages rapping about old times. It's a nice bar and we've got it to ourselves. There isn't another person around. You're aware of the barman, there if you need him, but he's out of sight. It's just me and Fran. This weird version of 'Everything I Do, I Do It For You' is piped through, sung in Mandarin. It seems to fit. You can hear the lads' coke-crazed laughter coming through in gales from the restaurant. I've never been that crazy about the floor-show element, to be fair. There's something about all that thing of a load of fellas with their cocks out, birds having to act like whores and that – I just don't like it myself. I don't mind saying so.

Fran's looking older. He looks grave. He comes to the point. It's about our Anthony. This thing with Purple Alphonse.

'Is there nothing can be done?'

I shakes my head. I know he's big and all of that now – he's fucking *yowge*, by the way – but Franner's my mate at the end of the day. He should know that I'd have explored every avenue. I'd've well explored it if there was a chance. He's not soft. He sees my eyes flicker, sees the annoyance and he's laid his hand on mine in a instant.

'I know, kidder.'

Mad, deep voice. Dead fucking gravelly, like he's smoked two hundred a day and had his throat cut. His accent's a mad mixture of Scouse and cockney. Not even a mix, by the way. He just goes from one to another, like he's Norman Bates.

'I've got to ask you, haven't I, lar.'

I half have to smile at him getting right back into the 'kidder' and 'lar' and that. He gives us his serious look. His eyes are wet and slow, buried deep back in his head under them lazy flappy eyelids of his.

'You know what this could lead to?'

I nod and clear my throat.

'Ask Mikey. I done it all by the book. I took a walk up to see him. He's all right with it. So long as everyone behaves themselves, there won't be no repercussions.'

He ponders this.

'Is there no way of doing it behind closed doors?'

I laugh. I can see his point. The thing with our Anthony and Fonzie isn't the problem. It's the aftermath. It's what all the seconds and back-up might do to each other.

'If there is, I'm all ears, like.'

'You know what them cunts are like, kidder. Just being there, stood off've each other'll make them want to have a fight. Can we have it so's there's no back-up?'

'There *is* no back-up.'

He looks surprised, then pleased – as much as Franner ever looks pleased, mind you.

'How'd you work that then? They'll all be chocker, won't they, that lot? They'd rather miss the Cup Final than miss a good straightener.'

He smiles to himself. His shoulders allow themselves a little twitch of amusement. He looks at myself.

'You could sell tickets.'

'Only about 10,000.'

He stands up and sighs, indicating that the meeting's over. He holds my hand and looks myself right in the eye with them slow, muddy Humphrey Bogart minces of his. Always did seem to be looking at you extra careful, half as though he thought you was having him off.

'Make sure they all behave, yeah?'

'I'll do me best.'

He nods. And as we're walking back to the restaurant he goes: 'Everything OK with Rats?'

Now I really do stop still. He never makes throwaway remarks. There's something in it. I turn and ask him.

'What's he up to?'

'I don't know.'

And that's it. That's as much as I'm getting. He puts his arm around us and steers myself back to the party. I stare hard at Ratter but he's into deep bullshit with this great-looking call girl. If there's something on his mind then he sure as fuck ain't showing.

Sunday

Ged

I might as well be a fucking party planner. No matter where we go it's me makes all the arrangements, me tells them where to go and me that gets them all up in the morning. Short of minding their pocket money for them and doling it out, I'm a fucking group leader.

It's their own fucking fault. They all had to sit there in the bar last night, didn't they, trying to impress the brasses with the expensive Armagnacs and the liqueurs and all of that. *Impress* the brasses, by the way!

To my great shame, I did take one back to my room. It was just for Bernie, mind you. He'd gone to all that trouble and, to be fair, it's a bit of a slap in the face if you refuse to partake of the host's hospitality. I made sure he seen me go up in the elevator with this one who looked like the one with the dark straight hair off've *Charlie's Angels*. The one with the little smile lines. Her. Cute as fuck but classy and all, too. She had a lovely fucking voice, this one. That's all we done, by the way. I did have a line in fairness and it's just like the talking drops for myself. I just sat there gabbing with her, asking her if the money's all right and if she's got anyone special and what does she want for Chrimbo and all of that. Didn't so much as kiss her but I still feel guilty as fuck, to be fair, just for having her up there in my room.

Still, what's done is done and that's all the more reason now why there's no way we're missing that train. Me and her have got tickets for that Celine Dion at the Nynex tonight. Some of the spivs have sorted it with the Salford lads. I'm not one for socialising with Mancs, to be fair, but it is Christmas at the end of the day. I'll do it for her. She'll love all that. She loves her music, Debbi does. Lighthouse Family, the M People, that Chris De Burgh and that – she's right into all that. Them Corrs, too. Anything mellow. Anything with a tune. I don't mind them Corrs myself, to be fair. I like the music, like. Everyone goes on about the sisters and that, what stunners they all are and all of that ballyhoo, but they wouldn't've got nowhere without their tunes. Is right and that, by the way. That Andrea's the one they all go for, but I've got quite a liking for the Sharon one. I'm half looking forward to seeing that Celine Dion myself, to be fair. I like the one off've the *Titanic* film on the sly. It'll do myself no harm, mind you, a night away from these beauts. It'll take my mind off our Anthony's to-do tomorrow. Starting to wreck my head that, by the way.

Moby

I made a proper fucking cunt out of myself. Thank fuck most of them bastards are getting a later train. This'd be one long train ride if they was all coming with us, and that's the God's honest truth. Brought it right on myself, I did. I'm there in the lobby with the others, aren't I, giving this poor cunt of a night porter down the banks. It was about half four, and he'd only serve us in the lobby and that. Taking fucking ages he was, just to bring through one bottle of port and a bottle of brandy and some more champagne and that. Fucking can not abide that champagne myself – most overrated grog in the world by my book. The brasses was all loving all of this, by the way. They was getting more and more cheerful by the minute – course they were.

There they are, getting bought all sorts of drinks and they don't even have to work for it – just giggle a bit and stroke our bald, stupid fucking heads. Most of them must know by now that they're not going to have to get on their backs and graft for it. Once the lads get up to bed they'll be off away to the land of nod, most of them, to be fair. Not my good self though, matey. If they wants a quiet time of it they better stay away from Mr Moby. It's a well-known thing – the more I bevvy, the more I has to find me some grumble. But not one of these, by the way. I'm not like that soft cunt Ratter, sitting in the corner necking the face off some brass. You don't *neck* brasses, by the way. He's a soft cunt, our Ratts.

My own stupid fault what happened, mind you. I'm making sure everyone gets on it, all hands are slaughtering him and I'm giving it the big one saying how I won't ever pay for it, not even if some other cunt is footing the bill. All sorts of shouts and cursing from the boys, but I'm not having none of it. And then, bang on cue, this great-looking lady gets out of a cab outside and totters into reception on heels. But unsteady and that, she is, little bit tipsy, to be fair – but a fucking boss-looking lady, no two ways about it. The lads go surprisingly quiet, in fairness – you'd expect them to roast a girl like that, coming home drunk on her own and nicely dressed and all of that. Looking back on it now, I should never have bothered. She'd obviously been ragged all over London, by the way. Could hardly stand up at all, in fairness, but I'd had a little go on the bugle myself by then and I was half looking for what I wanted to see. I seen that Kim Tate off've the *Emmerdale Farm*. I seen a horny, good-looking sort of blonde in a nice evening dress, stood at the hotel reception shouting for her key. Shouting, by the way – she weren't shy. The fella never come, the night porter and that. She turns around, looks straight at Mr Moby and goes: 'You don't happen know where the reception staff have got to?'

Nicely spoken. Not *posh* posh, but nice. She's slightly cross-eyed and all, too – that, or she's been fucking battering the ale. This attracts a few stupid remarks from the likes of fucking Jonah, but I keeps a steady eye contact with her – as much as you can do, to be fair. She doesn't flinch. Looks directly right at us, she does. I tells her the night porter one'll be back in a mo, he's just gone to the bar to fetch us some bubbly. I ask her if she'll join us. She smiles, really nice, lovely smile and that, but she goes no, ta and that – she's had a night of it and she has to be up in the morning. This gets a big, mad 'aaaagh!' from my witty amigos. Gang of pricks they are, sometimes.

The night porter comes back, all apologies to this Claire King lookalike for making her wait. She'll have none of it. She's not arsed. But here comes her big play, by the way. Still can't make no sense out of her. What happens, right, is she asks for her room key. Just asks the lad for her key but, I swear to God straight up, she raises her voice. She raises her voice and she repeats the room number. She says it twice – just to make sure that my good self has heard her loud and clear. She is keen for the company of Mr Moby, so it seems. So I gives her five minutes to get comfy then I'm straight up there. But not before I've made a complete cunt out of myself, mind you. Not before Mr Moby has clapped his hands together like he's the chocolate kid, called the boys all the fall-down losers in the world and wished them every happiness with their pay-per-view partners, by the way. Only then am I off to make love, sweet love, with Kim Tate. Who won't come to the door. Just pure will not even answer. I leaves it as long as I can and stand there in the corridor like a soft arse hoping she'll change her mind. More than anything I'm hoping them shower of bastards downstairs will have gone quietly by the time

I have to slope down again. Suddenly it's freezing up here and my room key is behind the desk at reception and I've got no fucking choice. And of course not one of the cunts has moved. To the loudest braying noises, by the way, noises of pure relief and happiness that some other Ted has fucked up and made a cunt of theirselves, I has to run the gauntlet and wait for Sydney Slowstreet to fumble and tremble and shakily find my fucking key. The lads are all singing that one: 'They call me mistah luvvah-luvvah!'

Shower of twats, they are. Their crowing voices was still ringing in my ears as I climbed under that heavy duvet and the flashbacks is haunting me right now, in fairness.

Thank fuck we're on this early train back. By no means ideal prep for a straightener, by the way. Far from it. Now that I've finally give the matter some thought, I could've done without a big weekend like this has been. Good job it's only Fonzie. I slide down behind the paper and hope none of these is in the mood for talking.

Ratter

This is a low. This is as crashing a cocaine low as I've ever known. I am nothing. I am filth. I deserve to be taken away and shot. Look at these two boys with me now. These guys are mensches. They're fucking kings, these boys are. But all's I do is plot. I plot against them and I plot for my miserable self and I plot for the day that I don't have to look them in the eye no more. They're worth ten of me. More. I'm the shit on the sole of their shoes. Praise be to God that Bernie don't see it that way.

Ged

Time is not on my side. Desperate as I am to see the kiddies, and much as I'm looking forward to Manchester tonight there's two big things I need to do on my way home. I need a quick pop in to the office to check everything's kosher with Trudi. Last night was one of the biggest Saturdays in the calendar for A-Line. I shouldn't have gone to London in fairness but fuck it – I did. I went and now I'm on my way back and I want to hear that everything went like a dream while I was away. Last thing I need is any them scabby drivers trying to hold out on us because the radios weren't working or whatever shite they decide to try this week. And that's just the half of it – a very minor half, in fairness. I'm meeting Coley for a very quick one in the Thatch. He's called us on the mobie – just needs a final yea or nay from the celebs for Tuesday. In all total fucking fairness I haven't done much more about it. I haven't had a fucking second what with one thing and another. I'll have a word with Moby now. I can't let fucking Coley down. That is not a option. This is going to be a party to remember for them kiddies and I intend to deliver for them. Our Anthony'll be able to have a word with some of the lads when he talks to them about their Liam's do. In the meantime I have, what – just less than two hours to see if I can fish out where Ratter's going.

Moby

It's starting to finally fucking dawn on us that I've got less than twenty-four hours until the thing with Alphonse. That purple cunt won't be taking this lightly, by the way. He'll be out doing all kinds of circuits, fucking roadwork, sparring, bags, the lot, he will. Starting to get a little bit para, to be fair. It's not just the beak, neither. I just haven't gone about this right at all. Fonzie's no mug, by the way. I can take him, no bother, but I'm going to have to take him quick, know where I'm going. I'm going to have to knock the lad out – and I'm going to have to do it pronto. Cos if I don't, if I lets him get away from me, if I start letting him get into a fight with me then it's going to come down to strength. Stamina. Training. I haven't trained proper for days. I haven't done none of that. I haven't trained proper for a long, long time. Fair enough, it's not the York Hall, Bethnal Green, by the way. It is a fucking straightener. But I could've gone out with Robbie and Willie Mac them few times. And I could've laid off last night. First thing when we get off this train I'm going straight the Adelphi for a good steam. Get all that gack and booze and shite out of my system. And then I'm going to bed.

There isn't no two ways about it – I'm going to have to knock the cunt out. Not a problem, by the way. Fucking deadbeat that I am, plonkie fucking half a playboy that I've become, I still do not see that soft cunt coming anywhere near my own good self. But I will have to knock him out.

Ratter

You can try to bury your worst thoughts. Memories of when you're a kid and bad things happen and you don't want to believe it was true – you just fight them things back out of your head. You chase them. When it's you's the victim, you *can* empty out the nightmares and try and replace them with good things. That's what I used to do. When I used to lie in that bed, shivering, *frozen* fucking cold – you can't *get* that cold in England, by the way, but I remember clear as yesterday that second of dread when I had to take my clothes off and dive into bed and it was so, so, *so* fucking cold I thought I'd die – there used to be a half a minute when I'd lie there, convulsing, sheets so cold they was wet, and I used to try and imagine that I'd broke out of Colditz and the Nazis was after us and I'd fled right through this thick forest and come out on a hillside, like Heidi, where a beautiful Swiss mountain girl agreed to hide YT in her barn. It was frozen cold but I was in love. And I knew she'd be back any moment with milk and biscuits and the warmth of her big breasts. I fell asleep like that night after night.

But when you are the baddie yourself, you can't chase the nightmares away so easy. Not when you have caused them nightmares yourself. Not when they was exactly what you wanted.

And I can not stop thinking about her. The image of the girl, her pretty face streaked with free-flowing mascara huddled in terror in the corner of my hotel room. It started with a kiss. She never thought it would come to this.

'What's up with you?' I'm saying. 'It's only a bit of fun.'

Even I know that's not true. I let her gather up what there is of her clothes, her torn dress and her shredded stockings and I let her back away slowly, let her think it's all over. It hasn't even started. I let her get as far as the door before I goes after her again.

Ged

I'm watching him. He's not all there. To be fair though, he's never been all there. He's never been there at all. From the moment my ma took him in, he was either out the house or he was in some kind of dreamworld. Never used to say fuck all, by the way. Never said a fucking word to no one. He weren't vacant – he done well enough at school and that when he could be arsed. When he first started seeing their Margueritte, to be fair, he got that fucking scholarly he could've went to uni if he'd've wanted. He weren't a emptyhead. He was just disconnected, know what I mean. That's him right now. Right at this very second he's exactly the same Ratter as he were when he was ten. He's here but he's not here.

The carriage is totally fucking empty, by the way, but I check to see that no one's got on, no one's around. Then I hits them with it, pure out the blue. I calls them over.

'Right, lads. This is the riff. We're going to go on Thursday. Yeah?'

Properly taken by surprise, mind you, the both of them. They wasn't ready for this. This, they were not expecting. Mobe's nodding, Ratter's nodding. And they pure don't want to hear it.

'John-Paul. I don't mean nothing by this, but I don't want you down the Mystery tomorrow. We're going to do this thing very softly-softly. There's nothing in it, lad. You know that, yeah?'

I watch him carefully. He pretends to be sore. He's fucking made up, by the way. I've let him off 've the hook big time.

'Moby. Let's just get this thing done tomorrow. We're

not bringing a crew with us, yeah? In. Out. Bang. Is that coolio?'

He's nodding, but he doesn't like the sound it. Does not fucking like it one little bit, by the way. Ratter comes in.

'How do we know *they* won't bring a crew.'

He's good. He's *fucking* good. Got the right blend of still half sore about being stood down and concern for Moby's welfare, he has.

'Just a hunch and that.'

Now Moby's in there.

'It better be a good fucking hunch, kidder.'

I wink and chew and try to look shrewd. I haven't got a fucking Scooby what I'm talking about here. I don't know what I'm fishing for. I just want to watch the both of them perform under pressure. See if there's anything that I need to be aware of.

'We'll be pukka, boys. We can do the Fonz thing real easy. It doesn't have to be a fucking tear-up for the lads and that, hey?'

They both half nod and that.

'I just don't want nothing distracting us from the other thing, know what I'm saying. You know we could've done without all of this, Mobe.'

That's got him, well. The big lad is double on my side now he's been reminded. This just leaves the slippery fella. Can't read his play, to be fair. Pure do not know what Franner's throwing us here.

'So, Ratts, Thursday, yeah?'

'Too much to expect any more detail at this point?'

I laugh and ruffles his hair. I know for a fact that he hates that. Anything just to soften him up a bit, get a bit of a reading off 've the boy.

'Dool's for brekky on Wednesday, right? Nine bells, everybody?'

Moby looks like I've personally told him he's too old to do a job for us any more. Let down isn't in it. He looks slayed.

'Dool's? How come and that?'

'It's got to be early doors, Mobe. I've got fucking loads on and loads more to do. Just fucking go with it, will you?'

'All right, lar – just asking and that. Bit unusual and that, isn't it, that's all. I'm entitled to ask, aren't I?'

He's starting to get a bit aerated, but I've half got a feeling that's down to tomorrow, the straightener and that, Fonzie and all of that.

'Make it ten, can we?'

Ratter. Won't take the first offer on nothing, that cunt. If a bird offers him a blowjob he'll go: 'Make it two.'

But he's half got a point. He has got a bit of a long haul in to Birkenhead from Grassendale, in fairness. Specially as this supposed meeting is the full phonus balonus. I takes a little decko at him. Still can't get no reading off've him. Lad seems straight as a die.

'Just get there soon as you can, Ratts. I know the tunnel's bad up until nine and that. We'll get started and you just come and join us, la.'

I looks at our Anthony.

'Mobe. You're going to be fine tomorrow, lad. Your main thingy is after. I'm going to take you right home to your doorstep afterwards, kidder. Don't go out. No matter how much you feel like you want to give it the big one and that, just don't do it. It's only a couple of days. Stay in. Rev your kids up. Make plans for the communion with your Marie. Just don't go out.'

Sullen nodding from the both of them, by the way. You wouldn't think I'm putting grands in their fucking biscuit tins, would you? You'd think I was taxing it out of the cunts. As we gets out at Limey I tells Moby I'll be round for him first thing and I give Ratter a big hug and tell him Wednesday at Dool's café. I'll give him the full riff about Thursday then. There is no Thursday, of course. I already have a prior engagement this Thursday.

Ratter

I am so fucking comedown para by the time we gets back to Limey that I don't even want Ged to go. I always hate that bit when the lads've been off somewhere together, when you all get off and go your own separate ways. You know the jaunt is over and done with when ones and twos start getting off. I always get a little bit of a lowie on when that happens, but today more than ever I pure do not want to be left on my tod. All's I can hear in my head is Mikey's voice the other night.

'That's the least of your worries.'

That, and his fucking mad-girl's laugh. I was half holding on there to see if Moby fancied one down the Pineapple or something – share a cab as far as Park Road and maybe stop off at one of the auld places. There's bound to be a match on at the Pineapple, but Mobe's not up for it. He says he's going the Adelphi for a sauna and that. Now, diminished as my mentality may be at the moment, the last place I want to be right now is a confined fucking sweatbox where any cunt could get at us. I try ours again to see if Margueritte'll come and pick us up, or see if she fancies lunch somewhere, anything – but it's the answerphone again.

So it's a wretched fucking shadow of old JPB that jumps in that cab in Lord Nelson Street. I pure can not stop myself from seeing things, proper hallucinating and that, palpitating, sweating, fucking DTs, the lot. All's I can see is cars pulling up next to the cab and putting one in my head. What the fuck did I say to Bernie last night? Was he all right with it? He did seem to see it from my own point of view. He would do, mind you – it's his point of view and all too, isn't it? His firm gets a bit off anything that comes through the port. That's how come I had to ask for his OK in the first place. So it's all pukka. I've done everything by the book. It's all hunky-dory – course it is.

I've half been pining for Margueritte all the way home. Times like this she always seems to sense I've been a naughty boy. She knows I have to do all of this shite to help us get on. She knows that. She understands. She'll just hold us next to her bosom and stroke my head and shush me down. She'll open up her blouse and guide my lips to them dark nipples. That's the only way we can make love now, after all these years together. It's only any good if I'm a little scared boy and she's a mummy that knows what's best. Right now I want nothing more. I want to get back there and tell her everything and tell her about the big one coming up and how, if I can just get away from Ged, I'll never ever have to get mixed up in shite like this again. We can just sell up and run away. I'd take her back to Haiti if she wanted. Whatever.

The cab is taking fucking for ever. There's roadworks on the stretch from the Kwikkie down to Ullet Road, but it shouldn't be taking this long. Not on a fucking

Sunday. I slump down low, my instincts suddenly telling me that them temporary lights are a prop. This is where I get zapped. Fuck, oh fuck, oh fuck! I am. I'm going to get it. I'm going to get popped any second now and it'll all be down to me and my big mouth. I've had this coming to me.

But nothing happens. No sudden noises, no screech of wheels, no gunfire. Nothing. The cab moves on, the throb of the diesel giving us some warmth against the cold outside. I feel a tiny bit better. I make myself a promise – if I get through this safe and well I'm going to change. I'm going to be a better man. I'll sack the caper – sack snorting the shite, anyway. I'll give Margueritte kiddies if that's what she wants – it's sly to keep holding out on the girl – and I'll get close to Ged instead of pushing him away. He's never done nothing but support me, that lad. I love him. I fucking adore the boy. It's not too late.

When I get in there's a note from Margueritte. One of her clients she's helped from the practice is having a social up in Mulgrave Street. She's says I'm to join them if I get back in time and if I'm feeling up for it. I couldn't be less up for it. Instead I lock every door and window and shut every curtain and cower in my bed with every fucking light on, believing that every distant car engine is bringing my executioner. I try to remember fields and trees and freedom, but even there I'm destroying things. Destroying lives. Come home soon, Margueritte. Come home to baby.

Monday

Ratter

Stuff and nonsense, by the way. The p's have gone, I've slept for eleven hours, I'm fresh as fuck and I'm about to conquer the world. Everything come to us as I was lying there. Every little bit fell into place. Quickly is how I moves from this point in. Quick like a cobra. No cunt is going to get in my way. Nobody, by the way – and in saying that I really do think the good times with Margueritte might've run their course, in fairness. Good while it lasted and that, but c'est la vie. And very good of our Ged to fill me in on that yesterday, by the way. I feel certain it's information the councillor's good friend Martyn Lid, CID, can put to good use. Shall bell the Bennett pronto. Nice knowing you, Gerrard Brennan.

Moby

I've never lost one yet. In fairness, I don't think I can be beat. Feeling fine, by the way. I've rested, I've stretched and that, and I've had a little think about how I'm going to do it. I'm ready for the cunt.

Ged

I always used to tell our Anthony he smiles too much. You can't get took serious as a musher if you're having a laugh and a joke all the time. He don't smirk so much these days, to be fair. He's fucking quiet, though. He's the quietest fucking fighter in the world. Even at school, *especially* at school, you'd get that thing where a kid wants to explain why he's mashing your nose all over your fucking kite.

'You called my sister a slag, you bastard,' he'll go, as

he slams your face into the playground. Wants you to know, by the way. Half giving you a clue why he has to do this bad thing to you. At away games, same thing.

'Come on, you Scouse bastards!'

People want to hurt you, but they want you to know why you deserve it. They need to unload the guilt from theirselves on to you. You deserve it and that. Brought it all on yourself and that. Fucking had it coming. Not our Mobe, though. Fuck, no. Not a peep out of the cunt. Bang! Bang! Bang! Done. Not so much as a 'take that, you cad!' I can see Fonzie trying to wind him up, but that stuff's only going to backfire on him. It will not work with our Anthony. That is a fact.

Moby

Fonzie looks much harder close-up in fairness to him – in the daylight and that. I've only really seen him inside of clubs and that. But I'm not thinking that. I'm not arsed about him at all, to be fair. All's I'm thinking about is why is this place called the Mystery. Doing my head in, it is. I used to know, by the way. We're stood here, circling each other, no one wanting to make the first move and all's I'm really aware of is the park. It's out of focus, rotating around as we fence each other, but it's the only thing I can think of. Not thingio, how am I going to go about this fight, but – why the *fuck* is this park called the Mystery, know where I'm going. It's not a tactic, by the way. I'm not trying to fade down and that, trying to relax or whatever. I've never really fought tactically. It's just what's going through my head right at this moment in time. It's a bit frosty underfoot. Bit crunchy.

Fonzie's coming across like that fella out of *Indiana*

Jones. I suppose it's the bare chest and that, done to make my good self think he's fucking rock, by the way, coming out topless on a day like this. And it is fucking nippy, to be fair. He's coming out with a bit of lip and all, Alphonse is, trying to get a rise out of us. I wish to fuck I could remember about the Mystery. Our John-Paul'd know. He was forever round here when he was first taken and that. He used to play out in the tunnels. He's in good nick for a older fella too, old Fonzie. His fucking biceps are like ten-pin balls, now he's close up, all covered in weird voodoo tatts, the beaut. And them hands of his *are* yowge, by the way. He's got his fists up proper, like he knows how to box and he's going to take his time and pick Moby off. Good plan. I deck him.

One thing I've got is one fuck of a dig with my right. To be fair, right, I'm not really a musher, myself. That's the truth, by the way. I'm not even a buck no more, not by a long chalk. I'd rather get along with people, have a drink with them, game of cards, how's your ma and that. Much rather that than knock fuck out of them. It's just that I can. If someone comes into range and they want it, then I can put them on their arse, no two ways about it. Fonzie come into range. It was just what I was looking for and that, just the little half-opening that I needed. Cunt was just leaning that bit too far forward, his chin and his head that little bit ahead of himself and in a one-on-one like this you don't wait for no invitations. I'm on it. Bang! He's gone.

Except he's not. Cunt gets back to his feet. There's no count or nothing in one of these. It's just two lads having a fight. I'm within my rights to put the boot in before he gets chance to stand up – could jump on the cunt and bite a chunk out of his grid, to be fair – but I want to beat Fonzie good. I want to do him proper. Doesn't matter to my good self that he stole it on us the other night after the thingy in Nirvana, but I want to be looking into the cunt's eye. I want him to know I'm a better man. Out of the two of us, I am the better man.

So I lets him get up. He's marked up bad. The thing when you don't wear gloves and you've got two lads boxing that's both got big hands and that, the knuckles can be lethal. Hurts the fella that's dishing it out and all too, by the way, but Fonzie's hurt bad. He's cut under his eye, his nose is opened up wide and there's something at the corner of his mouth. I've hit him good. I can finish this quite easy.

I let him come at me. Either he's a genius and he's got hidden reserves of strength, or he's coming at me with your basic prison-yard combo. Just as I'm about to bob under his right cross a panic flash skewers me. Just a half a recollection from the recesses and it's this: I'm playing right into it. The cunt's a southpaw. He's got a bit of a left on him and as I'm thinking it and before I can send the info down to my feet and fists he fucking crashes us under the jaw and rocks us right back on my feet. I'm like one of the kids in the comics taking a whack off've auld Bully Beef. Fucking hell of a dig, by the way – feels like I'm on a anaesthetic, stars and lines and headaches and that. *Hell* of a dig. Fuck this, la. It's a miracle I'm still standing. Fuck Saint Anthony, the gentleman boxer. Better get this finished.

Fonzie's got second wind now. He's half dismayed that I didn't go down from that one but he thinks he's got us, anyway. I'm just dancing, to be fair, just trying to get away from the cunt long enough to get my puff back – then I can come back and finish the job. Our Gerrard's screaming at us like I'm Stig Inge Björnebye or something, telling myself to do this and that, trying to have the fight for us. But I don't want to do nothing sly. I don't need to do that, by the way. I can still win this proper. Anyone watching knows I let up on Alphonse but, to be fair to the lad, he has taken good advantage. One-all and that. Down to old Moby to produce something big now.

Which I do, by the way. Again, I manage to let all the noise fade into the background. I'm aware of the blurry images of half-familiar faces as we circle each other again, but this time I'm on it. I'm focused. I feel strong. I duck under another of Fonzie's piledrivers and catch him with two hard jabs. The first breaks that cut in the corner of his mouth wide open, the second ruins his nose. He's fucked. He can't see. He's trying to brush the blood out of his eyes and keep moving, but the poor cunt doesn't know where the fuck he is.

'FINISH THE CUNT OFF!'

I don't want to make it too bad for him. He deserves a bit of dignity and that. But I am obliged to put the lad on his arse. I bang him right in the middle of the clock, not my hardest, to be fair, but it's a true dig and it's more than enough to KO him. He's well gone. Shattered. Face smashed, body fucked, over and out. Had us going for a minute, there.

Ged

I'm still not happy. Something, somewhere – I can sense it. Fonzie brought hardly any back-up with him. That is what we agreed, by the way. Mikey isn't even here himself. Dajun and a few other moody-looking cunts are over by the climbing frame trying to look naughty, but there must be more. They'll be in cars, dotted around outside, talking to each other on mobiles.

A couple of big black boys are helping a well groggy Alphonse back across the park, while Dajun and his crew give me and Drought the people's eye. If anything's going to happen it's going to be now. Right now. We stand our ground and look back at the cunts. I know a few of them. Gobshites at school. Think they're boys now. Half don't mind if a couple of them want to wander over now, by the way. I did make a promise to Franner, mind you, but it's not our boys trying to say something.

I look around. No sign of there being a crew of them. Maybe Alphonse is just pure unpopular. But what there is of his back-up don't want to go home. They're not walking out the park before we do. And then I sees them. Just over by the Welly Road side of the park. Loads of them just watching and waiting. I knew it. I could fucking feel it.

Fuck this. Am I having it off've that fucking no-mark Derek? Am I fuck, by the way. I tell the others to stay where they are. I gives the pistol a little squeeze, pull it up just a extra half-inch and that and I walks over, nice and slow. I go straight up to Dajun, one eye on the posse over there. They don't move. The whole thing is in slow motion.

'Did you want to say something to myself, Derek?'

He's taller than I am, by the way. A good bit taller. I'm making a effort not to push myself up on tiptoes. You don't do that. You just talk to his shoulder instead of his face, and you talk as contemptuous as you feel. If he wants some fucking respect, if he wants eye contact and that, then he's going to have to fucking look down and cop some. I myself am not looking up.

He thinks about what I've said, tries to look cool, takes a drag on his ciggy, looks up at the sky, amused.

'I got lots to say to you.'

If he'd've said 'boy' I'd've whacked him. Instead he stubs the ciggy, gives my shoulder a bit of a jokey punch and smiles. His eyes are laughing. Cunt thinks he knows something. What he knows is this: fuck all.

'Not today, though, huh? I say it to you some other time.'

He laughs, but his mates don't join in. This, again, is critical. If they had've done, if I'd've felt like as though they was having a laugh, I'd have had no choice. I would've had to do something about it. And if I do Derek now, then shots will be fired. Guns will go off. Even if they don't go off here, now, in fucking Wavertree, there'll be people shot tonight. Lads'll be getting picked out and picked off all over the South End. And if that's going to happen, I've got to be fucking sure I had no choice. If Dajun's little crew had all started rolling about laughing with him, then that's a clear green light. But they never. Maybe they just don't want to smile, but it means that Dajun's the only one laughing at his gag. As it is, I should still ask him for a one-on-one. But I'm growing up. Even though it kills me to let him walk away smiling, I can see the bigger picture. I'm phoning it in, though. Franner can talk to Mikey if he wants.

Moby

Am I glad to get that out the way. Probably haven't heard the last of it, to be fair, but that'll do me for now. I was well pleased with our Gerrard. Way he ambled over and fronted them pricks – fucking take my hat off to him. Very coolio. And he does know the score, our Gerrard. Even though we all said no mad ones, no celebrations and that, he knows that that was a important one for my good self, today. Gets us back on terms, know where I'm going. It was a important little go-around, in fairness. So we're all here in the Nutty, right back on the barrio having a quiet drink. A little livener in your own local with people that you know and trust – can't be beat, can it? There's Drought shadow-boxing with Georgie O'Farrell, Ged trying to get away from their Misty chasing him with the mistletoe, and I've even touched lucky with the lights, God willing. Freddy Woan's told us to hold tight and cross my fingers. He thinks he's got what I've been looking for. If that slippery no-mark comes up trumps, I'll kiss his fat head and that's the God's honest truth.

Ged

I'm not a great warbler at the best of times, not even at the match. I'd need a good few before you'll get myself singing and even then I couldn't do it on my tod. But the shite they all sing along to in here, by the way – Jesus fuck! It's all fucking Kenny Rogers and fucking Neil Diamond and that. Shirley Bassey. They don't play nothing trendy at all. 'Whole of the Moon' comes on the jukey sometimes when some of the younger crowd are in, and the Deacon Blue gets played but I get laughed down when I tell them I seen some proper fucking quality last night. I tells them I went and seen that Celine Dion and they all starts howling like a cat's chorus and shinging like they can't shay their eshesh proper. Gang of lunatics, they are. And then they start giving us 'Forever in Blue Jeans' even louder, right in my face. They're good people around here, but they need to move with the times a bit. You can't stay in the Nutty for ever singing 'Forever in Blue Jeans' and that. Moby asks us if I can give him a hand getting these Chrimbo lights round to his. I'm more than ready, to be fair. I don't mind getting out of there for a breather at all.

Moby

I feel humbled. When I gets back, Marie's sat there with Father Lacey, going through this big mad album with photos of communion cakes and dresses and horse and carriages and all sorts. They're both smoking Benson's. She's always loved the Benson's box, even when she was smoking loosies and that. She always used to go for Sovereign because the box was so similar. Golden, by the way.

I'm always very pleased to see Father Lacey. He's a priest who'll sit and drink a Jameson's with you and have a little talk about the match. He is a fucking filthy Blue by the way, but he's all right. I like him. But for my own good self this is a bonus having Father Lacey on the firm, because what he's going to see is auld Anthony Brennan, aka Mad Moby, bit of a Name, bit of a nudge-nudge persona, stunningly transformed into Moby the Family Man. Father Lacey is going to be here to help, or maybe just watch to be fair, as Family Man Moby toils and grafts to erect this big fuck-off full-size, illuminated Christmas frieze. That's what Freddie called it and he's only fucking right. This is no fucking *decoration*, mind you. This is Macy's! It's Santa *and* sleigh *and* a big gang of reindeer, by the way, and it plays 'Jingle Bells' loud enough for it to wake up fucking Alphonse over in Granby. Father Lacey's going to see Marie and the kids cry real tears of joy as Giant Santa and Rudolph and the gang light up in the night sky – and dwarf McKenna's pitiful fucking display while we're at it. Happy days and that!

Ged

I only went back to the Nutty to say ta-ra to everyone and to thank George again for his help in all of this. As soon as I got in there I could see he weren't well. Drought told us later that George'd been up with Misty, jitterbugging and that, trying to lift her up and whizz her through his legs and all of that. That gear's hard enough to pull off in the first place, but Misty? Forget it. That's fucking hernia talk.

Worse for George. I'd been in the pub for a minute exactly when he keeled over, rasping. We got him outside, got his collar and tie open, and got the paramedics down there pronto. He's OK. They're going to keep him overnight, but the word from Misty is that he'll be back home tomorrow, God willing it. I give her a big love and tells her to give us a phone on this private number, anytime, *anytime*, if she should need anything at all.

Tuesday

Ged

Today is going to be a bastard to get through, whatever way you go about it. But when it's all done and dusted, when I'm back here tucked up with AJP and nice glass of Baileys, I'll be a better person for it. Fuck knows how I'm going to get it all done. I want to pop in on Georgie first, make sure him and Misty are sound. Then I need to dart over to Armley to see Steady. Their Tanya was late coming through with the VO and all too, by the way. I was half going to let it go – it's one trip I could do without, in fairness. But I wouldn't've. I would've gone round there and got the fucking VO myself. After all Steady's done for me, I should be visiting him once a fucking week, not once a month.

I should leave now. I keep wanting to lash this tea, but I can't leave it alone. It's fucking gorgeous – dead hot, just right. Each slurp is fucking heaven. I stoop to pick up the mail and wander back to the kitchen, still sipping at my cuppa. I gaze out the window at poor Psycho. Psycho is the family squirrel, if you will. He's fucking horrible. Forget any ideas about cute little fellas with bushy tails that store up acorns and deliver letters to the woodfolk. Not Psycho. He's cock of our garden. Rules the fucking bird table, he does. Has done for a year or so, to be fair. Birds won't come near the bastard. Debbi still puts bread and that out, but only one freak of nature partakes. Poor old Psycho is one fucking horrible creature to look at. He'd give a rat the shits. He's evil enough looking anyway, but this poor lad's disfigured and all, too. The problem is one of his bottom teeth. In picture books, he'd have two extremely useful, goofy front teeth, good for chopping acorns into bite-sized chunks to store away for the winter and that. He'd also have a huge, red bushy tail and a sackful of letters. Well, Psycho is as grey as fucking vermin and has no front teeth. What he has got is one bottom tooth which he can not stop from growing, by the way. It's been growing since he first turned up on the bird table. Our Cheyenne come in screaming, saying there was a evil ferret out there. It was Psycho. He can't be long for this world, poor little cunt. The tooth has grown right through his bottom lip and curved outwards in a sabre shape. Now it's started curling back towards his face. It's on course to grow right through his eye. He's lost what there was of his other teeth trying to chip away at it. The RSPCA won't come out for a rodent, only to exterminate. I'll do that myself, to be fair. Let the poor little get have a few more days stuffing himself on our bread and leftovers and scaring the little sparrows and that, and then I'll go out there and pop him.

Psycho'll be the first thing Steady asks myself about. Fucking obsessed with him, he is. Never was a fella more properly named. Terry Steadman. Steady. That is one solid fucking lad, by the way. Totally took the rap for us, he did. His idea and all too, mind you. We had this bit of a altercation with some security personnel at the York Races, didn't we. Thought they was boys and that. I did take things a bit far with this one, to be fair – but the cunt had it coming to him. Jumping up and down like Bruce Lee, he were – fucking embarrassing, by the way. Didn't leave us with no option in fairness. Next thing it's Plod and fucking all kinds of ambulances and screaming and people running like fuck, panicking, fucking running for their lives. There was no problem.

It was only soft lad that was getting it. Place is overrun with Plod in half a minute, mind you – where are the cunts when some baghead's trying to screw your house? I was the only soft cunt in shorts, by the way, and next thing you know Steady's bundling us off round the back of one of the hospitality tents, taking his kecks off. His eyes look mad – he's half slobbering.

'Quick! Here y'are! Swop with us!'

I'm telling him no, I'll take my chances, but he won't have none of it. He's going: 'Here y'are, you soft cunt! The lads need you, don't they? They're fucked if you go down! Come 'ead – give us your fucking shorts. I'll only get two and a half.'

Poor cunt. He's *doing* two and a half, by the way. He got fucking four. Soft twat. Does look a little bit like myself, to be fair, Steady. You could see how the other Yorkie bouncers picked out the total wrong fella and swore blind it was him. If I can get up to him and out again by twelve bells, I should just about be on for the kids' party. One o'clock that's starting, and for myself it's pure hold-your-breath time while we see who actually fucking shows their face, know what I mean. Georgie O'Farrell said last night I should've just let him know. Could've got us that Craig off've *Big Brother* for starters. Could've had Mel C, the Steps, that Tinhead off've *Brookie*, all kinds. Said he'd have a word with Robbie himself and all, too – but it's a bit late for that, in fairness. But if even one of these lads turns up for the party then the fucking organiser needs to be there to shake their hand and get them a glass of bubbly. Not that I'm that arsed about meeting them, by the way. Our Cheyenne's asked us to get her that Mel C's signature, in fairness, but if these good folk are giving up their time to support our charity, then the charity's president should be there to greet them. Is right and all too, by the way.

I drains my mug and shuffles through the mail. Chrimbo cards and bills is all there is. There's a mailshot from Oxfam, putting us on a guilt trip about Christmas. I do more than my share for good causes, I think you'll find. I keep the free biro and lash the leaflet. Misty calls through on the direct line. Nice one, in a way. Helps us out big time, to be fair. Georgie's comfortable enough and that, but he's still sleeping. There'll be no visitors until this evening. Straight off to Leeds then, and don't spare the horses.

Ratter

Fucking irritating all this – could well do without it, to be fair. For starters, Byzantium Holdings has a meeting to work through loose ends on the health club deal. They're not massive things, but they're important and they're holding us up. Margueritte's saying she can handle it, but if she could handle it then why's there still a problem, knowmean. Plus there are a few very fucking tiresome things cropping up with South Village. They're making YT very angry, that crew – I really do get fucking cross when contractors try to stiff you, by the way. They approach Christmas as though it's some fucking newfangled concept invented to treble their inflated profits. That's what they think, mind you – think everyone's half pissed or too full of fucking merry cheer to fucking notice them slipping off've the job at one and charging fucking all sorts of extras for their trouble. Well, they're trying it on the wrong fella. I'll take a walk down there this afternoon. It might be a matter of giving the foreman a smack in front of the brickies, just to show them that he's not as smart as what he's told them. Then I'll sack him. Just when he needs the money for his lad's PlayStation 2 and his girl's little pony. Cunt should be fucking grateful he's got a fucking job, by the way – fucking fucking about with his paymasters and that. Soft cunt. Maybe I'll just sack the cunt straight off. Depends how I'm feeling. Depends how the real meeting goes.

This, out of all the shite I get up to, is the bit I like least. It doesn't happen that often, to be fair, but every now and then the Irish connection want to pop across and stare into my eyes. I can half understand them, mind you. Specially on this one – it is a biggie for JPB, to be fair. People are forever getting double-crossed. The Bhoys just don't mess about though. It's that simple. They should know that I understand that absolutely, but wherever the Turks are involved, the potential for double-dealing exists. They're notorious for it. They're forever trying to tap up bagmen like YT. I've just always worked on the basis that whatever I say and do is being filmed and watched. I know where the buck stops. I'm not a fucking idiot.

So I'll take them on the sloop, eat some oysters, drink some champagne and talk about the Reds in the knowledge that any one of these guys could shoot me in the head at any time for any reason. That's the game I'm in, by the way. During the course of the meeting they will ever so gently put it to me that the Turks have offered YT the same gear for four million – which they have, by the way. Fives at least, anyway. Got hold of us in London, didn't they? The Turks are forever offering us this and that, to be fair. I know them and that, but I do try to keep them at arm's length. Lairy bastards, they are. I half know this lad that collared us at the hotel. Just phoned us up and that. How's about it, and that. I hate that, when people just think it's normal that they know where you're staying, just phone you up as though it's dead normal and you should've half been expecting the call. I had to be extra careful with the cunt. I couldn't insult him and that. He wanted us to go up to his uncle's café in Haringey and I did manage to convince him that it was purely impossible with the boxing and that, the Gentleman's Evening and when I explained to him who'd be there he was a little bit more cautious. But he still insisted on meeting JPB. Had to have a coffee with him, didn't I. Like Ali Osman he were, moody half Ali Osman thing. Just kept staring at us and that, repeating himself, to be fair. Bit tacky, in all fairness. Bit of a fucking barrow boy, he were, kept on telling us what a ace deal he was giving us. Even if I was fucking half tempted I wouldn't entertain a offer put to us that way. That's no way to do business. So I just acted soft and that. What you on about and that. But they did offer us the gear for fives. Probably could've got them down and all, too.

So they'll ask us about that. I'll assume that they know and I'll admit that yes, I've been tapped up. The Bhoys'll smile slowly and ask us why on earth, then, I'm taking it from them at eights and at this point I'll just tell them what they want to hear. I'll tell them that I've always took it from them – which I have not, by the way. Show me a businessman that limits himself to one supplier and I'll show you a Year One failure. Course I takes gear from other sources – I'm just fucking choosy about when and where and fucking who is all. That's why I knocked back that Ali Osman cowboy. Fucking trying it on, he were. I'll point out to the Bhoys that they're not interested in who I'm laying it off to, or for how much. Why, then, should I wonder what price they're getting it from the Turks for? That's none of my fucking business, is it? What's my business is the knowledge that I can offload quickly and profitably and in a way that makes sense to YT. All other considerations are irrelevant. The Bhoys'll give it a deliberately strung-out pause to half remind us how moody they are, by the way, and then they'll start laughing and clap old JPB on the back and the champagne will flow and I'll know that we're still on. We'll agree to bring it in Christmas Day while the city's back is turned and I'll ask them if they won't stay over for the game on Boxing Day. That is exactly how it will go, mind you.

Ged

I shouldn't drive. I should not be behind the fucking wheel of a fucking car. I hadn't even got out of Davenport Road. Same sketch. Always the same fucking sketch. A little cunt in a baseball cap, thinking he knows something. I even let the cunt by. I didn't mind accepting that – it was his right of way, in fairness, even if the twat was going too fast. But I let that go, didn't I? I turned a blind eye to his fucking bully-boy-I-can-drive-dead-fast thing because, to be fair, the obstacle was on my side and so it's only right and that. Let the little cunt have his way. But did the cunt acknowledge that? Did he give us a little wave and that, little nod to say nice one, la? Did he fuck! Not only did the cunt not acknowledge, he tried to give us a look – a look that was meant to say: 'Good job for you that you didn't even think about trying to squeeze past us there, you cunt.'

That's what his look was saying to myself. Fucking snide little head-to-one-side-chewing-gum thing. Fucking pure insolent, horrible, baseball-cap fucking look. I weren't having none of that, by the way. Not for a second was I having one little bit of that carry-on. I jams into reverse hard as I can and puts my foot right through the floorboard. Pure lunacy, by the way – any cunt could've been crossing the road on the blindside or some immaculately shiny Moggy Minor could've been trundling round the corner, but I didn't give a fuck about none of that. I goes after him at sixty in reverse, engine screaming at us to stop, wheels ranting and squealing from side to side as I hits the bends. I starts to catch up with him and the penny finally seems to drop with him. He shoots off and I come to a standstill by the postbox. If I'd have caught him I don't know what I would've done with the little cunt. Made him go back and do it again, nodding his head nicely and putting one hand up to acknowledge my good road manners. Like fuck. I decide I'll go through the lanes and try and relax a bit.

Ratter

Far from ideal, but it's not the end of the world. It's still doable, although I'm fucked if I know what this does to the tides. The Bhoys have just told us they want to bring it forward. They're a terrifying fucking shower, by the way, them cunts. Forget your smiling Irish. Fucking monsters, these are. Bernie's firm is always laying it on thick with us how they're the RA and that, not to be trifled with that and that. I don't give a fuck if they *are* the Provos – they couldn't be no more scarier if they was, by the way. Scariest thing about them is when they laugh. They have a laugh that displays no pleasure. It's fucking horrible, it is – like a death laugh, knowmean. Each fucking one of them is yowge and all too, though success has done fuck all to smooth off their rough edges. For all that they must each and every one of the cunts be a multi multimillionaire they just look to me like big, rough country boys. Fucking forearms on the cunts, by the way – and they've got a look about them that makes you know that they've killed with their bare hands. They've strangled lads, they've cut their throats, they've stabbed them in the neck and watched them bleed to death. They're hard, hard men.

I'd prefer to be doing business in a sophisticated manner. I'd fucking well prefer it if we didn't have to meet, for e.g., by the way. But for these lads it's fucking horse-trading. They want to sit down and meet and look into your eyes and have a little tipple once all the naughty stuff is took care of. In different circs – e.g. if I was half interested in staying in this game – I could run rings around these lads. They don't scare JPB. They remind us half of our Gerrard – daft old dinosaurs and that. But time is one thing I ain't got – so on this occasion it's their rules that we're playing by. And for reasons I don't truly understand, they can only do this thing Christmas Eve. Mine is not to query them. Mine is to get my arse in gear and make sure the deal don't fall apart. It shouldn't be a problem. I need to get straight down the port and see Arturo.

Moby

She's being dead sound with us just at the moment. Since I stuck them Blackpool fucking illuminations up for her, in fairness – and she's dead excited about Sunday now. Everything that can be sorted has been sorted. I've caved, by the way. I have, I've just pure caved on everything. We're doing the whole thing the way she wants it. But that's sound. She's happy and that. She's being extra alright with my good self, which is just the way I likes it to be. I was just stood here before looking out the window waiting for the kettle to boil and she comes up behind us, puts her arms around us and slides her hand down my trackies and starts giving us a gam. Didn't have to press her or nothing. Fucking nice and all, too – properly caught Moby on the hop, it did. We can have thirty-grand communions every week if she's going to be like this.

Ged

Steady's on bob. He's fine. Bit subdued about being in there over Chrimbo and that, but he's starting to see light at the end of the tunnel. Won't be that long now. And I've told him he's walking right into a job at ours. No settle, nothing. Just drive the car, pick up his Billies, get paid. Least I can do for the lad. Half wants to just get his head down now, anyway. Fancies that, he does. Fancies a bit of a nine-till-five. Not that the taxis are, by the way.

I'm making good progress back down the M62. I'll be more or less bang on for the kids' do, but there's a little bit of a problem that's bugging me. Do not know what to do about it, to be fair. Just switched the phone back on and there's a message from Eli. He's saying he's heard there might be a change in plan. Sounds a bit cheesed off, old Eli. Wants us to call him *most* urgently, the head-the-ball.

Thing is, there IS no change of plan. We're going on Sunday morning, same as. There's only Eli and myself on this side of the outfit that knows that, by the way. So how's he got to thinking that's changed? Who else has any knowledge – or fucking *thinks* they have a knowledge? I want to reassure the auld cunt that I haven't lost the plot and it's still Thunderbirds Are Go – but I myself have a policy never to call a fella on the phone until I know I'm ready to talk to him, know what I mean. And with Eli, there's too many questions in my head still. I've known the lad a long time. In business, you like to think there are lads that are just unshakeable, lads you can totally rely on through and through – and Eli's one of them. You just know that this is one solid fella. If you're going to accept that some things can't be *proved* and that, you just go with them, then Eli is one that you would just go with. You can see it in his eyes and in every crease of his face. Lad's a bandit but fuck is he a honest bandit. He's the last of the gentleman rogues, Eli is, and I'm proud that he finds myself worthy of business. And yet – could I ever, hand on heart, say that I could trust any other cunt through the wind and the rain? Totally fucking trust them, that is – read their every move? Answer: you never fucking know.

And I've just got half a little feeling about something else, too. What Franner was saying to us. Everything OK with Ratter and that. I know full well that if I phone Franner to ask him what he meant by it, he'll give us some fucking baloney. It's his biggest fault, by the way – he thinks he knows what's best for everyone. Will not consult with no cunt, just goes ahead and does it. In asking myself if everything was strictly pukka with Ratts, he was giving us a gentle nudge, tilting us in the right direction. That's as much as I'll get from the fat bastard, mind you. Will he fuck tell me what's on his mind. He thinks he's give us enough to work with just by marking my fucking card. So when we was coming back on the train the other day, I just thrown it out that we was going Thursday with the job. Just thrown it out to see what'd come back. And what's come back is that Eli, quite rightly by the way, is going bonkers about last-minute changes. I only told our Anthony and John-Paul, so where does that leave us? It leaves us asking some very hefty questions, is where. Like how come Ratter's talking to Eli, for instance.

Eli the Mensch

What to do about this one. I just wish the boy would call. I hate it when I can't speak with someone. I can't think about nothing else. I just walk up and down the room, turn around, walk up and down the room. June has to get of the house. She can't abide me when I'm like this. I just wish he'd call. I want to know what is going on. I know Gerrard for a long time. I know him for a very long time and every time we deal he is a gentleman. A *most* honourable boy. Should be him who is called Mensch.

But I have to take all things into consideration. I have not done so well out of this caper that I can afford not to work. I *has* to continue working. And when I receive a call from Martyn Lid, I tend to take its contents most seriously. I should do. I pay him enough *not* to call. So when such a high-ranking officer of the constabulary calls me to see how June is getting along and to ask whether I has plans to be in the city over the holiday and he – rather rudely, I thought – wonders out loud whether I know of anyone who's stupid enough to try and spoil his Ramblers' Christmas lunch by making him work on Thursday, I starts to get very worried. Lid is dropping some very big hints. Like who is involved in this blag and what sort of money it might take to help make it happen. Very rude man, Martyn Lid. He just about stops short of ticking me off for trying to keep this to myself. Keep *what* to myself, I want to know! What *is* this! So great is my surprise that I do finally convince Lid this Thursday proposition is nothing to do with Eli. Nothing to do with Eli at all and, with my hand on my heart, nothing to with Gerrard Brennan. On this occasion, I swear it, Lid has been told wrong. I *tell* Martyn he's been told wrong and he must know that I mean that and he's very abrupt, quite surly about missing out on a Christmas bonus and bids me good Yule.

Now, what I want to know about is Thursday. What's this thing about *Thursday*? I do most sincerely wish that the boy would call.

Ged

'Forget that, Eli. Trust your old friend Gerrard, Mensch. You've got nothing to worry about. Just tell us this – did he seem to have any proper knowledge? Do you know what I'm saying to you? Is he taking a shot in the dark or does the bastard know something?'

Silence, then:

'Did not seem to have any real detail. Just sounded like something some wretch has phoned in. Only seemed sure something was happening Thursday – and seemed sure your name was on it.'

I think on this.

'Bingo. Mensch? You're a mensch.'

'Gerrard.'

'Eli?'

'You don't think maybe we leave this one?'

'No way.'

'No way?'

'Easiest blag you'll ever get. It's still on.'

'Oh my. Very good then.'

Ratter

Arthur thinks Christmas Eve can work even better. Better tide, whatever he means by that. Suits me well on the cash front and all. With the banks being how they are this time of year, I'm sat on eight million of our English pounds in cash bundles from close of play Friday. So going a day earlier is far from killing me on that particular score, in fairness. I can't stand to have that amount of tank sitting around. I start to imagine all kinds – people in balaclavas coming through the windows, everything. No bother and that, to be fair, I'll probably keep it up at the kennels or something. But I'm still jumpy as fuck. I have to make a proper effort to discipline myself. All's I can let myself think is that within five days I'll be away from here, looking for somewhere hot to live out my idle youth. And my dear, dear friend and protector Gerrard Brennan will be starting a twelve-stretch. Minimum. C'est la fucking vie, in all fairness.

Ged

This puts it all into perspective. The place is packed out with grimy, shiny little faces all squealing to be heard, hyper as fuck, wondering when the fella with the beard'll be coming round with the prezzies. They're not arsed that none of the footballers and that turned up, by the way. They're too busy squealing and throwing food and having a epic time. I feel good about it myself, I'm pleased that I've helped to make a difference. But that makes me feel shit, too. Shit about the shitty world I live in. Not just live in, neither – it's a shitty world of my own making. But this bunfight helps to stave off some of that – for a hour or two at least, anyway. Them kiddies' faces, lar – worth all the thingy of putting a do like this together.

I am a bit chocker about the celeb count, to be fair, but it's Chrimbo – folk have got commitments, what can you do? We've got the lad that played Growler Rogers going round the tables telling jokes and that, but in all fairness to the lad, the kids don't want to know. It is a while since he was on the telly and that, and the kids are half 'who's this cunt?' and that. I could've better spent that two ton on a extra prezzie or a film show. But Harry Rice has come around and helped us out at no notice whatsoever. He's sort of like MC-ing the party, but it's more like free-form stand-up comedy. He's a natural with all of that, Ricey – stick a mike in his hand and he'll rabbit for as long as you want. Funny, he is, too. His brother's the flamboyant lad off've the radio, but I think Ricey's well funnier. He's saved the day here and that, anyway. Won't ask for nothing, by the way, neither. Will not ask for one penny in exies. He's a cracker. He's a prize-guy, Ricey. Funny cunt, by the way. The stuff he does around the clubs slays me. Dead camp and that, mind you, but I don't mind all that – mincing and homming it up and that. Don't mind it. Makes me laugh. Couldn't really have him doing his proper half-a-hom act for the kiddies here, in fairness, but he's getting there. He's titillating them. Never know whether it's meant to be *titillating* them or *titivating* them, but they love him. He's saved the day.

Coley calls us over, all grave and that. Big, long, serious kite on the cunt. Beckons myself over to the side. Looks chocker, he does.

'Listen, Coley . . .'

I'm about to try to explain about the no-show from the players (bet you to fuck they'll be at our Anthony's on Sunday, by the way), but he puts up his hand to stop us.

'Gerrard . . .'

Zounds! Got to be something double bad, here. Just the way he's saying it and that. *Gerrard* and that, like a schoolteacher about to give us a load of toffee.

'Listen. I don't know – I really do hope this is nothing.'

He glances left and right, eyes darting like a ferret as though this kids' Chrimbo party is going to be wired for sound or something. He finally makes eye contact with myself. He looks chocker. He looks very fucking serious and very fucking, what? Saddened, to be fair. He looks disappointed as fuck. I make a encouraging face at him. Go 'ead, sort of thing. I'm all ears and that. He takes a big breath. Looks fucked, to be fair – betrayed. He's looking at us like I've badly let him down and I'm half starting to guess what this is about.

'It's Lid. He's had a shut-door about you. He's just called me in now.'

On mention of that name my heart sinks. I feel the life drain out of myself and that's the God's honest truth. I feel like I've been zapped. Ray Cole is looking at me like I'm trash. The way he's looking at us makes myself feel stripped naked and worthless, seen for what I am.

A buck. A hoodlum. A fucking South End musher. I tries to brave it out with him. I hold my hands up. I never was any good with guilt – it's wrote all over myself. Whatever I say, I know it's going to sound snide. I should say fuck all instead. Should just take my pride and walk. But the thought of losing Coley as a friend . . .

I try to busk it with him, try to sound like I've half got a downer on him for even thinking badly about myself.

'Lid. Yeah? And . . .'

But he's too long in the tooth for that. He just looks at us. He knows. His eyes are half saying 'tell us it ain't so' and that – but he knows. He doesn't know he's got the day wrong, mind you – but he knows I'm at it. Ray Cole knows I'm a blagger. I looks down, scuff the sole of my trainie along the floor, look up at him again. Caught out. Badly caught out. He offers his hand. Grave face. Very dejected man this, by the way. We shake.

'Good luck, Gerrard.'

I'm half not sure if he means the job and that – good luck with the heist. He peers long and hopeful into my eyes. He really likes us, Coley does. I know that he really *wants* to like me. He gives us that lovely crinkly smile of his. The smile of a good man. A good, good man. He glances around at all the overexcited kiddies and gives myself a little squeeze on the shoulder. Nice one and that. And then he's off. I have to stop myself shouting after him: 'What about the match? Boro? The box I sorted for you, remember?'

I'm like a tart, I am, but I manage to check myself. I don't mind admitting that I feel very fucking badly about it, but Ray Cole has just walked out and that. End of.

The kiddies are starting to filter out to the buses, all still rabbiting like fuck, all madly excited. Some of them are nice enough to stop and say thank you. Nice kiddies, by the way, some of this lot. Rough as fuck, but who could blame them? These are my people, these kiddies are. Not Heswall fucking Prep by the way, not Nina Perkins-West and not Raymond fucking Cole – it's these little faces from the Southern Neighbourhoods, out in force because some cunt wanted to do something for them for once instead of trying to keep them down and shut them in. I wish some of my so-called friends and associates had been here to see their faces today. For a few hours this afternoon them little street rats was kiddies. They was innocent. Even the ones with the hard little faces and the narrowed eyes – they was prepared to go with it. Some of this city's great and good might've recognised themselves out there, this afternoon – if they could've been arsed giving up their time. I thought I could've relied on Stan, at least. Him out of all of them glad-handing no-marks – I would've put my shirt on him being here. That's what depresses me. I'm so fucking low-key I'm invisible, these days. I'm fucking nobody in this city no more. No cunt feels obliged to Gerrard Michael Leo Brennan. And not only am I nobody, I've got a fucking snitch on my case and all, too. Depressing. Fucking bad one.

Moby

Wish our Gerrard'd turn his fucking mobie on. Where is the cunt? He'll be chocker. Georgie O'Farrell never made it. Honest George. Didn't pull through and that. Never did get over the effects of that first seizure.

Wednesday

Ged

I don't mind admitting it. My first thought was: 'Who're we playing?'

When Misty told myself the funeral was going to be on Boxing Day, the first thing that occurred to us was: 'Who the fuck do we play on Boxing Day?'

Shock, probably. It's Newcastle away, mind you, so no major worries. We always get shite fixtures on Boxing Day, these days. It always used to be Man U at home or City away. Now we get fucking Leicester at home or the furthest fucking away they can find you – Boro, or Southampton. Fucking Newcastle.

George is going to sort of lie in state until then. I ask Misty if she needs anything but she's too upset to think on it. The woman is pure forlorn, in fairness. She was dancing with the auld lad just a couple of nights ago. Now he's gone and that, the whole point of her being around. Gone. I feel a cunt, but I'm already late for the meet in Dool's. I'll pop back and see Misty later on.

Moby

Our Gerrard's late again. Don't know how he manages it. He must sit outside with binoculars, going: 'Must not be early! Must be last to arrive!'

I'm not that arsed today. One, I've got Spit here with us. We're having a laugh and joke and our Ged can take all the fucking time he wants. The cunt. Spit's going to be jockey on this one, by the way. Only got the call late last night, he did. He's made up – had no idea there was even a sniff of something coming off. He's keeping this one extra close to his chest, Ged is, to be fair. Even by his own p'd up standards he's telling us fuck all. And that's reason two: we'll get a proper briefing this morning. That is one of my real favourite moments out of anything. It is, by the way – getting the plan from Ged – I fucking love it. I couldn't see myself ever getting tired of that. It's something brilliant every time. If it was the olden days, our Gerrard would've made a fucking brilliant general. He's a genius, by the way.

Dool brings the brekkies over. Full hit, bacon, sausages, plum tomatoes – got to be plum, *can't* have fresh toms with your morning growler, just is not the done thing. Black pudding and all, three fried eggs, mushies, loads of toast. Fucking love it. Scalding hot tea out of a proper pot. None of them farting tin efforts where the tea leaks all over the fucking table the moment you pour. Real china teapot. Magnifico.

Dool asks if it's OK to join us. He's funny like that. Known the lad for years and that, but he asks permission to sit with you. Smashing lad, he is.

We gets to talking about good porno films, just the three of us having a laugh and a joke. We're all trying to think of ones with proper stories and that. Plots, as Spit keeps saying. He's fucking potty about films, by the way, Spit is. Loves them. Always going on about the plot and that, supporting roles and all of that carry-on. Even with the Frankies. But there is some with stories and that. Some good ones, to be fair. My favourite one is this one about a rich cunt in Boston who's in a wheelchair and his tasty young wife spends the whole time frigging herself daft and looking sorry for her rich, wheelchair-bound husband. She tries everything to get him hard but nothing works. Then a tennis instructor comes along. Bit of a beaut, to be fair. One of these fellas with massive teeth and spray-froze hair that the Yanks seem to go for. Half a tart he is, to be fair, but it ends up that the cripple can get a bit of a touch-on by watching his wife getting plated by the tennis instructor. Then she comes over and mounts him, still in the chair, while the tennis fella looks on, smiling with them teeth of his. That's about it, now I think on it. The scenes with her flicking her bean are fucking good, by the way.

Somehow this gets on to adverts. We're wondering why so many adverts finish with a line that starts 'because'. Well, Spit and Dool are, to be fair. They can think of loads. They're saying how the advert just ends with a mad statement and that, like as if the whole country's sat there going: 'Hmm, yes, I see your point – but why go to all that trouble?'

'Because the lady loves Milk Tray.'

'Because life's too short.'

'Because life's complicated enough.'

'Because you're special.'

'Because good things come in small packages.'

'Because eggs is Best.'

That was the one with Georgie Best in it. 'E for B and Georgie Best' and that. All's I can think of is the David Ginola one where he sounds like the fella off've *Eurotrash*. He goes: 'Am a futt-burr-lerr not a moddow.'

That gets them laughing. I'm made up, to be fair, because it's been all Dool and Spit, so far. Spit's on it right away.

'Beh-curss am worss eet!'

We all crack up and dig into our brekkies. Ged and Ratts come in together, and with that, the mood changes.

Ged

Didn't know it was him at first. Fuck! Did not know it was him, by the way. Coming back through the Birkenhead tunnel, I seen this prick in front of us talking on his phone and trying to drive at the same time. Swaying from one lane to the next, he was. I'm just trying to keep my mind off 've him, keep myself calm and focused on the meeting and that, but this cunt is pure doing my head in. I flashes him. He carries on rabbiting and swerving into my lane and back out again. I flashes him again. He cranes his head round, phone still tucked under his chin, trying to give myself the big one. He can't have got his head far enough around. He can't have seen us. But I seen him. Nice car, by the way.

Ratter

I'm just lucky. I'm used to it now. I'm one of these fellas that's just pure jammy. Things fall my way. This, for example. I goes to all the trouble of parking up right over by the old Priory and I'm walking back towards the café and suddenly there he is. He just walks out of a side street a few yards ahead of us and turns right for Dool's. I've just drove right past that very spot where he is now. In a nice new Shogun, by the way. A minute later and I'd have gone past him in the Shogun. He'd've deffo seen us like, no two ways about it. Fuck knows what would've come of that. But he never. He come when he did instead, and he never seen us. Luck was smiling on YT once again, knowmean. I gives him the stand-off's whistle and he turns round, all smiles, made up to see us. The soft cunt.

Ged

He's good. He's very good. If he's the fella trying to run myself in then there's not one single trace of guilt or treachery or nothing. Lad's a fucking pro, by the way. I've engineered this so's I'll bump straight into him just to see his first reaction, but there's not even a flicker from the cunt. I seen the whole thing in the shop reflection – didn't stop in his tracks, didn't hang back, nothing. The opposite, if you will – let on to us, he did. Whistled over to us. He's good. Let's see how good he is when I tell them all the news.

Ratter

Ged wants a minute's silence for Honest George, the phoney. I know for a fact that Georgie's missus couldn't get hold of him all day yesterday. I was round the hozzy the minute I heard. I wasn't close to him, in all fairness, but he was a legend. Everyone had time for George. When the word started to get round, it was like the three *Godfather* films run back to back. Every fucking face in town was there or thereabouts, wanting to pay their respects. All's his missus wanted was Ged, by the way. She couldn't get through. Give us his personal hotline to keep on trying. Which was nice.

Moby

I don't mind admitting it, I'm chocker. I've been looking forward to this since the meet in the Britannia. I'm gutted, to be fair. Our Gerrard must have his reasons. Para he is, by the way. Meticulous. If one little thing isn't right, he'll press red to abort.

Ged

I knew our Anthony'd be flattened by it, but fucking Ratts! Grid on him, by the way! Anyone'd think he was having a life-saving operation postponed on him. As good as he was just before when we was walking down to Dool's, he's fucked it now. His sneaky little brain is that bit too fast for his own good, too darting and diving for his kite to catch up on him. His eyes are darting everywhere while his mind is trying to think, think, think on his feet. It's a fucking treat to watch, mind you. It's like fucking face pinball, thoughts and reactions zapping around in his head. And all of a sudden I've got a fucking good idea of what the shady cunt's up to. Since we've been sat here, since I've been just sat watching Ratter's reaction, several fucking centuries of truth have come crashing in on myself. I've known, obviously I've known for years that Ratter had a little agenda going, but I've chosen just to look on it as his sideline. Just like auld Georgie O'Farrell with his allotment and his pigeons and that. A sideline. I never realised that *we* was the sideline. I never would have allowed myself to believe that one of our own could think so little of us.

But now I know. Now I know why my last-minute announcement that the job's off has fucked him right up the arse. He's the snitch, is why. The lad's been at it, hasn't he? Nice car, ambitions in other areas, friends in high places and that. He's a fucking cash-for-questions merchant, isn't he? He's fucking glad-handing fucking Martyn Lid, the low-life cunt. Jesus fuck – I knew he was fucking questionable, Ratter, but *Lid*? Lid is as low as a copper can stoop to, by the way. No cunt could be more fucking corrupt. Idi Amin had more to him, and our John-Paul is fucking flirting with the cunt. He has revealed my plans directly to fucking Lid in the most basic act of betrayal you could think of. The fact that it's all off makes him look a cunt, by the way – but that is not the point.

So I go further with him. Let's see how deep we're in, here. Let's see how many fathoms of shite deep we go with our little consultancy arrangement, shall we. If it's bluff he wants then this is now a game of double negative bluff. And if my news of the stand-down weren't bad enough, just look at the boy now, after my follow-up.

I've just looked at the table, cleared my throat and told them all that it was now looking like Christmas Eve. This has Ratter gripping the side of the table for the faintest split second. He nearly fucking fainted. It had them all going, to be fair. Moby weren't happy, obviously. Banging on about the fucking communion, he was. I had to keep telling the cunt we'd be well back in time. That communion IS our smokescreen. Half the coppers from St Anne Street are going to be there, so no cunt is going to expect us to be going over the wall Sunday of all days. Spit could've saved himself voicing his fucking unwanted opinion, by the way. I just phoned him up last night as a afterthought – just as a prop and that, to throw people off've the scent. I'll give him a few bob Sunday and stand him down. This just leaves Ratter. What Ratter has to do now is to think fast and to try and decide whether I'm telling the truth or not.

Fair play to the boy, he recovered good. He was only out for a minute before his sneaky snitch face was remembering to smile and laugh and joke again. But that minute told us everything. It's just what to do about it, now. Fucking upsetting, to be fair. That's two of us sitting here acting normal while our minds are racing ahead. Ratter doesn't want to leave while we're all still here, you can see that. He knows Moby's got a rehearsal at the church and he keeps offering him a lift. But it's not until thisavvy and Mobe's in no hurry and in the end Ratter pisses off on his tod. The snake. I tell Moby and Spit about the thing at my mother's place and they're all apologies. They both say they'll take a walk down there with us tomorrow, which is appreciated. I tell them Vic's at about eight bells.

Ratter

Too late to stop what I'm doing now. I'm already up to speed – to make another U-turn at this point would be plain disastrous. I just have to continue believing that dear Gerrard is as vain and as stupid as I take him for. I know this man. I grew up with the cunt. I'm fucking twice as clever as he is. The Gerrard I know could not fucking conceive of one of his own plotting to kill him. If I'm wrong, then I'm a dead man walking.

Moby

That's upset me, that has. I was a bit cut up about Georgie O'Farrell anyway, to be fair. He was good fella, George. But this thing with Auntie Eileen – I find it disgusting. That's all's it is – it's horrible. There's no standards in this city no more. People like me and our Gerrard, we're a dying breed. Even someone like Fonzie'll come outdoors with my good self and stand up and have a one-on-one. There's none of this behind-your-back carry-on. Anything with us boys, you know it's us doing it to you. These young fellas, though, they're wretches, some of them. It's all drive-by and guns and bullets in the back. Even there, they're shitehawks. They'll shoot the car or the house or the back fence instead of shooting the fella. That's the way these cunts'll end up. Any twat who can stone a old folks' home is going to end up shooting their enemy's front door to show him how bad they are. So they better get a good look at my kite 'cos from tomorrow night I am their enemy.

Ged

Feeling surprisingly chipper, to be fair. I've got nothing but shite to deal with, but I can see a way through at long last. I list the things I need to do today – flowers for Misty (what the fuck is her real name?); dedication in the paper; collect settle (yippee). Chrimbo shopping will have to wait until I'm in town tomorrow.

Wish I could've told Moby a little bit more about Sunday. He'll be made up when he finds out it's computer chips. Light as a feather. Easy-peasy. The courier's going to roll over for us but we've got to wear the uniforms and that, reflector bibs and that to help give the cunt a bit of a story. The chips are meant to be tiny. The whole package is the size of a bag of sugar. Nothing.

How it's come in is through one of the depot managers of the courier company. He's put us on to a few over the years. Maybe four or five good ones over about a eight-year span. Good as gold, he is. Never overdoes it. Gets it all absolutely spot-on from his end, he does, right down to selecting the right driver and that. He does get a good drink for his services, to be fair. He'll get thirty large out of this. The lad'll get ten. Makes a difference to them. Makes a big difference, money them poor cunts are on. Company's insured to fuck. Everyone gets paid. Happy days.

This one's going to be on a motorbike, which makes sense for the company. Makes it fucking hard for us, mind you. Not just from the blag point of view, by the way – it also makes it pretty fucking obvious that we've got inside info. Why else are we going to be hauling over a unmarked motorbike going a hundred mile an hour if we doesn't know what's on board? That's why the dropsie's got to be so rich – just a little bit of comp for them in case the company decides to get iffy. Coley's going to be chocker when he reads about it, but that's all gone now. Pip-pip, by the way, if you will. It was all take, take, take with that cunt anyway. He can't get me in that golf club. No way. No clout, Coley. He's more of a nobody than I am. I know what, though – if I went marching up there on Monday morning, walked into the club house and told them, 'Oh, the Pentium chip heist on the M6? That was myself done that one,' I'd be in like a shot. They'd fucking love it.

They won't scoff at the extra half-mill in my back bin and all. Eli'll have turned them chips into cash money before Coley so much as hears about it on the news. And I'll be back at the communion, my evil fire doused by holy water by the time Martyn Lid's been filled in on the morning's proceedings. Fuck them. I dawdle back to the Saab, folding up the flower receipt. I never can feel sure that the flowers I've paid for are going to get to where I've asked. And if they do, it still won't be the flowers I've ordered. It'll be something cheap, something shameful. I gets in and drives, my brain starting to feel like a sore, tired muscle. My brain's throbbing from all the pondering. I keep coming back to Ratter. It's my adoptive brother that's the unknown quantity. We now know that it's him trying to parcel me up for Lid with a red ribbon on. What we can't quite get to grips with is why. To be fair, I have always got more of the take than the lads, but that goes without saying. They'll get a hundred grand out of this for a half-hour's graft. More than Roy Keane, by the way. I'm going round and round with it, slooshing it round my head, but it's getting us nowhere.

I'm tired. I'm missing something. I can feel it just out of reach, but I can't reel it in. Instead my mind's flitting, offering me little titbits but refusing to stop still long enough to swallow them. Tax is due soon. Got it. Will have soon at least, anyway! They're not so bad, the tax goons. Nothing compared to the VAT. Them fellas are animals, to be fair. Savages, they are. I always think about my VAT when I'm off to score the settle.

I'm pulling up at the taxi rank now and feeling badly like a shag is the answer. Relax myself that little bit, just chill us out before the weekend. Even just a nosh and that – just a bit of a outlet'd do, to be fair. I know for a fact I can just walk in there and Trudi wouldn't even need us to ask. That girl would fucking love to suck my cock. That is a fact. She'd know how to suck a fella's cock and all too, by the look of her. Dirty isn't the half of it. She's cheap-looking and that, but she is sexy with it, I don't mind saying so. Like, she wears pink miniskirts whatever the weather. *Pink*, by the way, and so fucking flimsy you can see her arse cheeks through her knickers. One thing that gets me down about Deborah is the way she looks down on Trudi, thinks she's fuck all and that, asks myself if that slapper is the best we can do and that. But you couldn't say she's a slapper. She's a sexy girl. That's half why I have her there, mind you, though she is fucking fine at that particular twat of a job. More than capable she is, and I've no doubt she'd be more than capable of sucking myself off good style. But where does that leave you when you've shot your wad, by the way? It leaves you weakened. It means that she's got something on you.

Thursday

Ratter

Didn't sleep a wink to be fair, although the product of that insomnia is the knowledge it's all going to be fine. I've thought the whole thing through from top to bottom. Is right. Should've seen it straight away – I've got the cunt's own personal emergency-use hotline number, haven't I? Perfecto.

Ged

I used to love coming in George Henry's when we was kids. Not that we used to shop here, by the way. George Henry Lee was for families from the Wirral and Formby and Woolton and that. We used to come here once a year – for the grotto. George Henry Lee's grotto was always the best in town, no back answers. Owen Owen used to have a go, and Blackler's used to give out alright prezzies, but it was really between Lewis's and George Henry's. George Henry's was always best.

What I remember is being struck dumb by the thrill of waiting by them big old lifts. You would, properly, not be able to talk with excitement as them old brass cages come down to get you. You knew when it was coming because the cables'd loop over on themselves and there was this quiet hum. It was a confident hum, to be fair. You knew that nothing would ever go wrong with them lifts. As a kiddie, I was wary of lifts and was always glad to get out of them, to be fair, always thanked Our Lord that he'd delivered us out safe and sound – but I never had no qualms with the lifts at George Henry's. I always thought of them as rockets. They was my shuttle to the third-floor fantasyland.

It was a amazing grotto, in fairness. Looking back now, they couldn't've made no money on the thing. Decadent as fuck, it were. They'd have the whole floor decked out in white sparkle glitter and have loads of dead realistic, kiddie-sized rabbits and Bambis and that, dwarves and elves all waving as you went past, know what I mean. And Santa's grotto itself was all done out with shiny, glinting walls and these little hollows every few steps, little caves within the cave that had these scenes from *Snow White* or whatever the story was that year. I used to press myself right up against each one, trying to take in every little detail. My mother used to have to keep dragging us on – gently and that, by the way – but I was holding up the queue, in fairness.

I can afford to buy anything in here, but I always feel like a tealeaf when I'm in places like George Henry's. It always feels like I'm – not exactly not good enough to shop there, I don't feel like I'm being watched or nothing. That's not it – they're always lovely in there, especially the girls on the perfume. It's just myself. It's myself that doesn't think I should be in a place like this. I don't know what it is – I don't really feel like I've earned it, to be fair. I'm not a honest guy like the other fellas you see shopping in here. They've earned the right – they're all there spending the spoils of honest graft. The auld fella in the grotto that plays Kris Kringle, by the way – he deserves to shop here more than I do. Even the Father Christmas in the grotto is quality in this gaff, mind you. You don't get no auld plonkies hamming it up for their Aussie Whites in G.H. Lee. Their Santa Claus has twinkly eyes and big jolly red cheeks and a real, snow-white beard. Quality.

That's what Debbi asked us for. Something classy. Calvin Klein and DKNY and that's alright for kids to be fair, alright if you're going the Cream or something. But if you're after quality, there's only one contender. It's got to be Chanel, to be fair. The old classic. I stands there deep in thought, waiting for one of the half-tidy counter girls to approach us. I'm going to go through the motions of asking how much and that, and then I'm going to let her talk myself into buying the biggest bottle. Not the eau de toilette, by the way. Oh no. I'm after a full ounce of the pure Chanel No. 5 perfume. She asked for class, that's what she's getting – no two ways about it.

But none of them wants to give myself the time of day. I can't exactly be grafting here in front of the display, can I? They can't think I'm at it. It's all racked up there behind the counter, the good swag. I try to catch this one's eye. She's wearing about a ton too much of that full-on beige face powder. What makes it worse is that it stops just like that, halfway down her neck, like she's got a tide mark. She looks like she's wearing a white polo neck, but she's got nice eyes, to be fair. She actually makes eye contact then looks down and carries on chewing ever so slightly.

I'm half getting a touch-on from the way she looked at us when this pure fucking bandit comes mincing into the line of fire. Lily Savage is not even close. This lad's a monster – camp as fuck and right in your face with his Big Hom act. Makes Ricey sound like Tommy Smith, in fairness. He's so fucking Out his teeth are chattering – he's extremely gay and one of them that wants you to know it, in all fairness. I feel a cunt asking him for fucking perfume and that – would have to be scent, by the way. I try to deadhead his questions, but he seems to like the challenge. I keeps moving away from him, keep my eyes trained on the shelves and tell him I'm still looking and that but he's not having none of it. For our homosexual friend, these are the things that make his day go quicker.

'Is it for a lady?'

I try to make my voice sound dead gruff.

'Er. Yeah.'

What did he think it was for, by the way – a fella? He looks us up and down. He acts like that soppy cunt off 've *NYPD Blue*. At all times he has a finger in his mouth, like he's trying to solve some great mystery. And Jesus, is he cake! You couldn't get him more cake if he'd been to Dick Emery's Fruit School and eaten all the strawberries. He's having a laugh with us. He's got to be. You pure can not grow up in this city and put your little finger in your mouth and talk like a tart like that. He's doing it, though.

'Does she have a preference? I mean, if I showed you a few bottles would you recognise her brand?'

Ah, fuck this for a lark, I think. I can't listen to this shite. He's making myself queasy and that. Let's just get this over with. I tells him what I want and, in spite of him being nice and impressed and all of that, I can still feel myself getting a cherry on. There's fuck all I can do to stop that, by the way. The more I think about how red I must be going, the hotter I seem to feel. My hands are sweating. I can feel my top lip glistening.

He takes about a fucking year to wrap the thing but to be fair, it's a fucking beautiful job he's made of it. It does look *classy*. Them tart's fingernails of his have come in handy, well. He asks how I want to pay. One thing I haven't done is get cash. I usually put aside a few ton from the drivers' settle to see myself through the week, but it's gone like that with flowers for Misty and drinks and one thing and another. I pulls out my Switch card. I won't use no credit cards. 'Neither a borrower nor a lender be,' my mother always said. Is right and that, Mam. Is right.

Problem is I can never do my own signature. I'm alright in a petrol station or something, but any time there's a queue behind us, or if it's somewhere nice, or if there's half a chance someone I know or who knows my grid might witness the fucking farce then I'm fucked. That is fucked, by the way. Can not do it. Pure can not make the cunt come out anything like what my own autograph says on the card. This is how it's going to go in George Henry's now. I know all the symptoms, to be fair. My hand is like a oil slick, it's sweating that much. And my top lip and all, too – will not stop perspiring, in fairness. I use my own pen in the hope it'll make myself look confident, and I try to do it in one smooth stroke – but I know that my helpful, gift-wrapping quegg is watching us every step of the way. I hand him the slip like there's not even going to be a whiff of a problem and I stand back confident, not even looking at the cunt, paying *soooo* much fucking attention to putting my pen back in the right pocket. My inside pocket could pick me out in a identity parade it's seeing so much of my kipper. The lad sees no problem, though. He just goes: 'Thank you, Mr Brennan.'

Spits a bit on the 'thank you', to be fair. Makes a last little bid for eye contact and hands us the bag. Obviously his own commission on the sale was worth more than any petty concerns about kited cards. Good luck to the lad, by the way.

Ratter

Operation Offski is more than coming together. Soon as this is sorted – off. Gone. Vanished past vanishing point. Margueritte'll be sound. She's known for a long time what this was all about. There's no binlids to queer the pitch. She's got the gyms and South Village and that – she'll be sound. It's exciting, this. While every cunt in the city is getting fucking hysterical about Christmas, I'm preparing to fuck everyone and anyone who was near and dear to me and fuck off to Bermuda. I'm a louse. A twat. I can't help myself – I love me and nobody else.

Ged

I've got a hour to kill before I pick up the lads from Vic's. I picks up a *Echo* and heads up to the Buro. Their meatballs are to kill for, and that's the God's honest truth. That is a fact. They're proper fucking meatballs these and then some. Pure fucking delicious. My plan is to walk up there, plate of meatballs, little glance through the *Echo*. If the Count's around, pass a pleasant half-hour with him then off to meet the boys. And that's what I do, more or less. No Count, but the meatballs are epic and, once I'm done with the *Echo*, it's nearly eight. Honest George has got about five pages of obits. Straight up. Every cunt in town has put a tribute in. I thought ours was a good one, to be fair – nice big border and that – but I don't mind admitting it, there's some crackers here. Some real tearjerkers. The one from his little grandson Matty is too much. I can feel myself filling up, in fairness. It makes you realise that it weren't just talk – he was a proper fucking folk hero, Georgie. He died in his sleep and you can't ask for much more than that in this caper of ours. It's a lucky fella that dies in his sleep, to be fair. They don't make them like George O'Farrell no more. People have got no class.

Moby

Our Gerrard's right, to be fair. We've got to be careful not to go in too hard. We're teaching these kids a lesson they won't forget in a hurry and that, but that's all's they are – kids. He can see I'm fucking fuming about this one, Ged can. He knows me. I'm more pumped-up for this than I was over Fonzie.

There's just the four of us sat there in the grounds outside. When I say grounds, it's nothing much. A bit of a shrubbery and a half a front lawn and some trees by the wall. We're just by the trees, squatting down with our backs against the wall. It's fucking killer on the backs of your legs, by the way.

Ged

I can hear them coming. I know it's them. I can hear the stupid, selfish, show-off braying of the very young. It's not just lads, neither. I can hear girls, hear them making themselves coarse. I put my hand on our Anthony's leg, telling him not to go just yet. I want to be certain this is our boys. Spit and Drought are both trying to catch my

243

eye, but they know myself well enough. They won't make a move until I do.

Thud! A brick or a rock hits the wall of the main building, followed by delirious, put-on cackling. Some of them might be drunk or glued-up or whatever, but them cackling noises are pure phoney. Fucking braying, they are – the girls worse than the lads, by the way. They're saying: 'Look at me! I'm out of it! I'm fucking mad!'

And you're fucking dead and all, too. I vault the low sandstone wall in one and grab the nearest lad by the shoulder. Usual sort of thing. Trackie bottoms tucked into Pringle socks. Trainies. The girls are the same. Lowlife lite, they are – no finesse about them. No femininity and that. They seem to want to be lads – well, I'm here to show that they don't. This is what lads get. I drags him over to the main entrance.

'Don't you like people that's older than you, kidder?'

He's a live one. He's not going to back down in front of his mates. His face is all spite, all nasty, selfish spite.

'What you on about, you auld prick!'

A couple of his mates laugh, but it's muted. They're worried. They're more worried still when Moby and Spit come one side of them, Drought on the other, and they just stand there, arms folded as if they're just watching a gang of fire bobbies rescue a cat and that. The little hooligan posse shut right up now. They don't know what's happening. I gives the lad a shake.

'Ah leave him, ay!' goes one of the girls. 'Don't be tight.'

I turns to her.

'Don't you think it's tight terrorising old ladies? Ay?'

The penny drops. Now they know what this is all

about. Now it's just a question of what we're going to do. I was going to drag the lot of them down the drive and let them look into the faces of their lonely old victims. Shame them. I knew they'd hate it, and I knew they'd never come back again. But then the lad spat in my face. That was that. I throws him on the deck, face first. He screams.

'Fuck off, you! Leave us alone!'

I step on the middle of his back and hold him there.

'I won't. You're getting it, you, you little cunt!'

Some of the others try to make a run for it. The lads catch them and bring them back. I know the worst thing about things like this is the wait. What's he going to do? What's going to happen to us. It happened to me and our Anthony when we was about nine or ten, and I've never forgotten it. We was playing in Princes Park. Playing cricket, by the way, and these older lads, skins they were, Bennies, Comos, Flemmings, full kit, come ambling over. Never even entered our heads we was going to get done in. We was kiddies. Wasn't on the agenda. But as they gets closer, we can see there's young lads with them. In all fairness, we probably shouldn't have been there. We was off the patch and that – strayed away from the barrio, to be fair. We was in rebel lands. Some of the older skinheads starts uprooting our fucking pathetic little stumps we'd made, just a few shitty bits of stick and that – but then this older one come over and started talking to us. Where are we from and that. What school do we go to. And then he calmly tells us that we're going to get a hiding like we're going to remember for the rest of lives – but not just yet. They've just got to wait for some lad. And the waiting was fucking excruciating. This evil cunt knew exactly what he was doing. He just takes out a Numbo, sparks up and sits on the swing, enjoying the sunshine and smoking his ciggy. I'm stood there and the fucking indignity and the pure terror of it, man – untold it were. Fucking horrible, by the way. There's these two mini-skins, my age, nine or ten, holding myself by the wrists and they're repeating what the leader has said – you're going to get battered, boys. You're going to get done in so good that your mam won't know you. We was handy boys ourselves, by the way, no two ways about it – but there was loads of these little bastards and what they was saying to us was fucking sick. It was terrifying, by the way – our minds didn't work like that. We'd give a lad a dig and move on. This was something else. I'm starting to let my mind imagine what sort of damage we're talking about – are they even going to *kill* us maybe – when the parkie's van come round the corner. Now, you never *ever* seen the parkie's van in the daytime. You heard older lads talking about getting chased by it at night, but that was Sevvy Park. We all thought it was just a local myth and that – like Martin the Feeler and the Prinny Park Flasher and all of that. But here he was – Parkie to the rescue and that. At first it looked like they wasn't arsed – couple of them half let on to the parkie as though we was all mates together having a laugh, but thank fuck he never bought that. He starts walking over to us with his Ally on a short leash. The two little cunts just tightened their grip, started giving us Chinese burns. But the leader stubs his ciggy calm as you like and wanders back over and goes: 'Don't worry, boys. I know your faces now. We'll get you again.'

I don't mind admitting it – I was fucking petrified. Our Anthony cried which I never – but I did get a terrible attack of the shakes once they'd all fucked off. I had to try and walk back normal but I was fucking shook up bad, to be fair. Looking down every fucking side street I was, half expecting them to come running out at us again. But the lad was right. We did meet again. I stabbed him in the shoulder outside the Carousel a few years later. Let him know who I was first and all, too. He looked about twenty that day he caught myself and Moby, but he must've only been twelve or thirteen in fairness. I never did forget the way he went about us that day, though – and it took a long time before I could stop myself thinking about what they might've done to us if the parkie never come. Got to half respect the cunt for that. He did make his mark, in fairness, even if I made my mark better in the end.

I know we can't do these lads in. I can't stab this one in the shoulder, much as I'd dearly love to. But I can terrify him. I can humiliate him in front of his mates. I can make him never walk down this street ever, ever again. Even when he's thirty-five and he's got binlids of his own and this is all a dim and distant nightmare, he'll still take a detour away from here, just on instinct.

So while the other three make sure that his mates all stay, I just stand there with my foot pressed into the small of his back, and I tells him story after story about me mam. Every now and then I shouts over to Moby for back-up, just: 'That's right, isn't it, Micky?'

Didn't use his proper name and that, obviously. I never made one threat to the young lad, by the way. I just let his mind work overtime. Bit by bit I lets him know that my own dear mam, the subject of all these stories and fables, is also Micky's auntie. And she currently resides inside the very building we're stood outside. Not that he's standing. He's lying flat on his face and, from the smell of him, he's either pissed himself or he's shit or both. A little trickle escapes from under him and breaks away towards the gutter. There's a occasional shudder of his shoulders as he tries to disguise his sobbing. Then he doesn't bother trying to hide it no more. It all comes out. Sobs and sobs and sobs. He wants me to let him go home. He's not so hard, now. Neither am I, to be fair. Basta. Mission accomplished.

Moby

We're all agreed on that. Our Gerrard and Honest George is cut from the same cloth. When they made them two, they thrown away the mould. There isn't many like Ged left in the city now. I don't know how he does it, to be fair. I couldn't have stood off like that. That is a fact, by the way – I would've pure booted the lad up and down the street and stamped on his face to make sure he knew. Doesn't matter if he's fifteen, sixteen, whatever. Them kids can get guns these days. They wouldn't think twice on it. That's what I'm saying, mind you. That is my point. There's no morality no more. That's what it is. No cunt has got any morals left. Them boys, the real young ones and that, they're the ones getting guns. Lads won't have a one-on-one with you now, they'll get a gun. They'll get a gun and they will fucking pop you – and they'll fucking hold it sideways and all too, the little teds. Fucking designer gun stance, by the way. I don't know how our Gerrard can be so disciplined, I swear to God I don't. I couldn't do that. He's a one-off.

Ged

I've left them to it. It's all getting a bit fucking thingy in there. Everyone's getting a little bit emotional and that, what with George and tonight and all of that, know what I mean. There's all sorts of Judies in there, mind you, all fucking whacked on cocaine and white wine, all hanging round the lads, showing out for them good style. I've left them to it in there. I've got to get down to proper planning for Sunday, from this point in. I can't afford to be getting caned. Can not even afford just one little slip, by the way. One of the drivers is coming over for us and I've told him to bring another lad to drive my car back. And I've told them they can fuck the clock-and-a-half off and all. It may well be Chrimbo, but they're getting no favours off've the boss.

It's a cunt of a job getting a cab to pull up outside the Retro. Can be done and that, but you'd have to be a fucking phoney to make them come right to the door, in all fairness. It's easy-peasy to just walk up past the Revolution and get picked up on the corner there. Simple as. Bang, bang, bang and you're back through the tunnel and on your way home to deranged squirrels and deluded wives.

As I'm sat there on the corner of Victoria Street and Temple Court – just sat there waiting on one of them bollards that they've put up all round the Matthew Street area, I were – who does I see crossing the road but Mikey Green. Now then. And it ain't just Mikey himself, neither. It's Mikey Green and Al Stanton no less, heading up the jigger towards Nirvana. Hello, hello, I thinks to myself. Hello, hello.

Ratter

I know I can't trust neither of the twats. But then they can't trust me neither, can they. It's just that they don't know that, yet. If they'd just stop for a half a second and ask themselves why and that, then maybe they'd tumble. But they're not asking no questions, these two. They don't want to know why. By the time they do, I'll be well gone.

And Operation Offski is going well, by the way. I've been down to Marv's in Wolverhampton, picked up my snide passport. I've booked my flight and that. Bought a fucked-up Hyundai from a auction in Queensferry. It's got one good go left in it, that motor – which is all's I need. That car is getting ragged all the way to the airport and that's where it's going to bed. Fair dinkum, some of the Wolvo posse did help set this up, in fairness – and in fairness it wouldn't take that long for someone like Mikey Green to work that out. There's only so many places you can get a jarg passport and Mikey knows full well where the Yardies get theirs from. Marvin.

So let's say just for the fuck of it that Mikey knows I am now called Mitchell Hanson. Let's go further – let's say he's got a in to immigration and that. He finds out Mr Hanson boarded the Heathrow shuttle at Manchester. Caught another plane from Heathrow to Zurich. Then that's it. Trail's suddenly gone cold. He's fucked. He doesn't know I've got fucking Brewster's headed for a Swiss bank. He doesn't know that bank has got reps in the Caymans, in the Dutch Antilles, in Hawaii, in Canada, everywhere. He doesn't know that I've got a guy in Zurich who can give me any passport in the United Nations for 50,000 dollars. Any three for a hundred. He doesn't even know for certain whether it was me that got on the fucking Zurich plane at Heathrow, by the way. He knows it was Mr Mitchell Hanson, so he does – but who the fuck's he? For all anyone knows I could have a lad called Lee waiting for us at Heathrow, waiting to be given five grand and yet another jarg Mitch Hanson passport just to take the plane and take another one to Hamburg and come back into the UK by ferry. On his own passport. What I'm saying is, it's not worth their while putting the men and the hours into finding old JPB. Once I've left the city limits, it's needle in a haystack, knowmean. I can half lead the cunts round the world and they still wouldn't fucking find YT. He knows that. When the time comes Mikey will know it's not even worth his while. He'll shake his head and he might even raise a glass to the Ratter this one time.

Not that I'm counting on Mikey being around to pursue this, by the way. That is not my intention at all. My intention is to insulate JPB good and proper. Layer after layer of scheming and pre-planning will take care of each and any eventuality – even if Plod do fuck it, by the way. But I'm gifting it to them. I am fucking handing them these cunts trussed up like a Chrimbo turkey. That is my intention.

I've just had dinner with the both of them – Mikey and Al Stanton. Al Stanton of the purple SLK. Meathead. Fucking bully. From the moment he showed up on my tail in Kirkby that day I've known that Al Stanton was not rooting for YT. And after a day's tugging on it, I had to accept that Ritchie was fucking on it and all, too. Fucking depressing it were – I half thought Ritchie was all right and that. Did get to us, to be fair, that did – man's greed knows no rational bounds. It took the cull to sort my swede out that little bit and then I really did get down to some fucking pondering. What I could not fucking work out was who was pulling the fucking strings. Who would have the back-up or the front or the fucking stupidity to go up against Bernie on this? Half started to think maybe it was Bernie himself and that – and then Mikey goes and gives us the answer. He only fucking tells us himself, doesn't he – that night in the casino.

So once I'm on it, it's plain sailing. I phones Mikey and I goes to him – would be nice to work with you and Al on something one day. He doesn't even query the Al bit. Does not so much as take a extra breath. Pure buys it, he does – swallows the worm whole. Wants it big, by the way, Mikey does – wants it now. What did you have in mind, he's going. Pure Eubank, by the way. Putting the lisp on big time. Anything specific and that, like. Specific. Twat of a word to say when you've got a lisp and that, to be fair.

So we've just come from L'Alouette en Ville. That's one of the bad things about Mikey. He's ostentatious. He wants everyone to see him out and about. Half likes the idea that people will have seen us and will be trying to put two and two together. He does want to be talked about, by the way. Can't quite make the cunt out, neither. I think he's pretty stupid. I really don't think he's that bright. Tries too hard to be the big businessman, knowmean – did think he'd be a lot fucking cleverer than what he is, in fairness. Wants it though, he does. Wants it, wants it, wants it bad. Half admire the cunt, to be fair. For all that he's not that smart he's no shitbag, neither. He seems to know that this can only last so long. Seems to accept it that he'll end up shot and that. Maybe that's why he's so big time with it all now. Enjoy it while you can and that.

He's bought a lot of champagne and he's half tried to get us gabbing. But I've hardly touched a drop – I'd never talk business in a public place and no way would I open up in front of Stanton. Who is just sat there, by the way – just sits there like fucking I-am-a-hardcase and that. I won't breathe a word of it to them until we're over the road. We sits in the gardens behind St George's Hall. You can smell their excitement, by the way – they're double into this because it's a cross. It's the old guard getting fucked up the arse and I know they're going to be bang into that. It's the old fatal flaw. Ambition. Blinding ambition. Their desperation to take over, to get a proper slice of the proper fucking cake and that is preventing them from asking the obvious question. Why? Thank fuck I don't have a fatal flaw.

My plan is a simple one. It's this. I tells Mikey and Al Stanton that there's a major consignment of beak coming into the city on Sunday. I'm figuring they'll have had the arse end of a whisper about this, anyway. Just that *something* was happening, knowmean. You have to assume that nothing is secret in this city. But clock their faces when I tell them who's bringing it in. Sorry, Ged lar. Had to be done, kidder. Had to be done.

I've never liked the word, but them two twats are gobsmacked by the news. Chins pure hit the deck they do, no back answers. They're stunned. I have to tell them it's beak coming in, by the way – even these greedy no-marks'd never square our Gerrard being involved with gear. Mikey's loving it already.

'I knew it. I fucking knew it.'

Eubank. He's shaking his head half in admiration for

our Ged. He looks at us, thirsty, hungry, desperate for details. He wants it, by the way, this lad does. I tell him that's it for now. That's all. We'll get the true location and all the timings and that on the morning it comes in. All's they'll have to do is go down there with a firm and take the swag off 've them. Slowly, slowly they get their greedy minds round to my most immaculate self. What's my cut? What's in it for John-Paul Brennan?

What's In It For YT – What I Tells Them. I tells them that our Gerrard is dragging us down, has been for a while and that, badly starting to be a embarrassment to us. He's cramping my style. He's making it hard for YT to carry on the legitimate business interests in and out of the city that are half starting to make us a few bob, in fairness. Things like that fucking straightener the other day – episodes like that do JPB no credit whatsoever. It does pain me to have to hurt the boy, but he's his own worst enemy. I need him out of the way. Sorry, guys, but there it is. They're welcome to seize his merchandise if they can take it off 've him. Nothing personal – it's just business. Hopefully the first of many transactions between us fellows – a new era of understanding among a new breed of inner-city businessmen.

Mikey fucking loves that last bit, by the way. Nodding like a twat, he is. Grinning like Curtly Ambrose. I feel a bit sly and that. He thinks he's arrived. Thinks this is a proper hit and that, he does.

What's In It For YT – The Truth. I don't turn up for the blag with Ged and the boys on Sunday. Obviously. I'll be on my way to the sloop. I shall stop off for a quick bite with Martyn Lid, however – who will be dining with his good and esteemed friend, Councillor Bennett. From their table I shall call Gerrard Brennan on his emergency line. He'll see it's YT calling. I'll be straight. I'll tell him I got the number off've Misty the other night when she was trying to get through to him. He'll have that. And I'll tell him I thought I was being followed. He'll have that and all, too. He knows I'm always thinking that, half thinking I'm being followed and that. I'll ask him where it's going off. He'll tell us. I, for my part, shall tell Lid, then I shall wish the two friends *bon appetit*. On my way down to the sloop I shall be sure to phone through the same information to Mikey Green Esquire, colourful local entrepreneur. We do need two sides for a fight, by the way. And with the involvement of Mikey and Al, I think it's safe to say that firearms will be involved. I'd further venture that Mr Lid, while disappointed to discover no drugs at the scene of the shoot-out, will be only too delighted to have been on hand to witness a savage shoot-out and will be glad to remove such dangerous criminals from the streets of Liverpool. I, for my part, shall consider myself to have lit the touch paper and, equally, to have stood back at a safe distance. Then I shall fuck off out of there.

It's not a bad plan. At worst, the whole gang of them'll get nicked and get proper stretches. At best, they could all shoot each other before Plod gets to the scene and finally, beautifully, totally be out of my fucking hair for good. Finito, by the way. Whatever, I've got contingencies right up my sleeve as far as my back shoulder blade. Bottom line is this – I'm off, man. I'm gone. It's not a game of quit while you're ahead no more. It's a game of quit while you're alive. And that's what I'll be doing, come what may. Whether I bury our Gerrard or not, I'm out of here and he's out of me.

Ged

I'm not one for making my own problems someone else's, by the way, but this was one I just had to phone in. It's none of my business and that – except that it's totally my business, if you will. Individually, Mikey Green and Al Stanton are men as low as it is possible to go without getting carpet burn on your belly. Together, they are Semtex. They represent a clear and present danger to my old cockney mucker Francis Bernard, no two fucking ways about it. I've got no choice. I've got to phone it in.

Ratter

So that's that. Almost there, by the way. Just need to firm up with the Boro Brothers. They're smart lads and that, but I do need to make double sure they can get a banker's draft for that amount. I'm sure they can. They're very keen, them boys. All's they want is to be allowed to come out and play. It's a matter of pride for them. What their life is all about is being took serious by big-name hoods from Liverpool and London. They *live* for opportunities like this. They half want to be famous, by the way. They do – they want to be names and that. They wouldn't even think of turning up without that banker's draft. They'll be sound. So I won't worry about them. It's the Big One that's getting us now. Fucking Bernie.

There was no way around it, by the way – I pure *had* to go to Bernie on this. Did think it all through and that, half thought maybe I could've just took a flyer and that, could've just done a runner and hoped for the best. But it didn't hold water, not for a second – wouldn't have, neither. Just would not have got away with it, end of. What would've happened, by the way, is as soon as I told the Bhoys I was into it and that, quite liked the bigger deal, the eight mill and that – soon as I've gone yes it'd be straight back to Bernie, no back answers. And he'd've been scratching his stubbly chin – one of them and that, anyway – and he'd be going: 'What's Ratter up to, then? He's taking more than usual. He's taking a fucking *lot* more than usual, by the way.'

And that would've fucking been that. All kinds of glare on YT, no end of Q&A and that – and they would deffo have had a tail on us. From the moment I got hold of the gear they would've been on to us, on my case, on my tail. Far from perfect for a lad that's about to hop it, by the way. Not exactly incognito, slipping off to the airport with his eyes and ears calling it in, knowmean. So at the end of the day, I'm going to be briefing Bernie, aren't I? As risks go, this isn't even a risk – I didn't have no choice. I had to tell him what I was thinking. And I knew he'd go for it and all, too. I fucking *knew* he'd have it. He's half gone *Little Caesar* since he's been down there, by the way. Loves all of that shite, he does. *Loves* fellas having to make a appointment to see him and that, ask him for his advice and that, ask for his blessing on this and that. He's no different to the rest of them. They all want to be thought of as shrewd operators and that, and they likes to think that their head rules their heart. Not personal and that.

So I went and told him exactly what I told fucking Mikey – but different. Went about it brilliant and all too, if I do say so myself. Told him my fears about Moby's straightener and that, told him it could only lead to tensions in the city, not good for business, all of that carry-on. Got him right on board, mind you. Told him that, with all due respect for a great man – and I do revere our Gerrard, by the way – I'm thinking that Ged is just getting himself left behind the times. Obviously I don't tell the lad that I've got fucking plans that'll see Ged Brennan rubbed out if all goes well – I just tells him that, with his permission, it would not be a tricky thing to get Ged took out of the equation for a year or two. And he looked at us with them slow fucking never-blinking eyes of his and he never said yea or nay. He just goes: 'That could work nicely in a number of ways.'

So I've proper stuck my neck out. Calculated risk and that – I half knew Bernie'd see the sense in it, but it's getting close now. I've got to phone him. Just got to be certain and that – or I truly am in lumber then. I've been dreading this since last fucking Sunday, by the way. Burying it, to be fair. I need to be sure that he did mean what he seemed to be saying last weekend. I picks the phone up and, to my great annoyance, find words of wisdom from fucking Big Brother playing on my mind.

'Never make a big call until you're one hundred per cent ready. A few hours can't hurt – and they might make all the difference.'

Cunt's only right, mind you. I can hear how my voice would sound to Bernie if I made that call right now. Jumpy. Nervous. Jaunty and that – too eager to please. He'll know straight away that something's up. He just will. I'll sleep on it and give him a bell first thing tomorrow.

But of course I don't sleep. I can't sleep. All of this is not so much playing on my mind, it's fucking torturing me. My poor mind is aching with its responsibilities. Responsibilities to YT, myself and JPB, by the way, but it does hurt all the same. It badly hurts, what I've got to do. What I've got myself into. I don't know why I'm doing it. It's like I'm driving fast, straight at a tree. I know where the brake is. I know how to stop. But I like the drive. I like the speed and I keep on driving.

Ged

Franner's made up to hear from us, in fairness. Talks about Honest George for a while, says he's deffo coming up for the communion and Georgie's funeral. Gives us his usual funeral gag and that. Always does, by the way, he just goes: 'I take it yours'll be the car outside with the engine running.'

Funny the first time he said it, it were. He asks us what I think of his tribute in the *Echo*. Seemed a bit chocker that his weren't as big as the Mahers' and the Jacksons'. To be fair, Mikey fucking Green's was bigger. Well bigger, by the way – proper fucking tribute, Mikey give. Some fella from the council done the biggest box of all, mind you.

We gets on to Ratter. Franner's circling us and that – seems like he wants to bring something up, seems half to be fishing and that, see what I knows myself. He tells us Ratter roughed one of the girls up last weekend. Knocked her about bad. The boy is a pure scumbag, to be fair. I don't know that I can call him my own no more. I don't know what's got into the cunt.

I gets to the point, anyway – I tell Franner about what I seen tonight, Mikey and Stanton and that. He goes a bit quiet, to be fair. Then after a bit he tells us to do nothing, just wait for him to come up and all will be explained. Meantime say fuck all to any cunt. Goes a bit Harold Shand on us, he does – it will be dealt with and that. Daft I-am-a-gangster talk and that. We are aware of the situation with Mr Stanton and Mr Green and all of that. He forgets it's myself, sometimes. But we rap on about the match and what we've got the kids for Christmas and that and everything's sound. He says it'd be best if I didn't tell any cunt he's coming up, and if he could get his head down at ours and that, so much the better. Doesn't want no one to know he's coming up, now. He knows I want putting in the picture, to be fair, but he says he'll tell us everything when he sees us. Says it's a fucking long story and that, in fairness.

Ratter

Can't sleep. I go and lie in the sling. I'm imagining I'm here with the young girl from the other night. Young and firm and that, but experienced and all, too. I'm lying her down in the sling and I go: 'Trust me. Draw your knees up. Draw them right up to your chest. Now press your thighs together. Press them very firmly together and breathe in deeply. How does that feel? Does that feel good?'

And she does just what I say. She just lies there, dumb, and she obeys. But there's a flicker of a understanding from her. She knows what's going on. She knows what's happening in JPB's head and she wants to excite him and that turns her on, too. He can see her, now. He can see her smooth thighs parted slightly and he can see the pink of her young, small vagina, waiting. But it's no good JPB seeing all of that in his mind. There's ten, twelve girls like that out there now, just down the road. By the bridge and that. Young ones. Three minutes away. Young girls that's scared to go up by the cathedral or Mount Vernon where the auld pros are, these are kids

260

that'll take a chance so's they can get their next bag. If only they knew. If only.

I'm in the Shogun heading down Great Howard Street, shivering like fuck. The blaster hasn't warmed up yet and it is one fucking cold night. Doubt there'll be many out on a night like this, to be fair, Chrimbo or not. Should've just stayed in and called the Hom for takeaway.

I pass the usual spot, the junction with Blackstone Street and there's nothing doing, but I decide I'll head on. I say to myself that I'll drive as far as Millers Bridge and that's it. If I haven't seen what I want by then, I'll drive down to ours and spend the night with Margueritte.

In the event I go as far as Church Street and do a left to come back on the dock road. There's a place round there, by the way, a house and that, but standards have to be maintained. A man such as myself can't be seen going to a Bootle knocking shop for sex.

Just at the bottom of Boundary Street I sees a girl dart across the road. On the game. No doubt about it. She's gone in a flash, heading towards the little industrial estate. I cranes my neck to see which street she's gone down, flickering my sightline between the wing mirror, the rear-view and the passenger window.

I don't know what came first. The bang, the scream – more a muffled, resigned plea than a scream, to be fair – or whether it was just some sixth sense that I was about to hit someone. I definitely knew I was going to hit her before it happened, knowmean. Maybe a split, split, split second before, but not long enough to do nothing about it, in fairness. I seen her face perfect, lit up in the headlights. White. Shock white. Very red lips and very wide, very terrified eyes and that. Didn't scream, as such. She just sort of goes: 'Nooooo!'

I slows up, takes a look in the rear-view mirror, has a little look ahead. No other cars around. Nothing. As I move off, she's crawling, very slowly, to the side of the road. She might make it but no way will that baghead remember what hit her or what happened.

I've got to keep going. Whatever I do, I need to physically place myself as far away from this barrio as I can now. If I can get the other side of the Liver Building without getting spotted, even by casual passers-by or pissheads or whatever I should be all right. So long as I bypass the Tai Pan and that there won't be much other traffic at this time of night. My first plan is to go straight to ours. Chances are Margueritte won't be in anyway, so I'm laughing. Then I start to think about the car. What if the neighbours should clock us coming in and that? And what about the bodywork – what if there's a dent in it? Does it fucking matter?

I starts to curse myself. So close to everything and I has to go and blow it for the sake of a ten-bob fucking hooker. Fuck! I grips the steering wheel hard and hit the pedal. I don't know where the fuck I'm heading. Away. That's where I'm going. I weave up and down the streets and tracks between the dock roads, lights off for now. I cuts up Burly on to Vauxy and bangs the lights back on and hit the pedals. Whoosh! I go right over the little roundabout by the Eldonian – just like a fucking little nipple it is, hardly even there – but it sends us off balance for a sec before the four-wheel drive balances us up again. The jolt gets my mind racing again. One after another, plans and ways out enter my head only to be damned and shredded. And then I hear it. The helicopter. Could be going anywhere, but the longer I drive it's still there in the background, hovering, chak-chak-chak-chak-chak. I hate that sound. I do, I fucking hate it.

My first thought is that they've been scanning that barrio for kerb crawlers. It was in the *Echo*. All the young mams from round there got a protest together, saying not enough was being done. So the vice squad has put a chopper out. They've seen everything and they're on my case. Then I start to panic – is there any gear in the boot? There must be half a trace of something. But then I remember. It's round Greatie that the young wifies have been kicking off, round Everton and that.

I carries on down past the Harbour Club and fumble for the window button. A gush of frozen cold air. I try to get my head out far enough to see where the chopper is. I can hear it but I can't see it. I can't see nothing with that cold wind in my eyes. I decide to keep driving. I pass all our places. The Britannia. The Festival Gardens. Means more to them than me. They're forever looking back, them boys. Not JPB.

There's lights behind. Can't tell whether it's Plod or not. Fuck. Fuck, fuck, fuck! I takes a left into Jericho Lane and back out on to Aigburth Road and keep driving, right past ours, past the Kingsman and out towards Runcorn Bridge. The car is still on my case. I can see the badge now. Mazda. Nippy. I puts my foot down. The surge from this beast, no matter the size of it, its kick is stupendous. I'm off over the Garston flyover and away. But only for a minute. Them lights come screaming, round the bend, closer and closer. Now I know the Mazda's tailing me. Who the fuck is it! I don't want to panic. Can't let them see I'm losing it. I shoots over the bridge fast, bumping up and down like a mad cunt but the four-be-four soaks it up like it's fuck all. The Mazda can't plough across quite the same at the end of the day. I opens up a gap, but I'm still straining into the mirror. Who is it? Who is the cunt? I think and think and think, but I can't come up with nothing.

I've opened up a gap again now. If I can get on to the M56 roundabout without him closing us up again, I should be away. He'll have to guess which way I've gone. But no sooner have I thought that than the twat's in my mirror again – and he's gaining. Up ahead the light is green. I puts my foot right down on a road that can't really take it. I'm up to 125. The lights go amber. Fuck! Can't slow it down in time. Sixty, fifty, forty yards away. There'll be fuck all coming at this time of night. There'll be fuck all. I open my eyes wide and chill myself as I roar straight out and across and weave left on to the motorway feeder road. The Shogun screeches a little, tries to right itself, strains against the pull. I'm going about a hundred miles an hour too fast for this approach road. It's one sharp, continuous curve designed only to slow traffic down. I try to brake without slamming on but can't bring the speed down quick enough. I veer off the road and skid to a halt on the hard shoulder. In another car I might have been embedded in the crash barrier. I take a deep, deep breath and start up the ignition. The Mazda must've seen all of what happened. The Mazda, which is where, by the way? Cunts have vanished. Vamoosed. Properly have disappeared off've the face of the earth. And then I sees them joining the motorway on the other side, Manchester-bound. Just kids having a race and that.

I get myself safely to the transport mobile. This place IS a fucking transport café, by the way – it's nothing but. It's for lorry drivers. It's basically a car park with a caravan that sells tea and butties. I've been here loads of times, just to sit it out. It's a place I always find weirdly reassuring. No cunt belongs here. There's the huge oil refinery looming over it like a spaceship, mad, irrational jets of gas flame bursting from giant standpipes. Their fire lights up the night sky for a moment, enhancing that feeling of this being alien territory, but neutral and all, too. Safe. I parks away from the lorry drivers, but sit silent with my tea until first light, glad of their company. Not company, to be fair – just glad they was there and that. Driving back, dog fucking tired and thankful that I might at last be able to sleep, I ask myself again where all of this is taking us. Did I, John-Paul Brennan – no mug, by the way, in no sense a soft cunt – did I really think that fucking Bernie was going to rat out his best mate? I did, to be fair.

Friday

Moby
After last night, I'm going to stay low-key. It's got me to realising that we're not bad fellas, us boys. Them little cunts at the home and that – they did deserve the fright that we give them but, thinking on it, they was only playing the hand they was given, know where I'm going. We've been lucky. We've always had one another, right from the start. We've made something decent of ourselves. We should be glad of what we've got. So, apart from the match and that tomorrow, I'm keeping away from society. Until the job's done, I'm strictly a barrio boy. I'll take Benny and Blanco down

to Otterspool and they can run themselves into the ground.

Ratter

Made up, la. I. Am. Made. Up. Elation isn't in it, this is like being told the lottery numbers the day before.

This is how it goes. I don't even have to call him, by the way, he's on to YT first thing. I'm not long back, mind you, just lying there and that, half fucking cabbaged from zero sleep and endless nightmares when the phone goes. Bernie. Oh yes, by the way – it's only Frannie fucking Bernard himself. Sweet like chocolate he is and all, too – full of nice things to say and that, full of praise. Says he's coming up Sunday. Can't make the match tomorrow which is a real pity – Boro Brothers would've wet themselves getting the chance to meet Bernie and kiss his ringpiece and that – but he's deffo back Sunday for the communion and that and he's spending Christmas with his ma and staying over for the funeral. I feel a bit sly about the communion, to be fair, but I know he'd do the same in my place.

He's a pro. Doesn't directly refer to any of what we've spoke about, Ged and that, but it's quite clear he's rooting for JPB on this one. He's not heavy or nosy or nothing – just, knowmean, on my side and that. Supportive. Like, he asks us a little bit about Sunday – just looking out for us and that, wanting to make sure I'm not going to make a cunt of myself over such a big job. I let him in on it. Why shouldn't I? He is the Man, after all. He is the green light for all of us. So I tells him no worries and that. It's covered, by the way. I tell him I've already covered it with the Boro Brothers. Can tell he's impressed, to be fair.

'The whole packet?'

'Is right, Bernie lad, is right.'

He blows a low whistle.

'Them lads can cover that?'

'More than.'

I fucking hope they can at least, anyway. I believe them. They're good for it.

'Tell me when I'm asking too many questions, John-Paul. Are you doubling on this?'

I'm made up with myself. I'm so proud with what I'm telling him.

'Bit more.'

'Jesus.'

'I know.'

Silence from him now. He wants to ask us how much I'm looking to lay it off for. Anyone would. And why can't I tell him, by the way? That money'll be in fucking Zurich getting zapped all around the fucking globe by this time tomorrow. Meeting Bros thisavvy, I am. Wish the fucking Bhoys'd let us give *them* a fucking banker's draft. No way in the world, by the way. No fucking way.

'Twenties, I'm getting.'

Another low whistle.

'I'll see you right, Bern – obviously. Goes without saying.'

I can just see him, all them miles away in London wafting his hand at the imagined insult. He comes back at us in that half-cockney voice of his.

'Fuck that, lad. It's your deal. My end is all taken care of.'

Half knew the cunt'd say that. Would not have offered him otherwise.

Another big silence, then: 'Your lads, then. I mean –
how're they . . . is this *cash*, John-Paul?'

Get that, man! *John-Paul!* I have arrived. I'm enjoying
myself now, to be fair. I can hear the sound of his eyes
being opened up wide to the existence of John-Paul
Brennan, Player. I'm here. I'm in the game. But what
no cunt knows is I'm retiring right after my debut. Not
Bernie, not nobody.

'Fuck that, Bern! D'you know how much twenty
millioni weighs?'

Silence. I've got him.

'They're bringing a draft, aren't they? We're doing it
by banker's draft.'

I never knew relief sounded so loud.

'Nice job.'

'Isn't it, though?'

Now it's my turn to wait and think in silence. I can
do it. The time is right. He don't make it easy, though.
He says fuck all. Quite at home with the long silence
and that, he is.

'So, Bernie?'

Still fuck all. Doesn't exactly put himself out, this
lad.

'About what we was saying.'

Silence. He's play-acting now, the cunt. I know he
is.

'Our Gerrard and that.'

Eternal silence. Then he talks as though we're can-
celling the papers for a week or something.

'How d'you want to play it?'

I tell him.

Ged

Don't matter what time of year, I always prepare the same. It's a bit like a pre-season camp if you will. You've got to get your head right then, God willing, everything else falls into place. And what I do is, I takes my bike up to the start of Meols prom and I ride right across the top of the peninsula, past New Brighton and Seacombe, right down to Woodside and back. It's not that demanding a ride, to be fair. It's pretty flat, most of the way. What it is, though, is stimulating. It's focusing. It tells me why it's OK for me to go out and do what I'm going to do.

From the moment you get past Dove Point you can see right over to Bootle and Crosby and out as far as Formby. You can see the ferries and oil tankers and supply boats and that coming in and out of the port, going about their business. Just like me. And you can see the Dingle once you're past Seacombe. On a good day you can clearly see the Holylands up above the brow – the streets where I lived. I remember coming over here to summer camp. I loved it. Three years on the bounce we come. Barnston Woods the first year then two stays at Heswall. Naughty Boys camp and that, but the priests and the helpers were sound with us. Treated us like decent people and that – they gave a fuck about us, know what I mean. They'd send us up to the little village to get their ciggies and that. Sent us along for the Sunday papers from this half-timber auld shop, and if we got there after about ten bells they'd just leave the papers out in this little bunker and that to collect them. There was a honesty box, by the way, and we weren't even tempted. Bang – in goes the money, every time. I fucking loved it down there – did not want to go home.

From that first summer in Heswall camp, that was where I was going to live. Nothing or no one was going to stop us. When we finally did get the offer accepted on that plot of land and we could finally get started on building the house it was a emotional moment, to be fair – I don't mind admitting it. And that's what we done, by the way – we built our dream house. It is and all, too. It's nothing but. I've got my dream house in Heswall.

Ratter

It's ten minutes since he phoned and I'm still clinging on to the fucking handset like it's a gold nugget. He's said what he's said to me and it just feels – it feels like victory. Whatever, *who*ever I was fighting and that – I've won. I love it. Half wish I was staying, now. I think that YT and Bernie could do good together, to be fair.

I knew he'd go for me, by the way. I knew it. I fucking *knew* it. For a deal like this, in fairness, everything goes out the window. Nothing can stand in the way of business on this scale and even though I knew that would be the case I should never have doubted it. Makes sense and that of course, but you never can tell when it comes to fucking friends and family, knowmean. These lads have known one another for years. For *years*, by the way – and I was starting to think that maybe that couldn't be bought. How wrong I was. All's I needed to know is that Bernie will back us up and he has – he's gone for me – and that is fucking everything. I'm made up, la. Made. Up.

Ged

I've got another car and that. Just an auld bit of a Range Rover – not a boss one, to be fair, but it does do what it says on the label. It's a rough-rider. I use it for this and that – taking our Cheyenne down the stables and that, bung the bikes in the back or whatever. I've rode around the whole peninsula on that bike, but only slow, most of the time. Only for pleasure. Today's all part of the prep. I drive as far as the Green Lodge, parks up and gets the boneshaker out the back. Then I'm off.

Immediately – that's the God's honest truth, by the way, from literally the first few kicks of the pedals I'm taken over. All the shite that surrounds me is kicked away. The wind smashes into my face as I head down to the prom then, as I swing right on to the straight, all I can see is flat beach, zipped-up joggers, the odd lady out trotting on her hoss. Tide's right out, miles away – can just about see the white kick of the breakers. Way in the distance there's the gas rigs and feeder ships and that.

The smell is what gets you most, though. That smell of salty air and seaweed and damp sand takes you right back to easy days, long summer days, fuck all to worry about. I breathe it right in, right down deep inside of myself and hold it there, not wanting to let the moment go. Then I get a fuck-off gust of wind from behind and I hardly have to pedal. The bike is pure flying, propelling myself along past little clusters of auld men playing bowls and out past Dove Point and in minutes I'm on the cycle path and out along Moreton Shore. There's kiddies out there hunting for crabs. Their hands must be frozen, but they don't seem to feel it. No gloves or nothing. One of them's holding the rock up while the other two delve down, grabbing into the shallow water for the peelers.

The only sticky bit comes past the Leasowe dunes where the wind has piled the sand in over the cycle path. That bit is a grueller, to be fair, I'm right up on the pedals to keep myself going but I'm through it and back on the main New Brighton stretch in no time. Past the old pools, the Derby and the site of the big old New Brighton lido where we used to come as kiddies and terrorise all the local lads doing bombs off've the top board. Fucking magic. Whichever cunt decided to pull that old place down wants shooting. What have they done with the site? Fuck all. It's a car park. Fucking councillors, la – they give the people a load of toffee and feel hard done by.

With the wind behind me I gets down past Egremont and on to Woodside in good time. I stop up by the old Monk's Ferry and eat a salmon-paste butty. I think about what Franner and myself have said. I do feel fucking sad, thinking about Ratter when he was a lad and that. He just wanted to be one of us. I looks out across to the homeland. I can see it all clear as if I was watching through a telescope. I can see it all.

I drains my sachet of Lucozade Sport, suck it all up, bin it and then I'm off again, heading back along the coast. I'm driving head down, right into the fucking wind this time. If it's helped speed us down here on the tailwind it's a fucking fight and a half getting back. I'm riding straight into the gale, most of the way. It's not that bad on the flank up to New Brighton, but once you've done that left past the Chelsea and off along the front, you're fucked. It's no good. It's murder. I'm having to stand bolt upright on the pedals to get any kind of motion going. Glick-glick-glick. The pedals are fighting against us. I grips hard and turns my face away from the wind, heaving with everything I can throw into it. I'm not giving up. This is the whole point of the fucking circuit. It has to be completed. You have to complete the entire circuit or the thing means fuck all.

I push and push. This is a fucking grueller, by the way – no two ways about it. My hands are proper starting to ache now. More than any other part of my body though, it's my hands hurting most, to be fair. My arse is stiff, is right – but it's the actual muscles, the pads at the base of my thumbs that are aching like fuck now. I'm back on the stodgy patch by Leasowe beach. This is going to be the worst bit, getting back up on to the flat stretch past Moreton Shore. There's a little hill leading up to it, running alongside the golf course. Nothing more than a bit of a ramp, to be fair, but with this guster howling right in on us, it's going to be murder. Again I strain and stand right up on the pedals, straining every sinew in my legs to make the wheels turn. The wind is lashing my face and hands. Tears stream down my cheeks but I can't wipe them. The snot is starting to run freely, as fast as I can yock it out there's another load funnelling down. Sand is sticking to me, sticking to my tear-stained face, stinging my eyes. My ears are numb with pain from the drill of the wind. It's murder, but I'm getting up the hill. It's like treading water but, bit by bit, leaning forward and willing myself on, I get up the slope and on to Moreton front. My legs are fucking dead. Automatic rhythm keeps them moving but my chest is fucked, my eyes are sore and my hands are so stiff and numb I can hardly hang on. But I've got to complete the course.

The wind is wild now and rain is starting to slat in on us from the sea. Way out there, white horses are starting to whip up the surface. Face down, calves and thighs pumping, I grind on, grind on, grind on against the wind and the rain. It's a proper storm now, by the way. No cunt should be out in this. I'm past the fucking bowling green and I'm making the little turn into that last straight and wham! Fuck off! That is no wind – that is a fucking hurricane. That's come out of nowhere right off've the top of the sea, that has, in five minutes flat. Fucking monster. I have to stand right up straight and jerk the handlebar from side to side just to keep the bike upright. I jerk and jolt and stutter the bike forward. I can hardly breathe. My lungs feel like they've caved in. But still there, still getting tossed around with the seagulls, is that smell of salt and summer and fucking freedom. I make the Green Lodge's car park and I half don't have the strength left to lift the bike into the back. I done it, though. I done it. I never give in. I'm ready.

Saturday

Ged

From now on in, I'm like a spaceman or a mountain climber or something, know what I mean. I feel slightly removed from the real world. It's like I've took a step back. I know what's going to happen and how it's going to happen, it's now just a case of staying cool and that, understanding that it is me that's going to *make* it happen.

A lot has got to happen between now and the job tomorrow, but I'm on it. I'm taking it one step at a time and that. One thing I weren't counting on is pal Franner coming to join us this evening. No doubt it'll all make perfect sense but I do wish the cunt'd've told us a bit more about what's going on, in fairness. Meantime it gives myself a excuse to get out the house. I've told her we've got a guest staying but I can't tell her who it is and that and, in all fairness, she's not that arsed. She's half used to stunts like that now, Debbi is. I tells her I'll shoot up to Tesco's and get some swag in and she goes get some of that Thai red curry and I'm out of there.

Cutting through Dawstone Road my mind is trying to place everything that has to happen in its proper order. Tesco's. Home. Meet lads in the Salisbury. Match. Meet the depot manager at Birchwood for one last go-through then I'll drive down and meet Bernie at the place he's said. Take him to ours. Then tomorrow's tomorrow. Blag should be a piece of piss, in fairness, then it's back to the communion and all's well in the world.

I finds myself a parking spec quite easy, which is saying something, by the way. This place is fucking packed solid of a Saturday morning. They do a good fucking breakfast and that, though – the Tesco's café Magnificent Seven is something I do look forward to of a weekend, in fairness – and there are some very horny-looking Heswall wives to behold and all, too. I love them when it's Saturday morning and they're that bit hung-over – nice and natural and that. Dirty.

I'm just about to step on to that first zebra crossing in the car park when this cunt almost takes my toes off he's going that fast. Takes a while to fucking comprenday what's going on, by the way. Can still hear his bombed-out fucking engine now – can hear his tyres screeching and all, too. What a gobshite! This cunt is driving his shitty Fiesta through a supermarket fucking car park – a car park, by the way, kiddies, auld dears, disabled folk and all of that – and he's racing at fifty mile a hour and he doesn't give a fuck about no cunt but himself. He could've run us over back there. The place is full of auld girls pulling shopping trolleys along, mams with little ones on reins and that, trying to keep a eye on three or four kiddies crossing the way and twats like this come roaring through without a fucking thought for no one. He's dead, mind you. Tell you la, the lad is pure getting it.

I jumps up on to a bollard to see where he's got to and even in saying how he's nearly mown down half the fucking happy shoppers, I can not believe what the cunt is doing now. He's parking in the disabled bay. Not just that, he's parked right across two spaces, just took his shitty little car in at a angle and he don't give a fuck, he's not straightening up or nothing, he's sticking it there, right across two disabled places. He's a fucking dead man.

I legs it over and get to him just as he's getting out the car. Looks a bit caned, to be fair. Not out the game and that, but his eyes are red-rimmed and he looks like he hasn't had that much kip. I square him off and he stands back to see about having a little go-around with myself – and what he sees is that he's in trouble. Thing with me is for a long time now I'm used to fellas looking into my eyes and knowing they can't win. Done it from my first proper fight, in fairness. Cunt was a year older, done something at dinner time and I just waited for him outside school. Just waited, I did, like waiting for time to catch up. I knew what was going to happen – was just a case of *wait*ing for it to happen, know what I mean. I'm half possessed when it comes to a thing like this. I get took over – I'm half like a savage the way I tear into people – but I do half feel bad and that afterwards.

The lad backs off a step, still thinking he's going to slam me. I push him back on to his bonnet. It's not a hard shove, in fairness, but I've got good power in my upper body and he gets it. He flies back. I grabs him and pull him back and put my nut right up close.

'You're having that, then?'

'What you on about! You're off your head!'

He's looking round for help. Thinks people are going to step in. They won't. That is a fact. Will not come near it. But I raises my voice to let them all know who's the good guy here.

'You're going to park right across two disabled spaces, are you?'

'I'm only running in for ciggies!'

I draw my head back so's he can look into my grid and get a idea of what's coming.

'Running, was you? That why you went across all them fucking zebras at fifty? Didn't give a fuck whether some poor auld lady might've been crossing?'

'I wasn't doing anything like fifty! I know how fucking fast I was going!'

Mistake, by the way. He's swore at myself. I tightens my grip.

'You don't know nothing, lar.'

'Fuck off!'

I butt him and he goes down. I drags him back up.

'You want to park in the disabled, do you?'

I gets him by the shoulders and slam his head into the side of his filthy, shitty, horrible little car. That's it for this cunt. He hasn't taken the knock but he's down and fucked and groaning like a sick dog. There's a bit of a intake of breath from the people that's stood around, but they're not about to go and help the bastard. I makes eye contact with the nearest Auld Dear, who looks away.

'Wants to be disabled, this one,' I go.

I goes inside and orders a Mag Seven with extra bacon instead of the egg and pick a *Daily Post* off 've the paper rack. I can see that people half want to come over and go well done for that, by the way. But they're too embarrassed, in fairness. They just stand off and look at us with a bit of fear and a lot of admiration.

So I am properly taken aback when a security fella comes over and tells us that they don't know whether the lad's pressing charges but if he does the whole thing was got on their CCTV. I tell him, listen, lad, don't you be giving myself no toffee – I was just doing your job for you. And, in fairness to the lad, he goes, I know, I hate them lowlifes myself and that but we can't be taking the law into our own hands, can we? Then he half winks at us and goes, good job there weren't no tape in the camera and tells us I might maybe be best off doing one. Is right though – he can't do much more than that, can he, at the end of the day. I do still half feel gutted that it's myself being painted as the baddie here, but I slots the paper and goes back to the Saab anyway.

Moby

One thing I do love about Saturday mornings is that *Soccer AM* on Sky. I like that Hells Bells and that, but the bit I do look forward to is the Soccerette. Different Judy each week and that, comes on in her team's kit and just sits there looking ashamed. Marie and the kids always go down Greatie Saturday mornings and I can just sit there bollock-o and have a good play with the Soccerette. Can't be beat, in fairness.

Ratter

Fair to say that the Ratts is on top of the world. Didn't even have to ask Bros about that other. It was just like some lad repaying a debt – half embarrassed and that, didn't hardly make no reference to it – could've been twenty pound in fairness the way they just slotted us with it. So that's Part One done and dusted and I'm just sat upstairs in the Baa Bar with them enjoying a nice pre-match champagne breakfast and having a nice, relaxed time of it.

The Boro Bros are mad about champagne, by the way. 'More shamp-peen,' they keep going and who's going to argue with them? Jimmy Rico is getting slaughtered by all hands. He's one of these old-stagers that buries his dough in the back garden, he is. Had a big fucking lead-lined crypt dug under his back lawn and he's got it filled with cash. It's legendary, Jimmy's cash crypt. It's bespoke. Just goes and helps himself to a bundle whenever he wants some. But there was that one time when Plod got wind of it and seized a substantial amount of dough off've him. They couldn't prove nothing, by the way, why shouldn't a lad have Brewster's stuffed under his back lawn and that, but they made him wait years before he could get it back. Rico's getting hell over it.

'Didn't know you was a turf accountant,' he's getting. You got to hand it to Rico – he is a hard fucking fella but he can take a joke as well as he takes a dig. He's laughing as much as any cunt. It's Christmas Eve tomorrow and it's fair to say the atmosphere is catching.

'I wanna know who the fucking grass was though!'

The Boro Brothers are loving this. Buying champagne for all kinds, having a laugh and a joke with Liverpool's finest and a consignment of finest Turkish coming their way tomorrow. Happy days.

Moby

You don't expect nothing else, in fairness – our Ged's always on edge so close to a blag. I'm surprised he even come the match in some ways. Takes us to one side and gives us a big mad talking to again, don't go out and that, straight home to bed and all of that, but you can't blame the lad. Must be murder for him. Must come on top good style, specially the night before, know where I'm going.

Ged

If I was a cunt, if I weren't all fucking heart and that I could pull this blag on my tod. No trouble – I could pull it start to finish exclusively on my jack, Eli excluded. That's the God's honest truth – there is fuck all to this one, by the way. Quite why Soft Joe here has to complicate life and get all hands involved is a mystery, in fairness. I'm just a nice fella at the end of the day. Lads like Moby and Spit and that, they need a few bob. They always need a few bob in their back bin, specially this time of year.

Course my fucking insider, the fella from the depot, is now badly khaziing it. Convinced that his run of good luck with these is about to come to a gruesome end, he is. But I've just told him relax – think about it logical. It's Christmas Eve, we'll pull it off no problem and the chips'll have vamoosed long before Old Bill even gets wind of it. There'll half be a bit of heat on him for a few days – he knew that. It will be plain that there *is* a insider somewhere down the line, that goes without saying. But they can not prove who that is. So long as every cunt sings off've the same hymn sheet, Plod'll pure have to sack it. They can't go nowhere with it. They're going to think it's the lad himself, by the way, the courier and that – but they can not prove it. They can't. Everyone just has to keep a cool head and do it just like we said and there is no problem, end of. I pats the auld boy on the bonce and gives him a bit of a wink and sends him on his way.

So now that's done it's Get Franner time. Cunt's more paranoid than myself, he is. He's give us directions to this disused lodge on the edge of Delamere Forest. I thought I knew every fucking desolate spot within shooting distance of the motorways, but this is a new one on myself. If it's any good I will keep it in mind for future reference, mind you.

It's easy enough to find, in fairness. I just turns off by Hatchmere and you can see it, auld sandstone lodge and that, bit *Scooby Doo*, to be fair. There's a big long drive, dead, dead straight and all too, leading off through the forest. Must've been a big mad country estate at one time, but it all looks as though it's seen better days from what you can make out in this light.

No sign of Franner, mind you. It's that fucking cold I keeps the engine running while I listens to all the blue shite phoning in to complain about their latest fucking pasting. I do like the radio phone-ins – fuck knows what makes people want to pick up the blower and call it in, though.

I'm getting bored now. I switches to Radio Five to catch some more heartbroken maniacs taking it all out on that Littlejohn but I am half watching the clock by now. Franner's never late, in fairness. Early to a fault, if anything, by the way. For a lot of people, twenty minutes late is on time but for Franner this is unusual. Motorways might've been bad and that but he would've phoned to let us know. I checks my mobile for any messages that might not have lit up on the display. Nothing. Fuck all. He's just late is all.

Then up ahead, I sees lights approaching. Car head-lights. What I can't make out though is why they're coming from that direction – from the forest and that. Nothing's gone past us. They would've had to already be there. I think hard on it but I can't make out why Franner'd lay low in the forest for twenty minutes just watching myself sat here like a soft cunt – if it is him, by the way. Can't see what car it is yet. Could be kids and that. Could be shaggers. Could be any cunt. I feel for my little popgun.

The lights get to about a hundred foot away and then the car stops. Looks to me very much like Franner's Jag – don't get too many cars that shape around Delamere Forest of a Saturday evening is my guess. The lights flash us on. I don't get it. I stay where I am, but my hand is properly gripped around the pistol now. Not even dead certain that this cunt is my man. He flashes again. Can only mean that he wants us to get out and go on over to him. Can not read the fat boy's play, to be fair. Why's he wanting myself to walk over to him? Don't like it. Do not like it one bit. Why's he want myself out in the open?

I'm starting to think along the lines of vacating the area when he flashes again, impatient this time. Flash, flash, flash and that. Used to people doing what he says, in fairness. I still don't like it. I'm not having it. I screws my eyes up to try and see for sure if it's

282

Franner's jalopy. Fucking looks it – looks very much like his mad bell-head behind the wheel and all, too. Flash, flash, flash! Flash, flash, flash! Ah, fuck this for a lark – let the cunt try his fucking best! I shuts off the engine and gets out. I wouldn't do this for no other cunt, by the way, but Francis is a weird twat at the best of times – tend to find it's easier just to play along with the fat bastard, then we can all go home.

I gets about forty feet away and suddenly the car starts moving towards us. I hops off the track pronto, not at all fucking sure what's going on now. This is beyond me. Makes no sense at all. The car speeds up. It's coming right at us. If it doesn't hit myself then it'll hit a tree – then it swerves and stops. Pulls up right next to us and out pops Franner's big head.

'Sorry about that, musher. The old minces ain't so perfect in this kind of light. Wanted to be sure it was you and that.'

'What if it weren't me?'

He chuckles.

'Would've had to pop you, you cunt!'

We laugh and have a little tussle through the open window.

'Come 'ead, will you, I'm fucking freezing out here. Are you following us or what?'

'Nah. I'll leave this back up there. Should be sweet. Follow on behind but just stop and wait for us when I turns off to left. I'm just going to stick the car in a little place down there.'

That's how it goes. I wait five minutes for him, he hops in, apologises for keeping us waiting and that, says he had to make extra sure he weren't getting tailed and all of that. What he tells us next, though, is the weirdest thing I've heard in a long, long time. And the most shocking, the most upsetting thing, too. There's no two ways about it – it's sad, what he tells myself. So fucking sad that it makes me want to forget all about tomorrow and just sack the whole fucking thing – all of it.

Ratter

Can't put my finger on it. I was feeling great. I don't now, though. I feel like shite. I left the Boro Brothers in the Cream gabbing on to some *Brookie* babes – I know one of them to let on to and that, but I don't follow the show, to be fair. I think they half don't mind that, by the way. Think it's refreshing for them not to be fielding all kinds of Q&A, knowmean. Not that fucking Bros fit into that profile, mind you. Pure on their case, they were, made up that they was in company with three good-looking girls from off 've the telly. Big smiles all over their grids, getting their picture took and all of that. Left them to it, I did.

I got took over by this feeling that I wanted to go home and make love to Margueritte. But then I thought no, that's only going to complicate matters. I went down to the river and just thought to myself how there's been ships and gear of one sort or another took up and down that water for centuries. Significant cargoes and that – oil, sugar, spices, everything. Tomorrow's significant cargo will be my own, in fairness. A twenty-million-pound cargo and all, too. A little place for YT in Liverpool's long and glorious merchant history. I should be made up. But all's I'm doing is sitting looking at the cold moon glinting on the water and feeling like jumping in. We live to fight another day, though. And tomorrow is another day, by the way. Tomorrow is The Day.

Ged

I can hear the cunt snoring his fat head off. Doesn't have no problems with his own conscience, well. He was only up there a minute and next thing the walls was shuddering like a twister had hit big.

I'm sat here with a glass of Baileys that I haven't so much as pecked at, and I'm going over and over everything Francis has said to us. I'm trying to get it all in order, the order that he give it us and that, so's it makes sense – but whatever way you rack it up you can't make no sense of betrayal. He's laid it bare for myself – the whole rotten fucking picture of Liverpool low life that Ratter has gotten himself into. I can't, won't, don't want to get my head around it, but if Franner's even half right then this is the story:

Ratter's a smack dealer. No, worse – he's not a *dealer*. Ratter fucking *imports* the fucking smack. He's a big hitter – brings the shite into the fucking city, the whole nine yards, if you will. And he's in with Mikey fucking Green, no less. None other a mensch than Alan Stanton give him this info, by the way, so for me it's all still double dubious. Stanton is not a man, end of. Stanton is a bully. Stanton is a wretch. Franner knows this, but he says that Stanton is also – get this – one of his own. I'll say it again – Alan gobshite Stanton is part of the unit. Could've fucking slayed me with that one, by the way. Myself, I tends to think of solid fellas like Stratford Marty and that when I think of Franner's firm, not shite like that fucking no-mark.

He's just a eyes and ears and that, nothing big time, but here's the thing. Stanton's been on Ratter's tail for a while. Franner's been having Ratter looked at, by the way, because there's been half a feeling that he's sweetening his own deals, bit like pub landlords and that, if you will. They'll take a few kosher kegs from the brewery just to keep them off've the stoop then they'll get a load of cheap swill from one of the lads that does the beer runs. Franner can't reconcile Ratter's lifestyle with the amounts of dope he takes off've his people. He says he can only conclude that he's buying bad gear off've no-marks. He's set Stanton to watch his every move and he's set dicky guys on to him to offer him tasty deals and all of that. They never come up with nothing, by the way, until the other night. Downer. Fucking sickener. Still now can not get anywhere near comprehending the thing, but the bottom line is this: Ratter's fingered myself as Numero Uno on a upcoming beak deal. There's more: he's plonked myself right into the lap of who, by the way? Downer, lar. Pure fucking killer this – Mikey fucking sad-lisp and smiler Stanton is who my brother has give myself up to. Is this a low? This is fucking devastating, lar. One of our own – a lad that we took in and brought up and looked after – has sat down and come up with this. He's set myself up to get zapped. Can't believe him. Pure can not get my head around this at all. Tomorrow, if Ratter's plot goes true to form, I myself will arrange to meet him to divvy up the blag and walk right into a bullet wind.

That's about as much as Franner's told myself. He couldn't bring himself to go on. Could not speak, to be fair – them slovenly eyes of his started filling up and you could see he was fucking chocker. Kept swallowing and that then he just waved his big fat arms at it and went upstairs. Weren't so bad that it kept the cunt awake though, by the way.

I tries to sip some of the Baileys. It don't taste like

Baileys. Don't taste of nothing. Franner's snoring is fucking astonishing. Even at a time like this, there's something comic-book funny about it. He knows myself well, Franner. He knew full well that I'd want to settle this right now, one on one. He's tried to talk us through that particular one – the knock-on effect it'd have if I just go right ahead and do it – right through Mikey and all of them scheming desperados. Do I give a fuck? I must do, 'cos I've just sat there and listened to that fat nobody, the fucking gopher – the run-around, by the way – telling us how it's going to be. Him telling myself, if you will.

He's told us he's got a better way ahead. Wanted his kip and that of course. Just another day for Franner, if you will. Fat cunt says he'll run us through it line by line in the morning. As per fucking usual he won't tell myself any more than he thinks I need to know. I've just sat there, nodding my head. Numb, I felt. I weren't taking nothing in. Just nodding my head and that, numb, dumb, nowhere. But I'm coming to now. I'm coming round. And I'm thinking that I'll just get over to Ratter's now. Fuck Franner. Fuck how this'll upset his fucking seedy cartel. I don't give a fuck about that. If anything, by the way, I hope I do bring the whole fucking thing crashing down. Do not give a fuck. That's not to do with myself, all that carry-on. What *is* to do with me is this. Ratter. A lad that's been calling himself Brennan. I won't punch him or shoot the horrible cunt – I'll wring his fucking neck. I'll look into his eyes and throttle the life out of the wretch as he wriggles and writhes like a snake in my hands. I puts the glass down and looks for my car keys.

Ged

He may well snore like a cunt but he's one fuck of a light sleeper. I'd just got the porch door open and there he is in his undies, big fat lazy head growling at us.

'Fuck d'you think you're going, Ged?'

I'm not in the mood. He forgets who he is, sometimes.

'Fucks it got to do with you, you cunt? Get back to your bed.'

Way the lad reacts, he makes us feel sly. His face and that, properly hurt – not even shocked, by the way, he's pulled up short, wounded. Hurt, he is. I feel last. I go over and give him a playful little slap, grab a hold of his cheeks and look into his eyes. He knows what I'm saying to him. I'm saying sorry and that, but I'm telling him he can't come back here and sit with me and try and kid himself he's No. 1. He might mean something to his own kind but he knows that don't apply with myself. Now, I don't want to rub in. I love the big, sleepy-eyed dickhead but I'm telling him now just to leave well alone. And I'm telling him nicely. I gives his cheeks a chub and puts my arm around him.

'Never can sleep the night before a heist and that. Might just go for a little drive.'

Them fucking eyes slipping all over my face, like he's spotting things he's never seen before.

'Come 'ead, then. I'll keep you company.'

Got to hand it to the cunt, he's good. He's got that half menacing, I–am–a–player–do–not–fuck–with–me thingy off to a T. If you didn't know him from back then, you'd take him for the real thing. Well, he is and that – just not to myself, know what I mean. I do him the honour of taking him serious, though.

'Francis – I can't let this go, you know.'

'You've got to, kidder. You've got to.'

'No. I haven't got to do nothing. What I've got to do is finish the cunt off.'

'He'll get it. He will get it. But trust me, please, Gerrard, I'm fucking begging of you – if you go running in like this now you're going to bring down a whole house of cards, lar. Untold, it'll be.'

He spies a frog or a fucking spaceship just to the left of my nose. His fucking droopy eyes are looking just past my nose – just to the *side* of it, mind you. Now they're slowly, slowly moving to the hairs between my eyebrows. Fucking irritating, it is. I'm getting fucking bored of him. Fucking Fat Francis, by the way – Frannie Bernard, the fat lad that had to go in goal, stood here calling the SP. Don't think so, mind you.

'Tell you what, Franner. This is boring now. You've got your thing and I've got mine. I'm walking out of here now and I'm going round to his and I'm going to pop the cunt, yeah? There's fuck all you can do about that. D'you hear what I'm telling you, lad? I don't give a fuck about what your mates in fucking London and fucking Dublin and fucking . . . *Colombia* has got to say. You should know me better, lad. I don't give a fuck about them. They can come to my fucking front door if they want. You know the score, lad.'

Franner looks down. Now the boy's worried. Can see this is slipping away from him. He looks up again and suddenly he isn't Mr Big no more.

'Please, kidder. I'm begging you. This is going to be very bad for me. It's a disaster. Just listen to what I've got in mind.'

Lad looks desperate, in fairness. In that half second I

know it's not going to be me doing this thing myself. I push the front door shut and go back into the living room. I puts my hand on his shoulder.

'Tell us what's on your mind. Then I'll decide.'

Franner tries not to look too fucking grateful, but the relief is seeping out of his pores – along with a lot of perspiration. I lifts his chin so's he's looking directly at myself – his sludgy eyes on my angry beams.

'*I'll* decide, yeah, Francis?'

Franner nods. And we gets down to it.

Councillor Bennett

I feel like just tucking the girl up and telling her a story. But the story would be this:

'It's a sordid world we live in. You must take what you can, whenever you can take it. It's dog eat dog, darling – and only the cleverest dogs survive.'

And she's far too pretty and far too stupid to waste stories on, anyway.

Ged

He's starting to do my head in, Franner. Keeps on and on at us. Got this little pad out and that and he's scribbling down every little detail.

'What's your arrangement with Ratter? For tomorrow and that?'

'Same as normal. I phones them all at seven bells and gives them the story. Why?'

He nods. He seems excited, like that was exactly what he wanted us to say. He's still eyeing us, dead shady, *dead* reluctant to tell myself even the tiniest detail, even though this is all about myself and how my fucking brother is going to have me killed tomorrow. He looks at us long and hard. From the way that I look back at him, Franner knows that I will beat it out of him if it comes to it. This is what he tells us.

'Ratter's not going to be answering his phone, kidder. His intention is that he'll miss that call. He don't want to hear the story at seven bells. He needs a excuse so's he can hand you over to Mikey and co . . .'

'Does he really think we're that fucking stupid?'

He holds his hands up for shush.

'He won't be answering his phone. He might not even have it switched on but just keep calling him, yeah?'

In spite of the gravity and that, Franner's accent sounds mad. Never quite made his mind up who he is.

'Does your phone withhold ID?'

I nods. Yeah.

'So it'll show up just as a missed call, then. No matter, eh – he'll know it's you calling him, obviously, that time of day. Just keep phoning the cunt. Phone at five-minute intervals, like as though you really need him, really have got to get in touch.'

'Why all the fuss and that?'

Franner's starting to look impatient to be fair.

'All's I'm saying to you is that, from your end, you just make it real. You act like you have not got a fucking clue about what he's been up to, yeah? Far as you're concerned, you need him for the job, you do not know where the fuck the cunt has got to and you are genuinely starting to shit yourself about it. You keep phoning the bastard . . .'

I'm starting to see it, now. I'm starting to nod, in spite of myself.

'What then?'

'He'll phone you when he's ready. When it's just

that bit too late for him to reasonably get to wherever you're all meeting or whatever it is you cowboys fucking do . . .'

'Aye-aye!'

He's back in his stride, now. He's the kiddie again.

'Wherever you're meeting Moby and the team, Ratter'll phone you too late for him to get there on time. Trust me. Half blow up at the snake, go mad, call him all kinds of shitcunt and tell he's fucking finished and that. Then climb down a bit. Let him apologise and talk you round. Then you tell him – you tell Ratter to meet you at the car park at the bottom of Riversdale Road, yeah?'

'Otterspool?'

He nods and goes: 'It's Christmas Eve. There'll be no cunt around there. We'll make sure there's no cunt round there.'

'OK, I tell him that – but the cunt isn't showing up, is he?'

'No. Mikey Green and Dajun and no end of Granby heads will be there, instead.'

'Stanton?'

He gives us that same impatient look. I hold my hands up. Sorry, and that. Go 'ead.

'Al has got to be there so that Mikey don't smell a rat. But he knows what's happening. Al can take care of himself. Put it this way – he's being fucking very well rewarded to take care of himself.'

'He's going to pop Mikey?'

'Not as such, no. We need to make it look a whole lot more convincing than that, in fairness. An awful lot more convincing.'

He's lost us. Have not got a fucking Scooby where he's going with this. And he knows that, by the way,

Francis does. He knows this is all way beyond my ken. And that's just how he likes it.

'Just suffice it to say that Stanton is working off a debt. He knows what he's doing.'

I let all of this filter in.

'So Mikey's there, expecting my good self and a crate load of tartan. Then, soon as I turns up, him and his merry men are going to shoot us to bits and take the goodies. That right?'

He nods. Cunt is looking fucking smug though, by the way. I half feel like giving him a dig, just to show him. But I don't. Instead, I gives him the question I've been dreading asking him.

'So, Franner . . . who's playing myself?'

'What?'

'Who's going to be Gerrard Brennan. That's the whole point and that, isn't it? I'm the main course, aren't I?'

He's not looking that comfy, in fairness. I just carry on with it.

'Listen though, lad – all kinds may well turn out at Otterspool and that, but me and Moby – end of the day lad, I'm off to their Liam's communion being a godfather, end of.'

Now he does look wary. I swear I seen the lad gulp just then. He goes for it, trying to sound chipper, trying to sound like this is a wheeze.

'No, mate. This is where it gets a bit fucking otherwise. You ain't gonna like it but believe me, my old brain is tired trying to think of a way around it. All's I can say is that I done it for you, Ged. This ain't nothing to do with me or my interests.'

He gives us a big mad dead meaningful stare.

'This is me trying to pay you back.'

Half gone cockernee again now, he has. Looking at us dead intense, he is, tears in them eyes now, proper filling up and that. I'm trying to work out what can be so bad that it deserves his best Des O'Connor grid.

'Go 'ead then, lad – who you sending down as the oppo for Mikey's men?'

He drops his head.

'Jimmy Rico's brought a fuck of a lot of trouble on himself, kidder.'

Scouse again now.

'Fuck of a lot of damage, he's caused. Brought no end of glare on all of us, in fairness. This gives him a chance to go out with a bit of pride and that. And who knows? The odds is better than fifty-fifty. It's not fucking *Lock, Stock*, is it?'

I'm not hearing this. I'm not squeamish, by the way, but this is fucking way above my head. I do, properly, feel queasy. Not just because this fat cunt's stood in front of myself proposing to send some of the lads in as live bait, by the way, live fucking chess – it's because all of this has been going on around my head and I haven't had a fucking sniff of it. I'm fuck all, by the way. I know nothing, I see nothing, I hear fuck all. I'm the fucking History Man. I haven't got a lot of time for Rico as it goes, but end of the day the lad's one of our own. He's cut from the same cloth as me and Franner and now he's telling me this.

'You fucking what?'

'I know, la. But don't brood on it. He's sound with it. We've had a fucking good talk, me and Jimmy have, trust me. He knows he's been foolish. He badly wants to do this for you, Gerrard – and he fucking *hates* Mikey Green. He's half looking forward to this . . .'

I'm looking into the eyes of a lad I know well, who I've known from when we was boys and who was never, ever capable of having a fight or hurting no cunt. And he's evil. He's pure filth. He's stood here in my house telling us that he's sending some of the lads to almost certain death tomorrow. He's sending them into a gun battle where they are the fucking target. If they're very lucky they get away with bullets in their arses. And he's sanctioned this. He's saying this is for me. He might even half believe that it is for me. But we both know why he's done it. We both know. I turn my back on him.

'Get out, will you, Francis.'

'Done it for you, Ged.'

'Say it again and I will slam you.'

He just looks dead sad and goes back upstairs.

Sunday

Ged

Have not felt so fucking weird in a long time, to be fair. Franner just called himself a minicab and fucked off. I was changing my mind every two seconds – could not decide what to do next. I never hardly sleep the night before a blag anyway, but this is no way to prepare. This is fucking madness. I called Trudi straight away and goes to her here y'are, find out from the girl at Heswall where that cab's gone that's just picked up from ours, will you? Didn't take her a minute. They all know each other, all the cab-firm girls. Delamere, it were. So he's gone back to the place where we was before, up near Delamere Forest. Soft cunt's kipping in his car. But I never went after him. I wanted to think. He never did tell myself what was to become of John-Paul. We never got around to that. Suddenly all of the fight was gone out of me. All of the anger, too. All's I was was defeated – that's how I felt. Beat. I went to bed but I never slept.

The first thing I wanted to do this morning is cancel the job. I'm grieving, I'm knackered, I'm down and very nearly out and I pure do not have the heart for this – maybe not ever now, by the way. But the second thing I realised is that I can not undo this job, neither. Too much riding on it.

So I gets hold of Moby on the phone straight away and I tells him look, lad, just sit in your house until I come for you and do not answer the phone. Specifically, do not speak with Ratts. If he phones you wanting details of where the thing is happening and you do find yourself being stupid enough to get rapping with him, tell him you haven't heard nothing yet. Say fuck all, I tells him. Say fuck all.

This is tension I never normally get, by the way. Come the big day I am clear as a bell, finely tuned, fucking nerveless. I'm more tense at a fucking Cup Final, in fairness. But the danger now is that I am not thinking about our own little jobbie at all. Can not focus on it, to be fair. All's that's happening is that my mind keeps wandering back to the other thing. Him.

Fat Francis

I can understand Gerrard being thingy with me. He'll come round to seeing it how it really is. If I'd let him just fly out and zap Ratter, what sort of mess does that leave me to clean up, well? A big mess, to be fair. There's the Mikey thing. There's Rico. There's the Bhoys with a eight-million-pound bag and no buyer, not to mention two fucking pikeys from Middlesbrough who are running round the city looking for the gear they've paid for. Not pretty. Wore my old bonce out working out the solution, but I think we're getting there. I've had a nice breakfast at Mottram Hall with my friends from the Emerald Isle. We're all quite clear on where the land lies regarding naughty John-Paul Brennan. That has now been sanctioned. And we were always in agreement that something'd have to be done about Jimmy Rico. Can't say it didn't give me a little bump though, little jolt of something when I got clearance. Who's laughing now, Jimmy Richardson? Been a long time la, but a promise is a promise – especially one you make to yourself. Same with Mikey G and all. Lad's a cowboy. Fucking dirty bike robber, that's all's he is. Big bully no-brains, the pair of them. They deserve everything they fucking get, and by dressing this up as a spat, a black-on-white thing, it'll turn the glare back away from us boys.

So it's just these Middlesbrough kiddies, really. We're not sure whether to give them a chance to show us what they can do, or whether we just stiff the cunts regardless and keep the gear. We'll be driving over to Liverpool in a minute. We can talk about it some more in the car. Ged'll realise, once all the dust settles. I done all this for him.

Ratter

Excitement bordering on the khaziing myself. One of Mikey fucking Green's many fucking brats nearly blew the whistle on us this morning. I had to leave it until the very last minute to plant the drugs. Had to cover every eventuality, didn't I? Wouldn't do for Plod to arrive on the scene and find two sets of rudeboys all just stood off've each other, would it? Where's the crime in that, by the way? Now it's my fervent hope and expectation that the moment these mortal enemies catch sight of each other they'll start squeezing triggers, but one can not rely upon that. So just in case, I've taped a kilo of OK-grade smack under Mikey's motor. Worth a few bob, in fairness, but well worth it if it gets that cunt out of the picture. Lid will be given hefty clues as to the whereabouts of that pack. Did half fucking brick it though when I got back up from under his charabanc and his little girl's stood there asking us what I'm doing. It passes through my head that I should swipe the kid and bundle her away where she can't say nothing. But then I looks up and sees a cat on the wall down the road. I tells the little girl I'm looking for my kitty cos she ain't had no milk today. She smiles and says 'aaah' and that's that. I've got a way with kiddies, I have.

And if I'd had any last trace of sympathy or regret for our Gerrard, by the way, it's gone up in smoke now that fucking blagtime's arrived. Cheek of the twat, mind you. The fucking arrogance of one little fella with snow-white hair! So highly does he value my own contribution to this exercise that he's only just phoned now to give us the fucking details. Phoned twice he has, already. Not that he's left no fucking details, which is a fucking bore, by the way. Just left us a number where I've got to call him, urgent. Pity, that. I was looking forward to stiffing the cunt on his own private hotline. Wanted him to properly know that it was none other than YT on his case. Wanted to give the fucking number to Lid so's he could bamboozle the twat into giving his own game away. No worries, though. This'll do just as well. Fucking panic in the cunt's voice, by the way! Where are you, where are you, where are you? Have you overslept and that? Overslept, by the way – last time I overslept my ma was in her twentieth hour of labour.

But he's a fucking gobshite, Ged is. He's a class-one prick. He's phoning like I'm a arsehole that can't be trusted with nothing. Fuck him, well. I'll give it another half-hour and once they're on their way I'll give it the sob story. Cunt better give it up, by the way. And he will, of course. He fucking well will. He's a honourable man, our Gerrard. Fucking Robin Hood, by the way. This is him giving us our Chrimbo dropsie and that. Fucking gobshite.

Ged

There's still something missing, something nagging at us from the last few days or so. I know I should pull the plug on today, but I've got a fucking death wish now. If I'm going to get ambushed, if I'm going to get hoist, whatever – I want to know who done it. I want to see what happens. It's one of them where you've just to carry right on. You've got to believe in what you're doing and the way you've gone about it otherwise the other side has won. If I gets nicked, if I gets shot, if I gets killed, then at least I'll know. I won't be sat here suspecting all kinds of friends and foes of doing this and that. I'll know. That's how I've lived my life up until now. It's been myself calling the shots. Now I'm sat here dwelling on Franner. If it was him behind all this, he would've got us in that forest, wouldn't he?

Time to go get Moby, anyway. All's I'll be telling Mobe and Spit, by the way, is that things has gone pear-shaped. Moby'll be sound with that, mind you.

He'll half be made up because of his do later on and all of that. Spit might spy his arse a bit, thinking he's lost out on a drink. But I can't get the lads involved in a thing where I don't know the outcome, know what I mean. I can't bring them in when I'm not even sure what's going to become of them. How could I look their Marie and the kiddies in the eye if Moby got shot and I never, or he got hoist or whatever? I'll do it solo. I'll fucking pull it off and all too, and I'll go along to that communion and when we gets to the Britannia I'll weigh them in and explain about Ratter. Things should be a lot clearer by then, God willing.

Ratter

Otterspool, hey? Interesting. Might just be able to watch Señor Lid making mass arrests from the sloop. Might get to see a gunfight if the timing's right. Talk about live entertainment, mind you. Gerrard has said eleven so if I should tell Lid, say, quarter past, there should be some bodies for him to bag up by then.

Ged

Spoke to the cunt. Called us up just like Franner said he would, all apologies for missing the blag, cool as anything. Cold as fuck. Not a trace of anything from the cunt. Weirdest fucking thing I've ever done just carrying on with it, acting like I knew fuck all. Properly went mad with him, I did, give him fucking loads about letting the lads down, getting his act together and then I let myself get talked around. I give it all up to him good style, told him where the place was, where to meet myself and the boys and all of that, Otterspool and that. Fucking horrible, it were. He just lapped it all up, cold as death. How did he ever come to hate myself like that?

And putting the phone down on him, I'm overcome with a terrible grief. This is the real thing, the grief we feel for a loved one passed away. And it's him I feel it for. Because now I've spoke to the cunt, now I've got that last barrier out the way there's no more denying it. I know full well what Franner's going to do to him. I know what my brother has got coming to him.

Moby

I'm proud as fuck, to be fair. The carriage does look fucking cracker and Marie is pure filling up. She looks a fucking doll and all, too. Could half give her one here and now, if there wasn't kiddies in the carriage with us and that. All the neighbours is lined up to wave us off, as cold as it is this time of the morning. Even fucking McKenna's there, giving us a nice big wave, in fairness, big cheery smile on his grid. Don't half feel sly on them now. Should not have listened to her, by the way – I should've invited fucking next door, no two ways about it. When you sees them all lined up like that, genuinely made for you and that, it half does make you want to fill up. I wouldn't live nowhere else. The Southern Neighbourhoods is where it's at, la.

McKenna

Look at the phoney cunt wiping a imaginary tear from his fucking eye. Bob Monkhouse, he is. He's in fucking bits, the phoney! Thinks he's the Duke of Edinburgh, waving to us cunts down here. Kip on him in a white fucking suit, by the way – looks like fucking Soft Joe, he does. And the state of their fucking Marie! Grid on her, fucking orange sunbed tan grinning away like she's had ten tablets. You'd think the fucking *Hello!* was here. And what the fuck is the story with that white dress? Tell you, la, that is one twat of a outfit. She looks like a fucking Christmas cake – one that's been shagged repeatedly, mind you. Not by him though, the soppy cunt. Pair a gobshites!

Eli the Mensch

To think I doubted this boy as well. Tssch! This is extremely good quality merchandise – better than he had led me to expect. This is a Celeron chip, which is still an immensely saleable chip. I think I can better my price on this. I'm saying nothing to the boy right now, but if I succeed I will of course pass on some extra. If only everything in life could be so easy as this.

Ged

The job was a pure roll-over, by the way. I worry about myself. I'm no different to our Ratter. I just turn my mind off to things. It was like all of that with Ratter before on the phone, it never happened. I spoke to him. I went out. I done the job. Easy fucking peasy and all, too. Only hard bit was trying to make the lad take a slap. He's going: 'It's Christmas!' and that, and I'm going: 'You've just been robbed, you cunt.'

He half run away from us at one point and I'm thinking: 'Here y'are, this is where it really does go Pete Tong.'

This is where we get have-a-go heroes, by the way – that thirty seconds that weren't in the script, where the lad gets stage fright or whatever. Often happens, by the way. At least three to one something will happen that weren't meant to happen. So in doing that he'd got myself that bit mad and it weren't that hard doing what had to be done from that point in. Cunt was still lying there sparko when I got off with the gear. So that won't do his story no harm.

But dropping off with Eli just now, that has just dislodged one big fuck-off penny with myself. That's it – I know what the thing is that was eluding myself before. It's Lid, isn't it? Eli's already told myself as much, told us days ago, day of the kiddies' party, didn't he? And Ray Cole confirmed and all, too, in a way – told us Lid was looking at us again, anyway. That's what it is, then. Ratter's brought Lid in on this and all too, hasn't he? And fucking Franner don't know that. He's got his set piece with Alan Stanton and Mikey and that, but he knows fuck all about Plod. Far as Francis is concerned, what's going to happen is that Jimmy Rico and that are going to walk into a cul-de-sac where they're expecting bullets over Broadway with Mikey's posse. Mikey, on the other hand, is expecting none other than myself. The very last grid he'll be expecting is the ugly mug of Jimmy Richardson. So they're all going to be stood gawping at one another like soft cunts trying to work it out and it could well be that Plod gatecrashes the biggest non-event of the year. Mikey is crazed enough that he'll just start popping the first white heads he sees, no back answers, by the way, but I'd pure forgot about Lid. With Plod there, Rico's got a chance. He's got a good chance.

Ratter has not. Ratter is getting it. And for all that the cunt is a wretch and a lowlife, I can't just walk on by. I can't square this thing that somebody is going to go out and do something to my brother. Me and him are over, we're through – but no one else is going to do that to him. I'm thinking fast. If the twat's not answering his phone today, there's only one fella stands a chance of getting to him. Lid. I calls Eli straight away.

Eli the Mensch

I myself do not wish to call Martyn Lid any more times than is strictly absolutely necessary. Gerrard tells me this is emergency so what do you do? I call him once. I call him twice. I gets his voice telling me he ain't him. I got a flight appointment to keep. These private slots, you know, you can't fuck about here and there. You land when they tell you land, you fuck off out when they say go. I try Lid one last time and maybe hint to him that this is about Gerrard Brennan. That should bring him to his blower. If not, I don't know – maybe I can try one more time from the island – maybe it is too late by then. What are you going to do?

Ratter

To say that old Lidders is overjoyed with my information is drastically a understatement. He is beside himself with happiness. He is wetting himself, to be fair, wanting it all to be now, now, now. He's been quite stand-offish, in fairness, hasn't exactly been making twinkling eye contact. But now he's twigged the magnitude of all of this and what it can do for him personally, he's all smiles. He thanks YT and wishes there were something he could do in return and I just shrugs and says who knows? Maybe one day. I tells him that I fancy nothing more now than a little R&R on the river and begs my leave of the smarmy, gimlet-eyed, money-obssessed bastard.

In leaving them, I shakes hands with the councillor for what I know to be the last time and he does not.

He's already trying to screw another punyani date out of JPB, having only just had that little honey I put him on to last night. I'm looking at auld Bennett with the dancing eyes of the guy that knows something the other cunt does not. I could not be happier now, by the way. That little pre-match lowie is gone with wind. I feel on top of the world again. I am the smartest, cunningest, most clued-up cunt in all of this city and I am stood here pulling strings that no one nowhere could ever begin to guess about. It's not about who can have a fight no more – it's about who's got the best plan. They'll get on to that one day, them deadheads – shame that I won't be there to see their gormless kites when they do fucking finally tumble to old Ratter's plan. So fantastic does this rush of power and self-esteem feel that I digs into my pocket and fishes out that number for Lid anyway, in spite of the cunt not being able to hide his iffiness with old JPB.

'Might have some fun with that. Dunno. It's just for his missus and binlids to call him sort of thing. Emergencies and what have you. Might have a bit of a laugh with him at zero hour, what?'

Lid's cackle is as depraved as my own, to be fair. I tells him the Misty thing and he's double demented, clapping his hands together and showing his rotten teeth. Glee isn't the half of it, by the way. Loves it that he's somehow got this number courtesy Honest George, one lad he never did quite finger. He's fucking ecstatic about that. Looks at the number and places it neatly under the ashtray, and then he's stiff as a board again. Just like that. Very uncomfortable with YT, he is, in spite of his best efforts. He'd rather I just done one and, quite honestly, I'm not a lad that outstays my welcome.

Still, no regrets and that. All's I has to do now is toddle down to the sloop, ease out into the balmy waters of auld mother Mersey and go net myself some of her abundant bounties. I'll drop for Bros at Birchwood as per Operation Offski and then one slightly battered Hyundai Coupé will be seen headed at speed for the airport. Which airport, though? Only the Ratter knows. While his lovely wifie sleeps and his family is butchered, John-Paul Brennan will slip his ties and that, tragically, will be that. The final curtain. The last cut. The end of the lines – boom–boom!

Martyn Lid

What the fuck is that halfwit telling me? It's a typical Eli message, i.e. no info at all. Way too long in the tooth to leave anything on tape that could be used in court against him. I'd ignore the senile bastard but there's a chance, a good chance, that he knows something. Reptile that he is, you can't question Eli's nose. I play it back once more.

'Martyn. This is important. It is Christmas Eve, I know, I apologise, but that tells you how important. Could be there is change in the weather. Roads might need gritting. JP need to speak with GB. Over.'

Over. So quaint. Such a doddery, innocent old cove. Like fuck! And of course, I can not get hold of the old bastard now. Answerphone messages have been the bane of my life and are just one more thing I shall be glad to escape from. If I ever get away. If this fucking thing comes off. Oh fuck, fuck, fuck – I despise this job. I fucking hate it.

Eli's message'll be something key, of course. And there's fuck all I can do about it. The greaseball's well gone. I was glad to see him go. If it isn't bad enough having to break bread with filth like him and having to pretend to like him and come across like I'm on his level, I'm now being told that the play he's just given me might be subject to variation. My own stupid fucking fault. I didn't even ask the sleazy fuck to sit down. If I had, he'd probably still be here now and we could get to the bottom of whatever this hitch might be. Shit! And then, just like that, not so shit. My eye falls upon the scrap of paper he's left me with the brother's private line. Nice and easy does it, Martyn.

'Any good at impersonations?' I wonder of my companion Mr Bennett. And Bennett, to his great credit, asks me what I need him to do. What I need him to do is call up one Gerrard Brennan of this parish and pretend to be his greaseball brother – and find out what the fuck's going on.

Ged

In a strange way, that last ten minutes has given myself more a bump than anything in a long time. Twenty-four hours ago I was feeling down and out, washed up. I felt like a lad who'd had his day. All of that shite was swimming around my ears and I never knew a thing other than that he was up to something. Ratter. I never had a fucking clue. Me, by the way – one of the fucking untouchables. Fucking Paul the Hom knew more than what I did. And when I did find out, fuck – that was a mortal blow, man, tell you it was.

But just now I've pulled myself back up there again. With one phone call I've set people scampering. I've called Eli. Eli's called Lid. Lid's called Ratter. And Ratter's just phoned myself. Very poor reception by the way, but he's got the message. I've told him loud and clear. I've told him two things:

If you stay in this city today you will be shot by your drug brothers.

If you come back to this city ever you will be shot by me.

He called us up on the batphone, by the way, like we was friends that'd be pleased to hear from one another. Didn't sound himself, in fairness, but he certainly didn't sound sorry, neither. If he sounded anything it was extra jaunty. Callous cunt, he is. Fucking monster. No fucking trace of any guilt, no nothing – just this silly sing-song voice. He goes: 'A'right there, kidder – sorry to phone you on this one. Misty give it us the other day. Listen, is it still all as was? Otterspool . . .'

That's as far as he got. I stopped the cunt right there and just tore right in to him. He weren't saying fuck all after I was done with him.

'Shut the fuck up, you, you fucking lowlife! Listen very carefully to what I say now because these are the last words I ever speak to you. Do you understand that?'

Crackle, crackle, fizz. Would not have minded hearing some trace of shock or shame or some fucking thing but all I heard was feedback. I read him his fucking rights and that was that. Crushed the fucking phone under my foot. Get a new one after Chrimbo.

I gets out the car and takes one massive big deep breath and I walks towards the church. Shouldn't have missed that much. Moby'll be good as gold once I hands him two hundred thousand pounds and that. Give the lad Ratter's, eh? My hand's still shaking as I goes to zap the door locks.

Martyn Lid

Just more fucking big talk, Bennett said. Gun talk, tough guy threats – the sort of thing that's turning this city towards outlaw rule. You can't fight them any more. Girls of eight and nine swear at you on public transport and tell you their legal position if you reprimand them. Mothers put their ten-year-olds on the street, their twelve-year-old brothers have guns – there is nothing decent left to protect. All I see is bastards in baseball caps taking whatever they want. I can't stand them. I shall gladly pounce on these bastards today and lock them up for a very long time indeed – but I'd far rather they shot each other and saved me having to enter into their unspeakable worlds. One more significant pay day and I'm out of this shithole. I can't fight them any more. They've won. The outlaws have won.

Ratter

In different circumstances I could imagine myself happy as a fisherman. I know the water isn't always calm as this, but when it is it's purely bewitching. I mean that – I'm watching the trail fan out behind as the boat cuts through the river and I'm fucking hypnotised. It's as close as I know to total peace of mind. There may well be atrocities going on on the riverbank over there, but that's just the way it has to be. What's horrible to others is just fine by me. It's just another thing that happens in the world.

I drapes my arm over the edge and let my fingers drip through the frozen cold water. Beautiful but savage, it is – icy, icy cold. As cold as death.

Up ahead and making good time I can see the goodies chugging my way. That thin winter sun is backlighting the little vessel as it edges towards us. I drop anchor and sit and wait for them to pull up alongside – my last ever transaction of this nature. I feel that little bit nostalgic, in fairness – feel like it's the end of a era.

Ged

I feel last. I feel fucking terrible about it but I've decided I won't do fuck all. For once in my big stupid life I'll just leave well alone. I'm just walking over to the Britannia and I've seen three carloads going past, headed for Otterspool and that. I seen Jimmy Rico all nice and smart in his whistle, telling his self he's coming on here afterwards. Fucking Christmas Eve and all, too – I feel last on him. For a second I was going to go after them in the car and blow the whistle – but something come over us. Something like realisation – a knowledge that I, Gerrard Brennan, can not affect and fucking influence every single thing that's going to go down in this city. So I let them go on by. Old Bill should get there, mind you – they have got a chance.

And now I'm going to go inside this pub and I'm going to have a ace time with my lovely wife – who is going to *love* what I've got her for tomorrow, by the way – and my gorgeous children and all my soft, lairy mates and rellies and we're going to have a day to remember. That is a fact, by the way. I'm not thinking on that other thing no more. It's gone now. It's up to Ratter now.

Fat Francis

As we get closer to land I can suddenly see the place we used to stash the gear. It's uncanny – I've been back loads of times and never thought to look but now I can see the very spot, almost the same as it was back then. I can hear

Ged, always on the verge of exploding: 'Go-In! Are you there, la? Well, fucking shout back then, will you, you soft cunt – we've got all kinds, here!'

Funny thing with nicknames. People always think they've got them for different reasons. Take myself, for instance – Go-Inhead. Everyone always used to think that was given to me just because I was the fat lad and my head did used to look like a potato, in fairness. It was rounded at the top and just flared out like a bell and, with my chins and having a quite wide neck and that, my head looked like a jellyfish. Thank fuck only I seemed to notice that, but if logic were to prevail I would've got called Go-Outhead, wouldn't I?

Ged Brennan'd remember why I was called Go-Inhead, though. Up until I was about twelve, the two plates of my skull never met properly in the middle. Just like a newborn baby, in fairness, I had my soft spot where the two sides hadn't closed up proper. And my thing, because I was the fat lad and I wanted to be in with Ged and that, be one of the boys – my thing was to let them push my soft spot. Even the hard lads used to be fucking sickened by it – you could press your thumb right inside of my skull. Go-Inhead. Lads like Rico wouldn't leave it alone.

But then it did close up eventually and I was just Fat Francis, until Ged give us Franner and, because it was Ged, everyone else called us Franner. I was Franner from then on, though Go-Inhead still came up and all, too – mainly if I'd done something fucking stupid. But Ged was like a sort of sponsor to me. Fuck knows why, he just took me on and suddenly everyone was fine with me. I was still Fat Franner, but did he ever give me a leg up there.

Being a bit slow and not so handy with my dukes at that point in time, I was only ever any good for business. When all the little rogues was doing their thing it'd be myself fenced it off for them. But Ged saw something in me, took me to the gym, got me sparring and that, half got me in shape. And once I got started I found that I *could* throw a punch, I *could* have a fight – he gave me courage. Ged could do that for you, just by standing by you. I was a big lad and people were starting to be wary of me, to be fair. It was just the bump I needed.

So when I went to London I wasn't Fat Francis, I was a whole new character. I was Scouse Bernie, bit of a lad, bit of a chancer. I was bright as fuck, brilliant on the money side and streetwise to the top degree. Francis Bernard and that – Bernie. They wanted me, big time. They needed a boy like myself down there, in fairness. It was a shambles, the way things was being run. I'm not saying that I'm running things either, by the way – but it's fair to say they couldn't do much without me. If I went down it's fair to say we'd all go down, put it that way. To the lads back here I'll always be Franner. I like it that way.

But no one seems to remember Go-Inhead now and I myself am not displeased about that, either. Even the likes of Rico, though you can see in their eyes they don't like it, they're just waiting to get told that it was all a mad mistake, you don't have to shake hands with Franner no more – even he's forgotten. Go-In's gone, like he never fucking existed. I've got one lad to thank for that. I've never forgotten him.

Never forgot their Ratter, neither. Wrong 'un, no-mark, bad apple – wrote all over him, by the way. Because of his connection with Ged and because – I hate saying this but it is fucking true at the end of the day – because it was good business he was proposing, we let him work. We made it fucking easy for the cunt to work, by the way – easier than any of us boys had it at his age. Don't get me wrong and that – he was a bright fucking lad, Ratter. Very progressive thinking, very smart lad indeed. If it weren't for his hang-ups and his starting to think he was brighter than any of his elders and betters then who knows – maybe he could've developed. But he never. He went the other way. Turned gangster on himself. Started tricking his own self – just too clever by half, he was. Cunt had it coming to him.

And when he come to see myself in my own office with a proposition about the boy I love more than anyone in this world – well, it's curtains, isn't it, in fairness. Came close to having it done there and then, but these things have to be done proper. They always mature with time. What pains me now is that Gerrard won't know or understand the level of fucking brainwork that's gone into making this right for him. I'll just have to live with that. I can console myself with my own knowledge that we're straight now, me and Ged. We're equals.

The boat's pulled up and the auld Irish fella, who's stood through all of that and never once blinked, just carried on chugging the boat like nothing had happened – he holds the boat while I hop ashore. I check my shoes again. I've got most of it off. There's little spots and spatters but I done it right. Got the wind behind me. I makes my way up the grass bank and along the riverside walk, still snatching odd thoughts about us lot as little scallies. I used to have them off over the prices I got, by the way. That Freddie Woan'd give anything – better mug, he were. There it is ahead. The good old

Britannia. I spent many a afternoon skulking round that place, weighing the lads in, wishing I was more a part of it than just the gopher. Good times, though – good times. Maybe they'll continue, maybe they won't.

I take a good hard gulp of cold fresh air and make up my mind. Of course I'm going in. I don't belong in there no more, but they're still my people. I'll just step inside the old place and have a good drink with Ged and the gang and we'll act like we're still eighteen. We always said that the day one of us didn't turn up here for something big, that'd the day it was all over. I never thought it'd be myself that pulled the trigger, though.